SILVER BELLS

December is here and it's time to celebrate the holidays with a romantic collection of contemporary stories from three of Arabesque's most cherished authors. Each of these talented authors will introduce us to a special couple who have discovered the holiday magic of true love blended with undeniable desire. Rejoice in Gwynne Forster's tale of Christmas' glad tidings, relish the fruits of Kwanzaa with Carmen Green, and delight in Lynn Emery's New Year's Eve story. These three unforgettable novellas will touch your soul and are bound to warm your heart during the chilly winter season.

TIMELESS LOVE

Look for these historical romances in the Arabesque line:

BLACK PEARL by Francine Craft (0236-0, $4.99)

CLARA'S PROMISE by Shirley Hailstock (0147-X, $4.99)

MIDNIGHT MOON by Mildred Riley (0200-X; $4.99)

SUNSHINE AND SHADOWS by Roberta Gayle (0136-4, $4.99)

SILVER BELLS

Lynn Emery
Gwynne Forster
Carmen Green

Pinnacle Books
Kensington Publishing Corp.
http://www.pinnaclebooks.com

PINNACLE BOOKS are published by

Kensington Publishing Corp.
850 Third Avenue
New York, NY 10022

First Printing: December, 1996

Printed in the United States of America
10 9 8 7 6 5 4 3 2 1

Contents

CHRISTOPHER'S GIFTS
by Gwynne Forster   7

WHISPER TO ME
by Carmen Green   129

HAPPY NEW YEAR, BABY
by Lynn Emery   245

Christopher's Gifts

Gwynne Forster

"You begin work Monday morning, and I leave home at seven-thirty. I don't go anywhere late, so please be on time." A shadow crossed his face in what she supposed he'd meant as a smile.

"Yes, ma'am."

Nadine Carpenter watched the unassuming, very dark, tall man of about thirty-five years, who strolled out of her office nonchalantly, but self-possessed, jingling his pocket change and obviously confident of his place in the scheme of things. Chauffeur? She had trouble seeing him in that role, but he had answered the ad, and she was desperate. His eyebrow had arched when she'd explained why she needed one. Several evenings recently, after leaving her Manhattan office and driving to her isolated home upstate in Accord, New York, muggers had threatened her when she opened her garage door. Either she hired a chauffeur for protection or gave up her lovely stone house and move back to Manhattan, and she didn't see how she could do that. It was dark when she got home at eight o'clock and, with autumn approaching, it would soon be dark mornings when she left there. Wade Malloy had wondered about her; she could see that in his demeanor, relaxed though he had appeared, but he had taken the job. Still, she couldn't reconcile his ready acceptance of the employment terms and his occupation as chauffeur with his air of authority. But the employment agency had vouched for his references, so she wouldn't worry about his mixed signals and would just be grateful to have her problem solved.

She pulled her shoulder length hair farther down over her left ear, patted it self-consciously, and recalled that she'd done that repeatedly during the interview, a warning that she'd cared what he thought of her looks. She tried to get him out of her thoughts, but she found it hard to push aside the picture of him gliding out of her office with the posture of a man certain that whatever he left behind would be there if he ever decided to go back for it. Tremors of excitement flashed through her at the thought, and she cautioned herself not to let her tender-hearted nature soften her toward a man just because he might be down on his luck, as she supposed Wade probably was. She'd seen many chauffeurs, but not one of them wore the demeanor of Wade Malloy.

Her doorbell rang the next morning just as she reached the bottom of the stairs, briefcase in hand. She peeped through the viewer, saw Wade, and opened the door.

"I didn't expect you to start until Monday, but I'm sure glad to see you this morning. I hate driving in a fog."

He opened his big umbrella, shielding her from the windy mist. "I figured on getting settled in this weekend, so why not? Today's on me. My stuff's in the trunk of my Thunderbird, so I hope you don't mind if I park it in your garage."

She didn't mind, she told him, conscious of his finger at her elbow as they walked to the two-car, stone garage. He stood at the back door of her Crown Victoria, his left hand resting on the handle. "Back seat or front?" She opened the front passenger's door, got in, and closed it. They drove ten miles in silence, except for the tension of awareness that shouted loudly to them both.

She couldn't help being self-conscious about the rough texture of his pants touching her nylon-covered thighs and wondered if he sat with his legs spread wide apart intentionally or whether she had become paranoid. She groped for conversation to ease the tautness that simmered between them.

"The accommodations are simple, but I hope they're satisfactory."

"A one-room apartment over your garage is heaven compared to some of the places I've stayed." Her lashes flew upward, and she stared at him. However, he didn't elaborate further, and his tone said she might as well not ask. They reached her office on Park Avenue South fifteen minutes earlier than usual. He got out of the car and opened her door.

"The day is yours, Wade. Just be here at five." He nodded, and she turned to go.

"Hold on. Let me get this umbrella up. Wouldn't want you to get wet." She tensed at his firm grip on her arm.

"Thanks, but don't bother; it's only a few steps."

"I'll see you to that door." He did. Then, he tipped an imaginary hat and half-smiled in a way that made her want to use him for a pin cushion, but she immediately chastened herself for being mean spirited. She didn't see him, but she didn't doubt that he stood there until she got on the elevator.

Wade stuffed his son's letter in the inside pocket of his jacket and leaned against the hood of his boss's car, watching Nadine Carpenter as she approached. Tall, well built, and about thirty, she was choice. But her sepia good looks, lithe strides, and the gentle sway of her hips failed to entice him right then, though he appreciated beautiful women as much as the next man. He couldn't rid himself of the pain that his son's letter had caused, couldn't gloss over the meaning that it conveyed. Barely seven years old and already a genius at turning the knife.

"Dear Wade, my mother says I have to go stay with you, but I don't want to. Christopher." Wade stared at the childish scrawl and groaned. When would it end? He pasted a mask over his face as Nadine reached the car, greeted her, and began the drive home. Well, he was staying there. What else could he call it?

"Ms. Carpenter," he began, hating that he had to ask, "I have to have my son with me for a while. I don't know for how long, hopefully indefinitely. Is that alright with you? If not, I can get a place somewhere."

"Of course, he can stay with you, Wade. And please call me Nadine, otherwise I'll have to call you Mr. Malloy." He tried to cover his look of surprise.

"Where does he live now?" she asked.

"In Scarsdale with his mother. She's going on her honeymoon, and I get to keep him while she's getting a taste of true love." He hadn't meant to sound bitter, because that wasn't what he felt. He'd turned his life around so that he could gain custody of his son and teach the boy to love and respect him, and he wasn't looking a gift horse in the mouth. He felt her hand on his knee, glanced over at her, and knew that she meant to console him and hadn't thought about the intimacy of it.

"Does he split his time between you and his mother?"

"My son hasn't lived with me since he was six months old, but I aim to change that now."

She glanced at him just as he ground his jaw teeth and winced. He figured she ought to know that he felt more deeply about it than his words and casual tone suggested. "Scarsdale is a very upscale neighborhood," she began, obviously trying not to make him uncomfortable. "Do you think it's a good idea for you to bring him to that small room over the garage? He may make some invidious comparisons."

"It's all I've got right now."

Nadine didn't have much information about him, but she decided to take a chance. "You can have my second floor. It has two bedrooms, two baths, a sitting room, and a back porch. I promised you room and board as part of the deal, because I'm not paying much. You don't have to bring your son to that garage apartment. I'll move my office to the basement," she explained before he could comment, "and I'll sleep in the guest room. It's a big house, Wade. I'll also have the living, dinning, and family rooms plus the kitchen and breakfast room."

Wade asked her why she'd bought such a big, almost isolated house and learned about her practical side. The stone house was invincible to termites, fire, and hurricanes, the property had big beautiful trees, and bordered Rondout Creek, which was a trout fisherman's dream, she told him. She also wanted to live in the country, and the place came at a price she could afford. He accepted her offer to let him have her second floor and told himself that he wouldn't think of the implications of living under the same roof as this delicate morsel. He resisted the urge to whistle. He had nearly slammed his foot on the accelerator when she offered him her second floor.

She leaned back in the bucket seat and sighed. When Wade sensed that she might be troubled and asked what the problem was, she questioned the wisdom of telling him.

"You can tell the help," he needled, gently. "That's been acceptable from time immemorial."

She looked over at him and couldn't resist a smile, because his face shone with a wicked grin. "I can't find my plans for that model home in the Rolling Hills Village. It's the best interior decorating job I ever had, and if I don't finish it by January tenth, the contract is void. I've looked everywhere. The owner has tentatively approved it, so I can't make changes unless I have that plan."

"Where did you last see it?"

"On my desk. I came back from lunch, and it wasn't there." Nadine told him that she was one of the firm's four decorators, the only woman. He nodded.

"Let me know if I can do anything to help." She smiled as she entered the house. It was a nice gesture.

Nadine didn't tell him that she might not find the plans nor that one of her colleagues might have destroyed or misplaced them in order to undermine her position with the firm. She moved her things down to the first floor guest room, picked up the phone, and called Wade.

"Hamburgers, baked potatoes, and salad will be ready in twenty minutes. Tomorrow you cook."

"You promised me board."

"I promised food; I didn't say in what state."

"Modern man eats his food cooked."

"Sure thing. And in case it escaped you, modern man also cooks."

"Okay. I cook tomorrow, but don't be surprised if you lose the next round."

Fast tongue for a chauffeur, she thought, with some amusement and not a little surprise. "Don't worry. I have a housekeeper, but she's sick, so we'll take turns until she gets back."

"You bake a pretty good potato," Wade said, after putting the dishes in the dishwasher. "Good night." The wind swished in as he left by the back door, chilling her as she took in his slim, tight hips and easy gait. The door closed, and she sat down, suddenly melancholy. She had taught herself to be contented with her life. She had conquered the grief of losing her parents and had begun to pursue her dream of becoming a renowned interior decorator, maybe even the Billy Baldwin of the nineties. But right then, there was an emptiness in her that she couldn't banish. It was almost like last Christmas when she'd been unable to face the holiday alone and, though she wasn't impulsive, had decided on the spur of the moment to go to Madrid. If she was lonely there, she had reasoned, it would be for a good reason. She knew she was considered a beautiful woman, but she was careful—no, she was religious—about not exposing her left ear, which had been marred by a burn in her childhood. Her mother had always said that the effect on her looks was mostly in her mind, but her mirror denied that, and her one venture into true intimacy with her college sweetheart had proved it. The boy had pulled her hair back while ardently kissing her face and had seemed surprised when he saw her ear. She cringed at the memory. From then on, their tryst had deteriorated into the worst of disappointments. He'd said later that she had withdrawn, had turned away from him, but in her mind, it was he whose ardor had cooled. She hadn't had the courage to expose herself to the possibility of another such rejection.

I wonder who that turkey is, Wade asked himself as he stood at the curb waiting for Nadine, who approached the car accompanied by a man. His smile could only be described as feral, when the man stood back and let him open the door for Nadine and then waited for Wade to hold it for him.

Don't hold your breath, pal, he said to himself as he left the man standing there and got in the driver's seat. On the way to Accord, the man's obsequiousness with Nadine disgusted him. When he glanced in the rearview mirror and noticed the hand that tried to creep around her shoulder but failed when she moved away, he had to muzzle his temper and did the only thing he could do. He lectured himself. It wasn't his business who Nadine Carpenter spent her time with. Still, he reasoned, a woman like her deserved a better man than that one. He knew men, and this man was a gopher. He'd bet anything on it. He'd never been so glad as when Nadine directed him to let the man off at his house. He realized that he'd been perspiring and wondered what he'd have done if she had taken the man home with her. This job was not going to work out.

He turned into her driveway and, immediately, his finely honed sense of self-preservation—sharpened by years of work in hazardous areas of Latin America and sub-Saharan Africa—alerted him to danger. He flicked on the reflector lights and glimpsed two men dashing around the back of the house.

"Stay here and roll up your windows. If you here a shot, get down between the seats." He raced to the back of the house, but the men had seen him and were running toward Rondout. Later, when he let her out of the car, he noticed that she didn't seem the least perturbed.

"You've got to install some flood lights around here, especially out back," he told her, holding his hand out for her door key. "I'd better look around, see if anybody's been in here." He satisfied himself that she was in no danger and investigated the grounds.

"Wouldn't you like some coffee?" She wanted to show him that she appreciated the protection he offered her.

"Thanks. It's my night to cook, so I'll just go put on something casual while you get the coffee."

"Be careful, Wade. Those men may still be out there." She hoped the anxiety in her voice didn't register with him. She'd been horrified when he'd gone after those men, not knowing whether they were armed. *I don't know Wade Malloy,* she reminded herself, as she measured the beans, *but one thing is certain: he isn't afraid of much, and he isn't in awe of my status as his employer.*

* * *

The smell of garlicky, Italian meat sauce brought her to the kitchen just as he placed it along with spaghetti, French bread, and a green salad on the kitchen table.

"Does it taste as good as it smells?"

"So I've been told, but don't get happy; you're going to eat it every other day until your housekeeper gets back, because it's the only thing I can cook." He seemed to derive great pleasure from that announcement, jingling his pocket change as he stirred the sauce. She'd noticed that he habitually played with his change, doing it rhythmically as if to some silent tune.

"That guy you dropped off tonight. What does he do?"

Nadine explained that the man was an interior decorator and her colleague.

"I should have known. When he wasn't pawing over you, he was picking your brain, and you let him do it." Aghast, her lower lip dropped, and she stared at him in a silent attempt to warn him against casual familiarity. He stared her down until she told him she hadn't realized it.

"Of course not, because he's clever. He kept telling you what a genius you are, and you continued to answer his questions about your work. Believe me, he got things out of you that I would never have told a competitor."

She focused on her plate. "Imagine. All that time, I thought you were paying attention to your driving. I realize that you're smart and that chauffeuring is probably the least of your talents, but I would appreciate it if you would exercise a little restraint and stop meddling in my affairs." His careless shrug indicated that her remark didn't rest heavily on him.

She savored the last of her spaghetti and meat sauce, drained her wine glass, and pushed her chair back from the table. "Try it. It may distress you to keep your thoughts to yourself, but it won't kill you. Trust me." She spoke gently, but she meant it. It didn't make sense to get into an argument with her chauffeur. Weren't they supposed to be deferential?

He looked at her, winked and grinned. "You hired me for protection, didn't you?"

"Not that kind. Thanks for the dinner. You should bottle that sauce and sell it; you'd make a bundle."

His grin unsettled her. "Glad you like it. Look, if you were floundering around in deep water about to drown while I stood on shore, what would you expect me to do? Watch you? Or go in and get you?"

She folded her napkin and got up from the table. "You stacked that one in your favor." An unpleasant thought occurred to her and she asked him, "Are you saying that Rodney is a danger to me?"

He stopped smiling, and a frown creased his face. "In your cut-throat business, yes. He got as much information as possible about your work without telling you anything about his. What *do* you know about his work?"

She expelled a deep breath, impatient with the topic. "Alright. I'll take heed, but you still have to stay out of my business." A smile played around his mouth, and she couldn't help staring at it. A luscious pout. She licked her lips, imagining the sweetness of his full bottom one as she sucked it into her mouth. Shudders raced through her and she regained presence of mind.

"Thanks again, Wade." His wordless stare sent hot darts to every one of her nerve endings. She had to get out of there before she did something she'd regret. But as she turned to leave the kitchen, she remembered that he had cleaned up the night before. "I nearly forgot; it's my night to clean."

He continued to stare, and no smile lit his face. "Go on, I'll do it," he said with a harsh rush of breath. "I'll do it," he repeated, when she didn't move.

"I'll help." They worked in silence, but the tension

between them screamed for their attention. His pants brushed the side of her skirt, and both stopped as though electrified and stared at each other.

"Sorry," she murmured, but he didn't reply. His man's scent swirled around her, intoxicating her, luring her. His mouth twisted into a humorless half-smile, and she felt moisture settling on her thighs. He caught her gaze and held it.

"Wade. Wade, I . . ."

"Go on, Nadine, I'll finish this." Unaccustomed to huskiness in his voice, Nadine gaped at him and would have objected, but his stance, his entire demeanor told her that if she stayed, something would have to give. She swallowed the saliva that accumulated in her throat when his eyes blazed, and she could see the man in him fighting to get to her. She turned and fled, realizing that in doing so, she had acknowledged their mutual attraction. She went to her room and tried to concentrate on the whereabouts of her Rolling Hills Village plans, but her thoughts remained on Wade Malloy.

The following afternoon, wondering about the inconsistencies in Wade as she stirred the coals beneath the grill she'd set up in the backyard, Nadine looked up from her task as Wade walked around the house with a young boy, obviously his son. She smiled at Wade's introduction, though she marveled at the boy's stiffness and formal behavior with his father.

"I thought we'd cook out this evening. It's a bit chilly, but the fire will keep us warm. Would you like that?" she asked the boy. He looked steadily at her with Wade's light brown eyes, darkly handsome face, and impudent air.

"It's immaterial to me."

She glanced at Wade who seemed as shocked as she. "How old are you, Christopher?" she asked, pointedly ignoring his remark.

"I've been seven for a few months now, and I am considered very smart."

"Clever, maybe, but not very smart," Wade interjected. "Smart children are respectful." Nadine turned away. She had not anticipated that the child would be antagonistic toward his father. She walked over to him.

"Christopher, I spent last Christmas alone in Spain. I figured that loneliness would be easier on me there than here." The boy cocked his head and looked at her.

"Why couldn't you stay here with your folks?"

She knelt to his level and looked directly into his eyes. "I didn't have any folks, Christopher. That's why I went away; I couldn't bear being here alone. I hope that when Christmas comes this year, I'll be able to count you as my friend. Then, at least I'll have you. What about it?"

"Okay. I guess," he said, obviously less sure of himself. She grasped his hand and went back to the grill.

"You may start right now by helping me grill these pork chops." She started toward the kitchen to get them, looked over her shoulder, and saw that he followed her. She promised herself that she would soften him up, make him realize how lucky he was to have his parents.

Wade watched the two of them, and a smile spread over his face when his son jumped in front of Nadine and opened the screen door for her. Ellen might have raised him to be a stuffed shirt, but she'd taught him proper manners. He didn't know how he'd manage with the boy. Pain seared his chest when he recalled his son's refusal to go with him until his mother announced it was that or a babysitter. For years, he'd worked—sometimes in death defying circumstances—to earn a living for himself and his family, but Ellen had wanted it all: good living *and* a man who was home every night. He couldn't be home with her, because his work took him all over the world, and she disliked the instability of constant travel. Yet he didn't blame her, because youth was a one-time thing, and she wanted her man with her while she was young enough to enjoy him. Well, that was refuse down the drain, he decided. If he was going to win his son's affection and respect, he needed a plan, and the boy was too much like him to come around easily. Wade walked over to the grill and added some coals. Nadine and Christopher approached and, to his amazement, the boy bubbled with talk and enthusiasm. Until he reached his father.

Nadine couldn't help noticing the sudden change in Christopher, who had withdrawn emotionally and become sullen. She asked him if he would go back to the kitchen for a roll of paper towels and, for a minute, was certain that he'd refuse. He left, and she looked at Wade, hurting with him.

"Give it time, Wade." She spoke softly, in a voice that soothed. "He'll come around. Try to find out why he behaves this way with you; then you'll be able to deal with it. If I can help, just tell me."

He wouldn't have thought that a woman who went to work in Brooks Brothers type suits, spread collar shirts, cuff links, and bow ties would be so soft, feminine, and understanding. He inclined his head toward the back door of the house where Christopher had disappeared.

"Thanks. I may need help before this is over. There's a reason for his attitude, Nadine. I worked away from home and, when he saw me, it was never to my good advantage. I've got a lot to make up for, and I haven't got much time."

"What about school? Those in this area are excellent. I've a friend who'll keep Christopher until we get home in the evening. She won't charge. I keep her children sometime."

Wade gave the turf a hard kick with the toe of his left shoe, as he fought to bridle his emotions. He couldn't remember the last time anybody cared how he fared. "Thanks." If he said more, he'd expose his raw insides. Christopher returned from his errand, humming, and

Nadine asked him to sing something. The child demurred, and she turned to Wade.

"Do you sing, Wade?" The boy eyed his father as though something very important was at stake.

"Yeah. What do you want to hear? Classical, pop, or jazz?"

"Classical," they replied in unison. He sang the Toreador song from *Carmen* in a deep velvet baritone while they gaped in awe.

"Wow," Christopher whispered, when he finished. "Wow." That evening, Nadine noticed that Christopher sang when he thought he was alone and made a mental note to inveigle father and son into singing together.

Getting the boy enrolled in school was less of a problem than she'd expected, but when she asked her friend, Lorna, to keep Christopher after school, the woman's reaction to news of the boy and his father surprised her.

"You sly devil, you. Who would have thought it? If you'd been wearing mini skirts and tight sweaters, it wouldn't have come as a surprise. But I'll say this for you, you sure can pick 'em. That man turns my head, and I'm a happily married woman. 'Course what you do is your business, honey, but I'd be careful if I were you."

One evening about three weeks later, they stopped at Lorna's house to get Christopher. Nadine didn't want to expose Wade to Lorna's brand of wisdom, so she suggested that he needn't go in, but he insisted that he wanted to thank the woman for her kindness. Lorna looked him up and down.

"I sure am glad to meet you, Wade. Your son is a wonderful boy, though he's going to have to learn that I don't bake hard crust French bread. Besides, corn bread's got a lot more vitamins." Her glance at Nadine suggested that they shared a secret. "You two don't have to rush back here to get him every day, you know. Take a little time for yourselves."

Nadine noticed Wade's eyebrows shot up swiftly and his lips parted as though words might be forthcoming. Instead, he let the comment pass.

When they arrived home, Wade drove into the driveway and stopped in front of the garage door as usual. This time, he didn't get out but turned to Nadine and asked her in a voice devoid of inflection, "If we take time for ourselves, what will we do with it?" She shushed him, glad for Christopher's presence. The man didn't mind issuing a challenge to his employer, though he'd cloaked it in a demeanor of innocence. She didn't take offense at his directness; she'd learned that he said what he thought.

"Level with me, Wade. Are you testing my mettle, or your appeal? Which is it?"

He laughed. "I already know about the latter."

It was her evening to cook dinner, and she asked Christopher to help her. She didn't need his assistance, but she wanted to develop a spirit of camaraderie with him in the hope that he would extend that to his father. He hummed as he set the table. He turned a cup upside down, placed a saucer on it and sat a stemmed glass in that. She noticed that he searched through drawers and asked what he wanted.

"Something else to stack up here." They hadn't seen Wade lounging against the doorjamb. He walked over to the table, folded a napkin into the shape of a long necked bird and stuck it into the glass.

"Gee-whiz. Wade, can you show me how to do that?" Nadine gazed at Wade's face, the picture of love and joy, and her heart kicked over. His face glowed as though reflecting the morning sun and, when he glanced at her, she let him see the happiness that she felt. It wasn't hopeless. After dinner, she got a pad of multicolored drawing paper and gave it to Wade.

"Thanks, Nadine. You know, you'd look great wearing a halo, and I'd pin one on you myself, but mere man can't approach an angel." He winked and left her to ponder his enigmatic remark.

Two weeks passed, and they settled into an uneasy relationship, each well aware that at any time, the unexpected could push either of them over that fine line they'd drawn between them. Nadine knew it was dangerous to think of him as anything but her hired chauffeur. Yet, his problems drew her into his life. She watched him with Christopher, hoping that evenings of origami would have brought them closer together.

"You don't have to eat oatmeal," Wade told his son, "but you do have to eat the remainder of your breakfast. You have to—"

"I know what's good for me, because mother told me, and I'm not going to eat stuff like this. Our cook always made fresh biscuits or popovers every morning, and she poached my eggs."

"I'm not a cook, son, and we don't have one here, so you either eat what's in front of you, or stay hungry 'til you get your school lunch."

"I'll stay—"

Nadine interrupted him. "Christopher, you may enjoy hurting your father, but you are the one whose stomach will feel those terrible pains. Last night when you asked him to show you how to make figures with that napkin, what did he do?"

The boy hung his head, glanced furtively at his father and muttered, "Sorry," before tackling his bacon, toast, and scrambled eggs. Her glance at Wade found him distressed and unsmiling, and she couldn't help feeling his wound in her own heart.

When they stopped at Lorna's house to get Christopher that evening, the boy threw his book bag on to the back seat of the car, crawled in, closed the door, and presented them with another scenario.

"You don't have to come in and get me, Wade; you can just blow the horn and I'll come out."

"Forget it, Christopher," Wade told him, a little testily, she thought, "I'm going in and get you every day, and that's that." She watched the cloud of sullenness settle over the boy's face.

"Christopher," she began, reluctant to reveal so much of herself. "My father wasn't well for most of my youth, most of my life, in fact. But those days when he was well enough to come to school for me were the only times when I didn't feel different from other children. I'd run to him, and he pick me up and swing me around. It was wonderful. You don't know how fortunate you are to have a strong, healthy father who loves you." She only sensed Wade's sharp glance at her, because she didn't look toward him, knowing intuitively that his face would reflect pain. Neither of them spoke until they arrived home.

"Get your shower and a change of clothes while I get dinner together, Christopher, and then I'll drive you back to Lorna's place. You'll stay there tonight, and I'll pick you up tomorrow around noon. Nadine and I have to go to a reception."

"Why didn't you just let me stay there while I was there?"

"One hour, son, so don't fool around," Wade told him, and she marveled at his patience.

Seeing him struggle to draw Christopher closer to him, watching his trails with the boy, and eating with him at her table made it inevitable that she look upon him not as her chauffeur, but as a man. A handsome, virile, and capable man.

She dressed for the firm's annual charity banquet—the main source of funds for its interior design scholarship fund—and scolded herself for thinking that Wade would be a much more elegant and genteel escort than Rodney Ames. She didn't have romantic inclinations about Rodney, but he willingly escorted her whenever she asked him, and a woman in her position needed to put in an appearance at important social functions. Besides, Rodney was such an obsequious stuffed shirt that she could count on him to put his best foot forward around people whose good will be valued. She slipped into a shimmering, avocado green beaded evening dress, combed her hair in its usual style, added to her right ear a bunch of cascading zirconian stars and went into her living room to wait for Wade. He took her coat from the hall closet and held it for her.

"I hope the guy you put this on for is worth it," he mumbled, letting her see his irritation.

"I dressed for myself."

"Sure you did, just like you put on this mantrapping perfume for yourself." She attempted to move away, but he wrapped the coat snugly around her shoulders.

"Don't you ever keep your opinions to yourself?" she asked, furious with herself for having enjoyed the feel of his strong fingers on her shoulder.

"*Do I ever?* You'd be surprised."

She hated that her embarrassment was so obvious to him. "Come on." She started for the door, paused, and turned.

"Shouldn't you call Christopher and see if he's alright? This is the first time he's stayed away from home all night. I know he's gotten used to Lorna, but . . ."

"He's okay. As long as Greta's around, he'd stay over there indefinitely. That boy's gone head over heels about that little girl. Maybe he should have had a sister." His fiery gaze implied that it wasn't too late.

Nadine had to be joking, Wade decided, when she asked him to pick up her date and gave him the address.

"You mean you got all dolled up like this to go out with that guy who's only interested in picking your brain?"

"Wade, you're not my father, you're—"

"You don't have to remind me," he interrupted, "I know I'm your chauffeur. I'm also a man with sense, and you shouldn't waste your time on that guy. He's not worth it."

"You saw him once, so how do you know so much about him?"

"If you need proof that he's a wimp, I'll give to you." He parked, went in the apartment building, rang the man's bell, and waited for him. All the while he wondered at the anger that seemed slowly to build in him and that he tried unsuccessfully to shove aside.

To Wade's astonishment, Rodney Ames didn't even speak to him, but brushed passed on his way to the car.

"Just a minute, pal." Wade detained him. "In case you didn't know it, the blueblooded Robber Barons may have been notoriously harsh in their business dealings, but they were famous for their graciousness to the hired help. But then, you don't pretend to be genteel, do you?" He walked past Rodney before the man could retaliate, got in the driver's seat, and closed his door, leaving him to fumble with the back door until Nadine reached over and unlocked it.

Wade found a parking space behind the Plaza, let them out, got his high-beam flashlight from beneath the seat, opened his book to chapter eleven, and settled back. Three hours later, he noticed the crowds leaving the hotel, turned off the light, put the book away, and feigned sleep. The banging on his window alerted him to the couple's arrival, and he wondered how much alcohol Rodney had consumed. He got out of the car, opened the door for Nadine and assisted her in, but he let the hapless man look out for himself. Drunkenness disgusted him.

"Where to, Nadine?" His breath hung in his chest while he awaited her answer.

"Rodney's place, please."

The skin on his back seemed to creep up toward his neck, and he loosened his collar. What in the world had he gotten himself into?

"Rodney, would you please stop acting like an octopus," she whispered, hoping that Wade's gaze was glued to highway eighty-seven. His response was to show greater dexterity and imagination. She gave him a not too gentle shove.

"Come on, Nadine," he slurred, "I jus' wanna be friendly. What's a little friss between kins?"

"What's come over you? I want you to stop acting like a teenager." She'd moved as far away from him as the door would allow, but he took that as an invitation. "Mr. Ames," she said in her stiffest office manner, "get a hold of yourself. I'm your colleague, not your plaything."

"That's the problem, Nadine, honey. I don't want you to be my colleague. I want to play with you."

Wade eased up on the accelerator as he glanced for the nth time into the rear view mirror. He wiped the sweat from the side of his face and told himself that his concerns were in the front seat, not the back. Then she leaned against the door and had no further means of escaping the man's fawning and pawing, and he felt his blood heat up. He had learned with strenuous effort and practice to master his hot temper, but right then he felt it coiling its way to certain explosion. He hummed to himself, one of his old techniques for cooling his anger. But the man's hand went to her breast, and he skidded to the elbow of the road in a no stopping area and brought the car to a halt. He got out, walked to the back door and opened it.

"That Jack Daniels or whatever you've been drinking has made you pretty courageous, buddy. You'd better sit up front with me."

"You're not my date. Go back and drive."

Wade laid a very heavy hand on the man's arm. He kept

his voice low, cool and controlled, the voice with which he had managed hundreds of laborers in hot, insect and snake invested jungles and in scorching deserts. The voice that not even the most obdurate and mulish among them had dared to disobey.

"I said get up front. *Now!*"

"I'm not going to be ordered around by a chauffeur."

Wade grinned. "I'm not just her chauffeur, pal; as of now, I'm also her bodyguard. Get up front."

Nadine adjusted the straps of her dress and focused her gaze on the eerie shapes of trees and buildings as they whisked by. She didn't know whether she was more relieved or embarrassed. She did know that if she asked Wade to drive Rodney anywhere else, she'd lower herself in his eyes. Rodney had always been a harmless date, but this time, he'd overstepped the bounds of decency, and she would tell him about it when she next saw him. She felt sorry for Rodney, but she released a long sigh of relief when, without directive or discussion of it, Wade drove straight to the man's apartment building, parked, and turned to him.

"This is your stop, buddy. Hop out." Nadine viewed it all as though she might have been watching a movie. Her disgust with Rodney's behavior wouldn't let her do anything to help him salvage his dignity and, when Wade reached over, locked the passenger door and drove off before the man could tell her goodnight, she relaxed for the first time since she'd gotten in the car.

"I told you he was a wimp. No man would have let me get away with that without at least telling me where to get off."

"You know how to drive, Wade, but you're a lousy chauffeur. If you want to work for me, you'll have to improve your manners."

"Yes ma'am." She bounced out of the car as soon as he stopped, opened the front door herself and called good night to him over her shoulder.

* * *

"Good morning, Nadine. I didn't know whose turn it was to make breakfast," he said, as though they'd parted on the best of terms the previous evening, "so I high-tailed it down here as soon as I woke up." Nadine glanced at the kitchen clock. Nine-forty.

"How magnanimous of you!" She had a strange and compelling desire to box his ears, and she couldn't understand it, because she abhorred violence. Yet, her fingers itched for him. "I thought you promised to take Christopher shopping. He wants to buy Christmas gifts."

"Plenty of time for that. I'm going for him around twelve. What do you want for breakfast."

"I already ate two bananas and drank coffee. The pot's half-full, if you want some." What was wrong with him, looking at her like that?

"Then I'll have the same. Want to come along with Christopher and me?"

"I'd love to shop with Christopher, but I've got to work on my designs today, and I'll have to reproduce those plans from memory. What are you staring at?"

He swallowed the coffee with a gulp as though he'd burned his esophagus. "That dress you had on last night didn't do a thing for you. You look just as good this morning with your face scrubbed clean and that white shirt hanging out over your pants." He didn't move, but she backed up. Heat simmered in his darkening eyes. His aura had suddenly changed, had begun to swirl around her. His cologne, the scent of autumn woods, wafted to her nostrils, and she lost her breath, mesmerized.

Wade watched her rub her palms against her hips, unconsciously sending him the message that they were sweaty, and then rim her lips with the tip of her pink tongue. He swallowed the saliva that pooled in his mouth.

"Get out of here, Nadine."

"You're ordering me out of my own kitchen? Of all

the. . ." she stammered, thoroughly confused. "What gives you the right to—"

He stopped her. "Listen to me, Nadine. Don't bother to be outraged. You know what I'm talking about. Just go!" She spread her legs, and he could see moisture around her lips and on her forehead. Shudders tore through him.

"And if I don't?"

He started toward her, and he didn't care if she saw the fiery determination and hotly roused man that he knew blazed in his eyes. He walked around to face her when she turned her back.

"Why can't you face me now?" he tormented. "A second ago you were challenging me. Is it because I'm your chauffeur? Is that it? Your chauffeur is a man, Nadine. A man who knows that you didn't stay here in spite of my warning because you were standing on your right to do as you pleased in your own house, though that's what you'd like me to believe. You want to feel what you know will happen between us if you stay here." He advanced toward her slowly, nearly breathless when he realized that she still didn't move. His fingers grasped her shoulders.

"Either go, Nadine, or let me feel your arms around me."

"Wade . . . I."

His low voice didn't attempt to seduce, nor did it plead. It spoke of deep, compelling need and it reached her in her rawest, most vulnerable chamber. That secret place where she stored her longing to be needed, to have a man cherish and adore her, to need her desperately.

"Wade . . ."

"I don't care if you send me packing tomorrow or the next minute. Just hold me." He tipped her chin upward with his index finger, saw the compliance that must have glowed in her eyes and lowered his lips to her hungry mouth. She didn't know when she opened her mouth to him, only that the power and possessiveness of his strong tongue dancing in her mouth made her want more of him, all of him. Her whimper brought his arm tighter around her, and she melted against him, giving him kiss for kiss, caress for caress. The wind swished out of her when he gently withdrew his tongue from her mouth and kissed her eyes. She understood then what he needed, and she held him to her. Secure in the cocoon of protective warmth in which he'd cloaked her, she turned her face and touched his lips with her own. As though sensing that she desired more of him, he held her head for his forceful, passionate kiss. Her whole body blazed with the unfamiliar jolt of his loving, and she wanted it to last forever . . . until his full hand pressed her left ear through her hair. Abruptly, she whirled away from him.

"Nadine, what is it? Why did you move away from me? Have I hurt you?"

"No. I . . . Wade, we mustn't . . . I mean . . ."

"Shhh. Don't say anything. I know who I am to you."

"Do you?" He turned away from her, picked up his empty coffee cup, put it in the dishwasher, looked up, and flashed a smile. "No need to get bent out of shape. I can handle it."

She had to get out of there, something she should have done when he'd urged her to do just that. She put on a warm jacket, got a rake from the garage, and went to work on the blanket of leaves that covered the lawn. She raked until her arms ached, until she felt his hand gentle on her back.

"Let it alone, Nadine. Tomorrow's Sunday. I'll clean this up while you're at church. I'm sorry if I've upset you."

His arm lingered across her back in what she knew was an attempt to soothe her. She wanted to turn to him, to hold him and to let his strong arms hold her, but she did none of that. She smiled coolly and lied. "You haven't upset me, and everything is alright between us. I'm going in and get dressed. I have to go to my office this afternoon."

"Nadine, I try to tell the truth even when it hurts me. I don't believe you're not affected by what happened back there, though I'm sure you want to forget it; you're entitled to that, but please, tell it like it is."

"I think it best that we forget it." She hoped he wouldn't press her, because she didn't intend to tell him how she felt about their passionate exchange. She was already more vulnerable to him than she knew was good for her. He's not an easy man, she realized, when his gaze bored into her, scattering her nerves, while he stood mute before her. Scrambling for composure, she added, "I have to get to my New York office and do something about those missing plans. At least one man in my firm would shimmy around like a drunken sailor if I bungle this job, because he underbid me and still didn't get it." She couldn't fathom his demeanor. How could his posture be so loose while his face bore the tenseness of a man facing a jury's verdict?

"Then you have at least one suspect. What do you say we pick up Christopher, and I'll drive us all into town?" He must have detected her indecision, for he quickly added, "Then, if you should need help, I'll be there for you." She didn't misunderstand his phrasing. He hadn't simply said that he'd be there. He'd be there for *her,* and that implied something personal, a commitment to see her through whatever she faced. Unable to resist the kindness reflected in his eyes, she nodded assent.

Christopher explored Nadine's office while Wade leaned against the doorjamb watching her futile search for a roll of plans he knew she'd never see again. He wanted to say let's sit down and reconstruct them, but he wasn't ready to reveal himself. Instead, he said, "You may be wasting time, Nadine. If the contractor has already approved your plans, you don't have to worry about plagiarism, so why not borrow the contractor's copy and get to work? You did copyright them, didn't you?" Her look of surprise confirmed that he'd raised her curiosity about him, but he'd risked it because he wanted to help her.

"Who's your contractor?" he asked, while she was dealing with the surprise he'd given her. She hadn't copyrighted, she told him, because theft had never before been a problem. He looked at the contractor's card that she handed him and smiled inwardly; the man was one of his old acquaintances.

"How much do you remember?"

"Most of it. But I know I won't be able to reconstruct the fine points, those flashes of insight that wake me up at night." He could well appreciate that, because he'd gotten crucial inspiration that way more times than he could count.

"Well, why don't you get your stuff together, work in your office at home, and you can pick my brain as much as you like." He couldn't stop the grin that spread over his face when her eyes widened and her bottom lip dropped. *I'd better stop this, before I dig a hole that I can't get out of,* he warned himself.

Nadine looked from Wade to Christopher as the boy tugged at his father's sleeve. "Come on Wade," Christopher begged, "I want to see the Christmas decorations and the tree in Rockefeller Center."

"In a minute. The tree won't be up for a few weeks yet, but there's a lot we can do as soon as Nadine is ready."

Half an hour later, as they passed St. Patrick's Cathedral with its soaring spires and crossed over to Rockefeller Center, Christopher whooped with glee at the colorful flags of all nations, and Nadine wondered to what extent he'd been allowed the glory of childish expression. As Wade took his son's hand, pointed to the Cathedral, distinguished for him the towers, spires, and steeples and explained their architectural and aesthetic significance, she realized that driving a car was probably the least of his abilities. She was going to confront him with his secrets, too, first chance she got and make him tell all. Yet, an unfamiliar pain wound around her heart, pain for Wade in his struggle to win his child's affection and pain for the boy who had never grown to love his father. Neither parent seemed at fault, but the way they'd managed their affairs had hurt them all. She could see that the boy enjoyed his father's explanations about the cathedral, but she missed most of their conversation until she heard Wade promise to draw it for the boy when they got home. She stopped dead in her tracks. How could he draw that complicated building from memory?

Christopher skipped along trying to keep up with his father's long strides. "Are you going to take me ice skating, Wade? I can skate already. Mother paid a man to teach me."

"Sure thing." He must have known that she detected the resentment in his voice, because he shrugged as if to say, "so what?" The boy asked his father to let her join them. She smiled at his choice of words, but she noticed Wade's embarrassment.

"I'd love to join you if . . ." She looked at Wade. "Is it alright with you?" Her heart pitched in her chest when he smiled his gratitude for her thoughtfulness. She didn't need to be told that he hadn't explained their relationship to his son, and she'd tried to let him know that he had no reason to worry. What a mess. The wind blew her hair up over her head, and she quickly pulled it back in place and started walking. Children were too perceptive. She didn't want to hear what the boy was about to ask her, because she knew she had just raised his curiosity about her hair and the way she wore it.

They wandered through the miles of toys in F.A.O. Schwartz. "Look around Christopher and make your Christmas list. Things you want and things you'd like to give to someone else," Wade said. Nadine rolled her eyes upward in alarm, certain that they were about to spend hours there, but in less than half an hour, the boy had his list, though he didn't share it. She tried to banish the feeling of being alone, of being left out, of wanting to belong, as Wade explained to Christopher the houses that lined route eighty-seven on the way home.

"Why don't we stop at the first decent restaurant and have dinner; if we wait 'til we get home, it'll be pretty late by the time we eat. What do you say, Nadine?"

She and Wade had never eaten out together and, if they did it now, it would be a social occasion, not part of their room and board agreement. She should say no, unless she was prepared to risk an escalation of their growing intimacy. And who'd pay for their meal? It was a cinch he wouldn't let her do it and devalue himself in his son's eyes.

"Well?"

"Can I have a coke, Wade?" Christopher asked with an urgency that only a child could attach to such a simple request. "Mother doesn't like for me to drink sodas, but sometimes she lets me."

"If we stop at a restaurant, you may have half of one. What about it, Nadine?" The hope that she saw in his eyes nearly brought tears from hers; he wanted to please his son. She tried to make light of it.

"It's your night to cook. At least tonight, I won't have to eat spaghetti and meat balls."

"Why don't you like Wade's spaghetti and meat balls, Nadine? They're the best I ever tasted."

"She likes it, son; she just doesn't want to eat it every other day." His tone changed perceptibly to a soothing basso. "Of course, she can't say I didn't warn her." He drove off the highway at Ardona and found a neat little mom-and-pop restaurant whose owners willingly filled Christopher's order of one chicken leg, one hamburger and one hot dog. The boy chatted away, and she decided that the time had come to take a chance. If the idea didn't go over well, it would be too bad, because she felt strongly about it,

"Christopher," she began, somewhat tentatively, "none of the children I know call their father by his first name. I wince every time you do it. Your father deserves better from you. Much better."

"That's what my mother calls him," he replied, and she could see that her remark had dampened both their spirits. Wade didn't comment, and he didn't look at her, either, but she swore to herself that she wouldn't give up. Children should respect their parents.

The next morning, Sunday, Nadine drove herself to nine o'clock church service, hoping to avoid Lorna and her innuendos. But Lorna had apparently decided that the later service would be too crowded and had also gone to the earlier one.

"Honey, you're the talk of Accord. We were all at Alma's regular Saturday night bridge party—you really ought to go some time—and Hugh Cliburn said he'd always wanted to get to know you better, but you didn't give him any encouragement. Hugh's a fine man, and *he's* single. He's also very stable and has a *professional* job." She emphasized the word. "Did you know he's been our postmaster for the last eighteen years? Everybody respects him. Why, he personally puts up the community Christmas tree every single solitary year." Nadine wondered how far she could stretch the definition of friendship.

"Lorna, Wade Malloy is not married. In fact, his ex-wife is on her honeymoon right now. And another thing. I am not having an affair with him, so stop pretending to be open minded and modern, when you're really censoring me for letting him and his son stay in my house. They live on the second floor, and I live on the first. And if I wanted to sleep in his bed every night, Lorna, I'm past the age where I'd have to get permission from anyone other than Wade." She nearly giggled at the gaping mouth and wide eyes in Lorna's shocked face.

"Well, girl, you know I believe in live and let live. If he's got the music that makes you dance, far be it from me to interfere. I just don't want to see you make a mistake. He's a chauffeur, you know. *Your* chauffeur. And don't forget. Hugh is our highly respected postmaster." Nadine twirled her umbrella, suddenly wishing for a downpour that would offer an easy way out of that conversation. Lorna was a good soul with a big heart, but she'd had enough.

"I've got to hurry; it's my time to cook. See you tomorrow evening." Laughter bubbled up inside her and finally spilled over. Lorna's mouth could have received a tennis ball with ease, and her eyes nearly popped.

"You mean he cooks, too? My Lord, where did you find him?" Nadine waved goodbye, got into her car, and drove off. She already knew that Wade was good husband material, depending, of course, on what he was hiding.

At home, she found the kitchen clean and the house empty. Deciding that he'd taken Christopher somewhere, she changed into slacks, a cowl-neck sweater, and a big bulky coat sweater and hiked out to the Rondout where she found them fishing.

"I want you to stop calling me by my first name, son. I'm your father, and I want you to acknowledge that every time you address me."

"How come you didn't say anything until Nadine mentioned it?"

"Because I'm planning to correct your bad habits one at a time. Now that you know you mustn't brag on yourself, we can start on this."

"Gee whiz, Wade, I dunno. That's all I ever called you." Christopher paused for a moment. "Wade, where am I going to stay when mother gets back home? I don't like Casey, and I don't think he likes me."

"I'm going to try to keep you with me, son, and you start right now to practice calling me 'dad.' "

As though he hadn't heard a word his father said, Christopher prattled on. "Mother isn't going to like that, but she's got Casey, so I guess . . . Gee, I don't know. Wade, why is Nadine always pulling at her hair and playing with her ear, huh? Look! I think I got a bite." She wished she had let them know she was there, but she couldn't resist listening for Wade's answer.

"No. You don't have a bite; your hook's stuck in a weed. Why do you think Nadine plays with her ear? I've never noticed her doing it."

"Well, she does. All the time."

Nadine turned to walk away, stepped on a dry twig, and to her embarrassment, brought their attention to her.

As soon as he could do so inconspicuously, Wade curtailed the fishing expedition and took Christopher home. Nadine must have had a reason to listen to their conversation unobserved. He found her in her basement office trying to redraw the designs, her face so tightly drawn that he knew she wasn't capable of creative thinking. He lifted the telephone receiver after the first ring.

"Ms. Carpenter's home." He didn't like what he heard, handed her the receiver, and stood in the doorway while she talked. He watched the shifting play of the dying sun rays in her thick black hair and wondered about Christopher's observation. Her hand went to her left ear, and he realized that he *had* seen her pat that ear any number of times. She crossed her legs, leaned back in her chair and desire stirred in him. He didn't mind that, he told himself; he'd get upset when being around such a woman—warm, sensual, and surprisingly feminine—*didn't* send an occasional message to his groin.

"You've got some nerve," she told him after hanging up, but he shrugged it off.

"That's the same guy who showed so little regard for you night before last, wasn't it? I hope he called to apologize." He listened to her explanation that the man had been drinking and had never behaved that way before.

"Rodney is a highly respected interior designer," she continued, "and we've been professional associates for several years without his getting out of line. Well, not far out, anyway. He's harmless and, even if he weren't, you should have left the room while I talked."

"That guy bears watching, Nadine." He made up his mind to check on him, because he had a hunch that the man hadn't been that drunk, just pretending.

While Nadine was at work the next day, he did exactly that and learned that Rodney had recently signed a contract to design three suites in a newly renovated hotel. He asked for and got an appointment with the hotel's owner for roughly one week hence. That didn't mean the man was a thief, but he was at least a suspect in the theft of Nadine's place.

Several days later, Christopher brought a note from one of his teachers stating that he had been insubordinate in refusing to attend his swimming class. If he refused again, he'd be given a demerit that would automatically disqualify him from receiving any school honors. Nadine couldn't understand why he'd given the note to her rather than to his father. She soon understood the child's problem. Behind his braggadocio postures lay a deep-seated shame of an imperfection that he couldn't make himself share, not even with his father.

"No one's going to laugh at you because you have a large red blotch on your thigh," she told him when he confessed his reason for skipping the class. "Your classmates are only going to see what a good swimmer you are, so don't risk getting put out of school, honey." Those might have been her mother's words to her when she, too, had rebelled against going to swimming class, and she felt a little ashamed for asking the child to do what she had been unable to accomplish. Christopher bowed his head in an unaccustomed acknowledgment of defeat.

"You can talk like that, Nadine, because you're beautiful. Wade said you are. So nobody's ever going to laugh at you. But if it was your leg, you'd be ashamed, too." Without his arrogance, she saw a hurt little boy and risked putting her arms around him. To her amazement, he rushed into them and wrapped his own arms tightly about her. She held him close, suddenly aware that she needed him more than he needed her.

"I don't want them to laugh at me, Nadine. I don't. And I'm not going to that class." Her fingers stroked his young back as she wondered how to help him.

That evening, Wade walked into her office, speaking as he did so. "What am I going to do, Nadine? I've spoken with Christopher's gym teacher and explained to her that he's an excellent swimmer and doesn't need swimming lessons, but she says he can't be excused from that class."

"It isn't easy for him, Wade. Don't be fooled by his blustering; he's still very tender."

Wade's gaze perused her face in a way that suggested she might not be real. "He's becoming fond of you, Nadine."

"I'm just growing on him, Wade. Seems I have that effect on some people." She wished she'd swallowed those words. Wade's mesmeric, light brown eyes suddenly glowed as though they had become coals of fire. His hands dropped to his sides, and his fingers curled into a fist as his hot gaze sent rivets of heat throughout her body.

"Wade . . ."

"It's not going away, Nadine. Not now. Maybe not ever. And certainly not until we do something about it one way or another." She didn't know how she'd gotten out of her desk chair, fled past him and up the stairs to her bedroom.

She sat there trembling behind that closed door, wishing with all her soul that he'd break it down.

Wade sank into the recently vacated chair that still held the heat from her body. The floral scent that she always wore teased his nostrils and he rubbed the sweat off of his hands and on to his trousers. She didn't want to become involved, and he wouldn't pressure her; he'd never pressured any woman, never had to. But the more he saw of her, the more certain he was that he could drown in her. And love it. And the more certain he was that she had the strength to ignore her desire for him, to walk away and not look back. He got up and went to Christopher's room.

"Son, you have to go to your swimming class. Your mother never told me that spot bothered you so much, or I would have done something about it."

Christopher looked up, hopefully. "What could you do? You mean I don't have to have all those kids meddling with me?"

"Never mind the past, son. During the Christmas holidays, you're going to get a skin graft. When it heals, the spot will be gone."

"Really? The whole thing. It's almost as long as my thigh."

"Really. Now finish that story and get ready for bed."

Christopher didn't move, but kept his gazed fixed upon his father. "You're really going to get my leg fixed?"

"Didn't I say I would? I've never lied to you, and I never will." Wade turned to go to his own room, but whirled around as Christopher began to sing the Toreador song.

"I didn't know you knew that song."

"I didn't until I heard you sing it." The boy's smile warmed his heart, and he smiled in return. Then he quickly left; it wouldn't do for a boy to see his father's tears. Maybe they'd make it after all.

* * *

Nadine watched Wade and Christopher as they said goodbye to Lorna and walked to the car where she awaited them. She had the impression that the boy was becoming more at ease with his father, less inclined to behavior that denied their relationship. He didn't resist or show reluctance when Wade took his hand, though she had yet to see the boy reach for his father's hand. Her heart ached for them both. How had Wade allowed such an enormous chasm to develop between himself and his only child? He didn't speak of it, and she hadn't had the opportunity or the courage to ask him. She tried not to judge him, because she knew she didn't have some crucial facts, and what she'd seen of his behavior with his son—gentleness, tenderness, and patience, often suffering the child's hostility—reinforced her belief in Wade Malloy's goodness. Down on his luck, maybe, because he certainly hadn't made his living as a chauffeur. She unlocked the back door.

"How was school?"

"Not so good," Christopher mumbled. "I can't go back until I'm ready to go to my swimming class." She heard the unshed tears in his voice. "They're not going to let me be in the Christmas play, and I was supposed to sing 'O, Holy Night.'"

The grim expression on Wade's face elicited her compassion. He needed to bridge the gap between himself and his son, but he had to discipline him, too, and she knew that Christopher wouldn't take that well.

Her vision of it was borne out later that evening. Wade sat alone in his room trying to put himself in his son's place, to imagine what his own reaction would be to a stigma that was no fault of his own and of which he was ashamed. Still, he reasoned that, no matter the cause, he couldn't allow the boy to defy him and his teachers. As though shouldering the yoke of all the ages, he trudged over to Christopher's room. He was fighting for his child's affection, but children who loved their parents also obeyed them. He pushed open the door.

"I'm not going, Wade, so don't ask me to."

"I'm not asking you; I'm telling you. I can't let you skip school. I'd be breaking the law and ruining your future. You're a straight-A student, and that's a ticket to the best schools and prestigious jobs, and I can't allow you to ruin your chances."

"How do you know what happens?"

"Because I was an A student, top of my class, went to the best school, and had the best jobs."

"So how come you don't have an office anywhere?"

"The judge gave your mother sole custody of you because my work took me all over the world. I was never in one place more than a few months, and he ruled that a child needed more stability than I could provide. Well, I have decided to fight for my rights as your father, and I gave up that work. For the past two years, I studied law. I've finished, and I'm preparing for the bar exams. After I take Nadine to work, I go to school and study. As a lawyer, I'll be able to fight for my rights, and I'll be settled in one place. I'm not giving you up, Christopher, so you can begin right now to obey me. I mean it." He hoped he hadn't come on too strong. The boy had seemed awed by his tale of adventure, but the famous Malloy temper had begun to boil at the mention of discipline.

"I don't care what you say; I'm not going. Mother never makes me do things like that."

"You're going to school."

"I won't. I'm never going back."

"Calm down, son, and come downstairs tomorrow morning ready for school." He turned out the light, closed the door softly, and leaned against it. He'd tried to provide the best for his family, but his efforts had cost him his marriage, and it seemed that each time he made headway with Christopher, something happened to widen the chasm.

Nadine raced up the stairs. Christopher's screams had awakened her. She reached his door and paused when she heard the boy recounting his nightmare to his father.

"I dreamed you went away and left me, that you told Casey he could have me. I don't like Casey. You're not going to give me to him just because I won't take swimming, are you?" Wade sat on the side of the bed, trying without success to reassure him. She knew she should go back to her room, but she couldn't rid her mind of the desperation in Christopher's voice nor the pain in his father's eyes. She wanted to hold them both to her bosom, to comfort them and love them. She stood there, her arms folded beneath her bosom and tears smarting her cheeks. She couldn't hear Wade's soft, whispered words to his son, but she realized after some time that the boy had fallen asleep.

Wade looked up and saw her.

"How long have you been standing there?" His hoarse, emotion-filled voice quivered slightly, as he slapped both hands on his steely thighs, rose, and started to the door.

"Maybe twenty minutes. I know I should have left after I found you with him, but somehow, I couldn't. What happened?"

He stopped within inches of her, and she could feel his magnetic energy churning and swirling around her, warming her, pulling her into its orbit. As though against their will, her eyes lifted to his face, to the raw anguish there, and she drew in her breath.

"He acted up with me earlier tonight, and his guilt about it gave him a nightmare."

She heard his words, but she knew his voice proclaimed a different thought and mood. He thrust out his hand to her, quickly withdrew it and curled it into a tight fist. His lips moved, but no words come. Finally he closed his eyes, squeezed them tighter and drew in a harsh breath.

"Nadine, why are you standing here? You know I need to bury myself in you. You know it. Nadine. *Nadine . . .*"

She couldn't walk away from him. Her hands went to his stubbly cheek, and she stroked him soothingly. "Yes, I know that Wade. But can't you take what I offer without wanting more?"

He shook his head. "Not now. I—I need more. Much more," and stepped away from her, his palms thrust forward.

She watched him cross the hall to his room and knew that she'd never met a man who possessed greater dignity.

Christopher went to school the next morning, but when he wouldn't promise to attend his swimming class, he was made to spend the day in the principal's office. Wade looked down at the note without reading it.

"What does it say?" he asked Christopher.

"It says I'm not supposed to come back to the school building until I agree to take swimming. And you have to go and see the principal."

After dinner that night, Nadine walked up the stairs not fearful but very nervous. Until the night before, she hadn't been up there since she'd given the space to Wade, and she didn't know how he'd react to another visit so soon. There was no door, so when she reached the top of the stairs, she knocked on the wall as hard as she could.

"Wade . . ."

"Yeah." He ducked his head out of Christopher's room. "You need me for something?"

"No. I want to talk with Christopher about his swimming class, if you don't mind."

"Sure. I appreciate anything you can do, because I

haven't moved him an inch. He says he's not going, even if he's expelled.''

"Could you leave us alone?" He nodded, walked out and closed the door behind him.

"I'm not doing it, Nadine, so don't ask me.''

She sat on the edge of his bed and took his hand. "You said we were friends, Christopher, so I'm going to share with you a secret about myself that only one person other than my parents ever knew. Will you keep my secret?" He nodded. "You once told me that I didn't understand your problem, because I wasn't the one with the blotch. Suppose you had a spot that bad on your ear, right out in a place where everyone could see it all the time.'' He sat up in bed, and his stare told her that her words had touched him.

"That's why you wear your hair like that and you're always putting you hand on your ear?"

"Yes.'' She tried unsuccessfully to keep the tremors out of her voice.

"But you hide your eye, and Wade said you have pretty eyes. It can't be that bad.''

Suddenly, she didn't think she could go through with it, and she rose to leave. He held her hand, restraining her.

"Don't go, Nadine. I didn't mean to say anything wrong. It's just you're so pretty. Let's see.'' She shook her head.

"I feel the same way about showing you my ear that you do about showing me your leg.''

"Oh.'' He looked steadily at her for a moment. "I'm sorry.'' Realizing that she had only added to his insecurity, she gathered her courage and pulled her hair away from her left ear. He leaned around Nadine, braced his hand on her shoulder for support, and looked at her left ear.

"Gee Nadine, it's not so bad. And you look nice with your hair like that. I mean, you know, like normal.''

"You promised not to tell.''

His hand went to his heart. "On my honor. Not even Wade."

Especially not Wade, she wanted to add, though she didn't.

"I showed you because I don't want you to be expelled from school, and I want to hear you sing in the school play. I'll bet your scar isn't any worse than mine."

She smiled inwardly. Christopher hadn't lied about being smart. The brief anger that flashed in his eyes, before his mouth curved into a smile let her know that he understood her game. Slowly, his leg came out from under the covers until she saw his knee and the large red, skinless scar above it. She didn't lie when she told him that it was little more than a blemish, that his classmates might look at it once or twice, but they'd soon forget it. "Just like my ear," she added.

"You think so?" She leaned over and kissed his cheek. He didn't move away, but spoke to her in words so soft that she barely heard them.

"Mother says it's not good to kiss boys, because it makes them into sissies."

She kissed him again.

"My kisses are different. Now, do we take you to school tomorrow or not?"

"I dunno, Gee, Nadine. Well . . ., I guess. If you can show me your ear. Okay . . ., I guess."

Fortunately, Wade had the good sense not to comment when Christopher came to the breakfast table the next morning dressed for school and carrying his book bag.

A few hours later, with Nadine at work and at a time when he should have been cramming for exams, Wade used his established credentials and got an interview with the manager of the hotel for which Rodney Ames had the interior decorating contract. He took the long elevator ride to the hotel's tower suite of offices unable to get his mind off of Christopher's cheerful journey to school. The boy hadn't offered one objection, and he couldn't help wondering what had transpired between him and Nadine the night before. He was grateful for whatever had happened, but he intended to find out. Less than five minutes after entering the manager's office, he knew he was looking at Nadine's drawings. The initials "NC" were unmistakable. He told the man of his suspicions and asked him to remain silent about it until he could provide proof.

"Why do you want to know?" He knew he'd expose himself and face her questions if he helped her find the lost plans, but he hadn't seen an alternative; if he didn't step in, she'd loose more than a set of plans.

"Trust me, Nadine," he cajoled softly. "I'm not stupid just because I drive you to and from work. You said McHenry's your contractor? I'm on to something, and I need to be sure of my facts."

She leaned back in her desk chair and looked out on Park Avenue South. "He's the one."

"Tom McHenry. He's head of McHenry and Deaver Associates." He nodded, and gave silent thanks for his good luck. He had known McHenry professionally for years.

Several days later, when the contractor identified the plans as the ones he'd approved for Nadine's project, Wade had to stifle the desire to shout, and had to cloak his face in a bland expression. But it wasn't easy to hide his joy. He and Nadine took the plans and left McHenry and the manager talking in the manager's office.

They entered the elevator, and he'd have expected anything except the way she chose to express her happiness; with face aglow and eyes shining, Nadine grabbed his shoulders and kissed him on the mouth. He knew that she meant it as a kiss of thanks, but the feel of her sweet lips on him—gentle as a wisp of spring breeze—telegraphed an urgent message to his sensual center, and he wanted more, needed more. He didn't think to check his aggressiveness, and his hands went to either side of her face, tight over her ears as he took over the kiss and changed it into a fiery sacrament to their mutual need. He vaguely sensed an uneasiness in her, but her submissiveness fueled the fire that she'd torched with her innocent kiss. His tongue rimmed her lips seeking entrance but, when she gasped at the feel of his virile power pressing against her belly, he pulled back. He had let himself forget that they were in a public elevator, and she'd been so attuned to him that she hadn't even noticed his hand pressing against her ear. The roughness beneath his left hand told him that ear was different from the right one. He kept that revelation to himself, careful to remove his hand gently, suspecting that it could be one source of her reticence and unease, the reason for her, asymmetrical hair style. He meant to get to the bottom of it, if he could do that without hurting her.

He wasn't sure what he wanted from Nadine but having gotten past her business woman's exterior and glimpsed more than once her capacity for tenderness and caring, he had to admit that he needed more than physical release with her. Ellen was a good woman, but she wasn't a nurturer. She didn't envelope a man in a satisfied cocoon of sweetness and warmth as Nadine did. In all these years, he hadn't known he needed that. But he knew it now. And he knew it because Nadine gave it to him.

Nadine's company had closed for the Thanksgiving weekend, and she sat in her basement home office at work on her plans for Rolling Hills Village. Wade had taken Christopher into New York to buy Christmas gifts, and she had the morning to herself. She chewed the end of her pencil, and tried to figure out what she was going to do about Wade? She feared that what she'd thought was an old fashioned crush on an extremely masculine, good-looking man was beginning to escalate into much more. A sense of uneasiness pervaded her, because she knew nothing about him other than what she'd seen since she met him. She didn't doubt that he was honorable, a decent man. But every person his age had a past, good or bad, and only a foolish woman would let herself fall for a man of whom she knew virtually nothing.

She poured more coffee from the thermos into the horrible green mug that Lorna had given her for a birthday present. She hated the thing, but it had grown on her. She leaned back in her chair, thought about the kiss in which Wade had nearly drowned her that day in the elevator and began to squirm, embarrassed by the moistness of her thighs. If only she were convinced that he would accept her blemishes along with the rest of her, that her scar wouldn't shock him, wouldn't make him turn from her, she'd walk . . . no, she'd *run* into his arms. *And if you knew more about him,* her common sense cautioned. Work was now impossible. She left the plans on her desk, went up to her room and changed into casual outdoor wear. At least she could rake the leaves.

Wade looked down at the three gifts Christopher had managed to buy during three hours of shopping in some of the largest stores in the world. Patience was a virtue, but the boy had an oversupply of it.

"We can go now, Wade. Mother likes the Mormon Tabernacle choir, so I hope she'll like the two CDs of that and the sweater. I know granddaddy will love the fishing stuff. Can we shop some more next Saturday? If you don't want to, I can ask Nadine. I used up my allowance, though."

I'm not going to be jealous of Nadine and my son, Wade admonished himself, taking Christopher's hand. "We can shop next Saturday, but we're going to one of the shopping malls. And if you want something, son, you ask me; I'm responsible for you,not Nadine.''

"I know, but she likes me and she doesn't mind.''

Wade knew that, but he wanted his son to depend on him. While he'd been earning a living for them, the child had become so accustomed to going to his mother for everything that he didn't understand a father's role. He shook his head in dismay. How could he get the boy to address him as his father when the child didn't see him as one?

"Wade, do you think we can come back to Hunting World next week for just a little bit? I don't think I want to give granddaddy any fishing stuff for Christmas. He can buy that himself.''

"Alright, son, but you're going to have to learn to make up your mind about things. And let's get a move on. It's getting cloudy, and I want to get back to Accord before the weather changes.'' He noticed that Christopher skipped along with him, instead of dragging behind as he'd usually done whenever they went anywhere. And the boy seemed to be holding his hand, rather than the other way around. Well, it was something. He locked their seat belts and started home, suddenly anxious to get there. A woman as high up on the corporate ladder as Nadine didn't dally with her chauffeur, he mused, but he consoled himself with the fact that he wasn't an ordinary chauffeur. If he decided that he had to have her, he'd get her if he had to unmask.

Nadine tied the black plastic bags of leaves and dragged them into the garage. She hardly recognized the place, because she hadn't entered it since Wade began driving for her. The tools had been cleaned and polished, a shelf containing clean cloths, lubricants, and cleaning agents had been installed and the windows washed. Maybe he really was a chauffeur. She smiled, thinking that there wasn't much chance of that; he took control too readily, was too sure of himself and had too active a mind to have been content with a job that demanded so little of his mental acuity. She walked toward the back of the house against the rising wind, her arms folded for added warmth, and stopped beside the massive oak tree that had been an inducement to buying the property. She fingered her mother's wedding ring that always hung from an old gold chain around her neck. Get back to work, she told herself; time is running out. *Let him know you care and that you need him,* a niggling voice interjected. *He's my chauffeur,* an inbred instinct to abide by society's proscriptions insisted. She threw up her hands, admitting confusion, and went back in the house and down to her office. A few minutes later, Christopher's joyous announcement of his arrival put an end to her effort to accommodate her sponsor without sacrificing professional integrity. She was happy for the child and a little ashamed at her envy when he exclaimed excitedly about the gifts he'd found for his mother. She needed a child of her own, but she knew better than to hope.

Wade was due to cook dinner, but Christopher loved cookouts, and she decided to prepare his favorite meal. She built a fire in the stone oven and grill that nestled beneath a fireproof tent a few yards from the back door. The tent made it possible to use the grill in any type of weather, so she didn't worry about the overcast skies. She prepared the meat and vegetables for grilling and went back to her office to try and find a place in the Rolling Hills house for an oversized Persian carpet. Sometime later, she looked at her watch; she'd better get the ribs started. When she noticed the back door ajar, she knew a moment of fear, but it passed swiftly when she remembered that she had Wade to protect her. Where was he? She hadn't seen him since he and Christopher returned from shopping. She wondered whether the thugs who had threatened her weeks earlier had returned and geared herself for an unpleasant encounter. Cautiously, she stepped out on the screened porch intending to look around without exposing herself.

She was at first charmed by what she saw and then her adrenalin accelerated its flow as fear gripped her. There in the open garden, Christopher knelt beside a very young fawn, obviously lost from its mother and seemingly chilled by the rapidly cooling temperatures, for it huddled close to the boy and allowed him to stroke its body. She knew that the mother had to be trailing the fawn's scent and couldn't be far away, and she streaked out of the door, remembering the deadly power of a deer's hooves. Immediately, she saw the big doe spring from the thicket into the garden and head toward Christopher and the fawn.

"Wade. *Wade!*" Her screams pierced the silence as she, too, ran toward Christopher, though she didn't know how she would help him, especially since he didn't see the big animal.

"Wade! Christopher, run. *Run!*"

She stopped short as a chunk of wood whizzed past her and landed in front of the doe, disconcerting her. Seconds later, Wade lifted Christopher into his arms and crushed his son to him while doe and fawn disappeared into the thicket. Neither the pungent smell of charring meat and vegetables engulfed in the grill's smoke nor the gusts of wind that brought the odor to her dry nostrils and smarted her eyes distracted her from the scene before her. She stood riveted by the vision of a father's face wet with tears of gratitude, his eyes closed in prayerful humility while the son for whom he had desperately feared patted him as though to comfort him.

"Don't scare me like that again, son. If that doe had attacked you, if she'd hit you with those sharp hooves, I think I might have died."

Nadine knew she had to control her trembling, that she couldn't cry right then, because the moment belonged to

Christopher and she couldn't detract from that by calling Wade's attention to her. She thought her heart would bound out of her chest when Christopher gripped his father's shoulders and clung to him. And though she felt left out, she pushed back the desire to go to them and ease herself into the circle of Wade's arms. She found the strength to walk casually over to them.

"I guess you realize how lucky you are to have a father like Wade, don't you Christopher? He thinks fast. I ran over here with nothing in my hand, and I couldn't have done a thing to help." Still clutching Wade's shoulders, Christopher looked into his father's eyes.

"I didn't see her. Do you really think she would have hurt me?"

"As sure as the sun rises. When you go near a young animal, son, always be certain that you know where its mother is." He put Christopher down, but she noticed that he kept his arm protectively around the child.

"What on earth is that noise?" Christopher looked from Nadine to Wade before covering both ears. Nadine laughed heartily, glad for the opportunity to release her tension.

"Mr. DeVanzio is back from one of his tours, I see." At their inquiring look, she explained.

"He's an operatic tenor who's seen his best days. When he practices the scales, he always peters out by the time he gets to high C, and he can't make it. But he tries. Screeching, in fact. Caruso—that's his dog—always makes the note for him, and the whole neighborhood goes for cover." Wade's disbelieving sparkling eyes warmed her heart. She realized that, out of that near disaster with the doe and fawn, he had a greater sense of closeness with his son and that he was happier than she'd known him to be. Because she rejoiced with him, she let her eyes mirror her heart.

* * *

Wade noticed Christopher's efficiency when the boy helped him clean-up after dinner, but it pleased him so much that he didn't question it. He hummed his favorite tune. Christopher had volunteered to help with the dishes and had asked him if he was any good at geography, a subject for which the boy obviously didn't care much. If that weren't enough, he had seen Nadine shed tears of happiness for him while he'd held Christopher in his arms after their near tragedy. She couldn't have known that he hadn't held his son since the boy was six months old. All the times he had come home from working abroad, Ellen hadn't let him near the child, saying that he might be carrying a dreaded foreign disease to which the boy had no immunity. Christopher tugged at his hand.

"I have a geography exam tomorrow, Wade. I understand most of the stuff, but I can't figure out how water from the Nile river takes care of all of Egypt. It doesn't rain much. How come the river doesn't dry up? And how can the pyramids still be there after all this time and don't sink in the sand?" Wade raised an eyebrow, took the boy's hand, and started up the stairs jingling his pocket change as they went.

"You don't want to know much, do you?" He said, pleased with the sharpness his son's mind.

"We'll deal with those pyramids some other time, since you don't need that information for your test. Right now, you have to get to sleep." He tweaked the boy's nose, turned out the light and walked toward the door.

"Gee, Wade, you know more than my teacher. You sure know a lot. Thanks for helping me." Joy suffused him as he stood there in the dark. Maybe his fortunes were about to change. He had begun to gain his son's respect; now, he had to earn the boy's love and affection.

"No thanks needed, son. This is what fathers are for."

Wade made coffee and took two mugs of it down to the

basement where he knew he'd find Nadine at work on her plans for Rolling Hills. Her absent-minded nod of the head told him that she was deep in her work so, when the phone rang he answered it, grimaced, and handed it to Nadine.

"I'm sorry, Rodney; it isn't a good idea. You got out of hand, and I don't allow men to paw over me." She hung up and Wade asked for her to agree to the date if Rodney called again. She demanded to know his reasoning.

"You need to let him show his hand. He may be in cahoots with someone. I'd be willing to bet that this isn't the first time he's been involved in the theft of an interior decorator's plans, even building plans. Don't forget that he had the contract *before* the plans were stolen."

When Rodney called again, she agreed to go out with him.

Her frown of displeasure didn't appear to carry any weight with Wade, who could barely suppress his smirk as he held her coat.

"At least, you're not a siren tonight, though I don't expect that insensitive fellow to realize that you didn't dress especially for him."

She pulled away from him in a huff and put her left arm into the coat sleeve without his help, albeit awkwardly. "How could you live as long as you have without learning how to mind your own business?" She nearly laughed; her voice hadn't carried the outrage that she'd tried to put in it.

"The same way you learned to live as long as you have without ever revealing any of your own business."

She hoped he'd realize from her glare that he was out of line. *And speaking of secretive!* She whirled around, chin up in a stance of belligerence that she hadn't previously allowed him to see.

"I'm secretive? What about you? If you're a chauffeur,

the world is flat and Louis Armstrong was a college pro-
fessor."

"Let's go get your date. Why doesn't the guy pick you
up sometime? Doesn't he know he's at a disadvantage the
minute he gets into your car?"

That's the way I want him, she thought, but she didn't
ease Wade's mind by verbalizing it.

To her relief, Rodney's behavior proved exemplary
throughout dinner. But thoughts of Wade sitting alone
somewhere waiting prevented her from enjoying the meal.
Perhaps he wasn't alone, but was spending the time with
a pretty young woman. Maybe . . . Rodney had spoken
of nothing all evening but work as if he was fishing for
information about her plans and his contract with the
hotel. She sat up, more alert and now very suspicious.
Wade was right; the man was a gopher. He may have taken
her plans, but that was all. And he hadn't seen as much
of those hotel suites as she had. Satisfied that she had all
the relevant information he possessed and that she could
safely relegate him to the past, she smiled indulgently.

"I'm ready to go."

On the way home, Roger's behavior deteriorated by the
minute until she considered asking Wade to dump him
right on the highway. But Wade must have sensed that she
couldn't tolerate Rodney any longer for, without a word
he pulled over and stopped, got out and walked around
to her door.

"Will you sit in the front with me, Nadine?" Her answer
was to extend her hand. He dropped the man off at his
apartment and drove home without speaking to her. She
didn't have to guess his thoughts, because his barely
leashed anger radiated out to her. She tried instead to
decipher her own feelings, to understand her deep regret
that she'd gone out with Roger and to come to terms with
the nonsensical feeling that, in doing so, she had somehow
wronged Wade.

He drove into her garage, parked, and walked around

to her door, but she opened it before he reached her. She couldn't fathom his dark gaze, and she didn't welcome the hot darts that ricocheted through her while he held her arm until they reached her door.

"Stay here," he said when they entered the foyer and he started down the hall to search her rooms for possible intruders.

"Why should I?"

Without a word, he spun around like a man who had reached his limit and pulled her to him.

"Wa . . ."

He swallowed the rest of his name. She couldn't wait for his tongue and opened her mouth in a plea for it that ripped a groan from deep inside him. She pulled his head down to increase the pressure, as though to steep herself in the heat that had begun to erupt in her loins. His hands went to her buttocks, pulling her tight against him until his hard virile power nestled at the seat of her passion. Obviously frustrated, he lifted her until she fit him perfectly. Desire plowed through her and she sucked his tongue into her mouth and held it there, feasting on it, while his strong fingers stroked her back and her buttocks and his arousal quivered against her.

She heard her whimpers and knew that the sounds fueled his desire for her just as his groans led her to spread her thighs around his slim waist. He brought his hand from beneath her buttocks to the left side of her head, and she slid down from her perch in that faraway realm of sensation, back to reality and to herself.

Wade knew at once what had brought on the change in her and searched for some way out of his predicament. He had upset her when he caressed the side of her face, but he had also let their passion explode and get the better of them. Maybe he ought to be thankful for his innocent mistake, because if they consummated what they felt, she'd send him on his way in the morning. But he'd been almost out of control from the moment he saw Rodney Ames put his hands on her. He broke the kiss and drew a deep breath.

"I let it get out of hand, Nadine, but I don't think I'm sorry. At least I know that you want me as much as I want you. Just don't let me ever see Rodney Ames's or any other man's hands on your body."

She nodded as though barely aware that he still held her pressed close with his heat straining against hers. He carried her to the living room and sat down with her in his lap.

"You're sweet. No, don't move. I don't want to be separated from you right now. I . . . Nadine, do you realize what almost happened between us? Unless I leave here, honey, we can't avoid it. But it doesn't suit me to leave, and I don't want to. You know that I have to establish a permanent residence, but there's more now; my boy is settled. He's gotten used to the place and the school, and he's grown fond of you. I want him to see his father as a man on whom he can depend, not some guy who drags him around from place to place, breaking up his friendships, pulling him out of first one school and then the next. This is more important than I know how to tell you."

"I'm not asking you to leave, Wade, but you must know that I'm not comfortable with this relationship."

"Because you shouldn't consort with your chauffeur? Right."

She jumped up, not annoyed because he refused to see any agenda other than his own, but hurt because he either thought her a snob incapable of overlooking his status or didn't trust her with his truth. She had to keep her voice low and soft, because their passionate exchange was still so fresh and her emotions so raw that she couldn't manage a firm, assertive voice.

"I've come to believe that you are an intelligent, clever man, but right now you're behaving just the opposite. When you can tell me who you are and what you do for a living besides pretend to be a chauffeur, your lap may begin to look inviting. Right now, it . . . well, you figure it out. Good night." She couldn't suppress a smile when she looked back at him. "And thanks for burying Rodney."

Wade sat up straight. "You mean that's the end of him?" he asked, hopefully. She shrugged.

"Bad pennies have a way of turning up, but I think he knows you cracked his crown."

"Crown? I'd like to crack his . . ." She walked on to her room. "Good night, honey," he called after her.

Was he mocking her, or was that a deliberate endearment? She closed her bedroom door and slumped against it. Of course he had good reasons to stay, she thought, reflecting on his explanation, and she had nearly as good a rationale for his leaving. But the reasons why she wouldn't ask him to go were even stronger: he seemed to belong in her home and in her life.

Wade tried not to let his mind dwell on her seductive gait, the luscious curve of her hips and her lovely firm buttocks as she walked away from him. His predicament reminded him of a pool shark caught behind the eight ball. He laughed. This was nothing compared to some of the jams that he'd escaped. He started toward the back of the house to check it and stopped short; in those days he'd risked a lot, sometimes his life, and thought little of it. But with this woman, he risked his heart, something that hadn't been in his plans. And he couldn't make light of it.

He stopped by his lawyer's office Monday morning, collected his mail, and looked at Ellen's familiar handwriting. What next? He read her letter and relaxed. What were they going to do about Christopher? she asked for the first time since she'd sworn to the world that he wouldn't be a competent father because he couldn't provide a stable life for his only child. Now, she was asking his advice.

Would he be willing to keep their son a little longer while she got adjusted to being married again, and would he bring the boy to see her?

He didn't want to feel sorry for Ellen, but he couldn't dismiss the thought that Casey, her new husband, didn't want Christopher and that Ellen was buying time. Well, Casey could stop worrying about Christopher Malloy. He spent a few minutes with his lawyer going over his business accounts and conditions for reopening the divorce settlement. He advised the lawyer to ease Ellen's worries without tipping his hand and headed down to New York University, where he'd rented a cubicle in the Law Library. He stashed his sandwich, apple, and orange juice in a desk drawer, turned on his beeper and settled down for serious study. Exams began the week after Christmas.

He needn't have worried about the lawyer leaking his plan to keep Christopher permanently; his son had an agenda of his own, he learned, and wasn't seeking his advice about implementing it. He went over Christopher's lessons with him that evening, and sent the boy off to get his shower.

"Wade, would you please address my letter to Mother and mail it tomorrow? It's lying on my desk. I don't have any more envelopes and stamps."

"Sure." He picked up the short, clearly written note and read, "Dear Mother, I love you a lot, but I don't love Casey. If it's alright with you, I'll stay with Wade, but I'll come see you all the time and you can come see me, too. Love, Christopher."

Nadine wasn't certain of the wisdom of telling her boss that plans taken from her desk had been found with the manager of the palatial Sky Hotel chain. What if he were in cahoots with the thief? She wished she had discussed it with Wade, but she buttoned up her courage and went to the head office. Norman Perkins had once intimidated her, but not any more. Five years had done a lot of damage to the once daunting ladies' man. Receding and thinning red hair, puffy jowls, and an ever growing paunch had brought him down to the level of the human race, and she no longer shivered when his olive green eyes sent her the message that she was as choice a female as he was male.

"Why do you need an office up here on the executive floor?" He dusted his pungent cigar in a sterling silver ashtray, and she knew his stare was meant to make her ill at ease.

"Because I deserve it," she said with a flash of insight into the man's personality. "What is your biggest interior decorating account at present? Rolling Hills, right? Who got it for you? Me. Right?" She brushed a thick curl away from her face and let her leather booted left foot dangle from her crossed knee. "So, what about it?" He puffed strenuously without caring where the smoke went.

"You can have thirty-one twelve. Decorate it to suit yourself, except please, don't put any pink in there." She could afford to ignore his chauvinist remark, she told herself, wondering whether his ready acquiescence implied guilt.

"You're beaming," Wade said when they met that evening. "I'd say you're happy. Want to share?" She let him open the front passenger door for her, because he insisted on it, got in and waited. Waited for what? He didn't keep her guessing, but leaned over and kissed her on the side of her mouth before he started the car. She would have protested if it wouldn't have been such an outright lie. She looked over at him, smiled, and saw glittering sparks in his light brown eyes as he smiled in return. Thoughtlessly, she hugged herself, and what she'd communicated to him gave her a sense of unease, when he brought her hand to his mouth and kissed her fingers one by one. As though propelled by an independent force, she moved as close to him as the bucket seats would allow.

"What happened today?" He spoke as though he had the right to know. Maybe he did. She told him about her new office and how she got it, and he praised her presence of mind in not confiding in her boss. He stopped for a red light just before reaching the Major Deegan Expressway, leaned over and, with his hand holding her head still, gave her a full mouth kiss. She had an impulse to turn into him and hold him, but honking horns interrupted the moment. A bit unsteadily, she leaned away from him, straightened her coat, and cleared her throat.

"You aren't mad at me for kissing you, Nadine, so don't talk yourself into it." He patted her knee.

"I'm not angry with you, Wade, but I'm uncomfortable with this relationship. I've told you that." She glimpsed his twitching jaw, a sure sign of his displeasure. "Where did you get so much self-confidence? I get the impression that you think you can do anything you want to."

The twitching of his jaw stopped, and a smile played around his mouth. "That so? Well, I don't seem to be able to do anything about this traffic." Her hand light on his arm wasn't intended to sooth but to nettle.

"Then speed up, and let's fly. Getting airborne ought to be a cinch for you."

In a voice heavy with sarcasm, he warned, "Stop while you're ahead, Nadine."

She tilted her head sideways and watched him from the corner of her eye. "Could we change the subject? Why Santa Claus has reindeer, for example."

"What's the matter? Scared I'll find a chink in your armor? If you have questions about my competence, let's leave Christopher with Lorna tonight, and by the time you wake up tomorrow morning, you won't have any doubts. Not a single one, honey."

"Why should I believe that?" she needled. "After all, you represented yourself as a chauffeur. The only thing you've said that I can't question is that you're Christopher's father."

"Are you saying you doubt my virility?" he asked so softly that she barely heard him. "What's so sacred about *that*?"

He slowed and pulled into the right lane.

"What are you doing?"

"I'm going to stop over here and give you the chance to tell me to my face that you're *not* provoking me deliberately, that you're not maneuvering me into spending the night with you either in your bed or mine." He stopped the car. "Because that's what you'll get for issuing me that challenge."

"Wade, for goodness sake. All I said was—"

He interrupted, knocked her seat back to reclining position, and leaned over her, his hot gaze piercing and dangerous. Hypnotic.

"What you said in effect was that you didn't believe a night in bed with me could please you. Nadine, if you don't swallow those words, don't even bother to put on your gown tonight." His lips almost brushed hers, and the breath she took was his own. Hot blood pounded in her face when the tip of his tongue touched her bottom lip, and her mouth opened while her arms reached up to him as though of their own will. His groan set her temples to throbbing, and she wanted to curse the seats that separated their bodies when his tongue glazed her mouth with heat such as she'd never before experienced. She stroked his face and squirmed in her seat. A powerful desire streaked through her, scattering her senses, turning her traitorous body into a frenzy of wanting. He raised his head, and the sweetness of his smile shook her to the pit of her soul.

"You needn't worry. No matter how badly I want to, I won't go to your door unless you give me a very clear invitation." He smoothed her hair away from her face, and her right hand grasped his wrist so strongly that it brought a sharp look from him.

"Don't!"

He stared at her.

"What's the matter? What did I do?"

"Nothing. I'm sorry." He straightened up, raised her seat, and saw the dampness at the edge of her hair and the tiny beads of moisture on her nose.

"It's alright," he said, when he remembered what he'd done just before she panicked. But it wasn't alright or she wouldn't have frozen on him just when he'd thought, for the first time, that they might take a chance on each other. A real chance.

He eased the Crown Victoria onto the highway and headed for Accord, not sure that he wanted a deep involvement with a woman right then, when his priority was getting custody of his son. But he wasn't sure that he had a choice. His glaze swept over the sweet, and now troubled, face that seemed to have taken up a permanent place in his mind's eye, to be there for him to see and to relish day and night, no matter where he happened to be. He grimaced and focused his attention on route eighty-seven. She hadn't begun to interfere with his studying yet, but when she did, he'd get a cure. Maybe he'd better get one before he reached that stage.

He knocked on Lorna's door wearing the fixed smile with which he usually greeted the nosey woman, but Christopher opened it, yelled goodbye back to little Greta and dashed toward the car. He corrected the eager youngster, who rushed back and, to Wade's surprise and joy, grasped his father's hand. The child bounded into the back seat, greeted Nadine, and reoriented the adults' thoughts.

"Wade, can Granddaddy come here to see me Christmas? He always used to come see me at Mother's house. Nadine doesn't mind, do you Nadine?"

Wade hadn't thought of his father's annual, week-long Christmas visit with his grandson, a custom that he hadn't shared during his years of work abroad. He'd better make some plans. "Of course, my daddy can visit you Christmas, though I don't—"

Nadine interrupted him. "We'll be delighted for your grandfather to come for Christmas and stay as long as he wants to, won't we, Wade?" He felt her left elbow nudge his rib cage, and a bit sharply, too, he thought with amusement. But he didn't need prompting; she couldn't know how much her words pleased him and, considering the fragile nature of their relationship, it was just as well that she didn't know.

"Thanks, Nadine." He had to control his voice, because he had a feeling it might quiver. If anybody had told him he was an emotional man, he'd have laughed in their face, but something was happening to him, and Nadine was at the core of it. He assisted her from the car, and she let him do it, her attraction to him blazing blatantly across her face as he rested an arm possessively about her. He looked around. Not a chance; Christopher had glued his gaze to them.

They finished dinner and Nadine went to her office in the basement, while Wade checked Christopher's homework. Nadine taped her drawings for Rolling Hills Village to the wall beside her desk in order to study them better. Being without those plans for over two weeks had cost her valuable time, and she figured she'd have to work every night until midnight in order to make that deadline. She didn't hear Wade enter the room, and she jumped at the sound of his deep voice.

"You sure you want to put curtains on that living room window? Granted they're thin, but I think they detract from that awesome view." She turned slowly and looked up at the man who leaned confidently over her shoulder. She'd already thought of that, but there was a need for privacy even in living rooms. She told him as much.

"Frank Lloyd Wright wouldn't agree. One of his nearly all glass houses had no curtains or shades on the entire first floor. There weren't even any windows, just glass. So come on, be modern." The sound of coins jingling in his pocket told her that he was more than pleased with himself. A slow burn didn't begin to describe her reaction. She was certain that he wouldn't have been able to seduce her right then, not even if he'd stripped down to his birthday suit.

"Anything else?" she breathed, in what she hoped would reach him as heavy sarcasm. It didn't surprise her that he ignored her warning, thrust his hands in the back pockets of his trousers and thought for a while before answering. She'd learned that he took his words seriously.

"Well, I can't see a huge Tabriz carpet on that intricately inlaid living room floor. Why hide all that great work?" Furious as she was with him, his comment had merit and she couldn't help but respond in a professional manner.

"My firm never lays out the money for the research or the furnishings to test these arrangements. We decorators get sponsors, and one of mine is a dealer in Persian carpets, so I've got to use some of his merchandise." She turned around and switched on her computer, effectively closing the subject. Wade was not discouraged.

"Okay. Put a Royal Bukhara on the stair case and in the master bedroom. That ought to hold him. I'd leave the living room floor bare. Of course, I know you decorators don't believe in leaving *anything* uncovered, but this time less is more." She couldn't resist telling him what she thought of his "unschooled" ideas, and he made more than one reference to her pigheadedness. She didn't usually let herself get into arguments about individual judgments, but she was beside herself at his arrogance. Just like a man; he knew it better.

"How do you deign to tell me how to decorate a house?" she spat out in frustration.

"When I'm just your ignorant chauffeur?" he asked in an almost frighteningly quiet tone. She slumped in her chair. It always came back to his being her chauffeur.

"He isn't any chauffeur." They hadn't been aware of

Christopher's presence. "Wade's studying for his bar exams, aren't you, Wade? He's studying to be a lawyer." They both turned toward the child at the sharp tone of his voice and became aware of his fury, when they saw the tears that rolled down his young cheeks.

"Wade isn't your chauffeur." He repeated, though she could see that he was begging for confirmation. "He's a lawyer." She tried to breathe normally and to control her reactions, because she didn't want to expose Wade. But she couldn't hide her skepticism.

"Since when?" She asked, softening her voice.

"He told me that's what he's doing so he can stop living in jungles and airplanes, didn't you Wade?" Nadine knew that her face held a look of disbelief, but she couldn't hide her shock or her ire.

"Yes I did, son, and that is exactly what I am doing."

She couldn't make herself look at Wade, because she didn't know what he'd see. What her face would show. Right then, she didn't ever want to see him again. How could he have led her on the way he had? She flinched beneath Christopher's hard glare.

"There's no problem, Christopher, so . . ."

"You always say that," he screamed at her, "but you don't mean it, do you? If he's not your chauffeur, why can't you say so?" To her horror, he ran from the room and upstairs.

Nadine walked into the kitchen earlier than usual, dreading the morning. She'd been right all along in thinking that she'd given Wade his first job as a chauffeur. But that was not the issue. Who was he? So he spent his days studying for a bar exam. So what? After he'd left her the night before, she'd searched her library and verified his claim about Wright's glass house. And after sketching several good possibilities, she'd concluded that a red, Royal Bukhara carpet was just what that huge stair case needed. But how had he known that? She took a carton of eggs from the refrigerator, set out other ingredients for French toast, sighed deeply, and sat down. It was Wade's morning to cook. He walked in and stopped when he saw her.

"Can we meet for lunch today, Nadine? I know we have to talk, but we can't do it this morning, and I'd like us to get things settled. I think negative vibes are bad for children, and that's what's flying around here right now."

She sat up straight, started to push her hair away from her face, realized what she'd done, and slapped her hand over her ear. She didn't look at Wade, for fear of seeing recognition in his eyes.

"What about you and Christopher?" she bluffed, dropping her hand into her lap with apparent casualness.

"I straightened it out with him last night. I didn't make him happy, but he knows I'm not a liar. He thought this was my place, but he's just learned that it's your house, and that I work for you. To him, a chauffeur is a servant, thanks to Ellen's snobbery. He can't handle it."

"I'm not hungry this morning." Christopher stood in the door ready for school, his belligerence as visible as his face.

"You can't go out without breakfast," they responded in unison. "And I'm going to fix you some French toast," Nadine added. "You always like that."

The boy turned and walked away, and Nadine jumped up to follow him, knocking over her chair as she did so.

"Don't pander to him, Nadine. He's a child. Right now, he's a disrespectful child, and he has to learn not to be rude. The least you should expect from him is a civil greeting, angry or not."

She didn't pause, and found the forlorn little boy huddled in a chair that was so big he seemed lost in it.

"Casey doesn't like me, but maybe I should go back to my mother. Maybe Wade can pass his exams faster, and you won't have to bother with me."

Momentarily stymied, she searched for words of comfort.

"You can't leave with my secret, darling. Besides, this is your home. You have to stay here with me. I don't want you to leave me."

"You don't? What about Wade? Are you mad at him?" And what was the answer to that? She risked putting an arm around him and, when he didn't object, she hugged him to her fiercely.

"Don't worry. He and I will work things out. And Christopher, you must stop using your father's first name; it's disrespectful, especially since he asked you to call him 'dad.'"

"Okay. Gee, Nadine, I have to take my granddaddy's tackle back to the store, 'cause I'm not going to give him that for Christmas. Can I go shopping Saturday?" She wondered why he'd asked her rather than his father and suspected that she and Wade had confused him about his father's status.

"Darling, I can't answer that; you'll have to ask your father. Besides, I'll be working Saturday morning. Now, come on back here and eat your breakfast. We'll have to hurry, because it's getting late." As they walked into the kitchen, Wade placed hot French toast before his son.

"Wow, Wade. I didn't know you could make these," the boy said, appreciatively, as he savored a mouthful. She wondered how Wade had foreseen the outcome of her little chat with the boy, and couldn't help softening toward the man. He needed her.

Wade stood when Nadine approached the table. It had surprised him when she suggested a restaurant less than a block from her office where they might meet some of her colleagues. He didn't miss the heads that turned as she walked toward him. Stunning. She was *some* woman! He stepped around to her side of the table and held her chair.

"What's so urgent, Wade, that it couldn't wait until

tonight?'' He saw that she'd girded herself for battle and told his temper to take a walk.

"Thanks for coming. Let's order first." The waiter brought their menus and greeted her as one well known to him. Wade watched her eyebrows arch sharply when he gave his order of arugula and fennel salad, roast squab in pine nuts, and plum pudding. Alright, so it wouldn't tease some palates, but it was what he wanted. He declined wine. Nadine ordered chablis as an accompaniment to her salmon paté, broiled mushrooms, and redleaf lettuce salad.

"What's up?" he asked, when he noticed her intense perusal as though seeing him for the first time.

"You've got a rich man's taste buds." She paused. "But why should that surprise me? Everything about you is unusual, including your attempt to appear down on your luck when nothing could have been farther from the fact."

"I've never said or done anything to suggest that; you saw it that way because you wanted to. You wouldn't have hired a law school graduate to chauffeur you around, unless he'd just gotten out of school and was wet behind the ears. I needed two things: a steady job and time to study for my bar exams. What was more logical than chauffeuring for a working woman? I'd hoped to be able to sit in the car and study, but you gave me the whole day free, and I study at the NYU Law Library."

"Well, at least I know where you are in case I get sick and want to go home early."

He wrote his beeper number on the back of a napkin and handed it to her.

"You've even got a beeper? Have you got a Lincoln stashed away somewhere?"

"Nadine, I'm doing this so that I can gain custody of my son, something that I was denied because I had to work away from home in order to make a living for myself and my family. At present I'm only entitled to visit him once a week. A judge ruled that I wouldn't provide a stable life for a child and gave my wife sole custody. A man can't bond with his son once every two or three months and have it mean anything. It's now or never for Christopher and me, and if I don't stay in one place for at least a year, I'll still be considered unstable. I decided to learn domestic and family law so that I'll be able to handle my own case, because this is too important for me to entrust to another person. If you want me to leave, of course, I'll go. But I've more reason than that not to leave you." He watched her face for some sign of what she was thinking, though he knew and hated that she wouldn't be able to make an unbiased decision, because her feelings for him would interfere just as his did.

"I don't have any right to pry into your life, Wade. You answered all of my questions when you took the job. If I'm honest, I'll admit that there'd be no question were it not for the fact that we haven't kept personal feelings out of our relationship."

He picked up the fancy tweezers that lay in front of his plate, pulled the bones out of the tiny bird, took a bite and decided that candid honesty was in order. He was tired of pretense.

"That wasn't going to be possible, and I knew it before I agreed to take the job. You and I are the epitome of perfect chemistry." He reached over and covered her hand and, when she let him hold it, he told her, "When we acknowledge that, Nadine, we'll share something wonderful." Her failure to respond would have bothered him had she not turned her palm upward beneath his hand.

"Talk to me, honey."

"It would be best if you went away, but I don't want you to, even though I should fire you for not representing yourself properly. I was furious with you last night, because I felt you'd made a fool of me." She sighed heavily. "Well, that's water under the bridge. Anyway, Christopher has adjusted to his school, even to the swimming class, and you deserve a chance with him."

"I'd manage, Nadine, but you'd still be vulnerable to

robbers and muggers every morning and every evening, and I'd worry about that." He squeezed her hand, hoping to communicate the tenderness that he felt for her. "Can't we admit that we need each other, that life is better now for both of us. That doesn't imply intimacy though, mind you, I'm definitely not saying I don't want it."

"Alright, I'll admit I don't worry about muggers nowadays when I get home. So, let's let it rest."

Wade laughed. She could find numerous ways to avoid saying what he wanted to hear and still not lie.

He spread the side helping of hard sauce thickly over his plum pudding, earning a disapproving mug from his companion. "What's the matter? I like sweet stuff; you ought to know that." From her diffidence, he supposed he'd done an apt job of letting her know what he thought of her. He continued to let his gaze roam over her.

"This hard sauce could take lessons in sweetness from you," he told her, rimming his lips slowly with the tip of his tongue.

"Stop it! You're overdoing this." He meant his slow grin to unsettle her and enjoyed it when she squirmed. "Wade, have you forgotten that this is a public restaurant? Behave yourself. I could . . . I could . . . powder you, Wade."

Warm, prickling sensations began to spread throughout his hard, lean body. "Any time. Be glad to accommodate you." She looked skyward as though appealing to heaven.

"If we had some privacy right now, would you ravish me? If I put myself at your mercy and let you have your way with me, what would you do?"

"I'd box your ears." Her bubbling laughter warmed him throughout, and he wanted to push that hair away from her left eye so that he could see her whole beautiful face and both of her sparkling brown eyes. When her left hand suddenly covered her left ear, he knew that he'd been staring at her, and that he had ruined their precious moment. What the hell was it that made her panic about that hair and that ear? Christopher had stopped questioning him about it, and he suspected that the boy had somehow gotten the facts.

He paid the bill with his credit card, included a tip and gave silent thanks that she'd been sensitive enough not to suggest splitting the bill. He had invited her to lunch, because he wanted to be on his own territory when he tried to settle their differences. He wanted the advantage, and he knew he wouldn't have that at her home in Accord. And paying for their lunch with his gold credit card was part of the strategy. They reached the door as Rodney Ames entered it. The man nodded to Nadine.

"Seems I'm in the wrong profession. Chauffeurs have more fun and, when it comes to bodyguards, I wouldn't even guess."

Wade's arm automatically went around Nadine. He couldn't help it, and he didn't care what Rodney Ames or anyone else thought about it.

"Use a little horse sense, Ames, and stop overstepping your bounds with Nadine Carpenter. I don't like it." He moved closer, and Rodney backed off. "Oh yes," he continued, "I've been meaning to ask you how you initial your plans? You do use 'RA,' don't you?" The gaping hole that Rodney's mouth had become was all the satisfaction Wade needed. He kept an arm around Nadine until they got back to her office building.

"See you at five." He pondered whether to kiss her, settled for a stroking of his fingers against her cheek, and walked off jingling his pocket change and whistling the Toreador song.

Nadine got to the ladies' room as fast as she could, threw cold water on her face, blotted it with paper and leaned against the wall. Approaching voices and footsteps sent her scrambling into one of the booths, and she locked the door and clung to it for support. Finally, unable to hold them, she let the tears stream down her face. How had she let herself fall in love with a stranger? A complex, problem-saddled enigma of a man who possessed steely nerves, old fashioned grit, tenderness, and a powerful passion that drew her as sweet flowers draw bees. A stranger. And every molecule in her body wanted him. And loved him. And she could think of half a dozen reasons why she shouldn't. He was totally unlike the corporate types, the alpha males whom she had dated since graduate school. He showed his feelings. He hurt and wasn't ashamed to let her see it. And he was a strong, determined man. If she knew him, really knew him, would she still love him? Would she love him that much more?

The door closed and the voices receded. She stepped out and had no sooner begun to freshen up than Dilly, the boss's secretary and the executive floor's gossip courier walked in.

"Nadee . . . ine," she sang, "the whole firm is talking about your luncheon date. *Who* was that hunk? Lottie said she'd never seen anything that perfect—smooth dark skin, over six feet, gorgeous brown eyes, flat middle and nice tight behind, and a smile to die for. She swears she's going to thank the Lord for the pleasure of having seen at least one flawless man in her life. And she said he had his arm around you. You lucky girl! The best I can do is Roger Ames tomcatting behind me everywhere I go. But I'm not stupid; I know he wants to get in the boss's good graces. Well, later for him."

The one advantage of Dilly's company was that she did the talking. You weren't even required to answer or even to listen, because she didn't notice. She just talked. Nadine dusted powder on her nose and forehead, brushed her hair and applied a little lipstick, and patted Dilly on the shoulder on her way out. She swished past her own, newly acquired secretary, went into her office, and closed the door. Immediately, she pushed a button to get her voice mail and leaned back in her chair when she heard his sonorous tone. The first time he'd called her. She wondered why he'd never called her before and whether that meant he cared for her.

"You're wonderful, and I love being with you. See you at five." Nothing else. Not even their names. She could listen to his voice forever. But she had to work, so she punched numbers on the new combination lock she'd put on her desk, took out her plans and started to draw some bedroom chairs that she wanted to have made for her model home. To curve the arms, or angle them; she sketched them both ways, but couldn't decide. I'll see what Wade thinks, she told herself, then wondered why that thought had come to her. *Because you know he's clever*, an inner voice said. She argued the wisdom of discussing it with him rather than with one of her professional colleagues. He won.

Her secretary announced Rodney Ames, who entered without her having asked him to and seated himself without an invitation. She didn't correct him, because she wanted him to state his business and leave.

"The whole floor is buzzing about your brazen little caper," he began, and she knew he was seeking balm for the latest wounds that Wade had inflicted on his pride. She leaned back in her chair and eyed him steadily, giving him a warning that he ignored.

"When did you start dating your chauffeur, Nadine? How do you think Norman would take that?" Nadine stopped herself just as she was about to put the pencil in her mouth. Rodney couldn't make her nervous, she reminded herself, because she had his number.

"Rodney, I really don't care about the boss's opinion of my personal life. If you'd like, I'll ask Wade to come up after work and talk with you. And if you run out of conversation, I can always drop in and bring up the little matter of the plans that disappeared from my desk. Now, if you'll excuse me, *I* at least have to work." She imagined that she'd made his leaving awkward, but she didn't look up from her desk to verify it.

* * *

Wade buckled Christopher's safety belt, checked the traffic, and started back to Accord. The boy had bought writing paper, envelopes, and a ball point pen. He'd kept his one other purchase a secret, though Wade suspected that it was something for Nadine. Nadine. He cared for her; he no longer questioned that, but what was he going to do about it? He knew nothing of her other than what he'd seen. Her intelligence, warmth, gentle sweetness, compassion, grace, and yes, passion. Wild passion. When he'd been a young turk, that would have been sufficient to tie him to a woman, but he'd been through the battle-field of marriage and the swamp of a bitter divorce; he had to know more.

"Christopher," he began, though he hardly expected a straight answer from the boy while the radio piped out Johnny Hodges' saxophone, "you used to ask me about the way Nadine wears her hair and why she puts her hand over her left ear. What happened? Did you speak to her about it?" When the boy didn't answer, he repeated the question, lowering the volume on the radio as he did so.

"What about it, son?"

"What about it, Wade? It's her hair, and she can wear it any way she wants to." He turned the volume back up and hummed along with the music, raising Wade's suspicions.

"Alright. But I know you ask questions until your curiosity's satisfied, so let's admit that you know why she does it and that you don't intend to tell me. You're protective of her. Fine. I accept that; I even like it." Christopher's lack of comment was as much assurance as he needed that the two had talked about it and that a strong bond had developed between them.

The boy pretended to be engrossed in the jazz music. "Christopher, I want you to stop calling me by my first name. I am your father, and it's time you addressed me that way. I'm not giving you up, and I want you to remember that."

"Okay. Do you think we could stop at the farmer's market and get some chestnuts? Nadine said me and her could roast some under the grill this evening." A passing car diverted him.

"She and I, Christopher," Wade corrected.

"Okay. Gee whiz, Wade, would you look at that red corvette? Wow!"

Wade sighed deeply. He wished he knew what it would take or whether it was already too late.

He walked out on the back porch after dinner and watched the season's first snowfall. As a child, it had been his delight to roll in it, hide in it when he could, and play games with his imaginary friends, the fairies and sprites that he welcomed from the surrounding woods. He gazed out at the silver tipped pines that sparkled in the brilliant moonlight. So beautiful that it threatened to spark a tide of melancholia. No wonder he had so readily become attached to these surroundings; they were in many ways similar to his paternal home in northern Michigan. He had to share the night's beauty, and he needed to share it with his son. He stepped back to the door and called him.

"Christopher, throw on your coat and come down here for a minute." He smiled at the sound of his son barrelling down the stairs, noise that warmed his heart; things weren't perfect with them, but they were together.

"What is it?" He watched as a look of wonder spread over the child's face. "Wow! Those clouds look like little people running around up there. Gee whiz, Wade, it's awesome!" He grasped his son's hand, his sense of oneness with him tearing at his heart. The child had seen exactly what he'd wanted him to see—the mystery of the night as he had known it when he was a boy. He couldn't resist the urge to hug his son close to him, and they stood that way for a long time. Then he knelt to Christopher's level, held his shoulders firmly, and, in a voice so husky that he barely recognized it as his own, he told him, "I love you, son. I always have, and I will forever." He shook Christopher's shoulders gently. "Forever. Do you here me? Forever!''

Christopher's stare nearly unnerved him. In spite of the night's chill, perspiration beaded his forehead. He didn't know what reaction he'd hoped to get from his son, but none could have hurt more than the silence. With a light hug and a pat on the bottom, he admonished him. "Go back in and get into bed." Christopher lingered until Wade patted him again.

"Go on up, son. Good night." The boy turned quickly, grazed his father's cheek with the barest of kisses and ran inside. It was as though a shadow had vanished from his heart and a weight from his mind. He rubbed the spot idly and smiled ruefully. Wonder how long a man could get away with washing only one side of his face? His son had kissed him, the first kiss he'd ever had from his only child.

Nadine paced the floor of her basement office, the confines of which loomed like a prison, instead of the place where she had once happily practiced her craft. She didn't want to work, couldn't work; she wanted to go upstairs and find Wade, but that would be too easy. And she might regret it. She tried to come to terms with the fact that she loved Wade Malloy. She didn't try to talk herself out of it, or to diminish the depth and intensity of what she felt. She loved him. It was as simple as that. She turned off her computer, doused the lights, and walked slowly up the stairs, all the while talking herself out of searching for Wade and giving herself to him.

"If you're not working tonight, Nadine, could you help me do my science project?" Christopher called down to her. She readily agreed, because third grade science was definitely better than day dreaming, but she remembered Wade's crusade to win the boy's respect and affection.

"Honey, I'm bushed tonight, but I know your father would enjoy helping you, and he may be better at science than I am. Why don't you ask him?"

"He already went over my geography and my French with me, so I thought you could, you know, help me do my science." She understood then that he wanted attention from her, that he wasn't rejecting his father. She sat beside his desk and asked him to show her his work.

"Nadine, I don't really have to study." He hung his head and looked away from her before continuing in a tentative voice.

"Wade is going to get my leg fixed during the Christmas holidays. Do you think he could get your ear fixed, too? Then you could comb your hair away from your eyes. Could we ask Wade to get your ear fixed, Nadine? Could we, huh?"

"You didn't tell him about it, did you? You promised."

"Scout's honor. He asked, but I didn't answer him. If my leg's gonna be alright, I want your ear to be alright, too." She hugged him and enjoyed the feel of his arms around her, strong for one so young.

"I'll think about it and let you know," she told him, though she admitted to herself that she'd made an idle promise. "Now, hop in bed and go to sleep. It's late." He did, and she pulled the covers around him, paused, and brushed his cheek with a kiss. She straightened up, and he smiled. He's already got a mother, a niggling voice reminded her.

Wade remained outside, drinking in the soundless night, thinking of Nadine. His first marriage hadn't been a bad one; it just hadn't had the strength to withstand his long and frequent absences on overseas jobs. He'd tried his best, and he supposed that Ellen had too, but it hadn't been enough to keep them together. He didn't want to reminisce about the past, but if he stayed out there, that's what he'd do. He locked the outer screen door, went in the kitchen and gasped, flabbergasted at the sight of Nadine peering into the refrigerator, every line of her body revealed through a soft, pink silk gown and robe, a picture of feminine grace.

"Did you know I was out on that porch?" His own deep guttural sound warned him to rein in his passion.

Nadine looked up and saw him standing there. Wild and ready and wanting, and with the ravenous look of a man who had known only starvation in his whole life.

"Did you want me to see you looking like this? Did you?" She couldn't move, and she hoped he was out of control, because then, she wouldn't have to decide.

"I . . . I don't know. I didn't think." Tendrils of fear, excitement, and anticipation shot through her as he walked slowly toward her, his movements rhythmic, his gaze hypnotic. He stopped, spread his legs and extended his hands, causing blood to roar in her ears and her pulse to race while she stood glued to the floor, fighting her passion. He smiled and reached for her, and she sprang into his arms, grasped his head and wrapped her legs around him as he brought her to him, his kisses ravenous. In all her life, she'd never felt so free. So wild and so wanton. His lips moved over hers and she answered, surrendering to the fire that he built. She parted her lips, asking for more but, as though programmed to do so, he held her from him, his breaths deep and labored.

"Are we going to end this right here, or in your bed? Tell me. You're important to me, Nadine, and I don't want to make a mistake with you. I know you want me, but what are you asking of me right now? Do you want me now? *And can you live with it tomorrow?*"

Answering him wasn't easy. He was fully in control and forcing her to decide.

"I won't deny that I want to be with you and, if you hadn't slowed down, it would have happened. I don't know why you decided that you had to have my complete submission, but I suppose I should thank you for refusing to compromise."

He started to release her, but she held on. If he moved away, she'd have to look him in the eye, and she wasn't ready for that. She marveled at his intuitiveness.

"How do you know that I would have regretted it?" she asked, looking over his shoulder and into vast loneliness, the place where she'd spent most of her adult life. "How did you know?" she repeated. He put her way from him then, though he did it with care.

"Because you haven't accepted me as a man. I'm still your chauffeur. You care for me, and you want me, but you wouldn't mind if that weren't true. You'd just as soon I was someone else." She reached toward him involuntarily, but he didn't reciprocate.

"Wade . . . You're not just . . .," she couldn't finish the thought and had to watch helplessly as his face become a mass of bitterness.

"You don't know what I am to you, do you? Or maybe you know, and you don't like it. I am your chauffeur, Nadine. I'm the man you pay to drive you to and from work every day and to protect you here at night. And if you can't acknowledge your feelings for me, your hired chauffeur, where does that leave us? I am not going to quit this job just so you'll feel comfortable making love with me, much as I want it."

She didn't want him to see how vulnerable she was, to know that his words ripped her inside. How could he say that when she loved him with all her heart? She had to grope for composure and turned away to shield herself from his knowing eyes.

"Nadine. Sweetheart. Ah, baby, come here to me. I wouldn't hurt you for anything. Come, honey." They held each other gently until he stirred against her and, with a rueful smile, put her at arms length.

"I think I've set some kind of record for self-control since I met you, lady." His gaze pierced her. "If it's too much for you, I'll leave."

Idly, she stroked his left biceps, impressed with the strength that its solidness implied.

"I thought we already settled that. What's changed since then?" From the way in which he eyed her, clearly disbelieving, one might have gotten the impression that she lacked some essentials.

"Nadine," he said in a mien that suggested he was having trouble whipping his patience into line, "after the way we went at each other a few minutes ago, do you honestly believe that we aren't going to become lovers? That's what's changed. We suspected it earlier; now we know." She enjoyed the feel of his strong, gentle fingers as they squeezed her shoulders. "I think you ought to turn in." He smiled the radiant and loving smile that she loved so much, and then his face went rigid.

"If you need help to make it through the night, as the song goes, throw one of your shoes against the ceiling. I won't be asleep." He kissed her hard on the mouth and dashed upstairs. Her gaze followed him as he went; neither would she.

The next morning, Sunday, Nadine parked in front of Lorna's big, nineteenth-century white frame house with its wraparound porch, metal mail box beside the front door and oversized American flag that waved from a pole in the corner. That flag had always peeked Nadine's interest; she'd finally attributed its presence to Lorna's passion for keeping up with the Joneses; both the black Joneses and the white Joneses.

"Thanks for the ride, Nadine. I thought I'd see Wade and Christopher at service with you this morning. And we're still wondering when you're going to bring your . . . that delicious, honey of a man out to the Saturday night bridge party? 'Course, poor Hugh Cliburn will just die if you do.'' Nadine reached across Lorna and opened the door, not happy with the turn of Lorna's one-track mind. The woman had attempted to link her with Hugh at their first meeting and seemed to have made getting them together her one mission.

"Lorna, I have never said a word to Hugh Cliburn, nor he to me. Two, I don't play bridge, and three, Wade Malloy isn't mine to take or bring. Now, please drop the talk about Wade and me. It's not helpful.''

Lorna's tongue pulled air through her front teeth. "If you say so. But if you believe it, you ain't fooling nobody but yourself. Well, thanks for the ride.'' Nadine waved at her and drove off.

She changed into jeans, cowl neck sweater and a heavy woolen sweater jacket, ate an apple, and rushed outside for a look at the family of rabbits that she glimpsed through the kitchen window. The rabbits disappeared before she got outdoors, so she moseyed down to the creek, leaned against a tree, and watched the water swirl and splash in its rush to mate with the Hudson river. Solitude no longer suited her; Christopher and Wade could leave her at any time, yet she couldn't suppress the forlorn feelings that beset her whenever she came home and found them absent. She'd known that they planned to complete their Christmas shopping that afternoon, but she still wasn't prepared for the empty house when she returned from church and couldn't imagine that she ever would be again. Wade. Where were they headed? For a long while, she gazed at her reflection in the rushing stream, wishing that she knew the outcome. He wanted her, but did he care for her?

* * *

She didn't know how long she sat on that log at the edge of the stream. The chill and dampness alerted her to the sparse snowflakes, and she walked to the back door and turned the knob, but met with resistance and realized that she'd locked herself out of her house. She would have taken refuge in the garage but, when she put her car there, she'd followed one of Wade's iron clad rules never to leave that door unlocked. Hugging herself for warmth, she walked in the rapidly falling snow to her nearest neighbor, two blocks away, but got no response. She walked back past her house to the nearest one on her other side, but fear began to trickle through her: the entire neighborhood knew that when Mr. DeVanzio was at home on a Sunday afternoon, either he, his dog, or both could be heard trying to reach high C. Nevertheless, she knocked on his door and satisfied herself that he wasn't there. Deciding against the three-mile trek to the cross-road, she trudged back home in the now heavy snow, shivering with cold and hungry, because she'd eaten only an apple for lunch. She huddled up beside the front door to shield herself as much as possible from the wind and snow and hoped that her prayers would be answered. Wade and Christopher found her there much later soaked and suffering from hypothermia.

"What the . . .? Nadine, why are you huddled up here? Don't you know . . .? You're locked out." He unlocked the front door, picked her up and carried her inside.

"Are you okay?" Panic curled his insides when she slumped against him. He looked down at Christopher's anxious, frightened face and tried to assure him that she wasn't in danger.

"She just got too cold, son. Put your things down there and run some warm water in her bath tub, while I call the doctor.'' The boy scurried off to do as he'd been told. Wade pondered whether to undress her. Her clothes were wet, and he had to get her dry and warm, but did he have the right to take her clothes off her? Well, he'd better get her in that tub, so he had to take off her clothes, but he'd leave her bra and panties. He knew that the bath would make her uncomfortable, prickling her as though she lay on needles and pins, but her icy toes alarmed him.

He lifted her from the tub, still barely conscious, draped a bath towel around her and carried her back to bed, his gaze adoring her as she stirred and snuggled closer to his chest. His heart kicked over as her hair fell away from her face and he knew at last why she protected her left ear from human vision. He put her to bed and covered her carefully, then gazed down at her lovely bronze face, fully exposed to him without what he regarded as her "cock-eyed" hair style. Though rough textured, shriveled and smaller than its mate, in his eyes, it did not detract from her beauty. He started out of her room, remembered that she still wore her wet underwear, reached beneath the cover, and eased them from her body while the white satin comforter shielded her from his eyes.

The doctor's brief stay did little to ease his fears, for she still had not fully aroused.

"Wade, don't you want me to sing something to her?" Christopher begged. He'd kept the child out of her room, fearing that her semiconscious state would alarm him.

"Not yet, son. Maybe tomorrow she'll be able to enjoy it.''

"Tomorrow? Okay. I won't go to school tomorrow, 'cause I have to stay with Nadine.'' Wade wondered what kind of stunt the boy was about to pull.

"And you think both of us have to stay?'' he asked Christopher. He nearly laughed at the look of incredulity on his son's face.

"You're going to NYU to study for your exams so you can be a lawyer, and I'm going to look after Nadine." How had he lived apart from this wonderful child, this boy whose personality changed daily, who grew more like himself, it seemed, with each breath?

"She has a very high fever, son, and you may not be able to handle that. Let's wait until morning before we decide what to do. I'd better get us a sandwich or something."

When he went back to Nadine's room half an hour later, he noticed that her hair had been brushed over her left eye and looked around for further evidence that she had aroused and gotten out of bed. He couldn't find any. Maybe she'd turned over and her hair had dropped down because she'd combed it that way so often. He remembered that he'd have to call her office in the morning. How was she going to complete her Rolling Hills Village plan by the deadline, if he didn't help her? And if he did that, he'd have to unmask fully. He gazed out of the window at the thick white winter scene, shaking his head. When she learned it all, she'd probably never speak to him again. It was a chance he had to take.

He put a thermometer under Nadine's arm and waited. One hundred and four. He found a small white basin and filled it with a mixture of alcohol and ice water, sat on the edge of her bed and began to sponge her arms, neck, shoulders and face, pushing her hair away as he did so.

Her groans alerted him, and he leaned closer.

"Wade is so sexy . . . so . . . ." He listened closely, but she didn't say more. He pulled the covers up around her neck, but she knocked them away. "Christopher, Wade is so nice . . . Try to call him daddy. Make him happy . . ."

Wade placed the basin on her night table and leaned over her.

"Why are you worried about Christopher and me?"

"You're a wonderful father, and I want him to love you." She turned over, restless, and he sat down and stroked her bare arm, confident that the fever was dropping and he'd soon have her back.

"You're wonderful, too. And sweet," he told her. She turned over again, and he took her hand. "You ever been in love?" He was invading her privacy now, but he wasn't going to dig for anything that she wouldn't want him to know about. "Have you?" he whispered. The smile that caressed her face stunned him.

"I'm in love right now, silly. Nadine Malloy. Does that sound right? That isn't my name." She turned over and pulled her fingers from his suddenly cold hands. He'd had a few surprises in his life, but none so breathtaking as this. And, he wanted it to be true. In her conscious mind, she might not think or feel any of those things, but her words had struck him like a violent blow to his solar plexus.

"What's the matter, Wade? Isn't she any better?" What a time for the child to burst in there?

"She's perspiring, and that means her fever is breaking. So, she's better," he said, watching the boy's furrowed brow, certain now that the child cared deeply for Nadine. Wade saw that she started to throw off the covers.

"Hot ... It's so hot ... Wade ... Where is Wade?" Christopher huddled over her, gazing into her sleeping face. He had to get the boy out of the room, so he sent him to the kitchen for ice water. With Christopher out of the way, he got her gown from a hook on the bathroom door, quickly pulled it over her head and slipped her arms through it. The gown dropped no further than her waist, but that would suffice. At least, if she threw the covers off, she wouldn't expose her bare body to Christopher—or to him, for that matter. When the boy returned, Wade put a bit of the ice water in his palm and brushed it over her forehead. To his surprise, she stilled and a smile bloomed on her face.

"Wade? Christopher?" His pulse accelerated when she

abruptly sat up and looked around her. Then she slipped back under the cover and went to sleep.

Suppose she *did* love him. He walked upstairs to his quarters, pensive. If she'd gone that far, she was not going to forgive him. And if she didn't, he was in for some rough times. He changed into casual clothes and went back downstairs. He could barely believe his eyes when he reached her door. She lay on her right side, and Christopher had crawled onto her bed and, kneeling beside her, brushed her hair so that it fell over her left eye and covered her left ear. So that was how it had happened. He ducked back outside the room and tiptoed away. Christopher had done that at least four times during the evening, protecting Nadine, because he knew she didn't want her ear exposed. How had the boy known, and for how long? His chest swelled with pride. The two had a secret, and the boy protected her when she was unable to do that for herself.

"Wade, she's awake." He sprinted up the hall to her room.

"How do you feel, Nadine?"

"How do I . . ." He reached out to her when she sat up abruptly, fearing that she still lacked full consciousness. She gazed from him to Christopher.

"What happened? Why are you . . .? Oh dear." She slipped back under the cover, and he could see that she remembered having been locked out in the cold. It occurred to him, when he sat on the edge of her bed, that she might find that odd or even unacceptable. But they had attained a far greater degree of intimacy over the past six hours than she knew. He told her everything, except what she'd revealed in her delirium and that Christopher had tried to prevent his seeing her ear. She looked down and saw her nightgown, and he knew her next question.

"Did Lorna come over?" He looked her in the eye, and

her sudden diffidence was evidence enough that she knew he'd undressed her.

"I didn't violate your privacy, Nadine."

"Then, how on earth did you . . ." He interrupted the question that she couldn't finish.

"I undressed you in bed with the covers over you."

"Oh!" He couldn't resist the urge to taunt her. "Oh" was all she could say? He'd been in a state of arousal for six hours, and all she could say was, "Oh." If his grin was salacious, he didn't care.

"After what I went through to protect your virtue, don't tell me you'd rather I'd given myself the pleasure of a full frontal view." He winked suggestively.

Christopher reminded them of his presence.

He went over and sat on the other side of Nadine's bed. "I could bring you some more ice water, Nadine." She took his hand and squeezed it.

"Thanks, I'm thirsty." She drank the water and Wade sent Christopher back to the kitchen to put the glass in the dishwasher. The minute the boy was out of sight, he leaned across the bed.

"Kiss me. I'm dying for the taste of you."

"Wade . . . What happened to make you like this?" He let his finger slide over the silky flesh of her arm, then pulled her to him.

"You scared the living hell out of me. *That's what happened.*"

By mid-week, Nadine was out of bed, though confined to the house. She wrapped her heavy robe more tightly around her and sipped the hot lemon tea that Wade constantly forced on her. It might have been good for his mother, she thought sourly, but hers would have livened it up with a shot of rum. Bessie Carpenter had believed in a good hot toddy and a mustard poultice for colds. She could do without the poultice, but a little rum in that tea would do more than warm her. He walked in then with a bowl of tomato soup and two hard rolls.

"Lunch, madam." She blew her tender nose and took the tray.

"Thanks. I feel awful. You should be studying, not hanging around here looking after me." She sniffled and tasted the soup. "This isn't canned soup. Don't tell me you made it." He feigned humility.

"No way. I doctored it up. Nadine," he began, with all the spiritedness of a man facing the gallows, "You aren't going to have your model home ready by January tenth unless I help you. I'll take my bar exams on the twenty-eighth, and I'm ready for them. So let me help you. Your doctor wants you to stay home until after Christmas, but if you haven't finished those plans by the end of the week, you're in trouble."

"How can you help me? I have to finish revising those plans . . ."

He knew that he could put it off no longer; he had to tell her. He hadn't committed a crime, but she'd have every right to believe that he'd been laughing at her all this time.

"I have some skills in this area, I . . ."

She set the tray of food on the floor and stared at him.

"I was hoping you'd run out of surprises. Now you're going to tell me you're an interior decorator." She supposed that her face had a forbidding look, for she'd never seen him so solemn, nor so lacking in self-possession. He put his hands in his back pockets and paced the floor, and she waited for his next words, knowing that they were going to cost him something, cost both of them something. He stopped pacing and hunkered down in front of her.

"Nadine, I'm an architectural engineer." As though trapped at a formidable precipice, he took a deep breath, let it out and continued. "I'm C. W. Malloy."

"What? You're *who?* You mean to tell me you had the nerve to take a chauffeur's job when all of these unem-

ployed men needed the work? You've been having fun on me, haven't you?'' She nearly lost her breath. C. W. Malloy. As a graduate student, she'd used his book on home design. She stared at him, stunned.

"I should have realized it. Christopher. Wade. But I didn't put them together. Who else could have promised Christopher to draw St. Patrick's Cathedral from memory? And origami. Why, that's a natural for you. Well, I don't accept your nice offer."

"You have to, Nadine. Who else is there? I doubt you can lift that big roll, and who's going to arrange the furnishings for you? I'm not after credits, if that's what's worrying you. Let me help."

"Of course you don't want credit for it; the great C. W. Malloy would deign to decorate a model for a middle-class housing development? Would Prince Charles take his afternoon tea at Howard Johnson's? How old were you when you wrote that text book on home design?"

"Twenty-six, and you're making too much of this."

She drew the robe more tightly around her, shivering. Why was she suddenly so cold? He stood and attempted to gather her to him, but she extended her right arm full length, palm facing him, fending him off the way NFL ball carriers blocked their would-be tacklers.

"Don't touch me! You've had your fun with me. Pretending to be a chauffeur didn't satisfy you; you had to play with me, had to prove that I'm susceptible to you. You had to toy with my hear . . . uh, with my emotions. I don't like you, C. W. Malloy, and if it wasn't for Christopher, you'd be leaving here this minute. I can drop garlic and parsley into canned tomato soup as well as you can." *I'm not going to cry*, she admonished herself. *I won't*.

"Go away and leave me alone," she told Wade, struggling to control her quivering lips. She looked up at him, towering over her five feet seven inches, his hard muscled strength there if she needed it, his sensual charm beguiling her. She backed away and glared at him.

"If you think that all you have to do is open your arms, guess again. I've weathered bigger storms than you."

His eyebrow arched sharply upward. "If you want to be mad at me, okay. But don't cut off your nose just because you're tired of blowing it. I've never lied to you. You didn't ask what I'd done on my previous jobs, and I didn't tell. Be fair, Nadine. You needed a chauffeur, and I needed the job. If I don't help you meet your deadline, you'll forfeit that contract. So, let's put our personal feelings aside and do it."

"I don't want your help." She blew her nose again, and turned her back to him. "I feel so foolish." His strong right arm turned her to face him.

"You're saying that being in my arms, holding me and loving me, giving me what I needed and had never had humiliates you? You're ashamed of having held me and kissed me?" His face, the face that she loved, mirrored his pain and—yes, she had to admit it—his disappointment. "Whenever I've held you, Nadine, your response has been honest, but if you say you're ashamed of it, then I'm glad we didn't go further. Ellen was dissatisfied with our lifestyle, with the long separations, and she was honest about that, but she had no complaints about my behavior as a man. None. And neither do you." She faltered in her attempt to move away from him, and he held her, steadying her.

"I'm alright."

"No you're not. I'm going into Manhattan and get whatever you need there. Then, let's get to work. By the way, the manager of Sky Hotels reported that Roger was a small potato in a much bigger scam. Seems he was so delighted to be recognized by the big shot engineers and decorators that he fell into a trap and couldn't get out of it. Your firm is now short one decorator." She couldn't help feeling sorry for Roger. He wanted so badly to be recognized as a genius at interior decorating, and now he'd ruined his reputation.

"I can revise the plans myself," she insisted, and sat

down, her breathing heavy and her forehead damp with perspiration. He leaned over her, bracing his hands on either side of her chair, and she wondered whether he was imprisoning her or protecting her. His gentle, but persuasive tone settled it.

"Honey, you can see that you're too weak to do much. I'm here to care for you. So let me." She wanted to punch him when he grinned and winked seductively. Beguiling her.

"Anyway," he went on, "I'll let you vent your hostility later." She hoped he got the message of her censuring look, but as though he hadn't seen it, he added, "When you're feeling better and we can both enjoy it."

"Don't hold your breath," she replied, reaching up and shaking his shoulders. Try as she might to sustain her anger, she lost it all and laughed aloud when he straightened up, furrowed his brow, and exclaimed, "I never could figure out why women have to caress you when they're mad at you. Doesn't make a bit of sense to me. I'm going to reheat this soup."

He left for the kitchen, and she trudged back to bed. What choice did she have? If Rolling Hills Village didn't open on January tenth because she'd failed to deliver, she could write *finis* to her career. The governor had agreed to cut the gold ribbon at the front door, and he'd invited television camera men to record the event. She crawled into bed. What had he done that was so bad? *C. W. Malloy!* She could hardly believe it, but she knew that it was he. And which was worse? To love her enigmatic chauffeur or to love a certified genius? Maybe he hadn't lied, and maybe she'd been so glad to find a man who seemed trustworthy that she hadn't questioned him closely, but he should have leveled with her when he started kissing her, driving her crazy, pulling at the roots of her soul. She turned over and pretended to be asleep.

"Here you are." He helped her to sit up and handed her the warmed soup. "I'm going to run down to Manhattan. What do you need?" She told him, and he wiped the tomato soup from her bottom lip with his handkerchief, leaned over, and closed his mouth over hers.

"Things have changed between us, Nadine. Now that you know everything, I can mark my territory. I want you." He smiled, rubbed his lips softly over hers again and added, "I go after what I want." The jingling change and the sound of the Toreador tune zinging through his teeth as he left the house told her that, if a problem existed, it was hers, that he didn't have a care.

But Wade viewed it differently. It had been close; she'd been angry and on the verge of telling him to pack up. She still might do it. But more than Christopher's legal custody and well-being were at stake now, because he wasn't sure he wanted to leave her. Not then. Maybe never. He didn't know when he'd begun to care for her. Wanting her hadn't surprised him; he doubted that any normal man could live around such a woman and not want her. And he did. Sometimes he thought that if he didn't have her, he'd suffocate, but he wasn't a slave to it and he always shook it off; not that it was easy. Caring for her was another matter. When he'd found her huddled out there in the cold, he'd been upset and, later, when her temperature shot up to one hundred and four, he had prayed for the first time since Ellen had gone into labor with Christopher.

He spoke with her secretary, got what he needed from her office, and headed back to Accord. On the way home, he had to stop to get Christopher, but he didn't relish meeting Lorna with her insinuations. She never said it, but what that woman couldn't do with her eyes and the turn of her head! Biggest churchgoer in town, and he'd bet it never occurred to her to elevate her mind. She had decided that he was a stud, and got her vicarious thrills by attributing who knew what to Nadine and him. He knocked on her door.

* * *

"Come in, Wade. Christopher says Nadine's sick and only taking liquids, so if you'll just wait a few minutes, I fix some dinner for you all." Appalled, he grabbed the first idea that came to him and went with it.

"I appreciate that, Lorna, but I have to get going. I picked up Nadine's medicine and I'd better take it to her." Horror spread over the woman's face.

"She's sick enough for medicine? That's terrible." He could almost see her brain light up. "Can she keep anything on her stomach?"

Wade threw his head back and laughed. He knew he was about to upset her, but he didn't care. "I know you'll be disappointed to hear this, Lorna, but Nadine isn't pregnant and, to my knowledge, she has no reason to be." Her hangdog look warmed his spirit. "Christopher," he called, "get a move on." Christopher walked up to them holding six year-old Greta's hand.

"Hi, Wade. Can Greta spend the night with me?"

"Can she . . ." Nonplussed, he looked skyward and silently inquired why kids didn't come with an encyclopedia on childrearing? Seven years old and already moonstruck.

"Christopher, have you forgotten that Nadine has the flu? You don't want to expose Greta to that." That settled the matter; Christopher was protective of the little girl.

He drove up to the house, turned toward the garage, and stopped when the figure of a man dashed past the beam of his headlights. He swore. He couldn't leave Christopher and chase the man, and he had to get inside to Nadine. He turned to his son and told him what to do. The boy's speed astonished him. He followed carefully, opened the front door, and locked it behind them. In one second, he stood in her sitting room trying to breathe normally, to pretend that he hadn't just been shaken to his core.

"How do you feel?"

"Better. I even ate all of that soup." He didn't care about that, only that she was unharmed. That she sat there smiling at him. Glad to see him. He had to touch her, to let his senses verify what his eyes beheld. He let his hand skim softly over her face, stroking from head to chin, and immediately he regretted doing it, for she jerked away. He pretended not to have noticed, but he swore he'd put an end to that charade. And soon.

He went up to his room, reported the incident to the sheriff, and asked that he patrol the area. He still wasn't satisfied, but he couldn't search the back of the house, because he didn't know where they were nor how many were out there. He busied himself preparing a meal of hamburgers, baked potato, asparagus, and green salad. Cookbooks had their uses, he decided; five consecutive dinners of spaghetti and meat sauce had ruined his taste for it. He ducked back into Nadine's sitting room, formerly the family room, saw that she wasn't there and glanced toward her bedroom. He couldn't believe his eyes. Christopher sat on the side of her bed brushing her hair away from her face.

"It looks better like this, Nadine, and I don't even see your ear. But if you want to, Wade will get it fixed. I know he will if you let me ask him. Please, Nadine. I'm going to the hospital the day after his exams, and you can go to. Can I ask him, Nadine, huh?" What had happened between them? And how had they developed this deep trust, this level of sharing that he hadn't been able to develop with either of them? He went back to the kitchen, but he didn't feel like cooking. And he knew why. The pain around his heart wasn't going to respond to medicine of any kind.

"Feel like going downstairs and working on those plans for a while? I got everything you asked me to bring from your office." She looked down at her hands, and he saw the unsteadiness of her fingers.

"You don't have to draw. Just describe it, and I'll sketch and color for you. I'm good at that, Nadine. Can you trust me with something precious to you just this once?" Her eyes widened as she looked up sharply, and he regretted adding what she could assume was an accusation.

"I don't need help, Wade." Her voice lacked even a modicum of conviction, and he hunkered down before her, searching for the words that would heal her wounded pride and draw her closer to him.

"Maybe you don't need my help, but I need to help you. I *need* to help you, Nadine." He extended his hand, and she took it. Three hours later, they had finished the top floor of the model home, and she phoned in her orders for fabrics and furnishings.

She faltered as she started to climb the steps that led from the basement to the first floor, but immediately she knew the comfort of his strong arm around her. She didn't have the strength to climb the steep steps, so she didn't protest when he lifted her into his arms, carried her to her room and lay her on her bed. She wondered at the steely determination that glittered in his eyes, so unlike the sweet tenderness with which he had just laid her in bed.

He leaned forward, and panic gnawed at her when his hands went to both sides of her face, swept her hair back and caressed both of her bare ears. Thoughts of her deformed ear and her fear of its discovery vanished when his mouth covered hers in an urgent demand for her total surrender. She clutched him for support as wild tremors raced through her, alarming her and soothing her, shaking her and steadying her, pitching her into a cyclone of passion and need. Her parted lips asked for more, and he gave more in a statement of healing love that rocked her to the pit of her soul. Her five senses were full of him, and her body seemed to absorb him—over her, around her, beneath her, and within her. When his sweet mouth moved to her left ear, kissing, licking, nipping, cherishing, and healing, surely he could hear the wild pounding of her heart.

She brought her gaze to meet his when his finger tipped her chin, and she reveled in a new found sense of belonging as he kissed her with his eyes.

"You're so beautiful, sweetheart. Beautiful all over, head to foot and ear to ear. And you've no need to be ashamed of that ear. The skin is a slight shade darker and the flesh is a little bit rough, but—to my eyes—it's as beautiful as the other one. Most people wouldn't look close enough to notice a difference. So stop hiding behind your hair." She wanted to dissolve like a vampire at sunrise.

"How long have you known?" He dragged a green leather ottoman up to her chair and sat beside her.

"Known what? You mean about your ear? Ages. I suspected it early on, then I saw it the day you got sick, and I couldn't figure out what you were so obsessed about." He stretched out his long legs and relaxed, leaning against her thigh. "I had a genuine shock seeing my son sneak into your room when you were delirious with fever and brush your hair over your ear so that I wouldn't see it. He must had done that half a dozen times, and I resented his having a closer relationship with you than with me, but I'm proud that he tried to protect you."

Nadine wondered if she could hide anything from the man. Or if there was anything left to hide. He'd undressed her, bathed her, fed her, made her bed, and now, he was the only person alive other than Christopher who'd seen her ear. She felt his lips brush her cheek and realized that he drank her tears. She wanted to ask him if he loved her the way in which she desperately loved him, but her long habit of protecting herself against rejection stymied her. He suddenly wrapped his arms around her, laid his head against her belly, and held her. Not speaking. She gazed into his face. Radiant. Peaceful. Quiet. Like the setting sun. She held him to her. He must love her. He *had* to.

The day before Christmas Eve, Nadine put on a brick red, cowl neck woolen shift, her favorite style, combed her hair the way in which she always wore it and worried about what Reginald Malloy would think of her. Wade hadn't said much about his father; she knew only that Christopher adored him. Her tension was interrupted by the harsh ring of the telephone, and she answered it, hoping that the call had nothing to do with Reginald's visit.

"Miss Carpenter, this is Sheriff McGranahan. We've got two fellows here that we caught prowling around your place a little while ago, right after Malloy left. Do you want to come down here, or do you want to send Malloy? He's the one who called me." Wade hadn't mentioned that to her, and she wondered what had happened that prompted him to alert the sheriff. She told the man that she preferred to wait until Wade returned. Why hadn't he told her? She went into the dining room to rearrange the flowers for the third time, glanced out of the window and paused. So there *had* been an incident. Sometime, while she'd been ill, Wade had installed floodlights in the back garden. She went to the front of the house to see whether he had put any there and got her first glimpse of Reginald Malloy as he came up the walk with Christopher tugging at his hand and Wade on his other side. Wade opened the door with his key, and she met them there.

"How are you? Nadine," Reginald greeted her. "You're exactly what I expected." She took his extended hand and enjoyed the security of his warm and strong handshake.

"I'm glad you could spend Christmas with us, Mr. Malloy. Come on in; it's wonderful to have you here." She knew she was babbling, but the man was off-putting. Whatever she'd expected, it wasn't this. At sixty, Reginald Malloy's face was unlined. He had barely a gray hair and was his son's equal in height and physique. And looks. "Wade, would you please put his things in here," she said, leading them to the guest room that she had been using for her bedroom. Wade's surprised look must have been obvious to his father, for he asked whether he was inconveniencing her.

"I want you to be happy while you're with us, so you're to sleep in this guest room."

"Where're you going to sleep, Nadine," Christopher asked, his face shrouded in worry.

"Darling, the sofa in my office opens into a full-size bed. I'll be very comfortable." She picked up the man's suitcase and walked toward the room. Wade dashed after her and attempted to take it.

"You don't have to do this." She held on to the bag, her chin up in defiance, and Reginald Malloy laughed a deep hearty laugh.

"I can see that I'm going to enjoy my stay, Nadine." He looked down at Christopher. "Who usually wins?"

"Nadine," the boy announced, proudly. "She always wins, Granddaddy. Wade loses all the time."

Reginald gazed at his grandson and shook his head. "Son, if I'm your granddaddy, Wade is your daddy. I've told you this before: if you can't call him daddy, it doesn't make any sense to call me granddaddy." Nadine knew even before she looked at Wade, that his pain would be mirrored in his eyes. She hurt for him, but she didn't want Reginald's lecture, which Christopher certainly needed, to cast a pall over their day. She took Reginald and Christopher's hands and led them to the family room.

"Sit here while I get us something warm to drink."

Christopher jumped up. "I'll do it, Nadine. Let me help you. Wade said you're still sick."

She kissed his forehead and told him to stay with his grandfather. Alone with Wade in the kitchen, she told him of the Sheriff's call.

"What do you think's going on?"

"I don't know," he replied, a bit idly she thought, "but I'd better get down there. Thanks for making my dad welcome. This will be the first Christmas we've spent together since before Ellen and I married. Dad always visited Christopher for the holidays, but I was never able to get home; I had to work." She yielded to her need to touch him and let her fingers stroke his arm.

"Look at me," he urged in a voice that was at once sultry and commanding. She did, and a gasp escaped her as she stared at the blaze of passion that his eyes had become.

"Wade!" His strong arms folded her to him, and his lips found hers in a gentle brush, a tender softness that brought moisture to her eyes. She wanted to hold on to the remnants of her anger at him for keeping his identity a secret, but how could she when he offered what she needed.

"I'd better go. Look after them until I get back." She nodded. He spoke a few words to his father and went out. She stood where he'd left her, thoroughly discombobulated. If he kissed her that way again without telling her what he felt, she'd . . ., she'd . . . She'd what? *You'd kiss him back*, an inner voice taunted.

Nadine sat with Reginald and Christopher around the fire in her sitting room, formerly her family room, and ate hot roasted chestnuts.

"Can we save some for Wade? Can we Nadine?" Christopher begged.

Reginald asked him, "Who did you say?"

Meekly, Christopher replied. "Daddy."

"It didn't kill you to say it, now did it?"

The boy hung his head. "No sir, but Mother always called him Wade, so—"

Reginald interrupted. "Wade was your mother's husband, so she could call him Wade or whatever she liked,

but he's *your* father. She was wrong in not teaching you to
call him dad. You know what's right. Do it."

"Yes, sir."

Reginald turned to Nadine. "I knew from the things
Christopher wrote me about you that I'd like you. Tell me
about yourself." She did, and he eyed her steadily as
though sifting the information, making up his mind. His
smile nearly duplicated Wade's, and it unsettled her.

"A man is fortunate to find a woman like you when he's
already thirty-five years old. Fortunate indeed." She didn't
answer, only smiled. If he'd found her, he hadn't favored
her with the information, she noted, but she refrained
from saying it. She should get something together for
lunch, but she didn't feel up to it. She'd wait for Wade.

Wade returned and told her that the two suspects confessed to having been hired by one of her competitors for
the Rolling Hills Village contract to get any plans that she
had in her house. They hadn't found a way to get into the
house, and they had been instructed not to hurt her. Twice,
they had planned to force her to give them up when she
arrived home after work, but she had thwarted their goal
by driving off. She thought he seemed amused when he
said the men complained that hiring him to chauffeur her
had thrown a monkey wrench into their plans. Reginald
Malloy jerked around and gaped at his son.

"She hired you to do *what?*" Their story elicited a mild
exclamation from him. "Well I'll be. Don't tell *me* that a
leopard doesn't change its spots."

Tired after the early flight from northern Michigan,
Reginald napped while Wade and Christopher went into
the woods to find a tree, and Nadine took the opportunity
to wrap her gifts and put them away and to retrieve the
tree ornaments from their home in an old fashioned barrel
in which her family had stored them since her childhood.
She was glad that she'd done her shopping early, on her

lunch hour. What could she give Reginald? She searched through her treasures and found a pearl handled fishing knife that had belonged to her father and decided that it would make the perfect gift.

Wade and Christopher brought home an eight-foot douglas fir. She tried to imagine Wade's joy in these little daily experiences with his son, but she knew that her perception of it fell far short of it's meaning to this man who had turned his life around in order to gain custody of his son and for the sake of the child's love. He looked down at the boy and smiled broadly, and she saw the love in him. How he cherished that boy! A thought occurred to her, and she meant to ask him how and why he had let that situation develop. Surely, with his abilities and his reputation, he could have worked anywhere.

Reginald prepared his special dinner—baked pork chops, rice pilaf, and green beans—while Nadine and Wade helped Christopher decorate the tree. The boy's infectious glee filled the house as they hung the ornaments that Nadine had treasured throughout her life. A fire crackled in the stone fireplace, and fresh pine boughs and holly that Wade clipped from Nadine's trees gave the house a festive air. Bayberry scented potpourri perfumed the hallway, and gold-winged angels heralded the season as their light glowed in the windows. Suddenly, Christopher burst forth with "O, Holy Night," the song he'd sung at his school's Christmas pageant, and Nadine looked at Wade, praying that he would join the boy. But it was Reginald's stirring baritone that sent shivers up her arms as he walked into the room. She squatted on the floor next to the sofa and held her breath, waiting for Wade's wonderful bass baritone. The fire blazed, Christmas tree lights winked, and the angels seemed literally to have taken wing. Maybe not, but her world had become unreal. A wonderland. Caught up in the wonder of the moment as Wade joined

his father and son, her spirits soared, and she gazed at
Wade with a confession of love shining in her eyes. He
walked over to her and, without missing a note, sat down
beside her and covered her hand with his own. She wanted
to lean her head on his shoulder, but she didn't. She had
told him, albeit silently, what she felt for him, and the next
move was his.

They cleaned the kitchen after dinner, while Reginald
read Christmas stories to his grandson. "Grandparents
know how to keep children happy," Wade observed.

"They just fall short when it comes to discipline. Christopher is crazy about Dad, always has been, but Dad tolerates
things that I won't stand for." To his surprise, she became
solemn.

"Wade, I know it's none of my business, but how did
you become estranged from Christopher? I mean, your
name stands for something even among people who aren't
in your field. Couldn't you have gotten a job here, or at
least in the States? And how did you let it get completely
out of hand like this?"

He put the tray of flatware in the drawer and leaned
against a cabinet. He disliked discussing himself with anyone, even when he knew it was necessary, and his reluctance to do so frustrated the people closest to him. Ellen
had complained that she could never get inside of him, but
he knew that was because they were together too seldom to
form the kind of bond that true intimacy requires. From
the blunt way in which Nadine had phrased that question,
he realized that she, too, had a sense of frustration about
him. Where to start?

"Nadine, I had my credentials as an architectural engineer before my twenty-second birthday, but I couldn't get
a decent job anywhere. The big corporations weren't hiring
young black men, smart or not, and especially not if they

lacked experience. African-American companies weren't in need of help; what they needed were contracts. I wrote a hundred letters, but to no avail. Finally, I got on a radio talk show that had a Houston audience, and a fellow named Magnus Cooper called me. He's part owner of a firm that had building contracts with governments of countries in sub-Saharan Africa and southeast Asia. Two years later, I was head of a division. I designed and built schools, hospitals, office buildings, you name it. When I wrote that text book on home design, I had just built my first two private homes—as a thank you—for two Nigerian men who had risked their careers to get me the building materials I needed for my work.

"By this time, I could have gotten a job anywhere, but when Magnus hired me, I signed a contract to stay with him at least until we completed his West African projects. I had to keep my word; if he hadn't taken a chance on me, I'd probably be a chauffeur for real. Ellen didn't like to travel, and she refused to live where she wasn't assured of an unfailing supply of electricity and pure water, and the thought of snakes, mosquitos, and ten months of one hundred degree heat cooled her passion for me. I've never faulted her for it. I built us a home in Scarsdale, where she wanted to live, and I got there as often as I could." He looked at the hand that brushed his arm in understanding, and added, "It wasn't enough. She suffered three years of it, two of them after Christopher was born. Her story to the judge convinced him that I wouldn't provide a stable life for my son, and he gave her full custody. As soon as I'd fulfilled my contract with Magnus, I came back here to get my child. But what a legal morass! So I'm satisfying the requirements for stability," he couldn't help grimacing, "and getting a law degree so I can fight my own battle. I've got my son with me now, and I intend to keep him."

He looked at her hair, still hiding one of the most beautiful brown eyes he'd ever seen. What would it take? Christopher couldn't bring himself to stop calling his father by his first name, and Nadine couldn't believe him when he told her that she was beautiful, ears and all. He supposed it was human nature to feel vulnerability, even the strong. He felt Nadine's hand tighten on his arm.

"I've misjudged you, Wade, and I'm sorry."

"But not so sorry that you've forgiven me for not having leveled with you in the beginning. You're still sore as all hell with me, but if you kissed me right now, you'd give off enough heat to roast a pig. How is that?" He had to suppress a grin at the sight of her quivering lower lip which didn't necessarily forecast tears, he realized, but annoyance as well. That lip begged for his mouth.

"Did you ever watch a forest fire?" she asked. "Fire makes fire, and a burning tree lights the one nearest to it?"

"And?" In an unusual gesture of familiarity, she reached up, pinched his cheek and let her fingers trailed down the side of his face. She must have seen his suddenly rampant desire in his eyes for she stepped away.

"You can get hotter than fire itself," she told him, "so what do you expect from me? I'm a normal woman, and I'm not one bit unhappy about it. Don't want to burn, don't start a fire."

He laughed. They hadn't done much teasing and bantering, and he enjoyed it. "That's your attitude? Well, baby, we can burn together all night, and I'll just be getting started. Trust me." Her surprise showed in her big round eyes and their expression of bewilderment, but she could hold her own, he discovered.

"You're kidding. I've always heard that a fellow blows his own horn when nobody else is willing to do it. 'Course, you're studying to be a lawyer, so that may excuse you. I doubt it, though."

"Are you challenging me?" he asked, eager for an excuse to crush her to him. But she didn't bite.

"Me? Not this time, said the fly to the spider." He noticed that she glanced toward the kitchen door, conscious of possible intrusion.

His deep baritone laugh could be heard all over the house. He didn't know why, but he felt good. Happiness welled up in him, and he wanted to love her, to share himself with her as never before with any woman. But he stopped himself from asking whether she loved him, as she'd confessed in her delirium, because that would give her the right to ask the same of him. And his priority was Christopher. He wouldn't even examine his feelings for her until he knew Christopher was his.

Christopher bounded into the room, his face shining with anticipation. "Can I have the drumstick, Nadine? I always get it when Mother has turkey. Can I Nadine, huh?" She rested an arm around his shoulder, thinking how much he'd grown since she'd met him.

"Of course you may have it."

"I'm taking us all out to dinner Christmas day, son; you can have it only if it's available," Wade cautioned. The child's protruding lower lip reminded her of a habit she hadn't shed until she'd reached teenage.

"We're having dinner right here on Christmas Eve," she told them, adding that her housekeeper would shop and do the cooking.

"I thought she was sick," Wade said.

"She was, and she won't be back to work until the first of the year, but she called and said she'd get Christmas dinner for me. I'm glad, because I'd hate for Reginald to eat Christmas dinner in a restaurant." Christopher tugged at her arm.

"And I can have the drumstick?" She nodded. Tenacious. Like father like son.

*   *   *

At about five-thirty Christmas Eve afternoon, Wade took Christopher to see his mother.

"Christopher, darling. Oh, how you've grown in such a short time." The boy hugged his mother.

"I miss you," he said in words barely audible, as he glanced toward his mother's new husband.

"Oh, honey, I miss you, too. Terribly." Her tear glistened eyes confirmed the truth of her words. Their warm reunion gave Wade a sense of gratification. Ellen's love for the boy had been his one unfailing source of happiness in his marriage to her. Every child needed a mother's love, and Ellen was a good, loving mother. But one look at Casey was enough. If he hadn't planned to get custody of his son, meeting Casey Richards would have pushed him to it. The man did not like Christopher, nor did the boy like him.

"I'm preparing to seek custody of Christopher," Wade told Ellen. Her genuine alarm was precisely what he'd expected, though one of Christopher's letters should have prepared her.

"Wade, please. I only wanted him to stay with you while I'm . . . I mean while we're getting adjusted. Then I want him back."

He had to struggle to contain the anger that unfurled within him when Casey pulled her into his arms and soothed, "Darling, it isn't as if he was a girl. Boys need to be with their fathers. You don't want him to grow up to be a patsy, do you."

"But I thought you said . . ." Wade left them to their argument, satisfied that he'd have no difficulty gaining custody of his son. He supposed a man had a right to want his own children and not those of a previous husband. But if you loved the woman . . . He closed his mind to it, walked into the living room and gazed at the beautiful white artificial tree elegantly adorned with white angels and cherubs and shinning silver bells. Times had changed. Ellen had always demanded the biggest green douglas fir that he could get into the house. He stayed until he could politely leave and, to his amazement, Christopher was ready to go. He gave his mother her CDs and sweater, and Ellen gave Wade a large parcel for their son. Christopher hugged and kissed her and skipped off without looking back. Wade smiled sadly as he buckled the boy's seat belt. None of himself remained in that house he'd built when he still hoped for his and Ellen's future together. Worse, he was no longer certain that he had ever loved her. They were constantly together in college, and their friends had expected them to marry. Christopher's voice came to him from a distance.

"Wade, how come she married Casey? He's the pits." Wade squelched a laugh. The boy had voiced his thoughts exactly.

"Beats me, son. Love's a funny thing. You can't explain it; you can't create it; and you can't regulate it. It just *is.*" He glanced down sharply at his son when the boy wiggled closer to him and rested a hand on his knee. He tried not to interpret the gesture as one of love, because if he let himself hope . . . He put his right arm around the child's shoulder and, if his life had been at stake, he wouldn't have been able to explain why he suddenly began to sing.

"Sing the Toreador song, Wade." He did, and Christopher joined him in a clear soprano. His mind wasn't on the song, though he sang it joyfully. His thoughts were of getting home to Nadine. He couldn't bear being away from her right then, unable to share with her the powerful emotion that boiled inside of him. Reality struck him with astounding force; he needed her. He had to get to her, to see her and to satisfy himself that he was important to her. Parking in the garage took too much time, so he stopped in front of the house, unbuckled Christopher, and opened the child's door. Why had he done that? The boy could open the door with ease.

As he walked rapidly up the walkway, Christopher caught him and grasped his hand. Wade stopped as though immobilized, touched by the spontaneity of the gesture. He squeezed the boy's hand and walked more slowly. Had his heart beat run wild and his breathing become short ragged snorts because he'd see her soon? His hand paused above the door knob; he'd left her little more than two hours earlier. He looked down into the inquiring eyes of his son. Did he see trust and warmth . . . maybe even . . . He couldn't let himself *think* the word. Right then, he wasn't sure that his world hadn't begun to spin off of its axis.

"Can't we go in, Wade?" Christopher inquired, a little tentatively, still holding his father's hand.

"Sure, son." They walked into the house, and Christopher ran to find his grandfather, but Wade had a curious feeling of abandonment, bereft because she wasn't there waiting for him. That didn't make sense but, right then, *nothing did.*

"Why are you standing out here?" Had her voice always been soft and husky, and had it always had this soothing effect on him?

"Why?" He repeated. Her smile sent his pulse into a trot. He'd been looking at her for months, but he'd swear she looked new, different. And not because of her dazzling red velvet shift with its rhinestone shoulder straps that matched her spike-heeled shoes. He wouldn't apologize for staring at her; she took his breath away.

She reached for his hand. "Come on. Christopher's getting dressed, and you ought to start. Your dad's ready."

"Oh yes," he remembered, "Dad wants to go to candle-light service." But he only wanted to close off the world and lose himself in her. He corralled his thoughts, but he didn't intend to let many more hours pass before she was his.

"Where is he?" She told him, and he found his father in the family room, relaxed and well dressed.

"Could we have a word, son?" Reginald asked. Wade nodded and sat down, comfortable as always with his father.

"I've been trying to figure out what's wrong between you and Nadine."

"Well, I'm her chauffeur."

"Forget that nonsense," Reginald said, knocking the air with his hand in a gesture of impatience. "It's unimportant. Ellen is a good woman, but you weren't right for each other. Nadine is your soul mate. She brings you into line without even trying, and the heat between the two of you is so fierce it's almost embarrassing to a third person. Sometime I feel I ought to leave the room. I like her Wade; she's real people. Don't let her get away from you." He paused. "The problem is you're both too proud to open up and let your needs show. And you're so unsure of each other. Seems to me anybody could see that you care for each other." Wade didn't dispute that.

"She's been mad with me ever since you've been here."

"You don't say," Reginald drawled in disbelief. "I'd love to see you together when she's pleased with you." Wade glanced at his watch. Nadine was a stickler for punctuality, one of the things he admired about her, and she wouldn't want to arrive late for service. But he needed some answers.

"Dad, how were you sure that Mother was right for you? I think I married young hoping to find what you had. I loved being around you and Mother. Always loving. Always in the same groove. How did you know?"

"Same way you ought to know. She loved me, and I loved her. She didn't need me to rescue her or to take care of her. She just needed *me*. Want doesn't count for much, son; you can satisfy that in a couple of minutes. But need is another matter. Need and deep caring. I always wanted more for your mother than for myself, and I was happy when she was happy. What did Ellen say about Christopher?" Wade stretched out his long legs before the crackling fire, relishing the nearly rhapsodic feeling that washed over him. Sweet contentment. He knew what he wanted, and he'd get it.

"I'll get custody; I'm certain of that. Casey doesn't want Christopher around, and the boy doesn't like him. I don't say Casey is evil, I think he's unsure of himself and doesn't want to be reminded of me. I'll be generous with Ellen, because she's a good mother and she loves our son. If I have to spend every penny I've got, Christopher Malloy stays with me." Wade turned sharply as Christopher bounded into the room, dressed up, whistling the Toreador song and jingling pocket change. He glanced at his father, who nodded in awareness; the boy had copied Wade's habit of jingling change in his right pants pocket.

"Wade, Nadine says everybody's going to leave you here."

"You, too?"

"Yeah . . ."

"Yes, sir," Reginald corrected.

"Yes, sir. I want to hear the singing."

Nadine stopped at the kitchen door, not wanting her red velvet dress and jacket to soak up the odor of onions, celery, sage, and turkey that permeated the room. "We'll be back about seven-thirty." She told the housekeeper, "so you should be able to leave by ten. Wade or I will drive you home."

"No need for that. I drove myself." Nadine checked the dining room and went to the bottom of the stairs and called Wade.

"Hurry up, slow poke. We have to be seated in twenty-six minutes." She stood there anxious to see what he'd wear and how he'd look now that he'd taken off his mask. *Down girl,* she warned herself. But she couldn't banish her blissful anticipation, couldn't expel the breath that hung in her throat. She had plans for him. Never again would she let him take her to the brink and leave her there. She loved him. She needed him. And it was time he knew it. She wasn't disappointed. Her lower lip dropped as a small gasp escaped her. Wade Malloy in a tuxedo to celebrate Christmas with her! He loped downstairs and stopped right in front of her. Her reaction to the startling elegance that accentuated his good looks must have been mirrored on her face, because he rubbed the tip of her nose and winked.

"Like what you see?" She opened her mouth to protest his effrontery, remembered her game plan, and winked right back.

"Step out of line tonight, mister, and you'll get what you've been asking for." She surprised herself, not to mention Wade, whose eyes widened and eyebrows arched to a point. Don't back down, she told herself, shoring up her courage.

"I'll take that as an order, lady," he replied, his dark, husky tones sending shivers through her. She'd have been more sure of herself if he had smiled, but he didn't, and his mesmeric gaze made her feel as though she stood on quicksand. The scent of his cologne mingled with the odor of pine and bayberry, and she had to stifle the desire to caress his freshly shaved cheek, to loose herself in his masculine aura. She shook her head and grasped his hand.

"Let's go. We'll be late."

"But we'll be in plenty of time for what counts," she heard him mutter, and little darts of anticipation shot through her.

Nadine didn't question Wade's decision to drive them to the service in his Thunderbird, rather than her roomier Crown Victoria. She supposed he was telling her that he wasn't her chauffeur that evening, but her escort.

"Warm enough for you?" he asked, taking a woolen throw from the back of his seat and spreading it across her knees. "You're a knockout in that dress, but five feet of your five feet seven inches must be nearly frozen. Come over here." She moved a little closer, and he reached over and pulled her snug against him. "Isn't that better?" She noted the tease in his voice, but she didn't care. She was just where she wanted to be—as close to him as decency would allow, given that the gazes of his father and his son were probably glued to them.

She thought back to the year before when she'd been so lonely that she'd gone to Spain for the Christmas holiday rather than face being alone in her own home. Her fingers itched to touch him, but she told herself to be patient, to gauge his mood, to let him take the lead as he'd hinted he was ready to do. She closed her eyes, suffused with peace and contentment. Christopher's crystal clear "O Holy Night" was soon joined by the voices of his father and grandfather. She opened her eyes and looked at Christmas Eve. Gaily decorated trees adorned the windows of each house and, in many of the front gardens, a well-lighted Santa and his reindeer greeted visitors and passersby. The stars overhead shone as brightly as any she'd ever seen, and a lovers' moon raced from behind a cloud to kiss her soul with its unearthly brilliance. She hadn't realized that she'd snuggled even closer to Wade until his fingers grasped hers, thought only for a second.

They arrived at the little church with five minutes to spare. Christopher took her hand as they walked up the pavement to the front door, and winged angels with trumpets in hand greeted them as they entered. Hundreds of red poinsettias and unlit white candles adorned the altar and windows of the crowded little edifice, and silver stars dangled above the apse. Immediately, the angels marched to the altar, blowing their trumpets as the audience rose to sing "Hark the Herald Angel Sings." Chills ploughed through her when Wade took her hand and held it in a firm grip. *I want to be a part of this family,* she thought, *because I've never been so happy in my life.* On the other side of her, Christopher, too, held her hand and earned a reprimand from his grandfather when he jingled his pocket change. Wade smiled. She couldn't imagine why, but it was a smile of joy, and it warmed her heart. The story of Christmas was interspersed with the classic songs of the season and when, finally, they sang "Silent Night," the candles were lit, the lights doused, and the little church glowed in breathtaking beauty.

"Hugh, this is Nadine Carpenter I've been telling you about," Lorna exclaimed, waylaying Nadine as she left the church. Lorna's lower lip dropped when she looked at Wade. "And this is her chauffeur. Nadine is getting to be quite a pillar of our little community, and I know you'll just love getting to know her."

Nadine looked at Wade and laughed. Another inch, and he'd burst. She acknowledged the introduction and added, "Mr. Cliburn, Mr. Malloy is my date this evening." She introduced Reginald whom she noticed wore a smirk that she'd seen on Wade's face many times.

"I don't suppose you know anything about architectural engineers, but my son is C. W. Malloy, when he isn't chauffeuring Nadine." Nadine enjoyed seeing Hugh's eyes grow bigger; at least he was able to appreciate Wade's status. Reginald might as well have spoken Hindi to Lorna.

"I see you're busy now, but don't you forget," she admonished Nadine. "You come over Saturday night. Hugh's a good bridge player."

"In your dreams, Lorna," Wade told her, as he took Nadine's arm and walked off. She enjoyed Reginald's knowing chuckle. Several people walked away singing carols, and Christopher eyed them longingly.

"Let's go sing, Wade . . . I mean . . ." The boy hung his head shyly. "Can we go sing with them? Mother and me used to do that in Scarsdale."

"Mother and I," father and grandfather corrected simultaneously.

"Mother and I," the child repeated idly. Nadine nodded

in agreement to Wade's unasked question, and they walked through the little town that blazed with lights, hummed with the tingle of bells, and bustled with last minute shoppers. They gathered more carolers as they went, stopping at homes decorated for the season to sing carols, greeting those who opened their doors. Cold moisture sprinkled her face, and she looked up to see that the moon and stars had disappeared, and snow flakes swirled around them.

"Perfect, isn't it?" he asked, with a new urgency that made her feel as though he wanted them to be as one, at least for the moment. She nodded, wondering about his enigmatic smile. Then he stepped closer, gazing into her eyes as though he had a thousand questions, but she only wanted to answer one.

"Let's go home," he murmured, looking around for Reginald and Christopher. Snow blanketed the car's windshield faster than the wipers could clean it off, and he drove slowly. She looked at his tapered fingers on the steering wheel and saw the strength there, and the power. Her gaze fixed on his strong, square jaw, and she silently promised him: *you don't stand a chance against what I'm planning for you.*

Nadine had decorated the table with red and green candles, holly and pine needles, a white linen cloth, and napkins. Old fashioned Christmas carols filled the air, and they stood at their chairs while Reginald said grace. She asked Wade to sit at the head of the table to carve the turkey. This man is elegance personified when he wants to be, she thought, watching him dismember the big bird and serve their plates with dispatch.

"Am I getting the drumstick?" Christopher asked. Assured that he was, he focused on his grandfather. "Can you stay until school opens?"

The elder Malloy leaned back in his chair and said, "I don't think so. Three adults can be big crowd sometimes.

Another couple of days, maybe." They finished the meal of oyster stew, roast turkey with sausage and wild rice stuffing, turnips, red cabbage with chestnuts, candied sweet potatoes, and lemon meringue pie, the latter because it was Reginald's favorite.

"Time to open gifts," Wade announced, and they sat around the tree, aware of Christopher's sudden tenseness. The boy screamed with delight when his grandfather handed him a little golden retriever that had lived in the bathroom since his arrival. Inline skates from Nadine and a bicycle from his mother seemed to have flabbergasted him, a rarity, since the boy was never without words. He stared in amazement at the state-of-the-art MacIntosh computer, a gift from his father.

"I'm never going to leave my room now. Wow!"

"How will you ride your bicycle or skate?" Reginald asked him.

"Wow," was all the boy seemed able to manage.

Nadine's gift to Wade was a silver ID bracelet on which were inscribed the words, "To Wade with love, Nadine." With his eyes, he promised her his endless gratitude. Reginald's deep emotion was apparent when he opened her gift, her father's pearl-handled, stainless-steel blade fishing knife.

"Your father's?" She nodded. "I'll cherish this, Nadine, just as I'll cherish you." He thanked Wade for the gold pocket watch and quipped, "I see you got the hands large enough for me to read when I'm eighty."

"Sure thing," Wade shot back. "Foresight beats hindsight any day." The two laughed, and she supposed that they were enjoying a family secret. They all looked at Wade. What had he given her? He looked at her and wrinkled his nose.

"It's way up there in the top of the tree; I'll get it after a while." She only saw tree ornaments near the top, but he wanted her to wait. She'd wait.

Christopher made a loud ceremony of clearing his throat. "Granddaddy, I'd like to give you my present now." He opened an envelope, removed a card and read. "Dear Granddaddy, I had bought you some tackle, but I took it back to the store 'cause you can buy that yourself. I thought I'd just write you and tell you it's always Christmas when you come to see me, and I'm very happy. I love you, Granddaddy. Merry Christmas. Christopher." He put the card back in the envelope and passed it to Reginald who rose and gripped the boy tightly in his arms.

"I love you, too, son. Merry Christmas."

"Dear Nadine," he read, "If I didn't have a mother, I'd want you to be my mother. Ever since you shared your secret with me, I haven't minded going to swimming class. The kids don't pay any attention to my leg, and they all want me to be on their team, because I'm a fast swimmer. Thanks for my gift. But all I wanted from you for Christmas is for you to pin up your hair. You're so pretty, and my father says you have beautiful eyes, but he can never see but one of them. Pin it up, please. Nobody will notice. I love you. Christopher." Nadine brushed furiously at her tears, unable to say more than thank you. He handed her two unwrapped hair combs.

Christopher walked over to Wade, stood before him and read. "Dear Daddy, I'm sorry I wrote you that stupid letter telling you I didn't want to stay with you. Mother said today that I can stay with you if I want to, and I want to. I told her that I'm not going to call you Wade any more, 'cause you don't like it and Granddaddy and Nadine say it's not right. Anyway, you're my dad. I'll miss being with mother, but she said you'd take me to see her any time I want to go. So I guess it's us guys from now on. I love you, Dad. Merry Christmas. Christopher."

Wade dropped to one knee and embraced his child. "Merry Christmas to you, too, son. Nothing you could have bought or made could mean as much to me as this letter, these words. You're my heart, Christopher, and I don't want you ever to forget it.'' The boy hugged him, and Wade ducked his head to hide his raw, seething emotions. He couldn't help looking toward Nadine. He had his son, but he wouldn't be complete unless he had her as well. He blinked his eyes to make certain that he saw what he thought he saw. With unsteady hands and trembling lips, Nadine pulled her hair back and secured it with the combs Christopher had given her, exposing her face fully. He picked the boy up with one arm and rushed to her.

"You're more beautiful now than I've ever seen you. Lovely.'' Her luminous eyes showed misgivings, and he stroked her left ear. "No matter what you may think; to me, you're perfect.'' Reginald yawned.

"Christopher, we've had a long day, and you and I have to get you started on that computer tomorrow morning. So, say good night.''

It was now or never. She didn't know what to say to him, how to approach him as he stood before her, the epitome of manhood, every woman's dream. He fastened his unwavering gaze on her, his raw self exposed. If he needed her, why didn't he say so? Desperate, she stood on tiptoe and brushed his mouth softly and quickly with her own. "Thanks for a wonderful family Christmas, Wade.'' She would have turned to leave had his eyes not become pools of heat. Sensuous heat. Exasperated by his silence and steady stare, and hungry for him, she commanded more sternly than she had intended. "Wade, for Heaven's sake, say something!''

"When you were hot with fever and delirious, you told me you loved me. Those words sustained me while I fought for Christopher's love and laid plans to get custody. Did you mean it? Do you love me?'' He hadn't told her how he felt, but her words tumbled out of her.

"Love you? Oh, yes, I love you with my whole being. I don't . . ." In one quick motion, she was cradled in his arms, and her words were lost in his kiss. She thrilled to the feel of his fingers on her bare shoulders and arms as they moved ceaselessly over her. So long. Years seemed to have passed since he'd held her and kissed her. Since she'd known the loving security of his strong arms. She held his head in both hands to increase the pressure of his kiss, but he wouldn't be forced. She gloried in the drugging euphoria that settled over her when he slid his lips from her chin to her collar bone. Her nipples tightened when his tongue roamed every crevice of her mouth, and a strange aching settled in her limbs when his feathered kisses whispered over her left ear and across her face. An odd, inner excitement took possession of her. Then his murmured words of praise for her beauty and courage uncaged her need, and she surrendered to her passion.

"Wade. Oh, Wade. Darling. My darling . . ." Hot tremors course through her as he picked something from the tree, took her hand and strode swiftly down the stairs to her temporary room. At its door, he stopped.

"If I go through that door, Nadine, we'll make love. Do you want that?" She nodded.

"I need to hear the words. You're precious to me, and I'll risk not having you for my own, but I won't chance hurting you." His galvanizing look held a poignant message of deep caring. She opened her arms to him.

"I need you, and I want to be with you." He took her hand, walked in with her and closed the door. She dropped her gaze, unable to look at him.

"What is it, sweetheart? Tell me. I don't want anything to stand between us. I've waited a long time for you, and I want all of you." He put an arm around her and tenderly stroked her face with the tips of his fingers. "What is it love?" She studied the carpet, brushed it with the tip of her right shoe and finally looked up at him.

"You might be disappointed. My total experience at this amounts to one miserable failure when I was eighteen." The strength of his arms was there, holding her, comforting her.

"What happened? Tell me."

"He seemed to lose all interest after he saw my ear. He said that wasn't so, but he cooled off. I haven't risked it since."

"Forget that ever happened; you were both children." His lips brushed that ear and lingered there. "Don't you know that you're beautiful? Lovely? I've never known a woman like you." He changed the mood. "This dress has been driving me nuts all evening. There's nothing to it." He let his right hand find its way into the top of her dress. Hot spirals danced through her body and settled in the core of her passion until, in frustration, she undulated against him.

"Wade. Wade, darling. Please . . . I . . ."

"Alright, sweetheart, but don't chase it, just let it catch us." He asked if he could unzip her dress, and she nodded. It pooled around her feet, and he sprang to full readiness as only her red, spaghetti string panties, gartered stockings and shoes clothed her. At his gasp, she covered her breast with her arms, but he removed them and stood feasting his eyes upon her. Her brown aureoles tightened beneath his sultry gaze, and she moved against him in a frenzy of frustration when he brought her to him and loved them with his warm, teasing lips. Impatient now, he tossed the bed covers aside and laid her there while he undressed. She closed her eyes at his nudity, and then opened one of them. He laughed, joined her in bed and, with the skill of a consummate lover, he brought her to fever pitch, caressing her, murmuring words of praise and adoring her until she begged for completion. Slowly and gently, he made them one, loving, teasing and cajoling until she hurtled into ecstasy.

* * *

Satisfied that he'd given her something wonderful, that he had loved her exquisitely, Wade surrendered to the awesome surge that shook him from the soles of his feet to the top of his head and knew a completeness that he had never dreamed possible. His heart pumped wildly in his chest and, in that explosive giving of himself, he knew there would never be another woman for him. Her deep short breaths told him that she hadn't surfaced from the consuming power of their lovemaking, and he leaned over her and kissed tears from her eyes.

"Are you alright, sweetheart?" Anxious that he hadn't hurt her, he urged, "Are you?" Her brilliant smile warmed his heart.

"It was wonderful. Oh, Wade, I'm so happy. I can't express how I feel."

"Try," he teased.

"Now, you really are full of yourself."

"I can't help it; I just got something rare and precious from you." He reached down and got the small parcel that he'd laid beside the bed. "I love you so much, Nadine. I don't know the words to tell you how I felt when you said you loved me. Loved me even though you thought I was a penniless chauffeur. I know that you love me for myself alone, as I love you, and I want to spend the rest of my life with you. You, Christopher and as many brothers and sisters as you're willing to give him. Will you marry me?"

"I want to," she answered, snuggling up from her place beneath him.

"What are you grinning about?"

"It's a riot, Wade. I made elaborate plans to seduce you tonight, and it wasn't even necessary." He meant for his stare to signify incredulity. How could she be so naive?

"You wasted your time, honey. I was seduced by the time I walked out of your office the day you hired me. We've got to talk tomorrow, but I want to level about one thing.

I'm not anywhere near broke, and after I pass the bar, I'm setting up shop half a block from your office."

"You're giving up engineering for good?"

"We'll see how much of my time the law consumes."

"But you're at the pinnacle of your career. Won't you miss it?"

"No. I'll always have it; I'm in business with Magnus Cooper. Besides, architectural engineer is what I am, not *who* I am. My goal now is to be as good a lawyer as I am engineer. I need you in my life, Nadine. Take a chance on me?"

"I need you, too, Wade, and I've never thought that loving you was a gamble." He slipped his grandmother's and mother's engagement ring on her finger.

"If you look on the inside of this ring, love, you'll see the date, XII.24.1912. By some odd coincidence, my father and his father before him got engaged on Christmas Eve. This Christmas Eve is extra special to me, because I'm following their footsteps, because I have my son and because I have you. Love is the important thing in life, Nadine. And tonight, Christopher taught us all the meaning of Christmas: of all gifts, love is the most precious." He folded her in his embrace and loved her as he would for many Christmases to come.

Dear Reader,

Christmas has always been my favorite season, a time of love and goodwill, of bonding with family and friends. Thus, it was with enormous pleasure that I took the opportunity to write a love story that reflects the joys of this wonderful season. I hope you enjoyed this tale of the miracle of Christmas as Christopher understood it, and that you rejoiced with Nadine and Wade as they received this child's blessing of love. May your Christmas, too, be a time of love, health, happiness, and renewal.

I am glad to have this chance to thank the many individuals who purchased and read *Sealed With A Kiss*, my first book for Pinnacle/Arabesque, and *Against All Odds*, which Pinnacle/Arabesque published in September of this year. The response to both has been overwhelming, and I want to thank you for your wonderful support. I have recently completed a novella, *A Perfect Match*, which will be included in the Arabesque's 1998 collection of Valentine's Day novellas and a third novel, tentatively titled *Beyond Ecstasy*, which Pinnacle/Arabesque will release in July, 1997.

Your letters have encouraged me so much. Please continue to write. I try to answer each letter that I receive, and I especially appreciate your enclosing a self addressed and stamped envelope. My address is P.O. Box 45, New York, New York. 10044–0045.

Best wishes.

Gwynne Forster

Whisper to me

Carmen Green

Chapter One

"Daddy, did you look at my new list to Santa? I faxed it to your office this morning before I left for school."

Slightly perturbed at her father's preoccupation with his tie, seven year old Anika Hamilton stopped lolling in the center of his four-poster bed, propped up on her knees next to her twin, and fixed him with a penetrating stare.

When he didn't immediately respond, she exchanged an anxious glance with her sister.

"Did you get mine too?" piped Medina, in a nearly identical voice.

Cedric Hamilton glanced through the tri-paneled wall mirror from his dressing room, his gaze coming to rest on his two favorite women. The resemblance to their mother began and ended with their cinnamon coloring and brown eyes.

They bore the signature genes of the Hamilton ancestors with jet black hair and dark, half-inch-long lashes.

Dimples like his graced their satiny cheeks, while their intelligent eyes stared back at him with feigned innocence.

He couldn't resist the smile that tugged at the corners of his mouth. Ah, he thought, the gang-up-on-Dad approach.

Familiar with that technique of persuasion, he stalled, adjusting his tilted bow tie. When they began to fidget, he still delayed answering, taking his time to select and slip into polished dress shoes. He glanced slyly at the girls, feeling their unspoken frustration.

Cedric pulled at the sleeves of the starched white tuxedo shirt and crossed thick navy carpet to the armoire outside of the dressing room.

"As a matter of fact," he said, hearing them inhale. "I did receive something." He wiggled his eyebrows mysteriously.

They embraced and giggled and rolled on the bed.

Cedric smiled, wishing he could be so free. But ever since his wife's death, securing their future had been his primary concern. The smile slowly faded from his wide mouth. Things were good now, he constantly had to remind himself. He could breathe without fear they'd end up on the streets where he'd come from.

Contemplating throwing off the stiff white shirt and crooked bow tie, Cedric started for the button at his collar, then stopped. Duty bellowed like a horn on a foggy night.

The benefit auction was his baby. He had to be there.

Resigning himself to his evening's fate, he gave the crooked tie a final pat and pressed the mahogany armoire door. It swung open easily.

Tenderly, he pulled a worn gray velvet box from the drawer. Lenora had given it to him nine years ago. Thinking of his wife, Cedric lifted his eyes heavenward. He knew she was watching over them, protecting the family she'd been snatched away from.

The lid creaked as he tilted it up, and he became aware that the girls' giggles had ceased. They now stood beside him.

"Are those the cuff bl-, things Mom gave to you on your wedding day, Daddy?" Medina asked.

Cedric nodded, lifting the black and gold studs from the box. In order to keep their mother alive, he'd shared every memory with them. Except the most intimate. Those were safely tucked in a corner in his heart. Lately though, those memories had begun to grow fuzzy, distant.

Inquisitive eyes stared up at him. He finally answered.

"Links. Say it, Medina." Gingerly, he laid them in her palm as she rolled her tongue around in her mouth.

"Bw-bwinks," she stuttered, proud of her effort.

Cedric closed one eye, scratched his head, and gave her a nod of encouragement. "Close, and yes, they are the exact ones. Who's going to help me put them on?"

"I will," the girls replied in unison.

Cedric sat on the edge of the raised bed, waiting as they jumped from the hand-made footstool to sit beside him. His gaze slid from the stool to the dark mahogany furniture his wife had commissioned for them from her own designs.

It bespoke both their personalities in strength and firmness. Yet the hand-carved designs etched into the drawers and base were unique, complex. Looking at them reminded him of the love they'd shared.

Lately though, loneliness he'd felt only as a child had begun to creep in and steal his rare, private moments of peace. Those haunting childhood memories had ceased once he'd found love the first time. He believed he'd never be alone again.

Cedric stroked his chin, then dragged his hand down the front of his shirt, making sure it was straight. He wondered if he would ever find love a second time around.

Mentally, he pushed the thoughts away. So far no woman had been special enough to fit into his complicated world.

The demands of family and job were first and foremost, and that would never change. It wasn't likely he would find love again.

Cedric sighed, shrugging. Would be nice, though.

"Stay still, Daddy," Anika ordered.

"Sorry."

His gaze traveled over their bent heads, down their long braided hair. He lifted his shoulders and was fixed with a serious glare from Medina.

"Quit shrugging. I'm aw-most done." He held his breath when Medina's tongue jutted out as she concentrated on fastening the link.

"Lllll, links," he said, urging her to echo his pronunciation. Instead, Medina smiled adorably at him, dimples denting her cheek.

"You said it perfect. Very good, Daddy."

She bent over his wrist, her fingers intent on their mission, and he felt suitably put in his place. His mother's soft-spoken warning of pushing Medina too hard rang in his head. Difficult as it was for him, he tried to go easy on her. But he'd found out the hard way, life wasn't kind to those with weaknesses.

Anika's little hands pushed the air from his cheeks, making him turn toward her.

"Daddy, do you think Santa can bring all my presents on one sleigh and still fit everybody else's? My list is kind of long." She released his face and rested her hands on his shoulders.

"Wh-what?" Caught off guard, Cedric drew back, unsure he'd heard correctly.

"I think he should have one sleigh just for me," Anika said reasonably.

"Me too," Medina added.

Anika rolled her eyes in her head. "Okay," she said reluctantly. "He could probably attach a small one to mine and put your stuff on back."

Cedric stared at her, stunned.

"Daddy," Anika went on, "Santa might have to make two trips to the North Pole because he won't be able to carry our things and everybody else's too."

Anika held two fingers under his nose, forcing his eyes to cross as he looked down at them. "I need two life-size Barbie's, so they can be twins just like us. Two pair of roller blades, three pair of gold earrings. I saw this carousel when I was in the mall with Grandma and it wasn't that expensive. It had a two, six, zero, zero, dot, zero, zero. Can you get that for me? It's not really a toy, so I don't think Santa will get it."

"Twenty-six hundred dollars." Medina offered as she straightened his cuff, giving his arm a final pat.

"I need . . ."

"Stop!" His tone commanded silence.

"But . . ."

"Enough, Anika!" Cedric held up his hands to ward off the completion of a list he feared would go on forever.

Cedric paced in front of them, wondering if these two gift-hungry children were his. He wagged his finger at them.

"Santa is not, I repeat, is *not* going to drive one sleigh just for your gifts. Have you two forgotten the real meaning of Christmas?" When they shook their heads, a small margin of relief flooded him.

"No, sir. It's Jesus' birthday," Medina said solemnly.

Cedric breathed a sigh of relief, grateful at least one of his reasonable children had returned.

"That's right. It's also the season to give." His voice softened, and he lifted their chins so he could look into their identical brown eyes. "Not just receive."

"Yes, sir," they echoed, resignation weighing down their tone.

A quick glance at his watch indicated the late hour. Hurrying to the dresser, he pocketed his wallet, keys, and a few stray coins. "We need to talk, girls. Unfortunately, I have to get going. We'll have to do it tomorrow at breakfast."

"Are you going to make us bw-ueberry pancakes?" Medina clasped her hands together, a pleading look in her eyes.

More blackmail. Cedric did a mental check of pancake

ingredients, then nodded. "I'll stop and pick up some blueberries before I come home."

He glanced at Anika. Her chin was thrust upward and her eyes gleamed with determination.

"Daddy, we give away dresses and toys all the time. Isn't that right, Medina? And sometimes you give away money to those kids. I know it's just a couple dollars, but won't that count for us too?"

Cedric executed a slow turn toward his eldest child by two hours and thought he might see a spoiled debutante in her place. The couple of dollars she referred to was a fifty-thousand-dollar college scholarship he gave every year in his wife's name to a graduating high school senior.

"Anika Michele!" His voice rang with warning. Cedric stopped. Blowing up at her wasn't the answer. Her words went deep, farther than she could ever know.

"I said we would talk in the morning. Go tell Grandma Elaine I'm leaving. You too, Medina."

When the girls quietly closed the door to his room, Cedric shrugged into his single-breasted, athletic cut tuxedo jacket. One last look in the gold-rimmed, tri-paneled mirror revealed more than he expected.

For the first time in many years, he wasn't pleased with what he saw.

Chapter Two

"Iman, you aren't going to win the painting. Come on, I'm ready to go."

Iman Parrish linked arms with her sister, Aliyah, and dragged her into the crowd that filled the turn-of-the-century home.

"Don't leave yet, okay? I'm going to win." *If you believe, then you can achieve,* Iman told herself repeatedly.

"No, you're not. Have you forgotten this auction is to raise money?" Her sister looked at her with that "duh" expression on her face. "People are here to spend money for a good cause, not bargain. Your bid was so low, I could have bid against you and won."

Iman looked around at the guests. So what if the city's most prominent and wealthy were present? So what if most had enough money to make her bank account look like bread crumbs? So what? Nobody wanted a painting by an unknown child painter but her.

She stared at the painting and was grateful no one lingered near the table. It was perfect. And, she reasoned, it wasn't often she wanted something so bad.

Iman withdrew her arm from Aliyah's. "None of these people want it because the little boy isn't famous. Oh, shoot." Iman grabbed her sister's arm again. "Look at *him.*"

They eyed a tall, dark-complexioned man as he moved close to study the picture of children playing.

From behind, it was obvious his clothes were tailored and expensive. She eased to the left to see him from the side. His generous smile wasn't entirely lost on her. Her belly clenched uncharacteristically.

Everything about him spelled "I'm rich."

Rich enough to out-bid her.

To her dismay he stepped closer for a better look.

Iman's stomach jumped.

She had to stop him from bidding on her painting. Iman circled the table, approaching him head on. His dark eyes gleamed with appreciation. Her stomach plummeted. She'd seen that confident look before in other patron's eyes.

She'd felt it too—just before she'd placed her bid.

"He's picking up the pen," she whispered anxiously to her sister for no reason. The noise in the room was at conversational level.

"Told you," Aliyah knowingly replied. She tugged Iman's arm. "Come on. You lost."

Iman stared at the canvas her young friend had painted, longing for it. "I can't give up, Li. I promised Harold if he completed Kwanzaa class, I would buy one of his paintings. I want this one." She turned back to the man with the broad shoulders and long legs and smacked her lips into a determined line.

"He doesn't really want it. What would a good-looking man like that want with a picture of children?"

"Why don't you ask him why he wants it and explain why you have to have it?" Aliyah huffed impatiently.

"No."

"If that doesn't work, cry."

Iman drew in a breath of exasperation at her sister's suggestion.

"Bad joke," Aliyah shrugged, throwing up her hands. "Why don't you go say hi? Make pleasant conversation, use your feminine wiles, and he'll be putty in your hand."

Iman knew her sister was joking now. But she also recognized the devilish twist to Aliyah's brows and cringed. The matchmaker in her was rearing its ugly head.

She couldn't help considering the idea for a moment. The dark gentleman was something. Tall and broad across the shoulders, in a way she'd always found appealing in a man, his black hair cut close to his scalp, and the smoothness of his clean shaven face made her hand itch to caress it. He studied the painting with one hand in his pocket, the other hanging at his side, an aura of casual intensity surrounding him.

Iman felt the overwhelming sensation of wanting to take her place by his side. She stepped back, shocked.

He had probably come with someone. Probably not looking for company. Probably unavailable.

"Nah," she said, as offhand as possible. "He's not my type."

Aliyah's expression echoed her disbelief, but she kept quiet. Instead she pushed Iman ahead.

"Let's see if we can sneak a peek at Mr. Handsome's bid. Maybe you can beat it."

People filled the space between them, halting their progress. "Shoot," Iman exhaled in frustration when the lights began to flash.

"May I have everyone's attention?"

Reluctantly, she and Aliyah turned toward the aristocratic voice of the hostess.

"My name is Imogene Osborne, and I am the director here at Stone Manor. I'd like to thank each and every one of you for coming this evening to support the fight for a cure for children afflicted with the AIDS virus.

"We all know there is an answer but we need resources

to find it. Benefits like this help bring us one step closer to saving a child's life.'' Iman applauded while sneaking another look at the table. Her gaze was drawn away from the painting to the man beside it. He acknowledged her with a nod of his head. Iman bared her teeth in a semblance of a smile and returned her attention to Imogene, who had clasped her hands together gesturing with her index fingers pointed.

"Thank you for being so generous in your bids. It's for a good cause. While final bids are taken and the tallying completed, those of you with red tickets please convene in the west room to begin your tour of the house. Those with black, the east room, and those with green, remain here. Please respect the barriers protecting the rooms, and stay on the brown carpet. You will be notified after the tours are underway if you have won any of our auctioned items. Your tours will begin momentarily. Thank you for your support."

Applause rippled through the crowd and Iman turned back to the table. Her heart pounded. The collecting attendant picked up the book.

"Wait!" Pushing past a large woman in a red sequined dress and over the long wing-tipped shoe of her companion, Iman stumbled before she stood between the man and the attendant. A measure of satisfaction curled through her when Mr. Handsome, who'd been leaving the table turned and frowned. "Wait." She held up her hand to stop the attendant. "I want to place another bid."

"I'm sorry, ma'am. The bidding is closed." The attendant's sorrowful smile only made her want to plead. He moved to the next table leaving her to stare at his back. Aliyah walked up beside her.

"Did you catch him?"

"Yes. He said the bidding was closed."

Iman turned back to the man. "I was trying to catch the attendant," she offered, unable to hide her disappointment.

"I noticed." He stuck out his hand and she looked at long, strong fingers. "Cedric Hamilton. And you are?"

Her sister nudged her arm.

"Iman Parrish. Please excuse my manners," she said, grasping his hand. His warm touch made her shiver to the tips of her glittery shoes. She looked up and was captivated by caramel brown eyes, but she couldn't hold back her wistful tone. "I really wanted that painting."

His name rang a bell of familiarity and Iman searched his face until she realized how she knew him. Cedric Hamilton was on the board of directors of Stone Manor. He was one of the main reasons why she was there.

An elbow shoved into her side made her look at her sister. "Sorry. This is my older sister, Aliyah Easterbrook. Cedric Hamilton."

"Do you have to tell everyone I'm your *older* sister?"

Iman ignored the testiness in Aliyah's voice. The handsome Cedric was having a strange affect on her. He extracted his hand from hers to take her sister's. Their shake was brief.

"Nice to meet you," she heard her sister say. "Hope to see you again. Goodnight."

Iman snapped out of the spell. "Wait Li, where are you going?"

"Jerome will be back from Jacksonville tonight, so I thought I would slip into something more revealing and be home waiting."

Iman frowned at her sister's brazen announcement and gave her a disapproving look. "Li." Her face heated in embarrassment and she knew her nose was beginning to glow a faint red.

Cedric's laugh tickled her spine. "He's a very lucky man. I hope to see you again, too." When Iman turned a stunned expression to him, both he and Aliyah burst out laughing.

"Not like that." He touched Iman's arm, leaving a warm spot before sliding his hand in his pocket. "I meant socially . . . with her husband."

"I knew what you meant." Aliyah winked, encouraging Iman toward Cedric with a nod of her head.

Iman waited for her sister to stop grinning like a fool. "Aliyah, I'm not ready to go yet. Why don't you wait for me? You drove, remember?"

"Yes, I remember. Catch a cab, all right? I'm ready to go home. Good luck with the painting." She kissed Iman's cheek, then turned to Cedric and shook his hand.

"Goodnight, Cedric. Call me tomorrow, Iman."

Iman watched Aliyah's cream dress swish around her legs as she walked into the crowd that was headed toward the west room. Aliyah raised her hand to wave and Iman did too, wishing her sister had stayed. At least with Aliyah there, she would have an opportunity to control her roiling emotions. The intensity of her physical attraction to Cedric startled her.

Iman turned back to him and looked up. The blend of shadows and firelight cast from behind him gave him a familiar yet larger than life presence.

"She's quite a lady. Is she always like that?"

In the warm light from the fireplace, his smooth, dark skin looked as delectable as Godiva chocolate. She fought the overwhelming urge to press her lips softly along the side of his face. Iman didn't know she had a thing for sideburns until she noticed Cedric's.

His questioning gaze broke her reverie.

"Always. Nothing Aliyah says surprises me any more," she answered quickly hoping her Rudolph nose wouldn't betray her. "Should you be getting back to your date?"

"I *am* my date this evening."

"Oh," Iman said. *Yes!* She thought. "And by day?" Talk about brazen. Aliyah must be rubbing off on her.

He regarded her with a long, penetrating stare. "I don't usually date myself. I'm single."

"Really?" she asked, watching the movements of his lips, wondering how they would feel touching her skin.

He nodded.

"How . . ." their gazes caught and held, "How nice."

"I think so."

Iman pivoted on her high heels trying to get her bearings. She wasn't quite sure how to handle the explosion of desire that burst within her. She focused on the guests who entered the room using them as an easy distraction.

The lights dimmed. Unable to stop herself, Iman looked at Cedric. Something flickered to life within the dark brown depths of his eyes. It reached into her and warmed her making the backs of her thighs tingle and her knees wobbly under her gray and white evening dress.

He moved close and his jacket scraped her fingers. Intimacy was more than she'd bargained for.

His husky voice whispered close to her cheek. "Have you toured Stone Manor before?"

"No, I haven't had the pleasure yet." Iman inhaled his cologne, the faint bouquet of wine on his breath and felt lightheaded. She wanted to rest her cheek on his shoulder.

But her shoes were smart. They stayed rooted in place. His hand touched the small of her back and veered them away from the crowd to a door marked *Private*.

"Let me give you the grand tour. I'm an excellent guide." Iman found it difficult to say no. She nodded.

He opened the door allowing her to step through first. The hallway was long, narrow, and dark. Iman turned back in time to see Cedric fumble with something in his hands.

Apprehension snaked through her and she berated her hasty decision to follow him. Board of directors or not, she didn't know him. She took a step back.

"I think I should go back."

Cedric took her hand and placed a long object in it. He pushed a button. Light spilled to the floor. Iman stared down. *A flashlight.* Luckily the darkness shielded her tell tale nose and her guilty thoughts.

He pointed to the end of the hallway. "This is where the tour should actually begin. At the front door. Who ever heard of starting something in the middle?" His large hand closed around hers as he led her into the darkness, the round white circle their only guide. "There's nothing to be afraid of," he said softly. "I'll hold your hand the whole way."

As he led her from room to room, Iman listened intently to the history of the house and its occupants. She was most impressed with Cedric's knowledge of the antique European furnishings, and the unique sculpturing carved into the foundation of each room by black craftsmen. He knew every detail, even down to the year the silk damask wallpaper was hung in the dining room.

"Every room has a balcony but this one was designed to overlook downtown Atlanta." His fingers threaded through hers, his voice soft. "Isn't it beautiful?"

"Spectacular." Lights twinkled in the darkness and from this far away, the city noise eluded them, allowing them to witness its quiet splendor undisturbed. Iman loved the powerful feeling that she and Cedric were on a private island. "It's so secluded. So private."

"Like an island made for two." He looked down at her. "I feel that each time I come here."

It pleased her that his thoughts ran along the same line as hers. The mood shifted as they drew closer against a cool wind. Involuntarily, she shivered as much from the cold as from the budding emotions that sprang within her tonight.

"How long did the son live here after his father and stepmother's death?"

"Another forty years. Mitchell owned several businesses, and followed in his father's footsteps in philanthropy. He's one of my role models."

"How so?"

Cedric walked to the other side of the wooden balcony. His shoulders were stiff and he jabbed his hands in his pocket. He seemed troubled as he gazed into the cloudless sky.

"I want to teach my children those kinds of values. Mitchell learned from his father to never let adversity stop his dreams. His father was a slave, then opened a barber business in Atlanta and became a very wealthy man." His voice was awed. "Can you believe that?"

"It amazes me what people can overcome when they set their minds on a goal." Iman walked toward him.

"My girls are my pride and joy, but they're the most spoiled little people I've ever had the pleasure of meeting. I think their goal is to own the local toy store at seven years of age."

"Seven?" she shook her head, surprise making her eyebrows raise. "A precocious age. They must be a handful raising them alone."

"I'm fortunate to have both sets of grandparents to help whenever I need it. They help in the spoiling too, though. The girls love it."

This time Iman smiled. "Girls are made for spoiling. Don't be too hard on them."

He shook his head, his forehead creasing with thought. "No, they're worse than spoiled, and tonight for the first time, I feel the way I'm raising them may be a mistake." He finally looked at her. "Do you have children?"

"Not yet. One day."

Another breeze blew, this time making them step back with its chilling force. Iman shivered again.

"I wasn't thinking. Come back inside. You must be freezing." Guiding her by her elbow, he led her through the door and unfastened his jacket. "Put this on until you warm up."

"Thank you." She wrapped the coal black jacket around her shoulders, his body heat warming her. "I really should be going soon."

"What about the painting?" This time his eyes danced when he smiled.

Iman rolled her eyes. "You're trying to be funny, aren't you?" Cedric led the way back to the main area of the manor, a huge grin on his face. He left the flashlight in its original spot. "I'm sure my five-hundred dollar bid was slammed the moment you picked up the pen. Take care of it. A good friend of mine painted it."

Iman reluctantly slid out of his coat, handing it back to him. Their scents mingled enticingly, and the loss of its weight made her feel fragile.

He failed at looking wounded. "You make me feel guilty for wanting the painting." Iman knew he was joking. He didn't look guilty. He looked edible.

The centers of his eyes were dark pools and Iman felt herself absorbed by the black depths. She wanted to caress the masculine lines on his face, feel the sandy texture of his jaw against her palm, rest her head on his strong, broad shoulder. Instead, she had to look up several inches from her above average height to focus on his slightly crooked bow tie, Cedric's only outward imperfection.

Then their gazes locked. The house was now quiet, having been vacated by the other guests. Waiters quietly cleaned around them.

"I don't mean to make you feel bad. It's for a good cause." Iman stopped Cedric's fingers from drawing lazy circles on her arm. "Maybe if you win, you'll let me see it sometime. Right now, I need to get a taxi. It was an unexpected pleasure to meet you, Mr. Hamilton."

Iman squeezed his hand and hurried away afraid if she stayed any longer, she would embarrass herself by stepping into an embrace he would break. She retrieved her cape, spoke to Imogene for a moment, then looked over her shoulder before she called a cab.

No Cedric.

It was probably just as well. This Cinderella feeling had to be a warning. He probably *was* too good to be true.

Chapter Three

The outside of Stone Manor provided its namesake. Stacked stone walls installed in the early 1920s bordered the ground level of the house. Erosion made it necessary to relandscape the property, but the magnificent house had survived the years well. There remained the old southern style that made the house an unofficial historical monument in downtown Atlanta.

Iman descended the stairs into the parking lot and checked for her cab. A car rolled to a stop in front of her.

"May I play a humble second to a yellow cab?"

Iman shifted on cold toes, bent down, and stared at Cedric in the silver luxury car. The last car in the driveway pulled around them and Imogene Osborne waved goodnight. There were no yellow cabs in sight. Heat wafted from the open window beckoning her. She wanted to get in, but held back.

"I should probably wait."

"I don't want to leave you out here. It's your choice."

A brisk breeze swept up her cape, the imitation fur collar

doing nothing to protect her neck and head from the assaulting wind. She decided quickly. "If you insist."

Iman pulled the door handle and as elegantly as her stiff legs would allow, slid in. "I live near Piedmont Park. Were you really going to leave?"

His dimpled smile warmed her in places that hadn't felt heat in a long time. He turned the steering wheel and soon they were traveling down Martin Luther King Drive. "I saw your cab leave a long time ago while you were talking to Imogene. I was pretty sure I could convince you."

Iman nodded, remembering their brief chat. She fastened her seat belt and settled back in the luxurious leather.

"You didn't forget your purse did you?"

Iman couldn't resist teasing. "Imogene told me you won my picture, now you want my money?"

"I wasn't asking because I want your money," he chuckled. "You're very funny. It's been a while since I've found anything to laugh about." He pumped the brakes as they turned the corner. Iman enjoyed the rumble of his laughter and his eyes twinkled when he smiled.

"I didn't really think you were asking me for money."

"I'm glad to hear that. I asked out of habit. My girls are seven, and if we leave the house without their purses . . ." His brows furrowed in a pained expression. "There's hell to pay."

"You know all that tissue kept in those purses is very important," she teased. "What are their names?"

"Anika and Medina. Quite a combination."

"First grade, right?"

He regarded her from the corner of his eye. "Lucky guess."

Iman shook her head. "Experience. I worked with a group of seven year olds last summer in a reading program. I have a way with them."

He laughed. "You do, do you? My girls can change any

person's mind about kids with their antics." He laughed
to himself. "They're my life."

Iman studied him for a moment as they drove in silence.
He seemed to have erected a barrier around himself with
his pronouncement. A single father raising his daughters
alone was something she didn't see very often, but if he
handled them with the same smooth control he used to
maneuver the car, they were probably just spoiled, little
daddy's girls.

She thought of the close relationship she'd had with her
own father until his death several years ago. Being a daddy's
girl was very special.

"I think they've spoiled you. You wear fatherhood well."

He blinked several times, surprised. "Thank you." Iman
knew she'd caught him off guard with the compliment,
but parents were rarely patted on the back for a job well
done.

As the car slowed then stopped at the red light, Iman
noticed women hovering over sidewalk grates for warmth.

White smoke fogged them, obscuring their faces, but it
was obvious they would spend the cold November night
on the street. Cedric leaned over to watch as a short person
slipped out of a box. It horrified Iman to discover it was
a young girl.

Iman couldn't drag her eyes away from the sight of the
two homeless people, until she heard Cedric's voice in the
phone. He gave the women's location and description and
instructed the person to make sure they had a warm bed
for the night if they wanted it.

She released a pent up breath, and allowed the relief
of Cedric's actions to wash over her. How she viewed him,
grew disproportionately to his average male size.

A hero, she thought, his chivalrous attitude touching
her more than she thought possible. They pulled away
from a green light and the image of an old and young
woman fitting themselves into the box were left behind.

"What a life," Cedric murmured.

"Because of you, at least they won't freeze." Iman turned to look out the back window as the women grew smaller the farther away they drove. Eventually they disappeared, but the memory would forever be embedded in her mind.

She was a little taken aback at the harshness of his voice when he spoke. "There's nothing like being cold and not being able to do a damn thing about it."

The seat belt pulled across her chest and Iman adjusted it to a more comfortable position.

"Ever been cold?" His voice held more challenge than curiosity.

Controlled pain tightened the skin around his mouth. She sensed an underlying current of anger. It had something to do with the women they'd just seen. Iman reached out to comfort him. She answered cautiously, unsure of where it would lead. "I've been plenty cold. I grew up in Buffalo, New York."

He grimaced and patted her hand, as if to dismiss her response. "You were lucky. That was voluntary."

Iman remained quiet for a tense moment then asked, "Do you want to talk about it?"

"No." Cedric shut her out. She resisted the urge to try to soothe his troubles away. Iman withdrew her hand and watched the lights of cars passing on the other side of the street.

"I need to stop at the store before I take you home. Do you mind?"

"That's fine," she whispered.

Cedric turned the steering wheel and they entered the near deserted interstate. Fewer cars passed the further they drove. The store had to be an out of the way place because there wasn't much open at this late hour, in this direction, she thought.

Iman trusted the instincts that told her she was in good hands. Cedric Hamilton was known and well respected in the community. Besides, Imogene had spoken so highly of him tonight, the discussion had piqued her interest.

Iman settled back against the seat and let the smooth motion of the car calm her questions.

Finally, Cedric glanced at her, then returned his gaze to the road ahead of them. His voice was more relaxed when he spoke.

"How do you think the auction went tonight? We planned it with the hopes of raising money for AIDS research, but we also wanted to bring the needs of Stone Manor to the public's attention."

"Considering I lost my painting, I'm sure *somebody,*" she exaggerated, "left happy."

"You can come see that painting any time your heart desires." His fingers linked with hers and squeezed lightly. Tiny jets of sensation shot through her arm.

"Anyway, I thought it was a huge success. I was honored to meet the governor and the mayor. Even the police chief showed up. Imogene and the board really pulled out the stops on this. I know you're on the board of directors. How close is Stone Manor to being accepted as a historical site?"

His eyes narrowed thoughtfully. "The chairman of the historical society was there as well as several of the members. The board hopes to know something soon."

"Do you think tonight's event raised enough interest?" Iman asked. Stone Manor was too important to Atlanta history to be destroyed for lack of funds.

"Definitely." His voice rang with confidence. Cedric disengaged his hand from hers. As he wrestled with his tie, Iman watched. He looked immensely pleased with himself when he tossed it over his shoulder onto the back seat.

"Better?"

"Much." He grinned. "You want to—"

"No, thanks. I think I'll keep all my pieces on."

Their silence lengthened and Iman's thoughts gravitated back to the man beside her.

Cedric's work to save Stone Manor had brought him to her attention many months ago. Widely respected as a shrewd and powerful businessman, his fundraising abilities had saved the old home from the wrecker's ball.

Iman had been informed by chatty Imogene Osborne over lunch two weeks before that Cedric sat on the board of directors of several prestigious companies. She'd also reported that while Cedric Hamilton was a successful businessman, his personal life was a bit of a mystery.

At the time, Iman had listened with polite indifference. Now, she had a strong need to know. She cast a sidelong gaze at her riding partner and enjoyed what she saw. His warm eyes and gorgeous lashes made her think of relaxing in a smooth Caribbean pool. His reassuring touch and easy manner also didn't jive with Imogene's veiled assessment.

There was nothing mysterious about the way she felt about Cedric. Her attraction was bold. And though she hadn't known him long, his work had been one of the reasons she'd accepted the offer to teach a class about Kwanzaa at the manor. Something clicked in her mind. Iman turned to look at him.

"I really admire the work you did last year to open Robinson Community Center. I'd heard about the private investors not coming through with the necessary funds. Aliyah and I wouldn't be teaching there now if you hadn't stepped in and raised the money."

He smiled appreciatively. "You were a natural choice because of your teaching experience." His voice was velvet soft. "Of course, had I known what I know now, there wouldn't have been any competition."

"And what do you know? I hope my qualifications set me above the other candidates."

He leaned toward her. In the faint light from the dash board she saw the outline of his face and the firm set of his jaw. "There's no question about that. We had many offers to teach, but once Imogene reported to the board that she'd taken your class and how it changed her life, you were in." Iman felt relieved and proud.

While Imogene was chatty and a bit of a gossip, she and

many of the board members had worked hard this past month to pass along the principles of Kwanzaa at Robinson Community Center.

Kwanzaa was meant to bring families and communities together to celebrate the "fruits" of their labor and to set new goals and make plans for the next year. Cedric had been an instrumental part of that successful team of people who made it all come together. She wondered if he knew what a great effect his deeds had done.

"There are a few more reasons," he said.

Her stomach fluttered when his lips curled in a seductive smile. Somehow she didn't think her master's degree had been what tipped the scales.

"What are they?"

"We have the same taste in art, you're beautiful, single, and have a nose that glows. You were a shoe-in."

Iman touched the tip of her nose. Heat rushed to her cheeks. Soon she would look just like Rudolph.

She laughed. "So you've rounded out your resume' with comedian. I think somebody should keep his day job."

He hooted, laughing. "I think somebody should be nice to me, especially if said individual wants to see that painting ever again."

"I'm crushed you'd hold that over my head."

"I have to keep some leverage, don't I?"

"Tell me about your work at Dix."

"I'll tell you only on the condition that you tell me about Kwanzaa first. The other reason we decided to utilize Stone Manor's facilities for the classes was because of the over-whelming interest in the celebration. Refresh my memory. It sounds like something my daughters need."

Iman always enjoyed sharing the story of Kwanzaa's beginning.

"Dr. Maulana Karenga first celebrated the holiday in 1966. His intention was to give African-American people an opportunity to learn about their history and customs. Many of us fall into the commercialism trap that surrounds

Christmas. We spend money we don't have and buy things we don't really need. Kwanzaa isn't like that."

"How is it different?" He frowned. "It's on the tail end of Christmas."

"It's based on the concept of a harvest festival that was traditionally practiced throughout Africa. It brings communities, friends, and family together to celebrate the 'fruits' of their labor and to give thanks to the Creator for their blessings. As a collective group, you evaluate your achievements and set goals for the year ahead."

He considered this a moment. "I've heard there are rules you follow during that week."

Iman shook her head. "Not rules. Principles, and it's not just that week. It's a lifelong commitment. We start on the twenty-sixth with *Umoja*. It means unity. *Kujichagulia*, self-determination. *Ujima*, collective work and responsibility. *Ujamaa*, cooperative economics. *Nia*, purpose. *Kuumba*, creativity, and *Imani* means faith. When you have all those factors working in harmony in your life, you're physically, morally, and spiritually able to harvest success."

"It seems as if those principles are practiced by people everyday anyway."

"They are to certain degrees. Kwanzaa is about incorporating all those principles into one celebration and governing your life by it."

"Do you have a favorite part of the celebration?"

Without hesitation she answered. *"Kutoa majina."*

"What's koo-too-a-?"

Iman enunciated the words. "Koo-Tee-ah ma-JEEN-ah. It's the calling and remembering of ancestors and heroes. I always remember what a fighter my father was. He was a fireman. My dad was a hard working, but gentle man. He was my hero." Cedric took her hand seeming to sense her vulnerability.

Iman blinked back the moisture that gathered in the corner of her eyes. It had been a long time since she'd felt emotional about her father passing. She held onto

Cedric's hand and tried to catch a glimpse of the highway sign as they headed off the exit. The car wound up and around seeming to go in an endless spiral. Dense bare branches tangled on the side of the road, visible only in brief glances. She glanced at the dash clock, surprised to discover they'd been riding over two hours.

Iman looked out the window at the restaurant that stood at the top of the mountain.

"Pardon my French, but where in the blazes are we?"

Cedric answered solemnly. "Lookout Mountain, Tennessee."

Chapter Four

"Do you do this often?" Iman asked after returning from the ladies' room, taking the seat beside him. A fresh application of red lipstick coated her lips, and he drew his gaze away from them to meet hers.

Cedric felt himself relax for the first time since they'd entered the restaurant. Her teasing smile lightened the load on his mind. "I promise," he held up his hand in a Boy Scout's honor salute. "I've never done this before. You're the first woman I've ever brought to Tennessee for a date."

"I'm thrilled at the honor." Her voice grew husky and her eyes shimmered seductively.

Over entrees of fried chicken, loaded potato skins, and fried cheese sticks, Cedric took the opportunity to study Iman. Short, carefully styled curls, accented her smooth nut brown complexion. The dark warmth of her eyes was addicting, making him feel calm, at ease. Cedric resisted snuggling against the delicate curve of her slender neck and inhaling deeply of her. He just wanted to relax and enjoy her company.

She munched heartily on the chicken leg, oblivious to his visual examination. She finished and laid the bone on the extra plate. After she wiped her mouth with the cloth napkin she looked at him.

"You're not worried about your arteries, are you?"

Cedric waved his hand in a sometimes expression. "I like fried chicken. I know what doctors say about cholesterol. But the best chicken in Tennessee is served," he poked the table with his finger, "right here."

"You didn't have to bring me to Tennessee to get fried chicken. My kitchen would have done nicely."

"Seriously?" His expression bordered on disbelief. "Don't tease me, Iman. I don't get good fried chicken everywhere, so you'd better be prepared for a visit if you're serious."

"I am. Call first," she teased. "I don't do 'to go' orders."

"What's your number?" He was pleased when she rattled off the numbers and started in on her meal again.

She didn't eat much fried food, Cedric assessed. Her figure was too nice and shapely in all the right places. He was relieved she hadn't slapped him for damn near kidnapping her and bringing her to Tennessee.

Hideaway Mountain Restaurant was one of his favorite places and without consciously thinking about it, he'd wanted to share one of his private places with her.

His gaze glided over her figure hugging gray dress. She was quite beautiful. *Would she like my kids?*

Where had that thought come from? Cedric hurried to retrieve his clattering fork. The waiter rushed to replace it and scooted quietly away.

"Is something wrong with my dress?"

"Not at all," he said appreciatively. "I like your dress just fine," he scrambled for a graceful way out. "It's just that I would think you would be dressed more traditionally. More," he hesitated, not wanting to offend her.

She gave him a knowing look. "More African?"

"Well, yes. I suppose that's what I mean. I have to confess, I don't know much about the traditions." She wiped her mouth on her napkin again. Cedric couldn't explain his sense of regret at the gesture.

"I do dress traditionally on occasion. But that has nothing to do with Kwanzaa directly. I dress in traditional African clothes because I feel good in them. I think they accentuate the inner beauty of the person wearing them." She laid her fork on the table and looked him over in a way that set his pulse racing double-time.

"In fact, this evening, I imagined you wearing the traditional clothing." She eyed him from head to toe. "You looked quite handsome."

"Were you checking me out?"

Iman looked away, controlling a grin that revealed even white teeth. Her long earrings hit against her jaw. "No, I wasn't."

"You're lying," he said and shoved a forkful of spicy rice in his mouth to hide a teasing smile.

"Not."

"I can tell, Iman."

"Who are you, Santa? You can tell whether I've been naughty or nice?"

Cedric groaned, crossing his index fingers in front of her. "Bad word. Tonight my daughter, Anika, asked me if Santa is going to make two trips to the North Pole because the first sleigh full of presents will be hers. She faxed me an updated list this morning. She's sure she's getting that many."

"Is she?"

Her serious tone caught his attention. Cedric sat back in his chair. He rarely spoke of his girls. His mother and step-father, and Lenora's parents called him overprotective, but he didn't care. The girls were so important to him, in the past, he'd refused to share them.

Iman covered his hand. "Don't get quiet on me. I'm just asking if she has any reason to believe she's getting less than she thinks." Cedric looked down at her hand. It was soft and supporting in a way that if he weren't careful would have him spilling his guts.

He answered honestly. "No, she doesn't."

Iman resumed eating. "So, what are you going to do about it?"

"What?"

"Her theory that Santa will return to the North Pole after stopping at your place. Millions of children around the world will be disappointed if Santa gets too tired and doesn't get to deliver their presents."

Cedric felt a bubble of laughter build in his chest. He grinned sheepishly, leaned his head back and groaned. "That's crazy, isn't it? What am I going to do?"

"Can her mom talk to her?"

"Only to her spirit. My wife is dead."

"I'm sorry." Her gaze dropped to her plate. Cedric wiped his mouth and sipped his imported beer. "It happened during their birth. She began to hemorrhage, and the doctor couldn't stop it. She died two hours after Medina was born."

"I'm sorry," she said. An odd expression crossed her face. He wondered if she felt sorry for them. Cedric hurried to quell any such thoughts.

"Thank you. We've overcome it."

She smiled tenderly and his heart expanded. Cedric glanced at his watch, the late hour making him wish for once he could add more hours to the day. He signaled for the check and paid the bill. Iman said nothing when he left a large tip but Cedric noticed her eyes widen.

They hurried against the chill to the car and with relief got inside. Its comfort enveloped them as they drove back toward Atlanta. "Where do you live again?" he asked.

Her smoky laughter tickled his ears and he couldn't help reciprocating with his own chuckle.

"Near Piedmont Park. I'll direct you once we get close."

He nodded. "This may sound like a silly question, but do you believe in Santa at all?"

"No," Iman said quietly. "I believe in Christmas. I celebrate the religious aspects of the holiday rather than the commercial." She grew thoughtful. "But if I had children, Santa would visit our home. Aliyah and I used to have so much fun watching the snow fall in Buffalo hoping we would catch a glimpse of ol' Saint Nick. It was a wonderful time in our lives. My children deserve that thrill."

Cedric remained quiet. He'd never had a tree. Santa never visited the leaking, one-room apartment he'd shared with his mother. He hadn't had a reason to believe. Not as a child. Only through his girls he was able to recapture those lost moments.

"Now that I've talked your ear off about what I do, tell me about your plans for the future at Dix."

Cedric launched into a discussion on his dreams of finding medicines that would aid in the irradiation of diseases like sickle cell anemia, diabetes, and AIDS. He was surprised at how easy Iman was to talk to, but soon they were admiring the twinkling lights that draped bare branches throughout her neighborhood. Cedric stopped in the driveway she indicated. He left the engine running, not wanting her to go inside. He realized the evening had been the best adult fun he'd had in a long time.

Over the gray fur collar of her cape, she turned to look at him. His chest tightened.

"Iman I—

"Take my card." They spoke in unison.

"I don't—"

"Oh. You don't want it?" She fidgeted with the card, then dropped it. It fluttered to the floor.

"No—" Cedric shook his head. He bent to retrieve it, but she stopped him.

"I understand. I just thought . . . well," her brows furrowed and when she met his gaze, Cedric saw a flash of determination.

Iman held up her hands. "Cedric, I hardly ever give advice on raising children. But I've worked with kids and

I know that Kwanzaa teaches them responsibility, they learn to love and care for things, and they also learn how to earn them. Let me help you," she said softly.

He sank into her gaze. "Yes—"

Cedric stroked her bottom lip with his thumb. To his delight it quivered and she lightly caught it between her teeth, before letting go. Maybe he could let her know how much he wanted to see her again with his touch since his voice was failing him. His hand dropped to his side.

"I try to make class fun for them." She dampened her lips and went on. "You said yes, didn't you?" she whispered.

The shaking sigh of her whisper drove him wild inside. "I said yes."

Iman opened the door, the lights brightening the dark interior. "I'm sorry. You have to stop me sometimes. I can go on and on."

"Really," he said, a smile tugging at his mouth as he leaned closer. "I hadn't noticed."

Cedric lay in bed, head resting against his palms. He had been this way for over an hour since dropping Iman at home and picking up the blueberries for breakfast. Yet sleep hadn't come. The last few moments in the car with Iman replayed in his mind.

For an instant, he had been a tongue-tied kid again, and had blown his opportunity to ask her for another date.

Quickly, he flipped on the bedside light and hurried into his dressing room. Inside his tuxedo jacket pocket, Cedric found what he sought. Taking her business card back to bed with him, he crawled under the covers and stared at it.

Iman Y. Parrish. The scripted lettering looked whimsical and made him think of what a good sense of humor she had. Though easily embarrassed, she was charming.

At the bottom of the card were both her home and work

numbers. He stared at them until they were etched in his memory. So there was hope for his last minute loss of speech capabilities. At least he could call her.

When he'd leaned close before she'd gotten out of the car, instinct told him she was going to let him kiss her good night.

Only her lips never touched his.

Cedric resisted kicking himself. Some kind of businessman he'd turned out to be. His job involved controlled predictions, near perfect assessments, and precision. There was no margin for error. But those learned techniques had alluded him this evening.

In the darkness of the car, Iman had lifted his hand, maneuvered it over and around hers several times, then let it go. She was out of the car and into the house before he could react.

He hadn't caught on until it was too late. He hadn't even walked her to the door. Now, of course, he knew what she'd been doing.

She'd given him a soul shake.

"Can I pour the blueberries in now?"

Plastic high heels clomped against the floor as Anika headed toward them holding the cup of blueberries over her head. Cedric reached behind Medina to steady Anika's arm as she slid between them.

"Pour them in," he instructed, then let her arm go. He glanced toward her feet. "Must you wear those now?"

Keeping a watchful eye on Medina, who held the hand mixer precariously over the mixing bowl, he took hold of Anika's arm again and helped her to the chair. "Medina," his voice raised with warning.

"Yes?" they both answered.

"Be careful."

Cedric took one look around the kitchen and made a mental note to get an extra special Christmas gift for his housekeeper, Joan. How she did it everyday, he would never know. From top to bottom, the kitchen was a mess. He dreaded cleaning it.

Medina took his moment of reflection to raise the mixer. Pancake batter spewed everywhere.

"Stop!" he barked.

The order came too late. Startled by his voice, Medina lost her balance and slipped backward. The mixer flew across the counter spitting batter as it twirled.

Cedric bit back a curse, grabbed the handle, and pulled. "Sit down. Right now!"

The cord snapped from the wall and the kitchen fell into a stony silence. Cedric held the counter for support, counting to ten, then back to zero. The girls stared at him with worried expressions. Medina's chin quivered and her mouthed bowed.

"I'm sorry," he started, hoping to head off the inevitable. "I didn't mean to yell."

Cedric cringed when Medina let a loud wail rip anyway.

"You screamed at me!" Sliding on heels that matched her sisters, Medina stomped to the kitchen door. He wondered for an instant if she would storm out, something he absolutely forbid.

"May I be excused?" she asked tearfully.

Cedric decided they both needed a moment to cool down. "Yes, go ahead."

Anika crossed her arms over her chest in a way that reminded him of himself when he was lecturing them.

"You should say you're sorry."

Cedric bit his tongue as he listened to his seven year old offer him advice. He looked at her inquisitively. *Why was everything always Dad's fault?* He braced his sticky hands on the counter. "I already apologized, Anika. But your sister is stubborn. She'll be back."

"You always say stubborn is good. Is it bad now?"

The sticky mixture on his hands made him want to eat his words. "No. It's just that you have to listen to learn.

You girls have only been here for seven years. You don't know everything. I've been here thirty-two years, and I don't know everything.''

Wisdom-filled eyes stared at him. "You know a lot, Daddy. Otherwise you couldn't have passed to the tenth grade.'' Anika patted him on the back and then stuck her finger in the mix. She licked it off while he wiped at the drying goo on the counter.

"Thank you, sweetie. That makes me feel better.'' He rubbed her back in return. "Do me a favor and go get your sister, please.''

Cedric cooked as many pancakes as batter would allow while alone in the kitchen. When they returned, they wore their fuzzy bear slippers and had brushed their hair. The gesture was meant to appease him and it did. He hugged them both and waited while they quietly got their place-mats and set the table.

"Daddy? It's okay if you lose your temper and ye-yeww, and make me cry sometimes.''

Cedric had a fleeting flash of the future when the girls would have boyfriends and eventually husbands. He didn't want them to think any type of verbal abuse was all right. Silently, he damned his behavior.

Thick maple syrup oozed down the pancakes and onto the plate before he turned the bottle upright. He brought the plates to the table and sat down.

"Medina, it's not okay to yell and make you cry. I'm sorry.''

"I forgive you, Daddy.'' Cedric felt worse when her for-giving gaze rested on him. Children were so innocent. So pure. She actually felt sorry for him for yelling at her.

There had been a lot of yelling when he was a child, but nothing was worse than the silence that remained once his father had left for good. He pushed that memory from his mind. It didn't matter now. No one could turn back the hands of time.

They said grace and began eating.

Iman's declaration of having a way with children flew into his mind. He immediately remembered his decision about Kwanzaa. Cedric decided to broach the subject while they were eating.

"Girls, I thought it would be fun for us to learn about a celebration called Kwanzaa. It's *Kiswahili,* meaning 'first fruits.'"

"Why?" Anika asked between bites.

Cedric smoothed more thick syrup over his pancakes before he answered. "Because it teaches you about African-American culture and traditions." Iman's voice seemed to come from the air as it reminded him of the rich celebration he'd never explored.

"There are seven principles of the," Cedric searched his mind for the word Iman had used last night. "*Nguzo Saba.* I can't explain it all, but I think we should give it a try."

Both girls shrugged, looking unconvinced.

"Where are we going to learn it? Television?" Anika's voice was hopeful.

Cedric cringed. That was his weakness, especially old black and white movies. He shook his head to her question. "I met someone, a woman named Ms. Parrish." Cedric enjoyed the way her name tripped off his tongue. "She teaches the class. She's a very nice lady."

The girls started snickering. "Daddy, you have this goofy wook on your face. Is she your girw-friend?"

Caught off guard at the question, he stuffed his mouth full of pancakes. His jaws worked and he tried to stop smiling. "She's not my girlfriend. She's just a very nice lady. So, what do you think?"

The girls consulted each other and Medina nodded, while Anika regarded him suspiciously.

"We still get our presents from Santa?"

"Yes. One has nothing to do with the other. But I'm going to warn you, Santa doesn't take kindly to greedy children. And I know for a fact that any act of selfishness will not be rewarded. I haven't mailed your lists yet, but I think if you cut them down to four items, Santa will be pleased."

Dumbfounded, they stared open mouthed at him. He chewed thoughtfully then wiped his mouth. "Maybe three items."

"No, four!" they practically sang. "May I be excused?"

Before he could properly answer, they dashed from the kitchen leaving a puff of flour in their wake.

Cedric smiled and withdrew Iman's card from his pocket. Suddenly kitchen duty didn't seem so bad after all.

Chapter Five

"What did you do again?"

Iman sipped from an ancient tea cup as Aliyah paced in front of her. Shaking her head, she lowered the cup and bent low over her old Singer sewing machine, completing the edging on the *mkeke* mat. The phone rang and her gaze snapped to it. She held her breath, hoping, but not wanting to get her hopes up. They deflated when Aliyah lowered the receiver and continued her tirade.

"Why couldn't you just ask him to take you out again, Iman? Have I taught you nothing about dating men?"

"I gave him my card. Well, almost," she muttered, remembering her fumbled attempt. "Anyway, that's how it's done these days. You've been out of the dating scene too long," Iman informed her sister knowingly. "People give each other cards and hope the other will call."

"Did he give you his?"

Iman bent her head over the machine, her foot leveling the presser foot. Fabric spilled from the back of the machine. "No."

"See. He was probably wondering what planet you were

from," Aliyah scoffed. "He was probably wondering if you had dated anyone over eighteen recently. Only kids play games like that. Back in our day-"

"The man asked the woman out," Iman finished for her. She defended herself. "He must not have wanted me to have it because he didn't offer it."

"Well after you gave him the soul shake, can you blame him?" Aliyah pounded her chest and gave her the Black Power fist. Iman burst out laughing.

"You're a fool. Don't we have another order you can prepare while you advise me on the finer points of dating in the nineties? For which I might add you have no experience since you've been married this entire decade."

Aliyah gave her a sisterly kiss on the cheek and mussed her already destroyed hairdo.

"I just hoped you would get married before the next millennium."

"You're sooo funny."

"Tell me really, was he nice?"

"He didn't scratch his butt once." Iman straightened at her sister's warning glance. She didn't want to tell Aliyah she hadn't slept a wink all night. Correction, she reminded herself. All morning. And it was broad daylight before she'd even closed her eyes. Once she had, every gesture and facial expression, every shrug, and even the timber of his laughter replayed itself over and over in her mind.

"He was more than nice. Li, I've never met a more attentive man. He really listened. Usually, I yawn and sigh in that order when I'm out on a date because I'm bored to death listening to my date drone on and on about himself. Cedric wasn't like that. He asked about me and listened to my answers. Honey child, I could get used to that." She shook herself from the cloud. "He's got to have faults. Nobody is that good and still single."

"It's possible. I hope he calls, Sugar Baby." They slipped easily back into the names they'd made up for each other so many years ago.

Iman lifted the *mkeke* mat from the machine and held it carefully flat. The cardboard box lying on another worktable was half full of items needed to have a Kwanzaa feast.

"Aliyah, make yourself useful and give me the *kinara*. I already have the candles packaged, but I'm missing some things." Her sister brought the wooden candle holder that would hold three red, one black, and three green candles.

"Let's go down the checklist." Aliyah glanced at the contents in the box. They positioned themselves assembly line style. "Do you have the *Mazao* fruits and vegetables, and the *mkeke* mat?"

"Got it," Iman nodded affirmatively.

"Zawadi gifts?"

Iman hurried to the shelves lining the back of the room and retrieved the forgotten examples of gifts. "Got it."

"Condoms?"

"What!"

"You should always be prepared," her sister said with a leering smile. "I'll drop some off this afternoon."

"I can handle my personal business, Aliyah. What's next on the list?"

"The phone," Aliyah said to the ringing interruption.

"Got it," Iman answered, relieved to change the subject. "Hello?"

"Iman Y. Parrish, please."

"This is—" She shivered in anticipation. She knew immediately who it was. After all, once she'd fallen asleep this morning, all she'd heard was his voice.

"This is Cedric Hamilton."

"Hi." Iman fanned herself with one of the "Addie" books her company suggested as a *Zawadi* gift. It had suddenly gotten hot in the office.

"What does the Y stand for?"

"Mmm?"

"The Y in your name."

"Yvette."

"Very nice." His voice deepened, and she swooned for

Aliyah, who left the room with a huge grin on her face. "Does anyone ever call you that?"

"No. My sister calls me . . . Never mind."

"What?" he coaxed.

"I'm not telling," Iman vowed. Hearing Sugar Baby off *his* lips seemed too intimate. It was a natural defense, she assured herself. They'd only known each other for such a short time. But that didn't explain why her attraction felt absolutely right.

"Don't tell me," his voice echoed in her ear. "I like uncovering secrets." The challenge came through the phone lines, leaving her ear heated and tingly.

"Well," she teased to ease her discomfort. "This is one you'll never hear from me."

He laughed and the hope that she would be able to complete any more work flew out the window. There were orders to fill, but Iman knew she wouldn't be able to focus. His laugh and the sound of his voice through the receiver would dominate her thoughts.

"I called to apologize," he said.

Disappointment ebbed through her veins, slowing her thundering her heart. "You forgot to tell me you're engaged to be married, right?"

"No, that's not it."

"You're a wanted man and the police are at your door?"

He chuckled. "No, to both parts."

Her heart rate returned to its former drum roll pace.

"Well then, what?"

"I meant to walk you to your door last night, but I was stunned by your—"

"Handshake," she finished for him. "It surprises people sometimes."

He cut off her nervous chattering. "I enjoyed your company and I want to see you again. Do you have plans for later today?"

Excitement rushed through her. "No. I don't have any specific plans. What did you have in mind?"

He chuckled deep in his throat. Iman's lower body warmed in response. She sat straight up in her chair.

"I thought we'd go skating. Dress casual and bring a change of clothes for dinner."

"Sounds like an adventure. I'll be ready. Cedric?"

"Yes?"

Iman blurted before she lost her nerve, "Thanks for calling. I'll see you later."

"Cedric, got a minute?"

"Sure, Ronald," Cedric said, while depositing the receiver into the cradle. He waved his vice president into his office. "Come on in. What's up?"

Ronald sat in the chair across from Cedric's before he answered.

"A representative from an organization called Retired Seniors of Georgia or RSG is requesting to see you. I've talked with the gentleman on several occasions, but I don't think what I've said is satisfactory anymore."

"What does he want?"

"He wants Dix to lower the prices on twelve medications that are predominantly used by the elderly. Here's the list."

Cedric's eyebrows quirked as he stared at the neatly typed medications. He whistled low. "Does he want the shirts off our backs too?"

Ronald shrugged. "Eventually we're going to have to see him. He's threatening to picket if he doesn't get a meeting. He's here right now."

Cedric stood and buttoned his jacket. "Ask him in. Might as well deal with this now." Ronald rose from the chair and walked to the door. "Any kinks I should know about in the Blythe deal?"

"No sir. Business as usual." Cedric nodded and the man left.

Patiently Cedric waited for Jack McClure, president of RSG, to stop speaking. The elderly man was soft spoken, but had the eyes of an eagle. He seemed to sense whenever

Cedric wanted to interrupt and would neatly thwart his objection with a preplanned counter argument.

After fifteen more minutes of careful listening, Cedric tried to inconspicuously smooth frustration from his face. This was going on too long. "Mr. McClure," he cut in, "I understand your concerns, but from a business standpoint, I can't simply cut prices."

"Why? The cereal companies did it. You can do it."

"Yes, sir," Cedric said admiring the man's quickness. "But they're conglomerates. The levels in this company are far smaller, the profit margins are also. Really there is no comparison. I'm afraid Dix can't do what you're asking. Perhaps we can devise another program where seniors can go for blood pressure or diabetes checkups once a month."

The elderly man's smooth face broke into a smile.

"Appeasing will only get us so far without the proper medications. But, we'll take it. And a decrease in the drug prices too." Jack extended his hand. He spoke before Cedric could object. "We may have lost round one, but Mr. Hamilton, old folks are like pesky relatives. Everybody knows one, got one or gonna be one. We'll meet again."

Cedric shook the man's hand and saw him out.

Iman massaged her rear and watched with jealous envy as Cedric rollerskated, with great ease toward her. It seemed as though she'd spent more time on her bottom than on her skates.

"I used to be good at this," she grumbled when he dug in his stopper and halted by her side.

"You told me." Cedric's patience was exhausting as he helped her up for the fifth time. "The next skate is couples only. That should stop you from running over those bothersome kids again."

"That's not funny." Yet, Iman couldn't help laughing. She swallowed a groan when she straightened from the hardwood floor and held onto Cedric's waist. Relieved to be standing, she let him guide her. He bracketed his arms around her on the carpeted waist-high wall, while watching the skating monitor clear children from the floor.

Her body moved before her brain could send out the stop order. She lifted her hand to his jaw, turned his face to her and kissed his lips.

For a suspended moment, Iman thought she'd made a mistake. "Oh, shoot," she murmured against Cedric's mouth.

The air was squeezed from her lungs. His arms tightened around her waist until her skates left the floor.

Her hesitation evaporated with his words. "Don't move. This is right." His lips covered her gently, persuading them to accept him. Iman opened without hesitation enjoying the silky feel of his tongue as it lit fires within her depths.

Suddenly she was floating, the strength of his chest never separating from hers. Iman wound her arms around his neck and broke the kiss, but not the bond that forged itself between them as they skated around the rink.

Skating had been a dream compared to horseback riding, Iman thought as she slid off the back of the powerful animal and walked as if it were still between her legs. Her aching bones was why it took Cedric nearly two weeks of daily dates and smooth talking to convince her to give riding a try.

The stable hand led the huge brown mare away to be rubbed down in the barn.

Iman sighed, glad to see the horse go.

She groaned uncomfortably. Her body was paying for every ounce of pleasure she derived this afternoon.

She glanced back at Cedric, who was dismounting. Fluid grace, she thought with a tinge of jealousy. She had all but fallen off the back of her horse.

Cedric stood beside his black mare offering it carrots and worshipful pats. His face was unmarred by strain as he played with the animal. He looked at home on the ranch. Iman rather liked it too. She dragged her hands over her wind blown face and shivered. They'd started early that morning, but now the temperature had begun to drop.

"Cedric, I'm freezing."

He left the horse in the care of another stable hand and squeezed her shoulder, dropping his hand to her waist.

"You're always cold," he said gently.

Iman let her hand rest on his and enjoyed the leisurely stroll back to the house and the secure feeling his solid chest provided. The unexpected invitation to spend the weekend with his family gave her a special feeling deep inside.

Iman gazed up at him and reveled in the wave of tenderness that washed over her. That Cinderella, swept off her feet feeling claimed her again. Iman walked on more slowly. She had to admit Cedric got points for originality. She swung her arm around his back and hooked it into his belt loop.

He tightened his arm around her waist and looked down at her, warmth radiating from his eyes. "Sore?" he asked.

"Nah." Iman tried to cover her wince of pain with a smile. "These muscles are in great shape." They stopped and he looked down at her abnormally wide stance, and laughed.

"I can tell."

They resumed walking.

The girls and Elaine, Cedric's mother, greeted them at the porch. Anika jumped in front of Iman causing her to step back. Her body protested furiously.

"Miss Iman, did you like the horses?"

Iman tried to smile, but her face hurt from the cold air. Initially, she had trouble telling the girls apart, but she'd learned that Medina had a slight lisp, and the more she got to know them, it became easier to tell them apart.

She answered Anika's question. "Loved them." Iman reached for the porch railing and groaned.

"Help her, girls," Elaine said, taking pity on her.

Iman smiled her thanks at Cedric's mom and accepted the girls shoulders to rest her arms on.

"Elaine, you're a wonderful woman." Iman dragged herself through the screened porch door and into the large Afrocentric decorated great room. She immediately plopped down on one of the overstuffed sofas and laid her head back.

"Son, you had a call from Ronald Eubanks. He said there's going to be a huff on the news. Something about a deal you made going through. He said turn it on at five o'clock. Channel eleven."

Iman lifted her head and turned to Cedric who stood just inside the door. He looked so handsome in his cowboy attire. Faded denim pants hugged his body in all the right places. The red flannel shirt, covering a black turtle neck, was drawn taut across his broad shoulders and flat stomach. As sore as her arms were, Iman lifted them to reach for Cedric, but under strenuous protest, lowered them.

She prided herself for not acting on her wicked thoughts. He'd been the perfect gentleman, holding her hand, kissing her cheek, even draping his arms around her waist occasionally. Their relationship was progressing but there were times she saw a raw hunger in him. It matched hers. She wondered how long it would be before they acted on it.

Their days and nights had been filled with family fun. Cedric never conducted business when they were together.

Now, stress lines marked his forehead. Iman silently cursed Ronald Eubanks for bothering him. Cedric glanced at his watch then at her. He strode into the room.

"Why don't you soak in a hot bath with some Epsom salts? After that, I promise you some private time."

Distractedly, he glanced at the desk he kept in a corner of the great room. "I need to find out what's going on."

"Sounds fine to me."

He offered her a hand up, and to her embarrassment, her bones cracked. The girls giggled.

"Be nice," he scolded them lovingly. Cedric walked her to the stairs and swatted her bottom gently before he walked off hand-in-hand with the girls.

Iman climbed into the hot water and soothing bath salts and sunk into the luxurious heat. Her rear still tingled where Cedric had playfully touched her.

She soaked until the water cooled then toweled herself, her muscles no longer protesting so stringently. Cedric was a patient man. He had allowed their relationship to grow steadily, and now it seemed he was placing it in her hands.

She stared at her reflection in the mirror and the comfortable navy sweat suit she'd just put on. Iman looked into her own eyes and knew she was ready. She wanted the relationship to move to another level.

What that was though, was unclear.

The clock chimed five times and she walked on stiff legs back to the great room. She sat across from Cedric who had also showered and changed.

The newscaster's voice captured their attention. Iman gasped sharply when a none too flattering picture of Cedric flashed across the screen. It was made to resemble a mug shot.

"Another corporate hit man has struck. Cedric Hamilton of Dix Pharmaceuticals is a living Scrooge in the eyes of many Blythe Pharmaceutical employees. One hundred people got their pink slips today as they entered the building for work. Mr. Hamilton was reported to be vacationing with his family at his company's Helen, Georgia, ranch and was unavailable for comment."

Iman felt terrible for Cedric as they watched the newscaster interview an ex-employee. The woman called him insensitive, boorish, and claimed his heart was dead.

Iman barely heard the rest of the report as the girls' bickering interrupted the announcers words.

Cedric's mother asked, "Did you do the right thing, son?"

"I did what I had to do. It's business, Mom."

"I know, honey," she said loyally. "Come on," she said to the twins. "Let's go fix dinner."

Iman tried to forget the grimness of the announcer's voice, but couldn't. It permeated the air, thick as smoke leaving her to wonder about the man she wanted to get to know better. Cedric worked hard, she told herself. Certainly he had a good reason to let so many people go— particularly right before the holidays.

Silence surrounded them. Cedric swiped his head with his hands and brought them down over his face. Tension radiated from him. "It's business."

The curt words bored into her as did his gaze, seeming to beg her to understand. He stretched out his hand to help her up. "Come on," he said roughly. "We're leaving. I need to be alone with you."

Iman waited while he held her coat. She shrugged into her short wool coat and winced only once as she wrapped his scarf around her neck.

"Shouldn't we tell your mother where we're going?"

Cedric gently took Iman's hand. Sounds of his mother and daughters discussing dinner, filtered into the room.

"We'll be back," he called. He couldn't know how his words made her tingle.

In the fall, Helen, Georgia was a place vibrant with color and blooms. Now, it was asleep, preparing for the spring buds to restore it to its eclectic luster.

The bare brown branches seemed to float by as they drove unhurried through the quiet town, neither sharing their thoughts.

Cedric turned on the radio of the ranch's pick up truck, flipped around the dial, then turned it off again.

"Corporate hit man! Ridiculous," he muttered. "They didn't bother to mention that one hundred other employees still have their jobs."

"Why right before Christmas? Surely you can understand how the employees must feel." When he continued to scowl, Iman spoke in a measured, careful tone. "Would it have hurt the company to wait until after the new year?"

Cedric turned off the main highway onto a dirt path. It stretched endlessly ahead. Iman slid her arms out of her coat and stored it behind the seat.

"Is it ever a good time to lose your job?" He drummed his thumbs against the steering wheel as the car continued to roll over the hard, bumpy road. "Should I have let those parents buy gifts they couldn't afford? I guess you think it would have been better to do it after the new year, after everyone had gone into debt buying things they don't need."

He came to a stop in the clearing and Cedric eased the gear shift into park, letting the truck idle. He turned to look at her and his eyes sparkled with smoldering anger.

"Would it have been better to keep everybody on and in six months when I couldn't meet payroll, lay everybody off?"

Iman shook her head wanting to ease his frustration. This wasn't how she'd hoped to spend their first moments alone.

"No. You have to do what's best for everyone. I realize I work far from the corporate world, but I'm guessing that the timing could have been handled differently."

Iman stroked his stubbled cheek to soften the directness of her words. When he closed his eyes, she bathed him with her touch. She drew her index finger lightly over his forehead, down his nose and around to his cheek.

He looked so tired.

Cedric's chest filled then sank as he exhaled. "I tried

to keep the people who would best help both companies. We offered early retirement, and severance pay. Those that stayed, took a risk." He finally looked at her. "There wasn't much more we could do."

"Don't think about it now," she whispered. "Where is that happy man who rode his horse today like a champion?"

He captured her hand in his. "You're so beautiful."

Iman felt the familiar flush rush through her cheeks. Cedric leaned over to kiss her nose. His arms were around her. His mouth settled roughly against hers demanding a response. Iman's banked desire unleashed and met his fevered passion, but she yelped in surprise, when Cedric brought her to him.

"Seat belt," she muttered. His fingers grappled with the release, freeing her. He pulled her until she straddled his lap.

Iman groaned as much from the ache of her sore muscles, as she did from the pleasure of feeling the thick bulge of desire curving from Cedric's pants and pressing into her. He drank of her mouth, the trail of kisses on her neck burning silent promises into her flesh.

Iman sighed against his lips when he gently kneaded her thighs. He lessened the pressure to a caress.

"Still sore from skating?"

"And horseback riding," she breathed heavily.

He whispered in her ear, "Lean on me." Moving his hands up her thighs, he trailed a path to her back. Iman rested her cheek on his shoulder, her lips a breath away from his neck.

She closed her eyes languishing in his touch.

His callused hands massaged the sore tissues, eliciting a contented a moan from her. His fingers slid down her sides, then around her back to the waist of the sweat pants. He took hold of her bottom, kneading it into complacency. It felt so good.

Cedric then dragged the sweatshirt over her head. He

unfastened her bra and it fell away making her gasp at the exposure. Their gazes met briefly, before he decided which of the twin peaks to taste first. Iman arched toward Cedric's mouth when his eager tongue lapped at the right. He came up for air to nuzzle at her chin. "You're beautiful, *and* you taste good."

Iman chanced a look at Cedric's tongue when he went back to stroking her erect nipple. "Mmm" was all she could manage, when he claimed the other one.

Masterfully, he tasted her until she dissolved into a helpless, quivering mass on his lap. His mouth sapped her energy. All she could do was let him fulfill her desire.

She fumbled with the buckle of his belt trying to loosen the metal clasp.

Cedric held her and leaned forward to give her easier access as she slid the leather from the loops then dropped it to the floor. His flannel shirt was tucked inside his jeans, and Iman struggled to free it while he drove her crazy with his mouth.

She finally got the shirt half up his chest.

She sought the button at the waist of his jeans, then hesitated, her fingers tangling in his dark hair.

I'm going to do this in a truck?

Cedric blew on her nipple and it hardened into a tight nub.

She sighed. *Possibly.*

"Don't stop now," he urged seductively.

His gaze sought hers in the darkness and he pressed his erection into her softness. His hand stroked her once through the fabric and a shudder rippled through her. He passed his fingers over her desire again and her head fell back as she shook with anticipation.

"Having second thoughts?" he asked, but continued the rhythmic pattern. Her head dropped to his chest. She couldn't think straight under the tender assault.

"Yes." His thumb pressed the space where her opening was and she shook some more. "No, sweet mercy. No, I'm not." He stroked her there again. Iman caught his face between her hands and offered him her breast.

He obliged, much to her delight.

"It's up to you, Iman," he murmured, his mouth full.

Iman doubted that as his lips closed over her breast again and he shook his hand. Arrows of heat and desire tore through her. She couldn't deny him.

"I want you now," she said weakly.

Iman urgently helped him peel her sweatpants from her body. She tugged at his jeans, but her hands shook so, she let him work the zipper and drag the jeans over his hips. Their lips met again as he guided her above him.

The phone in the truck rang. Iman jumped at the intruding sound. Holding her close, Cedric reached around her and picked it up.

"Hamilton here." Iman felt him change immediately. He patted her rear. She stayed still.

His voice demanded an answer. "Was any equipment damaged?" His gaze flicked to her and he murmured out the corner of his mouth, *"It's business."*

Iman leaned to the right when he more firmly patted her side. Reality dawned on her. He wanted her off his lap!

"Did they arrest anybody?"

Iman kept her anger under control as she raised herself and moved off his lap. He never looked at her, while he pulled his pants over his bottom and carefully tucked himself in.

Iman drew on her clothes, anger blocking her pain.

"Johnson, from research was there too? Not surprised." He added, a grim tone to his voice. "I'll be back in the morning. No," he hesitated, looking at her for the first time. "I'm in to something tonight. See you in the morning."

You're in to something all right. Iman crossed her arms over her chest and sat as far against the passenger door as possible.

She waited until he hung up. "Everything that woman said about you is true. You're insensitive *and* boorish." Iman looked down at his waist, then up at him. As sweetly as she could manage she said, "You need me to zip those for you?"

Chapter Six

Two weeks of Kwanzaa class made a believer out of him. Anika and Medina had changed. They no longer talked only of Christmas lists and toys. Now their animated discussions were about all the new friends they'd made and *Zawadi* gifts.

Anika had even surprised him by asking if she could have five dollars from her savings account to buy books for Medina.

But what touched him deeper, was the close relationship they'd developed with Iman.

Cedric's gaze swung to her as she kneeled in front of the class, rehearsing dance movements with the dancers who would perform in a week at the *Karamu*.

He inhaled deeply, remembering.

So many wasted days had passed since their night in the truck. Cedric tried hard to forget his abhorrent behavior.

Iman had refused all of his apologetic overtures. Every gift he'd sent, had been returned. She'd only kept one thing. A card he'd finally written late last Friday night, while sitting alone at home.

It had been the first time he realized that he didn't have to be alone because there was somebody special in his life. Someone he enjoyed and who for some reason, liked him.

Those feelings were what had carried him to his desk and what had spilled onto the paper. Cedric grew warm thinking about his heartfelt apology. He hoped Iman would give them another chance.

Slightly off key singing drew his attention back to the children and Iman. The children sang the first principle harmoniously, but the second was a tongue twister. Several of them mumbled, and Iman nodded encouragingly singing louder.

"Umoja, unity. Kujichagulia, self-determination." They survived the five remaining principles, then Iman applauded them for their effort.

He waited until after the final call of *"Habari gani! Umoja!"* before making his way toward the throng surrounding Iman. His girls pulled Iman toward him.

"Daddy," Anika said, "Miss Iman said she would come over our house and work on our speeches with us, didn't you, Miss Iman?"

Cedric faced Iman. He wanted to apologize and make her understand how sorry he was. He wanted to pull her into his arms. To touch her intimately the same way the soft African material hugged her body, and to relive their near-union. To make the end of their evening together something beautiful, as beautiful as Iman deserved.

She held the girls' hands and looked away from him to Medina.

"Yes, sweetheart. I said I would help you. We can do it at my house, or stay here, I suppose."

He touched her. Her gaze snapped up. "You can come to our house, tomorrow."

Aliyah approached, halting Iman's response.

"Iman, Ada is asking for you." She pointed to the other side of the room. "I'll keep Cedric and the girls company while you see what she wants."

Cedric felt Iman's impatience. She dropped the girls hands. "We've got to talk," she said decisively to him.

"I'll wait here for you."

She nodded as she started away.

Aliyah stepped beside him to give his girls room to run around. "Long time no see."

Medina tagged Anika, who then turned to chase her. He didn't bother to stop them. They could have somersaulted over his head and he wouldn't have said a word. Iman was coming to his house, tomorrow. Thoughts of her telling him to get out of her life forever plagued him. He pushed them away. It was too sobering.

He turned to Aliyah. "How have you been Aliyah?"

"I'm always fine, Cedric." Her feline grin made him shake his head. Her humor was infectious.

The weight on his shoulder lessened.

"So, when are you going to ask Iman out again?"

His eyebrows shot up. Had Iman told her about their weekend? He grew slightly uncomfortable. "We're handling it," he said avoiding a direct answer. Something occurred to him. "What's her nickname?"

"Sugar Baby. Why?"

It was his turn to smile. "Just wanted to know."

Aliyah's thirteen and fifteen-year-old daughters fussed over Anika and Medina, giving him time to watch Iman and the older woman named Ada.

His gaze was riveted to her as Iman hugged the older woman. Iman broke the embrace, when the woman's body began to wrack with a hacking cough. There wasn't much to her slight frame but a colorful head wrap. But the frailties of her bony hands and wrists was obvious.

Cedric stepped forward to offer assistance, as Iman held her gently around the waist, a look of concern on her face. But the coughing spell ended and another woman assisted Ada into her coat. The threadbare wool, thinned with age, wasn't much protection from the cold winter air.

Cedric was taken aback when Iman unwrapped the scarf

that covered her own head and draped the woman's neck. Her generosity humbled him.

It was too cold to be without a hat or scarf, yet Iman gave without regard for herself. Her actions reflected how deep her beliefs lay. Iman had a way about her that attracted people.

Cedric was surprised at the strength of his attraction.

It was far more serious than he realized as he watched her from beneath hooded lids. He thought of her all the time, could describe her in his sleep, how she smelled and tasted. Everybody loved her. *I could love her too.*

The idea startled and provoked him.

His heart thundered against his ribs. *Not me,* he decided over his body's raging response. Too soon.

Iman returned with her bags of books and her purse in hand and silently gave them to him. They stood before each other in a face off.

"Daddy? Daddy?" Anika tugged on his hand to get his attention. "Can we go outside with Miss Aliyah?"

"Please?" She and Medina begged in unison. Cedric glanced from Aliyah, to his girls, then to Iman. He needed to talk to Iman alone.

"I think I'm outnumbered. Behave," he said more sternly than he'd planned. Anxiety always made his voice harsh when he didn't really mean it to be. He softened it. "Behave, girls." They ignored the warning, and ran toward the door.

"Wait. Anika, Medina," Iman called, snatching their coats off a nearby chair and shaking them. "Coats, hats, scarves, and gloves." She kneeled down waving them back. "I can't have my best speech readers sick, can I?" She bundled the girls up and tied their hoods tight.

When they resembled something out of an arctic clothing catalog, she patted their heads and let them go. They waddled off, barely able to move.

Cedric waited as she attended to each child who came within her reach, repeating the task until every child was bundled up.

He felt oddly out of place as it was he who usually attended to his girls. Yet a big part of him enjoyed watching her take care of the children.

Finally, they were alone in the room.

"You've been avoiding me," he stated without preamble.

"I know I have. I needed time."

Greedily he drank in the sight of her. Cedric shifted the bags in his hands to a chair.

"I've been trying to apologize for two weeks. It was my fault." When she didn't disagree, he smiled. "Why wouldn't you let me apologize face-to-face? Why did you return all my gifts?"

She looked up at him. "Because they weren't from your heart. Your card told me how you really felt." She rubbed her neck. "I forgave you days ago."

His brows knit in confusion. "Then why didn't you call me?"

"Because." She turned, but his hand on her arm stopped her. Her nose started to glow. "I had some things to sort out." The tip reddened. "I've been thinking about you." She looked at him, then away, "And me."

Her voice dropped, just above a whisper. "Sometimes you look so tired, I think you're going to tumble off these horrible metal chairs. But you still come to class, girls in tow." The flush spread to her cheeks. "I know it's hard, but you do it anyway. You're a devoted father." Her hand stroked her neck where the red had begun to travel like hot lava.

Cedric yearned to bury his face in the heat.

"I wasn't sure how to tell you . . ."

His insides clenched nervously. "Tell me?"

Iman fidgeted with her hands, her lips trembled. He reached out his finger to stop them.

"I don't know why I feel this way. When you're business, you're *all* business." He grimaced. "But I know that's only a part of who you really are. You were a sweetheart to those homeless ladies." She pointed to his chest. "I know there's a heart in there. So here goes."

Cedric got lost in the beauty of her gaze. He desperately wanted to tell her everything was going to be all right.

A nervous smile parted her lips.

His heart thundered when her voice dropped to a whisper. He strained to hear. "A part of me is falling in love with you."

Cedric pulled Iman to him, and pressed his lips to her matted curls. He wanted to share his warmth with her, to let her feel the beat of his heart. It felt as if someone swiped at the world and set it spinning on its axis. Her words set his whole body afire. Everything was going to be all right.

Cedric lifted her chin saying, "I think we should celebrate that good news." He lowered his head, their breath mingling. Her lips parted in expectation . . .

"Uh-hm. Mr. Hamilton?" the janitor interrupted.

"This better be good," Cedric's voice rang with irritation.

"I'm locking up, sir. Should I give you another few minutes?" Cedric took one last look at Iman's wonderful mouth and swore under his breath. He wanted to taste her so bad he could feel desire to the marrow of his bones.

Her breath quickened when he inched her closer to him. Because of her revelation, his heart hadn't stopped singing.

"It's getting kind of late. And Mrs. Winston will want me home soon . . ." the janitor's voice trailed off.

Cedric spoke loudly, while still maintaining eye contact with Iman. "No, we're coming now, Mr. Winston."

Iman backed out of his grasp and got her coat.

"I'll be at the door waiting," the older man called.

Cedric didn't hear him. He was too intent on Iman. He stopped just behind her. "Thank you for telling me."

She nodded and buttoned her coat. Black curls stopped at the collar of her bare neck. He unwrapped his long gray scarf from his neck and covered hers with it.

"I hoped you would join me tonight for a special date," he said, drawing her back against his chest. He felt a deep sigh leave her body.

She turned and a light burned in the soft depths of her eyes. "Where did you have in mind?"

"The mall," he said casually.

Surprise made her mouth O. "The mall? And Aliyah thought you were too mature for me. I think we're about equal." Her teasing lessened the tension that bubbled between them.

"I have to pick out some things for the girls, and I need a woman's opinion." He added in an off-hand manner, "No one can say you're not opinionated."

Iman pretended to pinch him. "I hope you're not implying that I'm not a woman."

"You're all the woman I need. How about it?" They walked out the door and checked on the girls. Aliyah stood watching over the brood.

"What about the girls?"

"My mother and step-father would love to watch them. How's seven o'clock?"

Medina raced by, bumping Iman as she went. Her apology was lost as Iman struggled to regain her balance. Their breath mingled into mist as Cedric firmly gripped her waist, steadying her.

"Thanks." She stepped away. "Okay. Seven is good."

Anika tugged on his coat, looking up. "Daddy, it's cold. Can we go home now?"

He tore his gaze from Iman's to look at his daughter. "Yes, baby. Go tell your sister it's time to leave." Medina appeared at that moment and took her father's other hand.

"Good bye, Anika. Good bye, Medina. *Harambee.*" The

girls looked at Iman quizzically. "It's a Swahili greeting," she told them. "It means, let's work together."

Cedric waited until she was safely in her car. A slow grin, like the slow heat rippling through him, curled his lips. He read her lips as she drove slowly past them.

"I'll see you later."

Chapter Seven

Iman glanced through the rows of clothes at Neiman Marcus and cringed at the prices.

"Great! They'll like these." Cedric picked up two dresses and checked the tags. "Do you see two size eights? Only in different colors?"

The fluffy dresses made Iman think of a bed of whipped cream. Not right for two active seven-year-olds.

"Cedric," she looped her arm through his and steered him away from the billowing ruffles. "Don't you think the girls would like something more, how do I say this," she considered out loud. "More playful?"

He stared at her. For a moment she thought he was angry. Then his face fell. "They hate when I shop for them. I like ruffles and fluffy stuff. It reminds me of when they were babies. But since they're big first-graders they don't like my style." He sounded hurt. "They beg my fifty-two-year-old mother to shop for them."

Iman held in her smile at his crestfallen look. He obviously took this issue to heart. She steered him toward a place she knew was a hit with Aliyah's girls.

Music pumped as they entered the store and Cedric visibly cringed at the attire on the mannequins inside the window.

"Come on, Dad," she said, hoping to lessen his reluctance. "Don't take yourself so seriously. Let's look for one outfit each. If they don't like them, you can bring them back."

"Kids don't like this stuff." He flicked distastefully over the baggy jeans and hooded shirts. "It's all too big."

"Kids do like this stuff," Iman countered. Her eyes drifted to the denim that covered his muscular thighs and bottom. He looked good in a suit and polished shoes, and great in a pair of jeans and shirt. Cedric needed to loosen up. He was definitely too upper crust.

"Just look at one outfit," she said convincingly. "You *asked* for my help, remember?" That seemed to straighten him up a bit as his lips pursed into a smirk.

Telling him her true feelings hadn't been so bad, Iman reflected, trying to keep things positive. Although, he hadn't responded the way she'd hoped. The fact that he didn't share her feelings stung, but the words were out. Too late to take them back.

"May I help you?" A young woman who looked about twelve bounced to Cedric's side. Iman held his arm so he wouldn't flee the store.

"No thanks, ma'am," Iman said around a giggle. "We're just looking."

"Okay. Let me know if you need anything." Happily she skipped away. Cedric stared at her with a disbelieving look on his face.

"Doesn't Georgia have child labor laws?"

"She's old enough. My, my, for such a young dapper dude, you sure have old fogy taste."

"Oh. Is that right?"

Iman offered token resistance but let herself be guided to him. When she was close enough, he slid his hand under her coat, and tickled.

Iman jumped, laughing. "Stop. People are looking. Cedric!" Giggling, she grabbed for the rack and in the process knocked clothes all over the floor.

"Now look what you made me do." She glanced around guiltily, enjoying herself immensely. Cedric's expression remained innocent. "I'll get you for this," she whispered.

"Is there a problem over here?" The young clerk demanded.

"I'll take each of those in a size eight, please," Cedric said casually, before moving away. Iman stared in amazement as the young woman's frown turned into a smile.

"Just a minute," Iman peered at the girl's name tag. "Sissy." She followed to Cedric. "There's at least ten dresses down there. Are you sure?"

"Definitely."

He pointed to the clothes. "I want all of those." Iman tried to hide her shock. He took her hand leading her toward a rack of expensive jackets. "Come help me pick out two of these."

Two stores and an hour and a half later, Iman sat under a mountain of packages, barely able to move. She stared blankly across the mall at a television that telecast a follow up report on corporate hit men. Cedric's picture filled a corner of the nineteen-inch screen. His photograph flashed away. The newscaster began talking about the phone company president.

Each time she'd seen a report on company closings, Iman visualized she and Cedric locked in a intimate embrace in the truck. But the dream would be shattered when he would say, *"It's business."* Iman wondered if he could survive without business. The answer in her heart left her cold.

"Hello, Iman? Are you sleep with your eyes open?"

Her stomach felt weak. "Mmm? What did you say? I was drifting."

"Do you like these?" He held up some earrings carved in the shape of the Black Madonna. Iman took them in her hand and was surprised at how heavy the beautiful pieces were. She raised them high and her eyes widened at the price tag.

Carefully she chose her words. "They're beautiful. But for two little girls, you might, perhaps, maybe you could go with something less . . ."

"They're too big, right?" His thumb caressed the earrings. "I thought so, too."

He turned to the salesman. "I'll take these and two pair of the smaller ones identical to these." This time her mouth gaped. The final bill was staggering.

"Are we ready?" Iman asked once the order had been packaged.

"Just about. I need to make one more stop." They walked to the valet parking attendant who took the packages and stored them away. Cedric took her hand and steered her back inside the mall. "I thought we could get something to eat, then make the last stop. Did you have any other plans?"

Her stomach growled in response. "Not really. I'm so hungry a box of rocks sounds appetizing." She fell in step beside him.

"Why didn't you say something before? We could have eaten hours ago." He stopped and turned fully to her. "Just tell me what you need, and it's yours."

"I didn't want to end up at the top of Lookout Mountain again."

He laughed and pressed his lips to the back of her fingers, chills chasing her doubts away.

The dimmed restaurant was crowded with other late-night shoppers but was festively decorated. Red and white stockings adorned the waitresses' heads, and holiday streamers hung from the ceilings. Holly-laced tablecloths covered the tables while red candles provided romantic light.

Quickly they were shown to a semi-circle booth, and a

waiter appeared to take their coats. Before they could slide in, the waitress stopped them.

"Now that you're comfortable, you know what to do."

For the first time, they both noticed the mistletoe arched over the entrance. Neither moved.

"The only people who get away without kissing are sisters and brothers. Are you two related?"

Iman's eyes were fixed to Cedric's lips. She shook her head almost imperceptibly.

"Then do it. I'll bring complimentary glasses of champagne in the meantime. I'll know if you don't kiss her," the waitress said to Cedric. "The bartender will make everybody boo you." She left them alone.

Images of hot fervent kisses filled her head. Involuntarily, she licked her lips.

"Shall we?"

Iman nodded. Cedric stepped forward and their lips met awkwardly. Her nose and his meshed together, then slid up, then down, until the fit became perfect.

Absolutely, blissfully, perfect.

His mouth tenderly touched hers, giving just enough satisfaction for the moment, but leaving sensual promises in its wake. He smiled against her lips before he broke away, leaving her body crying for more.

The bell clanged and people applauded, enjoying their embarrassment.

"That was unreal," Iman muttered as she slid inside the booth. He sat beside her and surprised her by placing another proprietary kiss on her cheek.

The champagne arrived and they took a moment to order.

Iman sipped from her glass and hoped her feelings were from hunger. No matter his blind side about business, being in his arms made her want to commit herself forever. Iman felt as if she had just dived off a very high cliff into darkness. She focused, when he repeated the question.

"Is Ada related to you?"

"Not really. We've kind of adopted each other. She's been a member of the Kwanzaa Association for a long time. Every fall, Ada heads up a fundraiser so members of the association can teach Kwanzaa classes at local schools and community centers.

"Recently, she's had a bad cough. The medicine her doctor prescribed is sixty-seven dollars a bottle! She just can't afford it. I called the pharmacist today, and they suggested I call around to get a better price, then they would match it. Can you believe that?" Iman shook her head, disgusted. "Bartering medicine prices. What are these drug companies thinking of?"

"The bottom line." He grimaced. "We have to stay in business."

"I wasn't making an indictment against your company," Iman said quickly. "I just can't help feeling the elderly are taken advantage of, when it becomes their job as the patient to find the best price."

He shrugged off her apology. "Unfortunately, competition in this field is fierce. You can have a drug that works well, but the company down the street has a generic brand. Every company has to fight to stay one step ahead. That's why they make you call around for pricing. Nobody is willing to lower their price and lose profits. I tried to explain this very thing to Jack McClure, president of Retired Senior of Georgia recently. What he's asking is impossible."

"What does he want?"

"Dix to do the unthinkable. Lower the prices of twelve medications." He shook his head. "Can't be done. No amount of petitions or pickets can change the current situation. It's business."

"Well, business sucks," Iman said distastefully.

Cedric laughed. "That's one way of putting it. Look at it this way. Nobody is sitting around with a room full of dusty dollars. Every drug company reinvests the money in new drugs to find new cures. We're still trying to help people. Despite," he gave her a candid look, "situations like Ada's."

"I don't think she'll be able to do the farewell for *Kuumba*. She suggested we find an eloquent, dynamic speaker who will wow the crowd. She suggested you."

"No." Cedric shook his head adamantly.

Iman went on as if he hadn't spoken. "I thought of asking one of the brothers, but when Ada brought up your name, I agreed, you're the perfect choice." She eyed him speculatively. Cedric began to suspect he was a specimen under a microscope, being studied by a mad scientist.

"I'll think about it," he said warming slightly. "Ada reminds me a lot of my own mother." Cedric stopped short, a black abyss gaping open before he could finish the sentence. He faced the dark hole, contemplating what lay on the other side. The urge to share his tragedies and triumphs with Iman was overpowering.

He waited for the feeling to pass as the waiter placed their food on the table and sprinkled grated cheese over his spaghetti.

Only it didn't go away. The closer Iman sat to him, the more her wonderfully female scent snaked into his senses, the more he wanted to bare himself before her and confess all his secrets.

"In what way?" The hollow musical strands of her voice reached inside him and unlocked his private room.

"My mother was sickly. Jobs weren't sympathetic to her illnesses, so just as soon as she got a job she'd lose it for absenteeism. It wasn't easy for us, but we made it."

"How did you live? That must have been very hard."

"Let's just say I have a working knowledge of how to fold a box just right to block the wind."

"The two women on the street . . ." she whispered.

Her expression was sad, stunned. She barely managed to utter her words. "I'm so sorry."

Cedric couldn't seem to stop himself once he got started. "Not long after that I got a job, and ever since I earned my first paycheck, I never looked back." He closed his hand and realized he'd linked it with hers. "It felt like gold bouillon."

She studied him. Her voice rose barely above a whisper. "You know that's not going to happen to you ever again, right?"

He breathed easier, drawn to the trust radiating from her dark eyes.

"Logically," he managed around an uncharacteristic croak. "But you never forget."

She slid close and placed her hand beneath his arm urging him toward her. Heat spread through him when his arms grazed her breast.

Her lips touched his ear. She whispered. "The girls are safe. It's never going to happen to them."

Involuntarily, he jerked, his body shaking once before he regained control of himself. She had found his biggest fear and confronted it.

Iman brightened an otherwise bleak place with her unqualified trust in him. Cedric grasped hold of her belief and let it rage through his blood. He tried to relax, but his stomach did violent somersaults. Her hands hadn't left his arm. He finally gazed into her eyes.

"How did you know?"

"Honey, you bought the girls ten dresses today." Her gaze softened on his. "Have they worn all the others in their closets?"

"No, but—" Cedric started to respond but she cut him off.

"It's natural to want to protect them, and you have. From what I can see, they're very well cared for. It's time to stop worrying, Cedric."

"I don't worry."

"Ah, well." She nodded. "But you can go too far in certain instances. If you want to improve their value system, let them follow their daddy's example." She patted his hand and gentled it into a caress. Love filled her eyes. "You turned out just fine. They will too."

She let him go, and resumed eating.

The enveloping darkness that once surrounded him, faded, leaving him glowing in her wisdom. He twirled his fork in his hand for a moment.

Iman was a very smart lady.

Cedric's thoughts turned to the upcoming Christmas holiday. He couldn't imagine a day without her. The past weeks proved that.

"Iman, do you have any plans for Christmas?"

"Christmas afternoon I always spend with Aliyah. My famous holiday goose is a hit despite what Aliyah says." She smiled at him. "Why?"

"I want you to spend some time with me and the girls. I want you to share Christmas with us."

Her eyes shined. "I would love to. 'Course, I'm hoping for a white Christmas."

"Why?" Cedric asked incredulous at the thought of not being able to go to work if snow fell.

"I guess my fondest holiday memory is the winter of seventy-seven. We were snowed in for days. I don't know how much fun it was for my mother and father, but Aliyah and I had a ball."

"Sounds like Anika and Medina," he said dryly. "They enjoy fanning the smoke detector when I burn something in the kitchen."

She shot him a wry look. "Kids are supposed to have fun. During that snowstorm, we must have played *Chutes and Ladders, Monopoly,* and *Candy Land* at least fifty times each."

The memories made her giggle. Cedric loved the light in her eyes. He wished he could have been there.

"The fourth day of the storm, my dad ran from the room yelling at the top of his lungs that he would fling himself in front of a snow plow before he played another board game. My mom suggested he tell us stories."

Her tone grew wistful. "Once he started, there was no stopping him. He told us all about his grandmother and grandfather. Then somehow we got on the subject of Kwanzaa. It wasn't as well known as it is now. But from those tales, I felt a connection."

"Tell me some," Cedric encouraged. He rested his head against the high back of the booth and folded his arms. Her voice was soft and melodious as she recounted the tale of a young African warrior who was brought across the ocean to America.

Some of the fables were funny, others were serious, but he was sure of one thing. Iman was indeed the best story teller he'd ever heard. Her voice truly entranced him.

"You should tell stories all the time," he said when she finished. "You're very good at it. Was this fable passed down from your father's grandparents?"

Iman nodded, her eyes still glowing, but she had grown sad. "Yes. I miss my father's interpretation, but I've added my own twists and style. To keep them alive, I tell my nieces and someday, when I have children, I'll tell them. I plan to tell a few at this year's celebration."

The waiter brought the check. Iman slipped into her coat, by-passing the mistletoe.

Cedric couldn't put into words how he looked forward to their goodnight kiss. He paid the bill and they started walking. "How are the plans for the celebration shaping up?"

Iman draped her head and neck with his long, gray cashmere scarf. He'd always considered the scarf efficient, useful. Now it was pretty because it protected the silky curls on Iman's head. Cedric shook his head in wonder.

"It's going to be the best celebration yet. A New York dance troupe has confirmed. We also have local dance groups performing, a drum selection, a karate demonstration. The children have planned some surprises."

"That's what Medina was talking about?"

"Yep. Oh, and our farewell speaker is going to dazzle us with his eloquence."

Cedric handed the valet attendant his ticket and glanced wryly at Iman. "Don't count on it."

She whispered, "You're going to be great." The valet stopped the car in front of them.

He raised his eyebrows inquisitively. "Why do you do that?"

Her lids lowered and a shy smile danced around her mouth. "What?"

He whispered. "Whisper?"

"Because then you can hear me."

Cedric stopped. She was right. She had his undivided attention.

It took twenty minutes for the men to decide how to pack the car with all the bags. Iman watched, careful not to offer advice as they loaded the trunk. Cedric's jacket hung open as he wrestled with a bag full of ornaments. Memories of being in his arms floated back to her as she paced the sidewalk to stay warm.

No wonder he was successful, she mused. He focused to a fault on whatever he was doing at the time.

"We'll be done in a minute," he said over his shoulder, just before he unloaded the car and started over.

Iman shook her head.

She focused on his hands as he piled in one bag at a time. Those hands were always gentle with the girls, quick to clap or praise them with fatherly love whenever they were near him.

Cedric turned a box sideways and cupped his hands to his mouth to heat them before grabbing another bag.

Those same hands carefully draped her in gray cashmere when she was freezing outside Stone Manor earlier tonight. And, she blushed, had strummed her intimately and made her keen with pleasure.

She followed the hands to the face of the man she had fallen in love with. It was more than a part of her that loved him, as she'd told him. Somehow, her heart had grown committed to him, somewhere over the last few weeks.

Iman felt strangely light.

Cedric's bottom stuck out of the car. He uncurled to his full height and looked at the bags at his feet, then at her.

"We've almost got it. Not too cold are you?"

"I'm okay, do you need any help?"

"No," he glanced at the valet, who looked annoyed. "We can handle it."

Iman waited fifteen more minutes then couldn't take another cold breeze attacking her ankles. "I'll hold those two on my lap," she offered when Cedric started to unload the car again.

"I'm glad you offered. That guy looked like he wanted my blood." Cedric started the car and heat bathed her cold feet.

Iman half turned in her seat and looked at the full back seat and then at Cedric who drove carefully away from the store and onto the highway.

"Where are you going to hide all this stuff?"

"I hadn't thought of that. The girls are at my mother's but they know every hiding place in my house. They go through there like gift-sniffing dogs."

"I did the same thing. We had a crawl space on our house and my parents hid our gifts there until I left for college."

"I can drop them by my office, then Monday, while they're at school, I'll sneak the gifts into the house. Of course that doesn't help about wrapping them. But I can do that the night before."

Iman smirked. "You smart guys sure know how to complicate things."

"What? I thought that was a very well thought out plan. Okay smarty," he challenged. "You come up with something better."

"You can bring them to my house and wrap them there. Then when Christmas Eve arrives, pick them up. The girls can search the Hamilton home to their little hearts' content, they won't find a thing. I'll even help wrap. Easy, huh?" Iman fought to hide her grin of satisfaction.

"I was going to suggest that as plan B," Cedric said, pasting on his best poker face.

"Yeah, sure you were."

"Really. It was on the tip of my tongue."

"Uh, huh. Sore loser." Iman savored the thrill of victory.

He started a slow grin. "I was just going to say that."

"Your nose is growing, Pinocchio."

They bantered lightly all the way to Iman's driveway.

Chapter Eight

Iman showed Cedric to the second floor bedroom where he stored the gifts. A worktable cluttered with *Kente* fabric and materials for *mkeke* mats covered one wall, while books spilled from shelves opposite it. The floor space was wide open until bags and boxes, colored wrapping paper, and clothes filled the hardwood. They backed out of the room, gawking.

"That's insane." Cedric appeared stunned. His usual cool, eluded him. "I can't believe we did this much shopping in one day."

Iman led him downstairs to the kitchen where she had coffee brewing. "That was you," she threw over her shoulder, her delicate fingers gliding over the black glazed counter tops. "I'm an innocent shopping bystander."

He spooned one sugar into his cup and sat at the glass-topped table for four in the cozy kitchen.

Cedric's presence in her home made Iman nervous. She straightened the pictures of her nieces that hung on the wall by the sink and wiped the stainless counter with her hand. She wiped her hand on her jeans.

"Are you nervous about me being here," Cedric asked quietly.

Iman washed and dried her hands, stalling. Finally she answered. "It's silly, but I am. I shouldn't be," she rushed on, her voice higher. "I mean, we just made up, I told you how I felt . . ." Iman stopped abruptly and covered her face with her hands. "I'm making a complete fool of myself."

"No you're not. I cornered the market on that the night in the truck."

Iman sat beside him. "I missed you," he said.

She looked at him. The words were plainly spoken, but had the impact of a one-two punch.

"I missed you, too."

He tugged her into his lap and she went willingly.

"I want to make love to you. No phones, no interruptions. No truck." He nipped at her ear lobe.

The promise in his voice turned her insides to mush. A yearning beyond conscious emotion seized her.

Iman brushed the soft curls that swirled on her head, with her hand her gaze on the floor. The checkerboard pattern of the tile, blurred under her penetrating gaze.

She'd forgiven Cedric, but she hadn't forgotten how hurt she'd been.

"We should take it slow." Iman had difficulty talking, with her ear in his mouth. His lips released her. "Cedric, this feels too much like we're teenagers. Like we're being careless. It feels too right," she whispered hoarsely.

She looked into his eyes, and found understanding. "I never used to believe in love at first sight. I never thought I would tell a man I loved him before he told me." She rushed on. "I'm not trying to pressure you."

"You're not," he reassured. "We'll take it slow." He gathered her closer to him, as sexual awareness swirled between them. His hand moved possessively up her side and around her back. His voice was uncharacteristically ragged.

"I'll wait until I can't stand it anymore. Until the sound

of your voice makes me so hard I'll just about explode at my desk at work. Then I'll come looking for you, Iman."

"I'm in trouble," she murmured once she looked into his eyes.

"You sure are." He kissed her tenderly.

Cedric was a patient, deliberate man. He wouldn't have to wait too long, the way she felt.

Iman was first to break away. "I can come over tomorrow about four-thirty to help Medina. If you need some help with your speech, I'd be glad to give you some books."

"I'll take all the help I can get. I'd better get going before I break my promise to wait."

Rising from his lap was difficult. Iman wanted to stay locked in his embrace, letting desire take them where logic had no place.

But she'd made the rules. Cedric steadied her on her feet. Iman retrieved his coat from over the arm of the chair. "I had a good time."

He pulled a new scarf from his coat pocket, brushing her breast as he looped it around her neck drawing her near.

"I had a good time too."

His lips descended on hers for a fiery reminder. Their good-bye kiss lasted another five minutes.

"I . . . I meant shopping."

A flush colored her cheeks when she came up for air.

"I didn't." Cedric's arms draped possessively around her back and they stayed close enjoying the feel of the other. She rested her head against his chest listening to the quickened beat of his heart. It matched her own.

He tilted up her chin. "Good night Iman Yvette Parrish. My Sugar Baby." He kissed her brilliant nose and walked out the door. Iman walked on watery legs back to the sofa and collapsed.

Chapter Nine

"Say it again, Medina. Take your time. Start here," Cedric handed her the paper and waited for her to start. He drew a frustrated hand over his hair as he listened to Medina recite her speech for the tenth time in two hours.

"Kwanzaa is a time to draw people into your homes and ask them to ce-webrate," she cringed but kept reading, "With you. Fami-wy and friends—Daddy I can't do it."

Cedric folded his hands in his lap and exhaled. "Stop saying you can't." He rubbed his temples, his nerves frayed. "You have to try harder. Practice the 'll' sound. Don't start crying. Why are you crying?"

"I'm tired and thirsty," she said rebelliously.

"You can get a drink, but we have to go over this again."

"I don't want to," she wailed, tears dripping off her chin. "Miss Iman's nice to me when she helps me. You're yeww-ing again and you promised to stop." She let the paper slip from her hands. "I don't want to do this anymore."

His patience snapped. "Well too bad. You made a commitment and you have to keep it. Iman's been coming over here all week to help you and in a few days, she's going to need you to do this speech. You're not backing out!''

Cedric heard the doorbell, but ignored it. He paced his study and watched his daughter.

"Daddy, it's too hard. I don't want to do it anymore. I quit."

"You can't quit!"

"Hello."

Cedric hadn't realized he'd raised his voice until he heard Iman's low familiar tone from the door. He cleared his throat and glowered at Medina who raised her chin stubbornly.

"Medina, can I talk to your daddy alone for a minute?"

The little girl nodded, then took off like a shot.

"You're coming back," he yelled from the door. Medina's bedroom door banged shut.

"I swear, Iman, why don't kids come with a manual? They give them to you and then don't tell you how to raise them." He stalked past her. "She says she's not going to do her speech." Cedric collapsed into the high-back leather chair behind his desk.

Iman entered the room and laid three bags beside the sofa on the floor. "Why do you always have so much stuff?" he asked with irritation.

"These are books I thought might help you with your speech on *Kuumba*. Don't attack me because you're being unreasonable about Medina."

He scoffed. "Unreasonable? She has to learn the same way everybody else does that if she makes a commitment to something, she has to keep it." He shook his head and waved his hand carelessly. "I won't have any of this fickle maybe I will, maybe I won't."

"I thought she was happy with her speech. Why did she change her mind?" Iman loosened the sash on her coat and sat down.

He glowered at her. "Because she has a speech impediment. She can't pronounce some of her letters correctly and she's shy about it. Practice," he announced. "She needs to practice."

"Cedric, I'm not going to tell you how to raise your children," she said softly.

"Sure you are," he cut in sarcastically.

Iman ignored him and continued. "But it seems to me that another way to handle someone like this is with positive suggestions. Give her positive encouragement. Tell her things like, you can do it, I believe in you, you did great." Her warm smile captivated him. She was whispering again.

Cedric felt himself falling.

"Iman," he warned.

"I believe in you, you're going to be great." She grinned sweetly. How he loved her mouth. Cedric shook his head.

"How come you think you know me so well?" Her smile widened victoriously. Cedric was hopelessly lost.

"I know you want Medina to believe in herself. That's why you work so hard to help her. But you get frustrated when she doesn't try as hard as you think she should."

He shrugged, agreeing. "I try not to be so intense with her."

"I know, I heard you. The housekeeper let me in. I listened awhile before I came in here. I know you want the best for her." Her voice was soft. "Try to take it easy on her. She's just seven."

"How come you know so much about children? You don't have any." Hurt and anger played across her face and he stopped short. "Sorry, that was unfair."

"I may not have children, but I've worked with them for years. And as you've said, they don't come with a manual. Any fool could do it."

His lips quirked. "I guess I deserved that. But if I have to give my speech, so does she, damn it." Cedric sighed raggedly. "What are you laughing at?"

Red looked so good on Iman. She slipped the wool coat from her shoulders and threw it on the couch. A brilliant red silk shirt was tucked into nicely fitting jeans with a complimenting vest hanging open in the front. Long earrings dangled from her ears and she wore a thin gold chain around her neck.

"She's doing it, damn it," she mimicked his deep voice. "Cedric, do you think your terrorist tactics helped? Positive thinking gets positive results."

He shook his head mimicking her silently and waved off her assessment. Cedric could see where this was going and he didn't like it one bit. Somehow he knew he was going to be wrong. He dragged his gaze away from her matte red lips and stared out the side window.

"I'm not the one that's wrong here. I agree my tactics may need some work." He scowled. "Medina made a commitment and she's going to keep it." He needed to change the subject. His body ached for Iman. "Come here."

Iman stayed where she was. She arched an eyebrow at him. "Ask nicely."

"Come here, damn it," he said, smiling. He was winning. He could feel it.

"Come here damn it, please," Iman tossed back.

Cedric pushed his chair from his desk and planted both feet firmly on the floor. "Come here damn it, please, Iman, and take care of your man."

Iman took her time closing and locking the door to his study before she came to him. She placed her knee between his legs on the chair and rested her hands on his shoulders. "That's much, much better."

She tasted exactly as he remembered only better, Cedric thought fuzzily. He slid his tongue over her lower lip, then sucked on the fullness. Her mouth eased opened in invitation and her breath rushed out. He sampled the velvet warmth, losing himself to her flavor.

"The girls," she murmured, when his hands stole beneath her vest and found the buttons of her shirt. He wrestled the silk shirt from the waist of her pants bunching it beneath her breasts. The vest fell to the floor.

Cedric dropped his head and sucked on her indented belly button. Iman gasped and writhed when he licked up her rib cage. Her fresh scent deepened into a powerful aphrodisiac as her temperature rose.

"Daddy? Can we come in?"

They both jumped off the chair. Iman fumbled with her blouse shoving it hastily into her jeans, bumping into the desk as she headed for the couch.

"Just a minute," Cedric called. "Iman," he whispered, waving her back. He tucked the flap of her shirt into the front of her pants, helped her into her vest, then grasped her face between his hands. He kissed her soundly. "I just wanted to make sure this wasn't a dream or a conspiracy against me for wanting you so much." His bulging pants relayed his desire.

"It's for real," she agreed, pressing herself lightly into him. "Open the door before they think we're up to something." Cedric got to the door and turned the handle but didn't open it. "I'm definitely up *for* something." Her nose brightened and a moment of silence hung between them.

"I . . ." The words stuck to his tongue, and Cedric didn't force them. He just couldn't say what lay on his heart. Iman smoothed her hair and looked questioningly at him. "Cedric, do I look okay?" She fussed with her shirt and vest, then smoothed her jeans. She was gorgeous.

"You look fine."

He flipped the latch and turned the handle on the door. The girls burst in and headed straight for Iman. Both spoke at once. "Hi, Miss Iman."

"Hi Anika, hi Medina." Iman inclined her head in their direction. "Let's leave your daddy to his work and go practice our speeches." They crowded out the door, leaving him alone.

Cedric stood in the doorway helplessly aroused with no

outlet readily available. He watched Iman disappear around the corner with the girls and resigned himself to work. If only he could manage to concentrate.

He worked on his speech for *Kuumba* and leafed through the books Iman had in her bags. He quickly completed the thinner books, saving the thicker ones for later.

The sound of giggling filtered into his office through the half closed door.

He laid his pen down, and contemplated joining them. The legal pad he'd been writing on held only a partially completed speech. With *Kuumba* only days away, there was little time to waste.

Cedric shook his head and tried to concentrate.

But the sound of Iman playing with the girls and their joyous laughter was too distracting. It didn't help his body recover either. He still wanted her.

Cedric picked up the warbling phone on his way to the kitchen. "Hello?"

"Cedric, it's Mother. Are you lifting weights? You sound out of breath."

Cedric refused to look past his waist again. It wouldn't do any good. "Something like that," he said dryly. "What's up Mom? Everything okay?"

"Of course it is," his sprightly mother replied. She claimed good health now, but he still worried about her.

"I'm just asking. How's Richard?"

"Richard's gone hunting with his son. Don't know what you could kill in the middle of winter but I said go. I called because I want my grand-bunnies to come over and spend the weekend with me. If you don't mind."

"Yes! Mom you saved my life." Cedric responded before he could think twice. The pulse in his lower region thundered in anticipation. Relief was just around the corner.

His mother laughed. "You must have plans. Got a hot date with Iman?"

"I plan to make one. Thanks Mom," he said before hanging up.

Cedric passed the picture he'd bought at the auction. The one Iman loved so much. It depicted children playing, their carefree spirit leaping off the canvas.

The first night he'd seen it, it had touched a lonely space inside him. He'd wished he could have been one of those children. Then he'd met Iman and he hadn't been lonely since.

The picture belonged to her. She'd seen it for what it was and she'd found something in him. It was her spirit that held the strings of his heart.

Cedric picked up the painting and headed for the basement, where he wrapped it carefully, then stored it in the trunk of his car. He'd surprise her with it later.

He headed up the stairs to the girls' room. The door was ajar and he peeked through. Iman lay on her stomach on the floor, with Anika on her right and Medina on her left.

"My dad is very smart. He graduated to the tenth grade," Anika said importantly.

Iman shook her head. "He went to college, didn't he?"

Cedric held his breath. For some reason, uneasiness crept through him.

"No. He went to work. He has extra skin on his hands 'cause he had to work so hard." Medina crinkled her nose. "Sometimes he peels it."

"Then we put lotion on it," they said together.

"Your daddy is a very good man." Iman's husky voice made his heart swell. "We'd better get back to work. Medina, I don't want you to worry about your L's. You did perfect, tonight. Absolutely, positively perfect."

"For rea-wl?" Hope surged in Medina's voice. She looked at Iman as if she'd hung the moon.

"For real," Iman reassured.

Cedric's heart swelled more than he thought it could.

"Anika," Iman went on. "Nobody told me you could sing. I think I have another job for you." Both girls giggled.

"Don't ask Daddy to sing. He sounds just like a rhinoceros," Anika giggled.

Cedric started to push the door open.

"Miss Iman, are you married?" He stopped and waited.

"Not yet."

"Are you going to marry our daddy?" Median asked.

Iman sat back on her knees away from the girls. They followed her up and sat beside her with their legs crossed. She seemed to be studying the cranberry colored carpet intently. Cedric held his breath.

"He hasn't asked me."

"If he did, would you?"

She laughed. "You two sure are inquisitive." She stood and reached for their hands pulling them up. "Let's just say that if he brings it up one day, I'd think about it. How do you feel about that?"

"Good," they responded unanimously.

"Really? Why?"

Cedric pressed his head against the door while they considered her question. It occurred to him they might be unhappy. His chest tightened, not knowing. Finally Anika spoke.

"Everybody in our class has a mother. We just want to have one, too. Daddy needs a wife so he doesn't have to be by himself all the time."

"I see," Iman said. "Well I'm sure things will work out for him."

Cedric knocked on the door. He wiped mist from his eyes before he walked in. "How's everything going?"

"Fine," they all responded. Cedric looked at Iman. She stared at the floor for a long time before meeting his gaze, briefly.

"Grandma wants you to come spend the weekend with her." Cedric pretended to shake from the girls squeals of happiness. "Since that's a yes, we'd better get some things together. But you have to practice your speeches while you're there." He walked to the mirrored wall closet and slid the panel open.

"Daddy, can Miss Iman help us?"

"Well . . ."

"I don't mind," she said coming to stand beside him.

Cedric touched her arm. "I'll be waiting downstairs." He walked from the room, closing the door behind him.

Chapter Ten

Iman stared at Cedric's long legs, which were stretched out in front of him. She'd come to know his favorite reading position as he crowded the corner of the couch with his lean frame, giving the book on his lap his undivided attention.

They had come to her house after dropping off the girls and he had assumed that position an hour ago working fervently on his speech.

Troubling thoughts assailed her. He was in her house, her life, but he hadn't said a word about her confession of love. What if he didn't feel the same way? Had she made a complete and utter fool of herself? Iman silently berated herself.

She tried to imagine herself without Cedric and the girls, but couldn't. Their reason for seeing each other so often would soon be gone.

What would happen to them?

Iman lowered the book from her lap and strolled to the window unobtrusively so as not to disturb him. The clear, cold, starlit sky held no fireworks, no exploding bombs, no blazes of light that scorched, "Love" in neon lights in the stars.

But they were bright. Luminous as if she'd never seen them before. Some formed a smile, while others danced.

Iman shook herself. Who'd ever heard of dancing stars?

"The stars are beautiful tonight," she remarked. Surely, if he looked, he would see what she saw.

Absently he glanced over his shoulder and nodded.

"Mmm."

Discontent swirled through her.

Iman settled back in the armchair to watch the man she couldn't imagine being without and wondered why he didn't see the same damn dancing stars she did.

Earlier in his study, she'd thought he might say he loved her. Instead, he'd opened the door for the girls and the opportunity vanished.

He loved her, she could feel it. But would he ever say it?

"I'm going upstairs to wrap presents," she announced, hoping he would stop her. Her hopes were dashed when he only nodded.

Iman took the wooden steps slowly. She gathered wrapping paper, clothes, boxes, and bows and dragged them to her room where she got comfortable on her queen size bed.

Methodically she cut, wrapped, and taped. Bows and ornaments in brilliant reds, greens, blues, and purples lay strewn on the bed and she peeled the backs off several, matching the perfect bow to each color paper.

Iman tossed the others in a growing pile of discarded wrapping paper which covered the top corner of her bed. A flash of guilt coursed through her at her wastefulness.

Her thoughts wandered to the woman on the television screen from Cedric's company. Iman knew it wouldn't help, but she folded several of the larger pieces to use later.

"Need anything?"

The door to her room was wide open and Cedric leaned one shoulder against the frame. Although his stance was casual, tension radiated from him. It made desire coil inside her like a hot spring.

His smoldering gaze caressed her bare leg that dangled over the side of the bed. Slowly it moved up and over the colorful caftan that gathered at her thighs.

She watched his tongue caress his lower lip.

Iman began to perspire.

His gaze lingered at her breasts, then locked with hers letting her know it wasn't Christmas presents he was talking about. Her concerns slipped away under the heat of his gaze. "I need you."

He started into the room. Iman slid both legs off the bed, her knees slightly apart.

She closed her eyes when his strong fingers tunneled through her hair, forcing her head back.

The long zipper on the back of her caftan made a cutting noise in the silence, broken only by the sounds of their heavy breathing. The caftan pooled around her waist.

His hands guided her up and the *kente* print dress dropped around her ankles. Strong fingers slid under the straps of her bra and peeled them down her arms. His forehead touched hers and his mouth was slightly open.

Their lips met and the tip of his tongue tantalized her.

Iman reached around and unhooked the back of her bra. It dropped between them, deep brown nipples peeking over the lavender lace.

"You want me?" she asked seductively against his mouth. His thigh nudged hers and his hand slid boldly up between her legs. Her panties were no match for his probing fingers.

Iman cried out, raising on her toes, wanting more.

He held her still and sampled her wetness. With the slowness of a predator stalking its prey, his fingers drew a moist path through her dark patch of hair, stopping long enough to make her left breast ache, then mercifully ending at her lips.

Cedric tilted her chin up and stroked her other breast lazily. "Do *you* want me?"

Iman nodded yes, mute.

He suckled, and licked the rest of the clothes from her skin. It was maddening, his loving was so good.

"I don't want to be naked by myself." Iman reached for Cedric, but he stepped out of her arms. She couldn't control her shivers of anticipation as he performed a slow striptease for her. Iman crawled to the center of her bed and waited.

This was what she'd dreamed about. Yearned for. Desired so much. Him. With her. Inside her. Taking her places she hadn't been in a long, long time. Iman silently thanked Aliyah's forethought as she handed him the little foil packet. Her heartbeat quickened when Cedric kissed her his thanks. She didn't know what she would do if they had to stop.

Wrapping paper protested under her back as he lay her down and loved her with such tenderness her eyes dripped tears from the splendid ecstasy.

Afterward he stroked her until the tears subsided and the pleasure began again. This time when the back of her thighs met the front of his, it was with an intensity surpassed only by their coupling of moments ago.

Iman lay on top of Cedric, her arms resting on his broad shoulders, her head against his chest. He held her still as he peeled another Christmas bow from her bottom.

"Ouch, what was that?"

"Christmas bows. Be still." She jerked when he disengaged the last bow from her skin.

"No," he groaned. "Don't be still. I like when you do that." His large hands rotated her hips against him.

"I tingle," she murmured.

"Is that *all?*" He slowed the movements and looked down at their bodies pressed together.

Iman grabbed the bow from the scattered covers. "I

meant my rear tingles from where you pulled this darn
thing."

He took it from her hands and pressed it on the tip of
her breast. Iman slapped playfully at Cedric's arms when
he swiftly flipped her onto her back and loomed over her.

"Hey, how are you going to make sure that doesn't hurt
when you take it off?" He lowered his head. "Oh, good,
yes," she sighed a moment later when he used his tongue
to remove it.

Chapter Eleven

Cedric reclined against the wooden head board and watched Iman sleep. She was beautiful in all her naked glory. Her skin was a soft brown, even in coloring from her head to her feet. Except her nipples. The tips were as dark in hue as his skin. And tasted better than any delicacy he'd ever sampled.

He'd had a chance to taste every inch of her over the last three hours. His body stirred, at the memories of their passion. She loved him. *She loved him.*

The next move was his. But what did Iman want out of life? Did she want to be a wife, an instant mother?

Those thoughts plagued him as he silently slid out of the bed and into his jeans. Her house was southern, comfortable in a way he'd experienced only later in his life. It hadn't been until he was grown and on his way to wealth that he'd been invited into nice homes.

Life was strange. Iman seemed happy with her life in a way few people were. She loved what she did.

He couldn't say the same thing. A long time ago, Dix had been a golden opportunity, a means to an end.

It didn't hold the same meaning anymore. The takeover of Blythe Pharmaceuticals bothered him more than he cared to admit. He couldn't get the faces of the people out of his head.

Company morale remained low and for the first time, his personal life was good. He wanted everybody to be as happy as he. Damn it.

Cedric hurried to the car and got Iman's painting from the trunk. At least he could do one thing right. He hung it in the spot she'd indicated the first time he'd come to her house and then went to the refrigerator. Something in his life had to change.

He provided a stable home and had secured a solid future for Anika and Medina. Not bad for a man with a tenth-grade education. So what was missing? Would having someone to come home to cure his restlessness?

"Are you trying to cool off America with that door open?"

Cedric closed the refrigerator door and leaned against it. "Just thinking." A long, white lace robe sheathed Iman. The darkest parts of her were still visible. He could feel himself growing and tightening beneath his half closed jeans. His gaze raked her. "Is that thing supposed to do something?"

She struck a pose, then slid her hand down from her waist to her thigh where she parted the thin material.

"It's supposed to titillate, tantalize, and tease the mind, body, and spirit." She walked forward slowly. "Is it working?"

He kissed her nose. "I'm completely under your spell."

Iman raised on her toes and kissed his mouth. "I know it's the middle of the night, but I want something to eat. Are you hungry?"

"Only for you."

Iman opened the silverware drawer, pulled out a spatula and swatted at him with it. "Back. I was talking about frying some chicken."

"Chicken is good, too. What do you want me to do?"

She handed him some potatoes. "Peel."

Iman had the chicken in the frying pan in no time.

Cedric dropped peeled and cubed potatoes into a pot of water on the stove, while Iman pulled two beers from the refrigerator and set them on the table.

When everything was bubbling appropriately, they sat at the kitchen table with their drinks.

Iman studied Cedric. He seemed so relaxed with his naked chest and bare feet.

The discussion with the girls that afternoon gave her a better understanding of him. She now realized he was so intense because of the immense responsibility he'd had from a young age. The knowledge that he'd only been educated to the tenth grade stunned her. His recent problems with the two companies merging came to the forefront of her mind.

"Have things settled down with your new employees?"

He shrugged. "Some are resentful their friends got let go. Others are grateful they still have jobs. Others are worried I'll fire them next month. Overall, it's been a cautious undertaking." Iman sensed something more, something he wasn't saying.

"Would you do it again?"

"Yes." He looked into her eyes. "It's not personal. It's business."

Iman shivered at his tone. "I know. But you must understand how they feel."

"What am I supposed to do? If it weren't my company it would be somebody else. I didn't let forty thousand people go like one of the Bell companies. I didn't pull something like that. It was one hundred people. Let's drop the subject."

He got up and stalked to the stove. The grease popped as he turned the chicken, then he slipped the metal cover over the snapping oil. It sizzled, then settled back into its regular bubbling level.

Too restless to sit, he leaned his shoulder against the refrigerator and crossed his arms.

"When did you discover teaching was right for you?"

Iman watched him closely. Cedric didn't like talking about himself. Whenever he was uncomfortable, he changed the subject. He'd done it before. She decided not to call him on it and answered.

"I've known since I was a six years old. What about you? Will you always run Dix?" Iman felt driven to know the "It's business" part of Cedric. For an inexplicable reason, it mattered.

He put the cooked chicken on plates and dished out the potato salad. "I don't know." His answer shocked her. They began eating. His potato salad tasted delicious.

"Have you ever considered doing something else?" she asked.

"No. I never have." Iman looked up from her plate at him. There was a finality to his voice that made her sad. He was bound to something she got the impression he didn't like. Iman felt sorry for people who didn't like their jobs. She loved hers so.

The overwhelming urge to cuddle with Cedric filled her. Silently, she eased onto his lap and wrapped her arms around him.

It took a long time before she felt his arms move. Then his body curved and molded to hers. Their strength, bonding.

"Let's go back to bed," he murmured against her hair.

"I'll race you." The seductiveness of his touch made her anxious to repeat their earlier pleasure and to forget the world.

Cedric swept her up into his arms. "We both win, we have all night."

"Ada, it's Iman. Where are you?"

Slightly out of breath from climbing three flights of stairs

Ada's apartment, Iman dropped her key on the table close to the door and stepped back.

Ada's apartment always overwhelmed her when she first entered. Having called the same place home for over fifteen years, Ada had long ago filled every corner to decorate out.

Now everything went up. Iman always had the sneaking feeling that something was going to fall off the wall and land on her head.

She heard Ada's answering cough and hurried to the bedroom. Her frail body was dwarfed beneath a mountain of ancient hand stitched quilts. The vaporizer hummed a steady cloud of steam, while crumpled tissues littered the floor.

"Iman," she wheezed. "Chile, what you doing here? We don't have much time before *Umoja*. You got everythin' taken care of?"

Iman took off her coat and dropped it at the foot of Ada's bed. Despite the woman's weakened state, the room was tidy. Iman threw the stray tissues in the can. She touched Ada's forehead, sucking her teeth at the dampness.

"Everything's fine. I came looking for you. I called you yesterday but nobody answered."

"I had a doctor's appointment at two o'clock. He gave me a new medicine, but I took the last of it last night."

"Why didn't you call me? I would have taken you." Iman caressed Ada's hand while she talked. She couldn't bear to think of her in the cold winter air by herself. Ada gave her hand a strong squeeze.

"I knew you were at the manor decorating and practicing for the *Karamu*. That doctor must be crazy to think I'm going to spend sixty-seven dollars for a bottle of medicine.

"Don't worry about me, chile. I mixed up something myself."

Medicine bottles, a cup with dark goo in it, and a half-melted candle cluttered the bedside table. Iman wrinkled her nose when she picked up the foul smelling cup and took a whiff of the concoction.

"Honey, what is this?"

She drew her nose back sharply from the pungent odor.

"It was good enough for you crumb snatchers," Ada said sharply. She coughed long and hard. "Only thing is, I didn't have enough eye of newt to finish it."

Iman laughed softly. That was Ada's way of putting her in her place. She was proud of her Haitian heritage and scoffed at conventional methods of healing. Only, the medicine she needed today was very conventional and very expensive.

Iman made her some tea and held her head so she could sip it. "Do you have any more sample bottles of medicine from the doctor?"

"No. He only gave me one."

Ada raised up on her elbows when Iman stood.

"Don't go rousting the pharmacist, Iman. They told me how you showed out last month trying to get that other medicine for me at a discount. They're giving me the best they can. It's my own fault I'm like this."

Iman held her through another coughing fit. "No, it's not. It's the drug companies fault for overpricing these medicines. And I intend to do something about it."

Ada's eyes followed her movements. "Chile, I smoked cigarettes for fifty-five years. These old lungs belong only to me. I made them this way."

Iman straightened Ada's covers, raising her chin stubbornly. "You would be well if you could afford the medicine."

Iman gently patted Ada's shoulder. She followed the phone cord to Ada's rotary phone.

"I'm calling Aliyah to come sit with you while I go pay our friendly pharmacist a visit. The last time I was there, he said the drug company was right here in Atlanta. I'll need this." Iman grabbed the bottle from the table and shoved it in her coat pocket. She braced the phone under her chin twirling the dial. "Don't you worry, I'll take care of everything."

"Oh, goodness," Ada groaned. "Have mercy on them."

Chapter Twelve

Iman stalked into the lobby of the Dix Pharmaceutical Company, Inc. Before she left, Ada had almost passed out from the coughing fit that shook her frail body. But like always, she refused to go to the hospital.

Iman was desperate and she knew of only one person who could help her. The ride up to the fourth floor of the washed stone structure gave her a chance to formulate her scattered thoughts. She squared her shoulders and stood tall. She would present her argument in a logical, reasonable way, and he would see reason.

The doors breezed open. Iman stepped into the lobby and walked the few steps to the receptionist desk.

"Cedric Hamilton, please."

The tiny receptionist flicked down the mouthpiece of her headphone and looked at her.

"Do you have an appointment?"

"No, but he'll see me."

The woman gave her a polite smile. "Mr. Hamilton is a very busy man. He operates on an appointment basis only."

Iman impatiently nodded her head. "He'll see me. I'm his—" she stopped. They hadn't defined their relationship with labels. She'd said she loved him, he'd said thank you.

"His girlfriend," Iman managed.

"Just a minute, ma'am." The woman hurried away and slipped into a room down the hall. Iman clenched and opened her fists. She reassured herself that things would be fine.

The door opened and Cedric stepped out. He approached her in long strides. Immense relief flooded her once her hands were within his.

"What's the matter?" His concern made her weak. Everything was going to be all right.

"It's Ada." He wrapped his arm around her shoulder.

"Did she . . . die?"

She hurried to reassure him. "No, she isn't dead."

"Then what is it?"

Iman looked into the eyes of the man she loved. In his arms she had found pleasure beyond her wildest dreams. Now she felt support. She knew why she loved him. Words spilled from her mouth.

"Ada needs our help. Cedric, your company manufactures the medicine her doctor prescribed to make her better. You have to lower the price so she can afford it." Iman retrieved the bottle from her coat pocket and pressed it into his hands.

The pencil the receptionist's had been writing with snapped.

Cedric took her by the hand. "Come into my office." He guided her down the hall and closed the door behind them. The expensively decorated office was a blur as Iman turned to face him.

"Cedric, did you hear me? Ada needs your help."

"I can't do what you're asking."

"Why?" She searched his features for a clue.

Cedric pushed himself away from the door and walked around his desk.

"Iman, drug prices can't arbitrarily be lowered. That's not how business is done. There are two hundred people that work for this company. Those people have families that depend on them. They count on me to make sure they get paychecks. If we're not profitable, then people lose jobs."

A steel trap seemed to be closing over her. Iman fought for air. "Cedric, this is Ada we're talking about. She's not some nameless, faceless person from RSG. She's my friend." Her voice quivered, but she continued to meet his level gaze. "Be reasonable." The words were more personal than she intended. Iman waited, hoping he would transform before her eyes.

His expression remained one of pained tolerance. "I'm being reasonable, and it seems as though I'm the only one who's doing so. What you're asking is ludicrous."

Fire rushed through her. Her voice came raggedly in impotent anger. "I know the medicine from that little bottle doesn't cost sixty-seven dollars to make. For goodness sake, senior citizens are the predominant market for this drug." She flung her arm out. "Most of them are on fixed incomes. How are they supposed to afford it?"

He settled behind his desk in the high-back leather chair, unfazed by her outburst. Iman's hope began to unravel.

"Most of the people who use this medicine have some kind of insurance or another. There's only a small number that actually pay market price."

She braced her hands on his desk. "Then what do the Ada's of the world do?"

His steepled fingers flew open. "It's not for everybody. Iman, this is business—"

Iman held up her hand. She resisted screaming at Cedric's tolerant look. "If you say that to me one more time, I swear, I'll scream."

Her throat constricted, but she forced herself to go on. "You know, that's your problem. You're so wound up in *business* you can't see your own face. Cedric, you've forgot-

ten what poverty is like because you're hiding behind
expensive suits and useless dresses for the girls." His eyebrows shot up, but he remained silent. Iman went on.

"You've reached a comfort zone that many don't ever
see. You're too *rich.*" Iman shuddered distastefully.

His voice was as sharp as jagged glass. "I worked my butt
off to get where I am today, and I won't just give it away
on a whim. I give back to this community the way I know
how. I do care. Lowering the price of a medication is
not the answer. Why can't Ada get on one of the social
programs?"

"She's afraid she'll be deported. She's not a United
States citizen." Iman's eyes watered. She made her final
plea. "Cedric, please. I've never asked you for anything
before. For Ada." *For me,* she said silently.

"Lowering the price of the medication isn't the answer."
His voice rang with finality.

Iman firmly placed her purse strap on her shoulder.

"My bottle, please." She extended her hand, she
couldn't look at him.

"What are you going to do?"

"I'm going to take care of Ada myself."

"You mean buy the medicine yourself."

She looked at him. "Yes."

Miles separated them.

All Cedric cared about was his precious bottom line. She
should have known. It was business. Shame washed over
her. The last time he'd said that to her, should have served
as enough of a warning.

Iman focused on the reddish-brown bottle in his hands
and waited for him to give it to her. She wanted to leave
before her tears started to flow.

Cedric placed the bottle on the desk between them.
Iman slowly took it and dropped it in her purse. She walked
to the door.

"Are you going over there now?"

She nodded. Breezy indifference failed her. Her voice wavered. "I'll be busy over the next few days."

"Let me come with you."

"No. I don't need—" Iman struggled with the words that pushed at her throat. "You've done enough."

"Will w-we—" he stammered. "Will I see you later?"

"No." She met his bewildered gaze. She deliberately whispered. "Good-bye."

Iman disappeared through the door.

Chapter Thirteen

"Mr. Hamilton, may I have a word with you, please?"

Cedric looked up from the computer screen surprised to find he wasn't alone. Most of the skeleton staff of employees had already left for the day. Considering it was the day before Christmas Eve.

Debra Gray, his receptionist, waited expectantly in the doorway. "What is it, Debra? I thought everyone was gone."

"I was leaving about an hour ago, but a delivery arrived. It's waiting for you in the conference room."

He rose from the desk, annoyed. "If it's a normal delivery, why didn't it go through receiving? I don't have to sign for every little package that comes into this office."

Cedric followed the silent woman to the conference room, further aggravated that she didn't defend her actions.

Ever since his showdown with Iman earlier that day, he'd been spoiling for a fight. He stepped through the door into darkness.

"What in the hell's going on here?" The overhead lights flickered and illuminated the room.

Cedric's jaw went slack. At least one hundred brightly wrapped Christmas packages spilled from the table onto the chairs. When that space ran out, the gifts covered the floor of the conference room.

All of Anika and Medina's Christmas gifts from Iman's house were wrapped and ready to be delivered.

Debra stood silently behind him. He finally spoke.

"When did she come back?"

"She left about five minutes ago. She said not to disturb you. You were busy . . ." The rest of the sentence died on her lips.

"She said I was busy doing what?"

"Fleecing the elderly."

Cedric pushed a gift to the floor and sat in a conference room chair. A bow and ornament stuck to his pant leg, and he pulled it off.

The brilliant purple glass ball distorted his facial expression. His head was wide, making the grim set to his mouth seem monstrous.

Probably how I looked to Iman and Jack McClure when I said no.

"Thank you, Debra."

The door closed quietly.

He caressed the thin glass. It was perfect in shape, pleasing to the eye. That was the main reason he'd chosen it. Cedric looked around the room.

Everything mirrored the same controlled perfection. Books stood upright as if monitored by a military general. His office, always impeccably neat and orderly. The staff at Dix, efficient and highly qualified. And it was all his.

On the surface, everything looked great. He'd even tried to have perfect children. Guilt over his behavior toward Medina assaulted him. Indeed, he had used tyrannical tactics to make her into the person he wanted her to be.

But the finely woven fabric of his suit couldn't hide his true identity. That poor, cold child from his past still lived inside.

Once a skinny kid, he'd been fattened, polished by strangers. People who stood to gain nothing personally. But they loved him enough to instill in him the values of hard work and achievement which later fostered his success. Those were the values he wanted to pass to his children.

Cedric rose from the chair and packed the gifts in his car.

Back in the office, the printer surged to life after he hit the command and signed off the computer. He stared at the numbers that declared Dix's hefty profits on all twelve medications, Ada's being one of them.

Cedric lowered himself into his chair. What had he become? Too rich, as Iman claimed? So far above others he no longer cared for their suffering?

A man of too much ability and means, but lacking the one thing money couldn't buy.

Where was his heart?

I can do this, echoed in his head. The pronouncement shook him to the core where his deepest fears lay. His past replayed through his mind like photos from a single framed camera. Highlights of the worst times flashed. Bitter cold, nonstop hunger pains that eventually ebbed into dull flatness. Hopelessness. Fear. He shut his eyes immersing himself in all he used to despair.

Then there was Lenora. Michael Dix. His beautiful children. His mother on her wedding day. Iman.

Iman. His love, his life.

I can do this. Cedric looked in the Rolodex and punched buttons on the phone. "Jack, Cedric Hamilton, sorry to bother you at home. I've decided to lower the prices on the medications on your list."

Cedric smiled when the man's buoyant laughter echoed through the phone.

"A Monday morning meeting sounds good. Goodnight, Jack."

Cedric grabbed his coat and drove slowly, making decisions that would change his life forever. He prayed Iman would want to share the future with him.

Cedric checked the doors as he locked up the house for the night. The girls were asleep, his house still twinkled with white lights, and the Christmas goose was a few pounds lighter than when it had arrived with his mother and stepfather hours ago.

But Cedric was alone.

Iman hadn't wanted to see him. She'd declined to spend Christmas with him. She'd taken time to call and speak to the girls, wishing them a happy day, but when he'd gotten the phone when they were done, he'd met a dial tone.

Today, unlike less than a week ago, there was no giggling. No anticipation growing inside him, like the last time she'd been there.

He was alone, and he hated it. Convincing her to share her life with him might not happen. Cedric shook off the depressing thoughts as he stacked the unopened presents under the tree. The girls had been so ungrateful. They'd only wanted two things, and when they found them, refused to open any more.

He shook his head.

"Daddy?" Cedric stood from his crouched position. He approached Anika and placed his hand on her forehead.

"Hey, there. You feeling okay?"

"I feel good. Medina went back to sleep so I came to talk to you about our plan." He sat down on the couch and drew her on his lap. "What kind of great plan could pull you from your bed in the middle of the night?"

She pointed to the tree. "We want to give our Christmas presents away."

Cedric drew back, stunned. Realization surged through his veins. When he found his voice it was emotion filled. He stroked her long braid. "Why?"

"Because we got a lot. More than other kids." Her solemn gaze met his. "We won't do it if you're going to get mad."

Cedric shook his head recognizing how they'd all changed. His voice filled with pride. "I'm very proud of you and your sister for making such a grown-up decision." He scooted her off his lap and held her hand as he guided her to the stairs. "You know, your old man could take some lessons from you girls. You're very smart." He tucked her in and kissed her forehead.

"You're very smart, too. I love you, Daddy." Anika snuggled next to her Addie doll and drifted off, unaware of the love glistening in her father's eyes.

Chapter Fourteen

Kuumba was upon them.

Cedric ran his hand nervously over his head and knocked off his *kofi*. Hastily he put it back on and dropped his hand to his side. He rolled his head on his shoulders and shrugged to loosen himself.

"Daddy, you're going to be great. Re-wax." Medina squeezed his hand, her eyes dancing merrily. Cedric knew he was acting uncharacteristically nervous, but tonight was important.

"I'm okay, sweetie." He kneeled down, a rush of paternal love filling him. Medina was a smart girl. And he told her so.

"Medina, I'm very proud of you. It doesn't matter how you do today, I just want you to know that I love you and . . ." Cedric stopped when her name was called to join her class.

"I love you, Medina."

She kissed his cheek in an exuberant rush and hugged him with a quickness that almost had him on his bottom.

She walked away then turned and said, "I love you too, Daddy."

Cedric barely controlled the tears that sprang to his eyes. She'd said it. The perfect L.

He turned his attention to the capacity crowd that filled the basement of Stone Manor. Just over a month ago, he'd come to the magnificent house alone, and incomplete.

Through his studies of Kwanzaa, he'd learned more about himself and the course his life would continue on.

Yet, there was one part missing.

Iman.

He'd spotted her earlier with Ada, who looked healthier and happier from taking her medication properly. He'd visited her several times during the week and had been pleasantly surprised by her snappy humor and straight-forward opinion on his and Iman's relationship. He held on to her confidence that everything would work out. Several members of RSG were present also which made him feel even better about his decision.

Cedric turned his attention to the program. Impromptu dancers from the audience dazzled the crowd during the drum-playing segment much to everyone's delight.

Then a libation was poured to deceased ancestors. Cedric wished he could hold Iman's hand. He knew she was thinking of her father.

Then all the children congregated in front of the stage for the lighting of the candles. Medina and Anika read their speeches and everyone applauded loudly giving the youngsters a standing ovation for their effort.

Iman hugged each child, exclaiming how proud she was of them. She told stories, just as she'd promised, captivating the crowd with her voice. She was a hit.

Cedric gave the New York dance troupe and karate dem-onstration only half his attention. His focus was on Iman and their future together as a family.

The Negro National Anthem music started, and the

crowd rose and sang, then a local dance group concluded the evening with uplifting African dances.

Cedric took a deep breath. He'd researched *Kuumba* and labored over his speech for days. It was perfect. He was ready. Finally, it was time.

He walked on-stage and shoved the speech in his pocket. The applause died down and he called, *"Habari Gani!"*

The crowd echoed its response.

Cedric stood before the audience in full African attire looking very kingly in gold, the color of prosperity and royalty.

"Tonight my charge was to be eloquent and moving. But I stand before you humble in my responsibility." He gazed out over the crowd and found Iman.

"When I was first asked to present the farewell, I said no. I thought, what do I have to say that's good enough to take our families into the next year? Then a little voice said to me, 'You're going to be great. I believe in you.' The funny thing is, the other day, I began to believe it too."

Cedric's voice reached inside her and stopped Iman's pacing. "I'll tell you what I've learned through Kwanzaa."

He folded his hands on the podium and looked out over the crowd. "Opening yourself up and stepping outside your comfort zone are the scariest things a person can do, because outside represents the unknown. It's where fear hides, doubt reigns.

"I used to believe that until recently. Someone I love challenged me to do my collective work and responsibility toward my fellow man. At the time, I didn't know what she meant."

Several people nodded. Others shook their heads. Iman stared, amazed. She couldn't believe Cedric was telling everybody their story.

He continued. "I felt I had served my purpose, done what I was supposed to do. Given all I could give." He shook his head. "I didn't know how much more needs to be done until I was faced with losing something . . . someone special.'' He looked into the audience and seemed to address each of them personally.

"Don't be like me and put worldly goods before things that really matter like imagination, trust, and most of all faith and love. My challenge to you is to utilize your talents, knowledge, and beliefs to help improve the lives of those around you. The rewards will come back to you one hundred times over.''

Through blurred eyes, Iman watched Cedric straighten and catch himself being eloquent and moving. He'd relaxed as he'd spoken and moved away from the microphone, his confidence captivating the capacity crowd.

He stood behind the podium again.

"Most important of all, listen to the voice that whispers. It's probably telling you something you can't afford to miss. Thank you.''

People applauded around her. Cedric left the podium and headed to the back of the stage. Iman tried to reach him, but it was time for the feast.

She didn't see him again until the entire festival was over and only a few straggler's remained. Elaine had long since taken Anika and Medina home with her, leaving them free to talk undisturbed.

Cedric stacked the last of the chairs, while Mr. Winston and other brothers completed the clean up.

"You two go ahead and leave, we've got the rest,'' Mr. Winston said.

Iman hesitantly dragged on her coat. She wrapped Cedric's scarf around her head and waited while he pulled his coat on. She turned to face him. "Thank you for the picture. I didn't get to say it before. You didn't have to.''

He stood beside her, staring intently into her soul. He reached for her bags, speaking softly. "It was your Zawadi gift from me.''

They walked down the long hallway which led outside. "Want to take a ride,'' he asked.

Anticipation surged within her. Her mouth quirked. "Sure."

This time she paid attention when they entered interstate seventy-five heading to Tennessee.

"I have a lot to say to you." Cedric drummed his thumbs on the steering wheel nervously. "Iman, I'm sorry about Ada. I know how important she is to you and I never wanted to hurt you or her. It's just that, well, when you asked me to lower the price of the medicine, I took it as a personal attack. I know how irrational that sounds, but, I couldn't get past the thought that my family would suffer the way I had."

He looked at her briefly before returning his attention to the road. His voice was soft. "Dix has been my life for a long time. I got my start there, and it's provided a stable future for my family. A part of me didn't want to disturb what's gotten me where I am today."

Iman broke in. "I was being unreasonable. I had no right to challenge your livelihood. It's just that I don't want to lose Ada. And I took my fear out on you."

"You didn't, you opened my eyes. I love you for that. I realized lowering the prices isn't going to hurt anyone. In fact, so many people will benefit, maybe other pharmaceutical companies will do the same. Even if they don't, I know I did the right thing. However, there is a question about our future."

Cedric guided the car to the side of the road and stopped. He turned toward her.

"What about it?"

He took her hands in his. "I love you. And I hope you still love me enough to give us a chance. I want us to start a life, together."

"I want that too. Do you really love me?" she whispered.

He gathered her in his arms, and touched her softly with his lips. Happy butterflies danced in Iman's stomach.

"Very much. I want a future with you," he whispered, "forever," then nibbled her ear and neck.

"Forever?" She asked breathlessly. "As in today and the rest of our lives? As your . . ."

"As my wife. Do you have a problem with that?" His deep voice rumbled close to her ear.

"Not at all." Her heart soared. His kisses were tender as they moved against her lips, marking his territory, leaving unspoken promises.

Iman responded with all the love inside her. She caressed his face with her fingertips. "How much farther to Lookout Mountain, Tennessee?"

"Thirty minutes. Why?" Cedric took her hand, love radiating from him.

"Because I can't wait for us to start our future where we began our lives together."

Happy New Year, Baby

Lynn Emery

Chapter One

"And Merry Christmas to you," the sales lady said in a weary monotone. She pushed a large bag across the counter.

"I hear ya, girl." Shani nodded her head in sympathy.

The woman, with the name Loreen on a black plastic name tag pinned to her jacket, nodded back. "If I hafta listen to that darn 'Jingle Bell Rock' playin' much longer, they gone take me outta here screamin' like a banshee and ship me straight to the nearest psycho ward."

"Folks shoving and pushing, stepping on your feet to get at the last Ninja Ranger Possum. Or whatever the heck this thing is." Shani held up the overpriced action toy that every child had to have this year. "Not to mention I haven't gotten through half my list yet."

"Tell me 'bout it. I'll be glad when it's over, child." Loreen gave her a long-suffering smile before dropping a receipt in Shani's hand and turning to the next in a long line of customers.

Shani walked to the crowded parking lot. She stood trying to remember which row she'd parked on. After wandering around for ten minutes, she stumbled upon her car. Just getting through traffic away from the shopping mall proved to be an ordeal. By the time she got to her condo, merry did not even come close to describing her mood. All she wanted was to slip into her favorite oversized T-shirt, curl up in the recliner in front of the television, and numb out watching a bad movie. Just as the whistle blew signaling the water for her sugar-free, low-fat hot chocolate had reached the boiling point, the door bell chimed.

"Great." Shani stomped to her bedroom. She pulled on a pair of sweat pants. The triple chime sounded again. "Don't push your luck!" she yelled.

"What kinda greeting is that? What a frown!" Terrilyn bounced in with an armload of packages. "You look like a combination of Scrooge and the Grinch that Stole Christmas."

"I had one lousy day. First—"

"As your best friend I must tell you, leave all that negativity behind. Take a deep breath and say, 'It's over and I can move on and up.' Come on now." Terrilyn put down everything she held and stood in front of Shani. "It's over and . . ." She waved her hands like a conductor.

"And as your best friend I must tell you that you're really getting on my last nerve." Shani spun around and headed back to her kitchen. "Hot chocolate?"

"Honey, you could deal with the holiday blues if you gave Dr. Falsum's techniques a chance."

"Terrilyn, don't start with me today." Shani held up a palm.

"I know it's tough getting over a relationship that lasted five years. Especially during this time of the year." Terrilyn shrugged.

"A year ago I was on top of the world. Then it rolled over me like an eighteen-wheeler. But I'm over it. And I didn't need Dr. False either." Shani put the black lacquer tray bearing two mugs on the coffee table.

"That's Dr. Falsum. Okay then, you're fine. Right?"

"Right."

"So what are you wearing?" Terrilyn took a sip from her mug. She looked down her nose at Shani with an air of expectation.

"Wearing where?"

"To the Ladies of Distinction Annual New Year's Eve Ball, that's where. Last year you had a good reason to stay home."

Shani sat back remembering that bleak night. Nothing tasted, smelled, or looked good to her at that time. Efforts by her friends and relatives to lift her spirits only seemed to send her deeper into depression. Her self-esteem had taken a nose dive. For years her sense of worth and attractiveness as a woman had depended on one man. And that one man had rejected her. Terrilyn, as usual, was the one person who said and did the right things. Maybe that's why they had been best friends since high school. Terrilyn let her vent without offering opinions. She allowed Shani to spend the first half of the night talking through her anguish. By midnight, they were sitting on Terrilyn's living room floor, on their second bottle of champagne and howling with laughter about some of the things she most disliked about Robert.

"I know it's been said, but thank you for carrying me through that awful night. You were there for me." Shani gave Terrilyn's hand a squeeze.

"Always, girlfriend." Terrilyn squeezed her hand back. "Now don't change the subject. Today is December ninth, you have less than a month to decide what fabulous outfit you're going to wear. So when are we going shopping?"

Shani took a deep breath. "I can't face that, Terrilyn. Robert is sure to be there with Claudia. No, I just can't." She stared down.

"Facing those two is one way to finally close the door on what happened. This is what you do: Get one hot dress, something in black or maybe red. Add one tall, good–looking man, and toss in some new attitude. Strut your stuff on in that place, and what have you got? A recipe for a good time, sugar.''

"That's not my style, Terrilyn. I'll settle for a quiet celebration at the Blue Circle Social Club banquet and dance. Mrs. Chauvin invited me again this year.''

"Girl pu-leeze! Ain't nobody in that club under the age of sixty. Most of the single men can't dance anymore. Shucks, most of 'em need help walking.'' Terrilyn wrinkled her nose.

Shani shook a finger at her. "You dated Jesse Fairchild for almost a year. He's a member and not that much older than us. Shame on you.''

"Okay, okay. That wasn't very nice of me. But we split up because that twenty-year difference was too much. We're not even in our thirties yet . . .''

Shani raised an eyebrow. "Only two years away, babe.''

Terrilyn grimaced. "Don't say it out loud. But like I was saying, we finally couldn't agree on anything.''

"I'm going to show my gratitude to people who've been a great help to the community center, not to find a husband.''

"But New Year's Eve is for celebrating a new day. A new beginning. To party until you drop.'' Terrilyn jumped up and begin to move in time to music coming from the radio. "Ooo-wee, let's par-tee!''

"Sit your butt down, girl.'' Shani laughed in spite of herself.

"The best way to ring in the new year is with a blast. Think about.'' Terrilyn did a fancy step as the music ended. "Move on and up, like I said.''

"Seriously, one thing you said is true. I'm not going to wallow in self-pity. Instead of acting like the whole world revolves around me and my troubles, I'm going to focus on others. Dozens of people walk through the doors of Mid-City Community Development every day who are a lot worse off than I am." Shani got up to put away the now empty mugs.

Shani's thoughts turned to My'iesha Campbell. That young woman had seen more in her twenty years than most see in a lifetime. Yet she and Shani had connected more than the other drug program participants. The fact that she had dropped out of sight filled Shani with dread. Terrilyn's voice cut through her morbid musing.

"Not work. Oh come on, Shani. You've been spending all your time down at the center as it is. Take time off at least for the holidays."

"Being executive director is not a nine-to-five thing, Terrilyn. We grew up in that part of town. You know how bad it was twenty years ago. Now that crack and cocaine have hit the streets, it's a war zone. There are just so many needs." Shani frowned.

Terrilyn gave a shake of her shoulders. "Yeah, you can't turn on the news without seeing bodies being carried away on stretchers. Horrible."

"Speaking of which, Mr. Carrington said there was going to be a story that might involve Mid-City. You know our board president, he keeps up with everything. It's time for the five o'clock news now." She turned off the radio with the remote and turned on the television.

"Got some of those cup cakes with the cherry-flavored frosting in the middle?" Terrilyn wandered into the kitchen and opened a cabinet.

"No. You got me hooked on those things and I gained five pounds in one week. Took me three months to lose it. You've got the metabolism of a hummingbird. How you stay a size eight is a mystery to me." Shani called out.

"Got it from my mama. That woman had six kids, ate whatever she wanted, and only just started wearing a size twelve. Daddy still can't keep his hands off her. Honey, it's shocking how those old folks behave—"

"Shh, this must be it." Shani turned up the volume.

"The Joint Health and Welfare Committee of the legislature has begun hearings on the looming budget shortfall estimated by the Legislative Fiscal Office as over 359 million dollars. It is expected that there will be significant changes in the next session. The elections last month resulted in a record number conservatives sweeping into office, defeating some career politicians. One of the most vocal is Eric Aucoin, the first black conservative to hold office in the Louisiana Senate since reconstruction.''

"Look at that." Terrilyn chewed on a cookie.

"Can you believe it?" Shani glared at the picture that flashed. A row of legislators stood looking earnest for the cameras.

"Yeah, girl. He's got it goin' on. My man is wearing the hell out of that custom-made suit. Umph, umph, umph." Terrilyn snapped her fingers.

"What? Who are you talking about?"

"That fine brother they just showed."

Shani wrinkled her nose. "I didn't see anything fine in that picture. Just a bunch of insensitive jerks."

"How could you miss Eric Aucoin? Every single woman in Baton Rouge has the hots for the brother." Terrilyn giggled.

"Take a cold shower. That *brother*, and I use the term loosely, is selling us out. He thinks programs like the ones we have at Mid-City are a waste of the taxpayers money." Shani snorted in disgust. She made a point of not looking back at the picture. "I've read about him. He's the token black conservative."

"The committee will meet tomorrow to consider those programs and agency budgets that will be reduced." The news anchor, a thin man with iron gray hair, went on to another news item.

Shani turned the sound back down. "Well I'll be there for sure to give them all a few facts about how much money we save the taxpayers. For every kid we keep out of juvenile court or a kiddie jail with our Teach One, Reach One program, we save the taxpayers over forty thousand dollars.

For every addict that stays off drugs by attending our Cocaine Anonymous group we save—"

"Calm down. You better save that intensity for those committee members. But listen, you know how I feel about the center. If I have to, I'll spend night and day with that mean old Senator Aucoin trying to convince him not to cut those programs." Terrilyn wore a leer.

"How kind of you." Shani folded her arms and stared at her.

"Hey, any sacrifice for you my friend. Now all we have to do is get his home address and phone number . . ."

"Terrilyn, this is serious."

"You don't think I'm serious about a man with his body? Did you see his chest? Whew!" Terrilyn pretended to fan herself.

"Talk about superficial. It's what's in here that counts." Shani patted her chest. "Obviously he's got no heart for the very people who need help the most."

"Well, maybe you're jumping to conclusions. All I'm saying is I'd be willing to let the man explain himself. Over dinner preferably." Terrilyn grinned.

"Oh he'll explain himself when I get through with him. The committee meets at two in the afternoon. I'll have time to get some work done, attend a staff meeting at nine o'clock, and have a quick lunch." Shani wore a wicked half smile. "I've got his budget cuts all right."

The wide hall outside the committee rooms in the basement of the state capitol was jam-packed with people. Shani nodded to several social workers she knew. A perfect swirl of red hair stood out above several dozen heads. Shani wove her way through the mob toward that hairstyle. Soon she heard the distinctive laugh that confirmed the identity of the owner. Paulette Gauthier was considered one of the best substance abuse counselors in the state. She was one of two contract group therapists employed by Mid-City for their drug treatment program.

"Hello, Paulette." Shani gave her a peck on the cheek.

"Hey now. Here comes the cavalry." Paulette put an arm around Shani's shoulders and pulled her close. "Shani, this is Susan Taylor and Joanne Lanier. They work with me at Save Our Streets."

"Hello. Well, what do you think?" Shani nodded toward a knot of men dressed in suits. "The Select Committee on Responsibility sent their big guns. They must be jumping for joy now that most of the candidates they endorsed have been elected."

"A bunch of men and women born with all the advantages who think they're morally superior to poor people." Paulette stopped smiling. "Look at Ed Parmalee grinning like a cheshire cat. He's the ring leader, though he keeps a low profile."

"Who are they exactly?" Susan gazed at the distinguished man with a receding hairline and expensive suit.

"According to them they're just a group of concerned private citizens who want good government. They organized three years ago," Shani said. "Ed Parmalee helped them raise over 600,000 dollars from corporate sponsors to pay a consulting firm to study state government. The report just came out two months ago."

"Talk about sending shock waves," Paulette broke in. "They made dozens of recommendations that include major cuts in staff and funding, especially at the Department of Health and Hospitals. Surprise, surprise."

"Staunch conservatives who think government has gotten way too big. They've been pushing for some of these changes for years. Ed Parmalee has been made it his personal crusade," Shani added.

"And now they've put their money to work with ads on television outlining why their recommendation should be implemented." Joanne took up the explanation.

"Yeah, and put up money to back their candidates."

Paulette shook her head. "With the latest round of scandals involving legislators and top state agency officials, the voters listened."

"We're voters, too. So are the people who live in Easy Town and the Bottoms. They're hard working men and women who are due representation just like the folks who live in Sutton Place Estates." Shani spoke with fervor.

"Power to the people!" Paulette grinned at her. "Didn't I say the cavalry was here? Shani Moore, you go girl. We're going to make sure you get a chance to speak."

"You both should speak." Susan glanced around and got affirmative nods from the crowd around them.

Shani swallowed hard. She did not want the ponderous responsibility of being a spokesperson. "I, uh, just came to say a few words about programs at Mid-City they want to cut . . ."

"Don't be modest. What you have to say applies to us, all of us." Paulette swept a hand around indicating the others. "Save Our Streets has been working to take back poor neighborhoods in south Baton Rouge from the crack dealers and gangs. Grants we've gotten to give kids an alternative are on the line. This is life and death, literally."

"I know." Shani glanced toward the committee room where decisions that could change lives would take place.

"Look, they're opening the doors." Joanne gestured to the Senate aides who had pulled open the double doors.

"I'll meet you in there." Shani did not follow the press of those trying to get in. "Be right back."

The thought of facing such a multitude hit her now that it was only minutes away. She had a strong urge to check her hair and the fit of her clothes. Going in the opposite direction of everyone was like swimming against a strong tide. When someone bumped into her, she dropped her portfolio. White sheets with her notes showered to the floor spilling around the hall.

"Excuse me," Shani said dodging another woman at the last minute. "Great, just great," she muttered as she bent to retrieve the papers from under several large feet. Without warning she ran headlong into a large object.

Seeing the charcoal gray fabric of a suit, she stepped back. Her nose was only an inch from a broad chest. "Excuse me."

"Here, let me help," a rich baritone voice said. "These must be yours, too."

He turned his back to her. In two long strides, he went several feet away to retrieve three sheets she had missed. Shani blinked at the muscular arms that reached down to pick them up. His shoulders rippled beneath the fine fabric. Brown hair in soft waves covered the back of his head and curled over the collar of the dove gray shirt. She drew a sharp breath when he faced her wearing a dazzling smile. Handsome did not begin to describe the chiseled features of his face. The word exquisite floated into her mind even as she examined the full lips and hazel eyes framed by dark eyebrows. But there was something familiar about him. *No, I'd remember having met him before.* Shani realized with a start that he stood holding out the papers to her, waiting patiently.

"Thank you." She forced her gaze away from him in an effort to collect herself. "Everything goes wrong when you're in a hurry."

"Happens to me, too. I was late getting out of a meeting to get here; took me ten minutes to find my car keys. And they were sitting on my desk the whole time I searched the floor and every inch of the rest of my office." He laughed. "Are you—"

"Senator Raymond is ready, sir." A young man spoke to him in a respectful tone.

"Thank you, Carl." He lingered looking at the floor then at her. "Got everything? I . . ." A voice began talking into a microphone. "Excuse me."

He seemed apologetic about the need to rush off. Shani felt a sudden gap in the atmosphere when he walked away, as though the wonderful fresh air surrounding him was sucked away with his leaving. She followed him feeling somewhat dazed by their encounter. A strong urge to be near him pulled at her like a magnetic force. This man she had never met before seemed not only familiar, but someone she knew intimately. With a strange certainty, Shani had a sense that they would like the same music, movies and be able to talk for hours with no awkward silences. *Get it together, girl.* Seeing Paulette waving her over to an empty seat, she sat down.

"Ready?" Paulette spoke into her ear.

Shani could only nod. She scanned the audience looking for the man who had shaken her tenuous composure. Craning her neck, she looked for the gray suit among the assembly of representatives from community action agencies. There were many familiar faces, but the newcomer was not among them.

"Did you see the tall man in a gray suit? Which agency does he work for?" Shani tried to make herself heard over the buzz around them.

Paulette leaned closer. "What? I couldn't hear you."

"Good afternoon ladies and gentleman. This is the Joint Health and Welfare Committee. I'm Senator Harold T. Raymond of Sunset, chairman of this committee. We will be hearing testimony regarding items included in the budget for the Department of Health and Hospitals. Specifically, those funded with block grants and Medicaid funds. We have cards with the names of those who wish to present information. If you wish to do so, please complete a card. Each speaker is limited to three minutes."

The chairman continued for several minutes laying out the rules. Shani did not pay attention to him as she was still looking on either side behind her. Convinced she would have to wait until later to complete her search, she faced forward in time to hear the other legislators sitting around the dais introduce themselves.

"Senator Eric Aucoin, district eighteen."

"Oh my!" Shani groaned. Her mouth dropped open.

Paulette touched her arm and frowned at her with concern. "You all right, babe?"

"No, yes." Shani shut her eyes. "Just my luck," She ground her teeth in frustration and anger at herself.

"Huh?" Paulette's arched eyebrows came together in a puzzled expression.

"Nothing. Forget it."

Shani pushed away the warm thoughts of him. Her own harsh words to Terrilyn came back to her. She, too, would do well to look beyond the attractive packaging and remember the threat this man posed to programs vital to poor communities.

The hearings began with Ruth Frazier, the Secretary of the Department of Health and Hospitals, giving a detailed description of the agency's budget. This was followed by fifteen minutes of sharp questioning by the senators. It became clear which senators were sympathetic to social programs and which were skeptical of their usefulness. Shani became angrier by the minute as Senator Aucoin criticized program after program as having shown rapid growth with no evidence that they were effective in reducing the problems they were designed to address.

"With all due respect, Madame Secretary, these programs have shown an average increase of eighty-five percent in the last four years. Yet we've all read in the newspapers that control and regulation of them have been severely lacking." Eric held up copies of the Baton Rouge *Advocate* and the New Orleans Times *Picayune*. "Furthermore, even you have admitted that those most in need are not getting the services." Gone was the radiant smile that had so captivated Shani only a short time ago. He wore a serious, searching expression as he waited for a reply.

Though it was only about twenty minutes, the grilling of Secretary Frazier seemed to go on for ever. At last the microphone was free for comments from others. Paulette's name was called.

"Senator Aucoin is one tough nut." Paulette pursed her lips. "I'm going to pass. You go." She nudged Shani.

"Hey, wait a—" Shani began.

"Ms. Paulette Gauthier." Senator Raymond called her name a second time.

Paulette stood up. "Ms. Moore will speak next, sir. You should have her card behind mine." She clapped her hands causing a smattering of applause to increase until everyone in the audience joined in.

"Oh my," Shani mumbled.

Now she would have to give up the protective cover of the crowd. Worst yet, she must face Eric Aucoin, an opponent she had drooled over like an over heated moron. She walked to the table dreading each step. She looked up from her notes to find him staring at her with a slight smile. Humiliation and anger flooded her. Shani sat up straight and fixed him with what she hoped was a cold blank expression.

"Good afternoon, gentlemen. My name is Shani Moore and I'm the executive director of Mid-City Community Development, Incorporated. We're a private nonprofit social service agency that operates a range of programs that address needs of the very young to the very old. For example, we have health screening for at-risk infants and home delivery of meals to the elderly. Certainly we acknowledge that mistakes have been made in the implementation of programs. We providers deplore the lack of controls that results in funds being wasted since it means less for those truly in need. But we will not stand by while those who have a conservative agenda use this as an opportunity to plunder agencies that have kept blighted, abandoned neighborhoods from complete despair."

Shani looked at each of the senators in turn. She stared at Eric whose smile began a slow fade.

"Those who should, better than anyone, remember the barriers they faced now suffer amnesia. Certainly as you wield power and enjoy your success, keep in mind that you have left others who still struggle against tremendous odds." Shani pushed back the chair to stand.

"Ms. Moore," Eric said into the microphone in a voice strained with controlled indignation. "Do you have proof that your programs result in measurable positive change in the neighborhoods you serve?" He went on before she could answer. "It seems the only answer given by those who favor such programs is to promise results if more money is given. And the result is to foster dependence on welfare rather than use it as a springboard of opportunity to be self-supporting."

"Senator, it's simplistic to look at such a complex issue as the poverty rate and lay all the blame on the welfare system. Economic and social changes have led to displacement of large segments of the workforce. Not to mention inequities in education and employment opportunities that have existed for generations." Shani spoke in a measured tone yet her dark brown eyes flashed with anger.

Eric shook his head slowly. "It's time for us to take responsibility for ourselves and not behave as victims. What we need is to spend less time wringing our hands about life being unfair and more time working."

His words brought a smattering of applause from the audience and nods from most of the legislators on the committee.

"That's what our agency does, Senator Aucoin. But to ignore the causes of a problem makes no more sense than for a doctor to ignore the origins of a terrible illness. No treatment can be effective without at least an understanding of the forces that work against a cure." Shani's voice rose with force. Loud clapping and voices of assent burst forth. "Most of you oppose our programs without having visited the communities we serve. I challenge you to look into the faces of those whose lives you will change so drastically." She got up and strode back to her seat beside Paulette.

For the rest of the comments she sat stone faced. There

was testimony from others who advocated cutting funding for many programs. Many echoed the words of Senator Aucoin. Shani fumed at the man she saw as the worst kind of traitor. The man had no compassion. She glanced up to find him watching her. A tingle went through her body as she gazed into those arresting eyes. With effort, she looked away. Not again. She was not going to repeat falling for the wrong man. And he was more than the wrong man, they had nothing in common. He was the antithesis of everything she looked for in a man. Not that she was looking. *Of course I'm not looking. Now forget it. Stop thinking of that.* Shani clenched her teeth with determination to focus on her work and saving the center.

After the hearing was over, she stood in the hallway being congratulated by her colleagues.

"Perfect aim. You hit him right between the eyes with a nice mixture of facts and emotion. I hope the news cameras got that expression on Senator Aucoin face when you started talking. Oo-wee, he was steaming." Paulette chuckled.

"Yes, you were fantastic in there." Joanne nodded.

"As long as they can demonize the poor, their consciences are eased. They give welfare to the rich claiming it trickles down," Shani said. Murmurs of support and agreement fortified her.

As she continued to talk with her friends, Shani pushed away thoughts of his eyes and lips. She welcomed the return of her wrath. How could she feel anything but repulsion for the man? All of the work done for years by dedicated men and women would be undone with one stroke if he had his way. Senator Aucoin was the enemy. And that was that. Shani's small sigh of relief was cut short when a rich voice brought back that tingle. This time it shot up her spine when he spoke right over her shoulder.

"Ms. Moore, I accept your challenge. How's Thursday?"

Shani turned around to find those eyes and lips only inches away. For a heart beat the nearness of him mesmerized her. The tall, muscular frame filled her vision. She felt a wild urge to take his hand. Paulette's voice brought her back to the present.

"Senator Aucoin, I'm . . . we'll be happy to meet with you then. Right, Ms. Moore?" Paulette shook Shani's arm.

"What?" Shani blinked at her.

"Senator Aucoin would like to visit the center next Thursday. You have your planner right here. Our meeting with the city Human Services staff was rescheduled. I think you're free." Paulette raised an eyebrow at her.

Shani fumbled with the leather planner, flipping to the daily calendar after several seconds of searching. "Uh, yes. I don't have anything in the morning."

"Good. Ten o'clock?" Eric stood looking down at her. He wore a "put up or shut up" expression.

Shani nodded. "Yes. That's fine."

"Then I'll see you Thursday. Goodbye." He held out his hand.

"Goodbye." Shani steeled herself not to react, at least visibly, before shaking his hand. It did not help to feel the smooth flesh. She assumed the most grim, cool look she could muster.

Eric strode off followed by several other young African-American men. His shoulders moved above most other men through the crowd.

"Well, I thought we were going to need smelling salts for a minute back there," Paulette whispered into her ear.

"What do you mean?" Shani brushed the front of her suit and looked away as they walked outside ahead of the Joanne and Susan.

"Honey, don't even try it. I've known you for a long time. That good-looking man reached out and touched you with those gorgeous eyes. And in more places than just your heart." Paulette laughed deep in her throat.

"He touched me all right. Here." Shani pointed to her stomach. "I'm still nauseous from exposure to his arrogant, insensitive views."

Paulette held her back. "Y'all go on; we'll catch up," she said to the other two women then faced Shani with a knowing squint. "There was real heat bouncing between you two. Senator Aucoin was checking you out, baby. And he liked what he saw."

"Oh, please. He was fired up all right. Ready to burn my butt and Mid-City." Shani waved a dismissal of her words. She walked off afraid Paulette would see the excitement her words had caused. So, he was attracted to her, too. Interesting.

"Listen to the voice of experience. The passion of opposing opinions, the clash of two strong wills is a potent aphrodisiac. Just don't get swept away."

Shani stopped walking and looked at her friend with a defiant smile. "Eric Aucoin is a legend in his own mind as far as I'm concerned. Don't worry. I won't be used ever again. Not by him or anyone else."

Paulette had scored a direct hit on a sore spot. The hurt Robert had caused her came back with a vengeance. Shani wanted to make it clear that Eric did not have her so enthralled that she could not think straight. But was she trying to convince Paulette or herself?

"Whoa! Excuse me." Paulette eyed her. "Guess I was wrong." She looked skeptical still.

"Yes, you are. And next Thursday will be a day Senator Aucoin won't forget for a very long time. We're going to hit him hard where it hurts. He'll be dizzy for weeks when I'm through with him." Shani smiled with wicked glee as a plan formed.

Chapter Two

Eric stared out the window of his office at the yellow, red, and brown leaves trembling in the chill wind. One hand rested on the pile of papers on his desk. Since arriving in at eight o'clock that morning, he had struggled to concentrate. Somehow it was difficult to make sense of the facts and figures. The rough draft of a bill he planned to submit to the Senate was far from complete. One bill in particular caused his mind to wander. It would result in deep cuts to a grant program that funded community agencies in poor urban areas of the state. The words brought back a vivid image of a beautiful face with dark brown eyes flashing with outrage. Eric was confused by his reaction to her. Based on their encounter, he should want to steer clear of the woman. Yet he kept thinking about her. At odd moments for the past two days she came to mind. Never had he let what anyone thought bother him. He was used to being lambasted by other African-Americans for his conservative view of such issues as the welfare system and affirmative action. Yet her accusation that he did not care about his own community chafed like a piece of sandpaper on a now raw conscience. It disturbed him that she had such a low opinion of his motives. But why? Having dated some of the most attractive, talented women in the state, Eric was peeved that this one female could set off doubts about his positions. Doubts that had never surfaced before.

"Knock, knock." Dalton Aucoin, tall with iron gray hair, strode into the office. He sat down in a large red leather chair opposite Eric's desk. "How are you, son?"

"Fine, Dad. What are you up to this morning?" Eric shifted the stack of files a little to the side. He hoped his perceptive father would not pick up on his pensive, ambivalent mood.

Dalton Aucoin owed his success in the construction business to his skill at putting up sturdy and attractive buildings at a reasonable cost. But his reputation for refusing to sacrifice quality was legendary. At fifty-six, he had achieved the success his father had always wanted. Dalton liked to tell how he fought his way to the top in spite of being born into a poor family of fifteen children. And as he told his children, he let no one tell him what he could or could not be.

"I had to light a fire under that Tellwood crew. Subcontractors can be a real problem. Before I got so big, Landmark Construction did it all, you know. Oh well, the price of success." His father leaned forward to pluck a several sheets from the pile. He peered at them for several minutes. "See you've made solid progress. Good start, son."

"Yes, I'm still studying some of the research done by the party consultants."

"Any surprises? We know most of the programs are top heavy with high-paid paper pushers. Those folks are more interested in getting plum jobs for their relatives than helping the poor." Dalton snorted with disgust.

"Not all of them, Dad. A few could get rid of administrative layers that are clearly unnecessary. And some have questionable management of funds." Eric thumbed through a report that summarized data on twelve of the largest agencies.

Dalton stabbed the air with a forefinger. "What we need is a better business atmosphere. Lift all these regulations so businesses can operate more efficiently. Profits will go up, jobs will be created, and we can put people to work. Handouts only keep a man down."

"But we do have to have a safety net for some."

"I don't argue with that. There are elderly and disabled folks who need support. But things have gotten way out of hand with all these give away welfare type deals." Dalton stood and glanced at his gold wrist watch. "I know you'll do the right thing. I'm off to a meeting with the mayor on that urban renewal project."

Dalton waved goodbye without looking back. He hurried off though he would probably be the first to arrive. He was also famous for being punctual.

"Bye, Dad." Eric sighed with relief that Dalton had a lot on his mind this morning. But he could not relax just yet. His friend Chris exchanged a brief conversation with Dalton in the hall then headed for his office.

"What's up, dude?" Chris sauntered in. He was dressed in the latest, casual designer clothes. He draped one leg over the chair Dalton just vacated. Chris had his own telecommunications company. Tel-Com, Inc.'s offices were on the same floor on the opposite side.

"Nothing much." Eric grunted and tapped the folders. "A little light reading."

"Better you than me." Chris wrinkled his nose. "Give me a set of blueprints any day over that."

"Come on. I've seen you handle the most complex government manuals. You could whip through this stuff in no time." Eric took up his familiar theme of trying to convince Chris to run for office.

"No thanks. I'll leave the job of steering the ship of state in your able hands. You've got ideas on how to turn this state around."

"Depends on who you talk to." Eric muttered.

"Yeah, I saw a news clip from the other day. Some lady." Chris laughed.

"Yes indeed," Eric said.

"She sure knew her stuff. Not the impractical do-gooder you were expecting." Chris watched Eric closely. "What's her name?"

"Shani Moore. Eric gazed out the window again. "She works for that big community service agency in Easy Town."

"Lovely name. Shani means 'marvelous' in Swahili. In Kiswhahili it translates as 'an adventure.'" Chris rubbed his chin with a thoughtful expression.

"Really?"

Eric felt a pleasant flush. He thought of the curve of her full lips when she smiled up at him. The perfume she wore was spicy and sweet at the same time. Or was that the natural scent of her skin. It would be nice to get close enough to ... *What's the matter with me?* Eric shook his head as though to clear it. With a start, he noticed Chris examining him. He frowned and looked at the papers again.

"Ms. Moore has some misguided ideas about what the black community needs. Liberal policies of the past got us into this mess. African-Americans don't need handouts, they need opportunity." Eric spoke in a gruff voice.

"Got to you, huh?"

"Nonsense," Eric said with too much force.

"She is one fine babe." Chris goaded him. "Silky, smooth skin the color of cinnamon. All the right curves in all the right places. Yep, she's got it goin' on."

"She did not 'get to me' as you put it," Eric snapped. "The woman has a mouth on her that won't quit. She all but called me an Uncle Tom." He slammed down a heavy manual, which caused several sheets of paper to fly off his desk.

"Got under your skin for sure." Chris picked up the papers.

"You damn right she did. Any black person who doesn't spout the traditional liberal pap, who shows some sense of being able to think on his own, has to defend his racial credentials. It's preposterous." Eric's jaw muscles clenched. This was infuriating. The woman had him daydreaming about holding her close in one instant and enraging him in the next.

"And you're going to tell her so next week, right?"

"How do you know about that?"

"Trumaine told me. He says you've got a deadline to get proposed bills in so the party can move early in the session."

Eric ran his fingers through his hair. "Which is why I've been working twelve-hour days for over a week now. Trumaine is getting more notes from the lawyers now."

"Senator Raymond breathing down your neck to take a strong stand, eh?"

"He wants to get the wheels turning fast. He's long been vocal about the waste in the budget." Eric thought of the veteran politician who at long last saw his party rise to power on the national and state level. Senator Raymond and other conservatives were impatient to proceed with their brand of reforms.

"This complication won't help then." Chris lifted his hands.

"Complication? What complication?"

"Falling for the opposition. Those guys don't impress me as the kind who would understand that sort of thing. You know, sleeping with the enemy." Chris studied his fingernails.

Eric's mouth flew open. "What ... No way." He arranged his expression to be one of relaxed disdain. "Sure she's attractive. But ..." He let the sentence hang, implying he was more than capable of dealing with the wiles of pretty women.

"So the only reason you made a point to arrange another meeting is to set her straight." Chris raised both eyebrows in a skeptical expression that spoke volumes.

"I'm going to lay some hard facts on Ms. Moore that she'll find hard to refute." Eric dug a folder from underneath the others. "When I'm done, she's going to eat her words. When I'm through, she's going to be agreeing with me." He smiled with confidence.

"Smart move. Then getting next to her will be a snap. Still, I've never seen you respond with such . . . intensity to any woman before now. Ms. Moore is something special."

"Forget it, man. If I was ready to get serious with anyone, and I'm not, it would be someone who shares my values." Eric waved away his suggestion. "My only focus is to make sure we have a reasonable budget and show social workers like Ms. Moore that the old way of tackling social ills does not work. Next Thursday will be a real education for her."

"If you say so." Chris gave an amused grunt before leaving. "Have a good time."

Eric searched for a smart comeback, but could think of nothing to say.

"Aunt Shani, look what I made for you." Colin held up a large red Christmas stocking with her name written in gold glitter on it. "It's for hanging on the mantle." His small upturned face searched hers for approval.

Shani wanted to squeeze him tight, but knew better. Now that he was a grown-up ten-year-old, he resisted such gross displays of affection. She was surprised at the tears that threatened to spill down her face. His gift touched her heart.

"I love it, sweetie."

"I made Mama and Daddy and Kara one, too." Colin held up the other stockings.

"Magnificent. Can old auntie give you a tiny kiss?" She could not resist at least one surrender to sentiment.

Colin grinned with satisfaction at pleasing her. He offered his smooth little face before darting off to play again.

Shani sighed as she watched him. She sat in her older brother's spacious den waiting for her sister-in-law to return with their coffee. The radio played jazzy holiday tunes. Shani mused at how much Colin resembled her youngest brother J.J. at that age. A brief spasm of pain touched her chest at the thought of J.J. sitting in prison on Christmas day.

J.J. was serving a ten-year sentence for selling cocaine. Shani and Brendon long ago adopted an attitude of tough love toward him. He was only two years old when their father died and had no clear memory of him. And he was only fourteen when their mother succumbed to breast cancer. J.J. had always been the wild rule breaker of the family. Sadly, he graduated from mischief as a young boy to breaking the law as a teenager. Now at twenty-one, he all ready had a long criminal record. For years Shani spent lots of time and money getting him out of trouble. Brendon finally convinced her that she was enabling J.J. to continue his self-destructive lifestyle.

Shani gazed at the family photo displayed on the bookcase. Brendon seemed solemn despite the slight smile on his attractive dark brown face. While the grief at losing both their parents so soon had caused J.J. to strike out at the world through law breaking and Shani to fight for those in need, Brendon found solace in his career as a computer analyst. He also worked very hard at making a warm, loving family.

"Hello, sis." Brendon patted her shoulder.

Shani blinked in surprise at his presence. So lost in thought, she had not heard him enter the house. "Hi."

"What are you thinking about so hard? All those gifts you got for your wonderful older brother, I hope." Brendon began to sort through a stack of mail.

"You wish," Shani shot back.

"Here we are." Janine swept in. Tall, she still moved with the grace of a model even though she had been a full-time mother since the birth of Kara four years ago. "Hi, baby." She kissed Brendon after putting the tray down on the end table near Shani.

"Hmm, thanks." Brendon took a cup of steaming coffee. "The perfect wife. Greets her husband with a treat when he gets home from a hard day."

"It's the least I can do since you're taking us out to dinner." Janine flashed her famous dazzling smile at him.

"I am?" Brendon laughed.

"I spent all day wrestling with your little dynamo of a daughter while shopping. Thank goodness she's still napping. She wore herself out. Anyway, I got the art supplies J.J. wants. It will be a wonderful surprise for him when he opens his gift."

Brendon's mouth turned down at the mention of J.J. "All his talent and what does he do with his life? Nothing. Worse than nothing."

"Brendon, please." Janine glanced at Shani with a look of helplessness. "J.J. says he wants to turn his life around."

"Sure he does. Now that he's serving hard time." Brendon shook his head.

Shani could see through Brendon's anger to the real pain at losing his brother to the streets. "You did all you could, Brendon. We both did. We were barely out of our teens and still dealing with Mama's death."

"But J.J. has to take responsibility for his choices, too," Brendon said.

"I agree. Still, we could have used something like the 'Lean On Me' mentor program operated by Mid-City." Shani grimaced. "Which is why I intend to fight any cuts to our agency and others like it."

"Let me know if I can help. I'll write letters, send faxes and e-mail those jokers to let them know we won't take it lying down." Janine nodded.

"Thanks, you're a real pearl. Well, I better get going. I

have an early day tomorrow and Saturday I'm going to visit J.J.''

"Good, you can take our gifts to him." Brendon pressed his lips together and began to open his mail.

"What! You've got to go see him. J.J. will be so hurt if you don't." Shani stood in front of him with her feet apart, hands on both hips.

"Shani, I don't want another Christmas tainted by having to visit a prison. J.J. was in jail this time last year and I bailed him out."

"You're right but—"

"The year before he showed up at my house with a lot of expensive gifts and some hooker on his arm, in front of my children. Expensive gifts bought with blood money. No, my family will have a normal Christmas this year." Brendon's jaw was set in the way that indicated he would not be convinced to alter his decision.

"But Brendon please . . ." Shani felt the urge to cry return, this time for a very different reason.

"That's final, Shani."

Driving home, Shani tried to be furious with her older brother and failed. The truth was she could not blame him. Brendon had spent more than one holiday traversing the criminal justice system on J.J.'s behalf. Feeling tired and dispirited, Shani put on her pajamas first thing when she got home. She spent the rest of the evening staring at the television. It was midnight before she knew it. Lying in bed for hours, she went over in her head how to tell J.J. Brendon would not visit him.

"So you see, we have no choice. Sources tell me Senator Raymond has the votes to push his plan through the legislature." Harold Carrington IV, president of Mid-City's Board of Directors patted his gray mustache with the linen napkin.

The dignified architect sat across from Shani in his favor-

ite restaurant overlooking the Mississippi river in downtown Baton Rouge. He picked at a large shrimp and
crabmeat salad while breaking the bad news that several
programs would be scaled back July first, the beginning
of the fiscal year.

"I don't think we need to make such definite moves yet,
sir. We had a lot of support down at the hearing." Shani
had pleaded for the better part of an hour. Her lunch, a
bowl of chicken gumbo, sat untouched.

"I'm sorry, but we have to be realistic. Walter and I have
feelers out to get some limited corporate funding, but for
very different kinds of projects. Batton Chemical prefers
less . . . controversial things such as planting flower gardens
to beautify streets and parks. Projects I favored all along."
Carrington shook a finger at her.

"And as I've said all along, the problems of the Easy
Town are much bigger than cosmetic touches can help."

"When folks have a pleasant environment, they take
pride in themselves. It's been done in other cities with
great results."

Shani swallowed a lump of frustration. "But we need to
focus on more immediate problems first."

Carrington twisted his wrist to stare at his fancy watch.
"I have an appointment with some people from New
Orleans. I'm sorry to bring bad news and run. But really,
Ms. Moore, this may be a blessing in disguise."

"But can we meet later?" Shani tried to get a commitment for further discussion. The look on his face said it
would be fruitless.

"I suppose." He shrugged. "I'll get back to you. So
long." He left after giving the waiter his gold card to pay
for the lunch.

Shani sat alone, oblivious of the chatter of the full dining
room around her. Somehow she must make the board
members see that giving up was not the answer. She sat
brooding over this new menace when a familiar voice
jarred her back to her surroundings.

"Ms. Moore, how are you?" Eric Aucoin's posture, he was some two feet from her, seemed to be one of caution. Close enough to be cordial, yet far enough for a graceful exit if rebuffed.

Shani was too depressed for another confrontation. "Fine and you?" she said in a mechanical voice. Her face mirrored the distress churning inside.

"Fine." Eric cleared his throat. "May I join you? Of course, if you would prefer . . ." He backed up a few inches when her eyes went wide.

"Oh, no. Have a seat."

His request caught her completely off guard. Fortunately, her mother's etiquette lessons put her on automatic pilot. For several minutes they exchanged small talk about the food at Angelle's. Shani recommended he get the soup and salad special. She noticed how his hands, large with smooth skin, made the silverware look tiny. The delicate scent of Armani cologne floated toward her as he waved to the waitress for more iced tea. Eric looked at her and smiled. In an instant, her gloom lifted. Shani smiled back at him.

"So, here we are sharing lunch and you haven't tried to strangle me for being an insensitive traitor to the community." Eric watched her reaction closely.

Shani fingered the cloth napkin. "Yeah, well it's been a bad month. Look, some of the things I said the other day may have been . . ."

"Insulting? Over the line? Down, dirty, and personal?" Eric dark eyebrows went up. But his lips twitched with amusement.

"Okay, okay. It's just that the programs you're targeting can mean the difference between life and death for some." Shani leaned forward.

"Can you deny some of the abuses that have occurred? Look at that Project Neighborhood Uplift scandal. Hundreds of thousands of dollars unaccounted for. Huge salaries, so-called consultants paid exorbitant amounts to study the needs of the Banks area. Most of the consultants were Marvin Gravelle's relatives and friends.'' Eric's jaws tightened with outrage.

"I know. But—"

"And that's not an isolated case, Ms. Moore. There is a serious lack of accountability. This voter backlash can be traced right back to the actions of those of you in the human service profession.'' Eric drew in a deep breath. "I mean . . .''

"You're right.'' Shani put down her soup spoon.

"What?'' He blinked at her in amazement.

"I've seen darn good programs made useless by so-called leaders using them to pay back supporters. Those of us trying to get the money to folks who need it have been as mad as the voters. But what could we do?'' Shani tapped her fingers on the table. "They've got low friends in high places.''

Eric threw back his head. Rich deep laughter came out. "I love it. Ms. Moore, you're priceless.''

Shani felt a rush of pleasure at the approval in his clear eyes. How splendid to know she could make him laugh.

"Well, we want fiscal responsibility, too. But I'm sure your party members don't think so. And the work we do isn't valued at all I'm afraid.'' She tried to get back to the subject that divided them to counteract the rising desire inside.

"Talking to you has been a real eye-opener. It seems we share common ground after all.'' Eric leaned closer to her. "I'd like us to—"

"Senator, I made it after all.'' A tall thin young man bustled up to their table. "My goodness but Representative Brella can talk. A simple planning session with the other aides became a long lecture when he wandered in to the office. Oh, hello.'' He stopped short seeing Shani. His voice was cool.

Eric patted the younger man's arm. "Have a seat. Trumaine Delacrosse, this is Ms. Shani Moore.'' Eric turned to

Shani. "Trumaine is a political science major at Southern University. His father and mine were at Tuskegee together. Trumaine is my able assistant."

"Nice to meet you." Shani nodded at the wary young man.

"Uh, are you okay?" Trumaine gave Eric a long, meaningful look.

Shani chuckled. "Don't worry, I haven't hurt your boss."

"In fact, Ms. Moore and I actually agree in a few areas. Something neither of us anticipated. I certainly didn't." Eric gazed at her. Several seconds of silence hung between them. A trill of beeping broke it.

"That's me." Trumaine glanced at his pager.

"There's a phone up near the cash register, Trumaine. Go use it." Eric did not look away from Shani.

"But they could bring me a ph . . . Uh, right." Trumaine cleared his throat and stood. He pointed in the direction he was headed. "On my way."

"Wait for me there. I'll be out in a minute." Eric waved at him.

"Yes, sir. Nice meeting you, Ms. Moore." Trumaine wore a knowing grin as he glanced at Eric then at her.

"I really look forward to visiting your center, Ms. Moore." Eric fingered the long-handled teaspoon in front of him. "But you know, I'd really like to have more in-depth background information about the origin of Mid-City Community Development and its staff before I get there. It would make my tour more meaningful."

Shani steadied her breathing. *Don't be such a fool. This is all business. Isn't it?* "I'd be happy to provide whatever you need." She blushed. Shani prayed the possible double meaning of those words that sprang to her mind was not written all over her.

"Excellent. What about lunch on Tuesday? I know a little restaurant on Nicholson that's very quiet. Rick's would be perfect." Eric beamed at her.

Shani was impressed in spite of herself. Rick's was quiet

because the prices on its menu meant only a relatively small clientele patronized it. Though she had never been there, Shani knew it was a favorite among the politically powerful and wealthiest people in Baton Rouge.

Shani checked her planner. "I'm free."

"Then I'll see you then. Goodbye." Eric held her hand.

Shani felt a tingle at the contact of warmth that spread up her arm into her chest. "Bye." Her voice sounded weak. She cleared her throat. "Goodbye," she said in what she hoped was a stronger voice.

Eric walked away with that long-legged, graceful stride. Shani shook her head. She wondered where was her resolve to keep men at arm's length. Eric had chipped away at her wall of resistance. Who was she kidding? He'd blown it away like dynamite with his smile. Well, she would just have to be cautious. But even as she finished her lunch, Shani felt anticipation at seeing him again.

Thursday morning dawned bright with promise. Shani sprang out of bed humming to the tune that played on her alarm clock radio. As she went through her routine getting ready for the office, she remembered the lunch with Eric. How right he had been. After a few moments of feeling each other out, they talked for over two hours barely touching the food in front of them. To think, only last week they met for the first time and clashed in front of the entire city! What a difference a few days made. She sang along with the car radio on the drive to work.

"Hello everybody. Umm, that coffee smells good, Elaine." Shani swept past her secretary's desk brimming with cheer.

"Yeah." Elaine exchanged a puzzled glance with another clerical worker. She waved goodbye to her friend and followed Shani into her office. "Mr. Carrington called. You've got a call from Mrs. Lomax; to complain again no doubt. Will that woman ever get over not being elected chairperson of the Summer Youth Festival?"

"Well, we need to be patient with her. She's given a lot of time to the center. Mrs. Lomax is used to having an active role in the festival, after all it is one of our biggest special events."

"Used to ordering folks around you mean. After three years of misery, the committee got up the guts to vote her out." Elaine put one hand on her hip. "Remember how she changed your order on the decorations two weeks before the festival dance? Boy, you were breathing fire." She giggled.

Shani shook her head with a sigh of regret. "Yes, I could have been more understanding."

"You all right? Maybe we should take your temperature." Elaine placed the back of her hand to Shani's forehead.

"I'm fine." Shani pushed her hand away. "Now let me get busy before the senator gets here."

Elaine shrugged and left. For two hours, Shani made phone calls, completed reports, and consulted with staff about the day's activities. Soon it was ten o'clock.

Elaine came to the door and closed it behind her.

"That Senator Aucoin is here." Elaine rubbed her hands in anticipation. "He's on our home turf now. Let him have it, honey." She winked at Shani before opening the door.

Shani came around the desk wearing a large smile. "Welcome to Mid-City Community Center, Senator." She shook his hand.

"Thank you, Ms. Moore. Impressive building." Eric held her hand as he spoke.

"The nephew of one of our founding board members designed it. At a reasonable cost, of course," Shani added. "He's an outstanding architect."

Eric nodded. "Philip Ricard. He's done wonderful work all over the south."

"Let me get you some coffee." Shani went past a wondering Elaine.

Elaine shut the door with care and fell in step behind her to the coffee machine. "Is that the same Senator Aucoin you creamed on television about two weeks ago?"

"I didn't 'cream' him, Elaine. Senator Aucoin has a different perspective on certain issues. We exchanged opposing views." Shani put cream and one teaspoon of sugar in a mug. The other cup held black coffee.

"Say what? Hey, how did you know how he'd take his coff—" Elaine's eyes stretched wide. "*Oohh.*"

Shani wore a mysterious half-smile. She left a now flabbergasted Elaine. "Excuse me."

"Here you are." Shani handed him a mug.

"Thanks. Trumaine should be along any minute. If you don't mind, that is. He'll take a few notes, talk to staff." Eric took a sip of the hot liquid.

"No problem. I hope the material I gave you Tuesday was a help," Shani said.

"Lunch was great. I mean . . . very enlightening," he stammered. An embarrassed look of alarm flickered across his handsome features.

Shani felt emboldened by his admission. "I enjoyed it, too."

"Really? Then maybe dinner Friday. If you're not busy. I mean . . . if you're involved with someone. Are you involved with someone?" Eric groaned. "Real smooth, Aucoin."

"It's okay. Yes to dinner tomorrow night. And no, I'm not involved with anyone."

Shani marveled at how easy she felt accepting a dinner invitation. It had taken her months to begin dating after breaking up with Robert. And it was after agonizing indecision. Only a couple of the men had been persistent in pursuing more dates. But both gave up in defeat at the cool, even suspicious treatment they received. Shani was relieved each time when their phone calls stopped. The last date had been over three months ago. Since then she had been careful to give a wide berth to any single man who gave the slightest hint he might ask her out.

"Great." Eric looked up at the ceiling with an exasperated laugh. "I don't usually mumble 'great' to everything like a college freshman. But you've taken me by surprise to be honest, Shani." He gazed at her with an earnest expression.

The dulcet tone of that voice saying her name made her heart rate go up several notches. Shani had to steady her breathing before she could speak. "I have?"

He put down the coffee mug. "Yes. Let's spend time together. I want to know you, really know you."

"I . . . I'd like that." Shani soon found her face only inches from his. Elaine's voice made them both start.

"I did knock a couple of times." Elaine stuck her head in the door. She eyed them in open speculation.

"Fine, Elaine. What is it?" Shani tugged at her jacket. When she noticed how Elaine stared at her, she stopped.

"The senator's staff person is here."

"Thank you. We'll start with the library." Shani sprang from her chair and led the way.

For the next hour, they went throughout the building. Shani was gratified Eric seemed to grasp their attempts to support while encouraging self-sufficiency. His questions were thoughtful. Trumaine asked pointed questions about program evaluation, which Shani answered promptly. Eric did not fail to offer support even when Trumaine appeared dubious about the effectiveness of their efforts.

"The center has been open for seven years, right? Hardly enough time to effect lasting change in an area that has been hard hit by a slow economy and drugs for over twenty years. Still you've done a tremendous job." Eric looked around the adult education classroom in admiration.

"Thank you, Senator. By the way, Mr. Delacrosse," she turned to Trumaine. "We have a seventy percent completion rate in our high school equivalency program. Unfortunately, job placement is a much bigger challenge."

"In this job market, it's no wonder," Eric put in before Trumaine could speak.

Trumaine snapped his notebook shut as they headed back to Shani's office. "Humph, well that about does it." He arched an eyebrow at his boss.

"Thank you so much for taking time to show us around, Sh . . ., Ms. Moore." Eric shook her hand.

"You're quite welcome." She walked with him to the lobby.

Trumaine lingered behind. "Looks like I'll be seeing more of this place," he said in an undertone to Elaine.

"Count on it," Elaine whispered back.

"What did you say, Trumaine?" Eric called over his shoulder.

Trumaine scurried to join him. "Just saying goodbye to Ms. Moore's secretary."

Shani spent the rest of the day dealing with all manner of concerns that usually left her feeling spent and irritated. But nothing could pierce her buoyant mood. After work, she headed for the China Garden restaurant to meet Terrilyn.

"Whew, I'm so hungry. How are you doing, sweetie?" Shani beamed at her friend across the table.

Terrilyn sat back to examine her. "Who are you and what have you done with the real Shani Moore?"

"Don't be silly." Shani snickered. She waved the waitress over. After ordering, she sat back with a satisfied sigh. "What a great day."

Terrilyn wagged a forefinger at her. "Tell me what you're up to right now."

"I don't know what you mean."

"I've got it! Today you met with Eric Aucoin and publicly humiliated him again. His crushed ego is still splattered all over the walls at the center. Go, girl." She raised her glass of iced tea in a mock toast.

"Actually, it wasn't like that at all." Shani squeezed a slice of lemon in her tea.

"Not one insult?" Terrilyn looked skeptical.

"Nope."

"Not even a little jab?"

"Uh-uh." Shani grinned at her.

"I'm in an alternate universe." Terrilyn closed her eyes for a few seconds before gazing across at Shani.

"Eric seems to truly understand what we're trying to do now that we've met twice to discuss it." Shani watched with glee the reaction to her words.

"Eric?" Terrilyn's mouth hung open.

"He just feels strongly that programs should be accountable to the taxpayers. I can live with that." Shani spoke with confidence.

"I knew it! I just knew you wouldn't be able to resist that tasty morsel of masculinity. Bet I know what area you and *Eric* agreed on first. Dinner, Saturday night," Terrilyn said.

"Friday." Shani gave a delighted laugh. "It's strange, Terrilyn. After spending time with him, I found out he isn't at all the kind of person I thought he was. He's so . . . nice."

"And you're sure getting next to him is a good idea?"

"Have you heard something about him? Don't tell me he's left a string of destroyed women all over this town." Shani stared at her friend in dismay.

"No, no. He doesn't have that kind of reputation. It's just . . . Are you sure the differences won't become a problem? I don't want to see you go through another let down." Terrilyn gripped her hand.

"I'm taking it slow, girl. Don't worry." Shani pressed Terrilyn's hand for a second in reassurance.

Still, nagging doubts tugged around the edges of her consciousness as she kept up light chatter through the rest of dinner. Alone at her apartment, Shani pondered all the possible consequences of letting Eric into her life. She made a promise to hold back and not let her heart rule her mind. But the thought of how those large hands would feel against her skin, pulling her close lingered.

* * *

"This is my favorite restaurant in the city." Eric swept a hand around the dining room.

"It's beautiful," Shani agreed.

Though she loved Lebanese food, this was her first time eating at the upscale Serop's. The carpet was fashioned in rich jewel colors just like a fine Persian carpet. The chairs were plush and upholstered in the same ruby red, emerald, and royal blue. The soft sound of Eastern music floated around them.

"You're going to love the Mousaka. Of course, the kebabs are great too, especially the beef." Eric pointed to the menu, leaning toward her with enthusiasm.

"I love it all," Shani replied. She could feel the heat from his skin. Not wanting him to pull away too soon, she asked a question. "What about the kebbi?"

"Delicious." Eric's gaze shifted from the list of entrees to her face.

Shani looked up into those clear eyes. "Maybe I'll give it a try," she said in a soft voice.

"You won't be sorry." He put down the menu.

"What will you be having today?" A short round waiter held his pad, pencil poised.

The magic moment, a brief time only the two of them seemed to exist, dissolved. They took their time choosing entrées, exchanging experiences at other restaurants. After ordering, conversation flowed between them. Shani marveled at the comfortable fit of being with him. It did not take long for them to share family histories, where they went to school, and other personal information. She loved to see his eyes light up when he laughed. Or the way his heavy, dark brown eyebrows drew together when he was discussing a serious subject. Shani found herself contemplating the joy of being a part of this man's life in a serious way.

"Excuse me?" Shani blushed. She missed what he was

saying, so vivid was the image of lying in his arms amidst smooth cotton sheets.

"Hey, look at me. I've been rambling on for so long, you're bored stiff." Eric stared down and fiddled with his napkin.

"Oh no, not at all. I'm sorry, I was just thinking . . ." Shani hesitated. She did not know how to go on. How to tell him without coming on too strong? *I can't believe I'm here feeling like this. I hardly know the man.*

"Yes?"

"This is so strange. A few days ago I wanted to slash your tires and publicly humiliate you. And now I'm laughing at your jokes." Shani gazed at him.

"And I know my jokes aren't that funny," he said with a grin. "So that means we like each other. We're Eric and Shani, not Senator Aucoin and Ms. Moore." He took her hand.

Shani felt sweet yearning flow through her body. A yearning stronger than she had ever felt before, not even for Robert. "You're very different from how I imagined you to be."

"I haven't evicted any widows or taken candy from a baby in weeks." Eric's eyes twinkled with mirth.

"See, I've had a positive influence on you all ready." Shani giggled. "You might even vote liberally next election."

"Hey, let's not get carried away." He let out a musical laugh. "Maybe you'll vote conservatively."

"Depends on the candidate I guess." Shani's eyes softened with affection.

Eric gazed at her. "I want to spend more time with you, Shani. There's something strong between us."

"I feel it, too. But you don't think our views will be a barrier?" Shani wanted to touch his face.

"Not if we talk it out. I don't know any couple who agree on everything. Besides, it's worth it. Well?"

"Let's do it. I mean . . . uh.." Shani's eyes went wide. "We'll get to know each other, not . . ."

Eric stroked her hands to calm her fear. "I don't want to rush anything this important."

"Me either." Shani stared at their entwined hands. His touch both comforted and excited her.

"Now what do we do?" Eric smiled at her.

"I've got an idea. Let's go downtown to see the Christmas lights." Shani wanted to share one of her greatest pleasures at this time of year with him. Being with him would make it even more so.

"You've got it. I haven't done that in years." Eric's face brightened at the prospect.

They strolled around the governmental complex admiring the lights and displays set up by the city. Shani loved walking beside him, her arm looped through his. They bought hot chocolate from a street vendor. They even danced the two step as a zydeco band played on the levee plaza overlooking the Mississippi River. The huge bridge spanning the river between Baton Rouge and Port Allen was strung with white lights that shone against the deep blue night sky. Shani felt a kind of enchantment in the air. When they returned to Shani's apartment, he came inside but would not stay.

"I had a fantastic time. But it's time to go." Eric stood near speaking low.

"You're working on Saturday even?" Shani felt dazed by the force of his presence.

"Yes, but that's not why I'd better leave. Believe me taking it slow with you isn't on my mind right now. Goodnight, Shani." He covered her lips with his, exploring with slow movements.

"Goodnight," Shani said.

From the moment the door closed behind him until she sank beneath her down comforter, Shani relived the sensation of his kiss. Being in his arms was more electrifying than she'd imagined. Yet she relished the process of getting to know him. It would make the first time they made love even more passionate. The days ahead seemed luminous with the promise of love.

Chapter Three

The sky was several shades of gray, dark lead to silver in spots. A fine mist hung in the air. Shani shivered even though the heater in her Toyota Camry was working well. Trips to the Angola State Penitentiary sent chills through her no matter what the weather. She would never get used to this. The long winding drive only added to her dread each time she went to visit her younger brother. It was depressing in the summer when the trees and bushes of rural West Feliciana parish were resplendent in deep green, sunlight painting the rolling hills bright yellow, and blue skies stretching for miles. Then she thought of how much J.J. loved the outdoors. How awful that he had to see such beauty from such a dreary place. But today the scenery was a perfect match to her mood.

Shani went through the routine search at the gate. She was searched again before she was allowed into the visiting area, a large room scattered with tables and hard metal folding chairs. Four or five guards took turns strolling around the big room or standing along the walls observing. All the prisoners were dressed in pale blue denim shirts and dark blue jeans. J.J. wore a crooked smile that was a shadow of the radiant boyish one he'd once had. Shani could see the progressive change with every visit during the first six months of his sentence. His face was thinner and his eyes dull.

"Hello, J.J." Shani hugged him tight.

"How ya doin', baby. Whew! Look at you. Getting prettier every year. Just like Mama." J.J.'s face softened for a few seconds before the veil of hardness came back. "So how's the family?"

Shani shifted in her chair. "Doing fine." Too soon to tell him Brendon would not come. "The kids are growing like weeds."

"Wish I could see Colin. And Janine was pregnant with Kara when I was sent up the first time."

Shani brought out the small photo album. "Voilà. The Moore family in all their glory."

"Oh, she's lovely. My main man Colin." J.J. drank in the photos like a man taking a refreshing drink after being parched for a long time. "Brendon and Janine always did make a good-looking couple, didn't they?"

Shani glanced at the picture of the two sitting on her living room couch, Brendon's arm draped around Janine. "Yeah, they do." Shani bit her lip. Now?

A full minute passed before he spoke. J.J. did not lift his head, but continued to gaze at the photo. "He's not coming, is he?"

"No, he's not coming." She put a hand over her mouth to stifle moan of sorrow. Her family, already left with a huge hole caused by the death of their parents, was slipping away it seemed.

J.J. straightened one or two photos then closed the album with care. "I understand."

"Well I don't." Shani fumbled for the purse-sized pack of tissues she knew to always have on hand for these visits. "It's enough that you're locked up for what you did; Brendon is wrong to punish you this way." She wiped tears from her eyes.

"Shani, listen to me . . ." J.J. said taking her hand.

"No, J.J. I won't forgive him for deliberately hurting you."

J.J. held her hand for several minutes until the quiet sobs tapered off. A burly, black guard approached.

"Everything all right here, ma'am? Y'all need anything?" He eyed them with concern.

Shani, expecting some censure, feared for J.J. The compassion in the big man's rugged face touched her. "I'm okay, sir. Really." She sniffed.

"Thanks, Officer Crawford. Come on now. Cut that out." J.J.'s voice was tight with emotion. "You're being too hard on Brendon. Besides, what kind of role model am I for Colin? Brendon is trying to raise two kids in a world that's got high mountains for black boys to climb."

"What kind of message does disowning his brother send to Colin and Kara?" Shani said with force.

"Shani, I don't think you realize how much I hurt him." J.J. sighed. "When Daddy realized he was dying, he had a talk with Brendon. He was only nine years old, still he took that promise as seriously as any grown man. In Brendon's mind he's not only failed me, but Daddy."

Shani's breath caught in her throat. "J.J., I never knew . . ."

"All these years every mistake I made weighed on him like they were his, too. Brendon can't face me, Shani. And it probably scares the hell out of him that he'll repeat his failure with his own children." J.J. took a deep breath.

Shani gazed at him with new respect. "J.J., I've never heard you talk like this."

"You mean think about somebody other than me for longer than three seconds?" he said with a grin that almost recaptured his youthful fun-loving expression.

"I'm embarrassed you had to tell me, a clinical social worker by training, what should have been obvious all along. You are one perceptive man." Shani took his hands in both hers.

"Shani, tell Brendon how much all he tried to do for me meant. Maybe I didn't see it then, but now I do. The one thing that has made a difference is remembering all the ways he stood by me." J.J. sat up with his shoulders back. "I'm going to earn back his trust, respect, and love. I'll make you both proud of me."

Shani brushed his chestnut brown face with her fingertips. "You don't need to earn our love, J.J. That's something I can say for both of us."

For the first time since coming to the prison, Shani left with spirits higher than when she arrived. The crowning good news was J.J. felt sure he would be released on parole in January. The parole board would meet in another week to consider his request. Based on his good behavior, recommendations from several ministers and others, the chances were good he would be home before mid-February. She said a silent prayer of thanks. As she crossed the boundary line back into East Baton Rouge Parish, Shani swore again to build up the children's programs at Mid-City Center. She thought of all the boys who had no one trying to lead them in a positive direction. But there were people ready to reach out. Shani thought of the men who spent time with young boys at Mid-City's recreation rooms. And now she could look to Eric for help. The memory of him sent a thrill up her spine. How marvelous to know they would be fighting together against forces tearing the African-American community apart rather than each other. Thoughts of sharing Christmas with Eric planted a smile on her face.

Everyone at the office marveled to see her breeze through several trying situations with uncharacteristic ease. Elaine shot sidelong glances at her when she thought Shani was too busy to notice. The secretary almost dropped the morning mail when she returned to find Shani humming

"Jingle Bell Rock" and taping Christmas cards to her office door.

"Look, Elaine. This one is my favorite," Shani said waving a card with a large white dove in flight surrounded by embossed green and gold foil paper shaped to resemble ribbons. "Of course, this one with the little kids listening to a bedtime story is so cute."

"Yeah, it is." Elaine scratched her head. "You feeling okay, Shani?"

"Certainly, Elaine. Now it's perfect." Shani stood back to admire her handiwork.

The colorful cards against the background of red, green, and gold wrapping paper did brighten up the place. Shani made one last minor adjustment before going to her desk, still humming.

"Hi, Jesse." Elaine's beginning smile of greeting froze at the look on his face.

As head of operations and maintenance, Jesse supervised janitorial staff. He also made sure the building was kept in good condition.

"What's wrong?" she dropped her voice. The short muscular man gave a grunt of vexation.

"We gonna hafta fire Carlina Brown. I caught that woman loading some of the food from our kitchen into her trunk. Had the nerve to give me attitude when I told her about it."

Elaine screwed up her plump face. "Oh man! You're coming in here to mess up her good mood. For the first time in months she hasn't been snappish."

Jesse threw up his hands. "Hey, don't blame me. She's got to know this. I can't fire nobody without telling her. I ain't lookin' forward to it neither."

"Hi, Jesse," Shani called through the door. "Merry Christmas."

Jesse looked up at the ceiling. "Why did it have to be me first thing this mornin'?" he muttered in a low voice.

"Hi, Shani. Merry Christmas. 'Course you ain't gone be so merry when I tell you what I have to tell you."

"He's a damn lie!" a gruff voice yelled. Carlina, thin and wiry, marched past Elaine into Shani's office.

"What's going on?" Shani glanced at Jesse then at Carlina.

Carlina jabbed a finger at Jesse. "This no good dog is a liar, that's what's goin' on. Them was bags Miz Craig told me I could have," she shouted.

"Lower your voice, Ms. Brown." Shani closed her office door. "Now, Jesse—"

"I been working 'round here off an' on for four years. He been on my case since I got here." Carlina started blubbering. "It ain't right, Miz Moore."

Shani handed her a wad of facial tissue. "Let me—"

"You ain't no good, Jesse. You know you wrong." Carlina said, her voice muffled by the tissue. "Miz Moore, I need my job."

Jesse shot her a smoldering look of condemnation. "Last month I saw her puttin' some liquid cleaner from the storeroom in big bag. She saw me watching and put it back."

"That's a da—" Carlina broke in.

"Be quiet please." Shani held up one hand. "Go on, Jesse."

"She tried to tell me she was goin' to clean, even though it was five minutes before quittin' time. Claimed she hadn't noticed what time it was. I let her go with a warning to be sure all materials was put away before she left."

"What he doin' spyin' on people anyway? Musta been scared somebody was gonna see him do somethin'." Carlina glared at him. "Betcha you search his house you find some center stuff."

"I don't need to be no thief," Jesse spat at her.

"That's enough," Shani said in a commanding tone. She stood between them. "We can settle this if Mrs. Craig confirms she gave Ms. Brown permission to take the food."

"Here she is now." Jesse wore a look of satisfaction. "I asked her to come, too."

Lucille Craig, the short, round kitchen supervisor, came in still wearing a hair net and apron. "Mornin', Miz Moore." She nodded to the others. "What y'all need?"

"Did you tell Ms. Brown she could have those bags Jesse saw her loading into her car?" Shani folded her arms.

"Sure. She said she could use 'em. No sense lettin' it go to waste." Mrs. Craig shrugged then frowned seeing Jesse's expression. "What's wrong with that?"

"Nothing. We'll talk later." Shani meant to point out that helping employees in need was admirable, but should be done after consulting with her to avoid just such a misunderstanding. "Well that's it then. Jesse, it seems Ms. Brown was not stealing the food."

"Told ya so." Carlina gloated. Her eyes sparkled with malice. "Now I want him wrote up for startin' this mess."

"How was I to know Miz Lucille gave her all that meat and stuff?" Jesse mumbled.

"Meat and stuff? I ain't gave her no meat. And what else you sayin' she had in them bags?" Mrs. Craig's question caused them all to freeze for a few seconds.

Shani looked at Carlina, whose gaze darted around the room as though searching for an escape route. "Jesse, tell us exactly what was in the bags."

"Two canned hams, frozen chicken legs, three boxes of powdered milk . . ."

Mrs. Craig placed both hands on her hips. "All I put in them bags was some vegetables. They from my uncle's farm an' we had more than we needed for the dinners. I brought 'em intendin' to share with some of the workers."

"Uh-huh! Just what I figured." Jesse planted two meaty fists on his hips.

Mrs. Craig faced Carlina with a glower. "You decided to get slick an' pack them bags with other food. Come to think of it, food been dissappearin' for three months now. Ever since you come back."

"Sure has, Miz Craig," Jesse put in.

"Thank you, Mrs. Craig." Shani gestured for her to leave.

"You welcome. Humph." Mrs. Craig threw Carlina one last look of scorn before walking out.

Shani faced Carlina. "Ms. Brown, you will be terminated effective immediately. Elaine will prepare your last paycheck." She opened the door and stared at Carlina.

Carlina shot them both a venomous look before stomping out and down the hall.

"Thank you, Miz Moore." Jesse started to leave. "I hate this happened. By the way, that guy was over here a few days ago been wanderin' around the halls. He's in the library now I think."

Shani's heart skipped a beat. She headed for the library full of anticipation. Her face must have shown obvious disappointment when she found Trumaine chatting with the librarian.

"Sorry, just me," he said. "I decided to take more time to fully investigate, I mean, explore all facets of the community center. To make sure all the work you're doing here gets adequately presented in my report." He flashed a winning smile.

Shani shook his hand. "You're welcome anytime, Mr. Delacrosse."

"Trumaine, please. Miss Zeno was telling me about your story hour for children. What a wonderful oasis in a desert of crime and immorality." Trumaine shook in head.

Shani felt a streak of irritation at the condescension in his tone. "There are hundreds of hard-working, church-going people in Easy Town. Being poor does not equal moral deficiency."

"Of course, I didn't mean all residents. But crime is rampant. And most households are headed by unmarried mothers who can't get the fathers of their children to support them." Trumaine held up a sheet of paper. "It's here in the grant proposal your organization prepared."

He held a copy of the center's application for a Ziegler grant established by the wealthy Louisiana family of the same name. Shani wanted to snatch it from his hand and hit him with it. Unlike Eric, the more she got to know Trumaine the less she liked him.

"It's wise to appreciate that a community is more than a compilation of statistics and graphs. You have to walk among people to really understand their plight." Shani kept her voice calm. She even managed a smile.

"Which is precisely why I came back for another visit," he replied in a suave manner. "Well, I think that should about do it. Thank you so much for allowing me to impose, Miss Zeno. Goodbye Ms. Moore."

Shani grimaced at his back as he left. "What was he asking about exactly, Denise?"

"What kind of special events we have here at the center, who my boss is, things like that. He was only in here a few minutes before you came, Shani." Denise wandered off to help a teenager in the reference section.

Shani walked back to her office slowly. Why was Trumaine snooping around? Something about Trumaine Delacrosse disturbed her. She had a feeling he was looking for dirt. Maybe she had been wrong to assume Eric would break from his conservative leanings. For the rest of the day she went over their previous conversations. She was still feeling wary when he picked her up for dinner.

"Hello." Eric pecked her cheek lightly. He was impeccable in a heavy wool sweater the color of burgundy wine, navy pants, and leather loafers the deep red color as his sweater. "Looks like we're going to have cold weather for Christmas."

"Hi. Have a seat. I'll be ready in a minute." Shani went back to her bedroom.

"In fact the weatherman says we're going to have cold weather through New Year's day. Perfect for the holidays," Eric called to her.

After several minutes, Shani came back into the living room with her purse and sweater jacket. "Yes."

Eric stood and pulled her close. "It's going to be a very special Christmas for a lot of reasons," he murmured into her ear.

"Will it?" Shani's face was impassive.

"Um-hum. And you're most of them." Eric nuzzled her neck with his lips.

The faint brush of his mouth on her skin set tingles of desire through her. Yet the suspicions brought on by Trumaine's visit to the center caused Shani to tense. "I'm really hungry. Let's go."

Eric blinked in confusion. "Wait. The temperature is pretty low in here, too. Have I done something wrong?"

"No, it's . . . Forget it. You ready?" Shani tried to move away, but Eric tightened his hold.

"We're not leaving this apartment until I get some answers. Now talk to me," Eric said. The firm set of his jaw gave his handsome face stern look.

"Your fact finding seems to be very meticulous. Trumaine Delacrosse made a second visit to Mid-City without letting me know he was in the building." Shani bristled at being treated like an errant child. "More like he was digging for dirt."

Eric loosened his hold. "Honey, is that all?" He smiled.

Shani grew even more incensed by what sounded like a patronizing note in his voice. Honey indeed! She put several feet between them. "All? Do you think this is some game I'm playing? Funding for programs that are critical to that community are under attack. Don't imagine we haven't been through this enough to know some of the tactics you've used."

Eric grew serious again. "Now wait a minute—"

Shani pressed on as her angered gathered steam. "You take things we tell you and turn it against us. Maybe I've been a bit naive."

Eric stood with his feet apart and arms folded over his broad chest. "Shani, you are—"

"Trumaine knew exactly what to look for on his second visit, I'll bet. He looks like a real budding spin doctor or should I say junior hatchet man?" Shani faced him full.

Despite her words, Eric appeared calm. His voice was even when he spoke. "Can I say something now?" When she said nothing, he walked to her. "I'm sorry Trumaine didn't go by your office first, but your administrative assistant told him it would be okay."

"Elaine?" Shani was taken aback.

"Yes, Elaine. She was sure you wouldn't mind since you did tell us both we could visit to get information anytime." Eric placed both hands on her shoulders. "Trumaine told me he missed a few details during the first tour."

"Oh." Shani let her arms fall to her side. "I didn't know."

"Let's sit down for a second." Eric pulled her over to the sofa. "It is very important that you believe what I'm about to say. We don't agree on some issues, but that's not news to you. If I ever oppose anything that involves Mid-City Community Development, Inc., you'll be the first to know." He wrapped a muscular arm around her.

"Eric, I'm sorry I jumped to con—"

He put a finger to her lips. "I'm not finished with you, woman." His face was inches from hers. "What I feel for you is so strong it's hard to put into words. And nothing is as important to me right now. I want, no, I need to have you in my life."

A heat wave started in Shani's toes and traveled up taking full control of her body. Strong was an understatement. This feeling eclipsed anything she had felt before for a man. She felt giddy with desire, willing to risk all. Watching his full, delectable mouth hover ever closer mesmerized her. It took considerable effort to speak.

"When I saw you the first time that day at the state capitol, I felt . . . so good being near you," Shani said in a small voice. She struggled to put into words the strange magnetism he exercised over her.

"Yes, so very good. And it's been growing ever since," Eric said.

Eric's touch was tender as he caressed her face. He kissed her long and hard. When they parted, both were breathless.

Shani fell back against the large cushions. "My oh my." She fanned herself.

Eric puffed a few times. "Have mercy."

Shani's eyes were aglitter when she looked at him. "There's a great Chinese restaurant nearby. They deliver."

Eric closed his eyes. He pressed his lips to her forehead. "I love Chinese takeout," he murmured.

Dinner was a delightful game of tease. Shani took great pains serving their plates. They sat across from one another at her dining table. She lit candles that gave off a mild scent of spice that went well with the meal.

"Umm, this shrimp Schezuan is tasty." Eric put down his fork. "But I'm stuffed." His plate was more than half-full.

Shani savored a helping of moo goo gai pan. "China Garden is the best in town. Is that all you're going to have?" She pointed to his plate. "Have another taste."

"All right, I will."

He came to her in one quick motion and lifted her up from the chair. Swinging her around in slow motion to the rhythm of a blues ballad playing soft and low, he let his tongue roam across her lips. Pressing her body to his, she matched his movement to the music. Shani no longer wanted to play the game. She wanted to feel his bare chest against hers. Her hand guided his fingers to the front buttons of her sweater.

"What about going slow?" Eric said between short gasps.

"Oh we will definitely go slow, sugar. Nice and slow."
Shani led him to the bedroom.

True to her word, even their undressing was a sweet,
sensuous ceremony. Shani ran her tongue down the middle of his chest and around each nipple until he cried out.
Yet still she took her time as they stood naked in front of
the full length mirror near her bed.

"What are you doing?" Eric watched in fascination. Her
hands moved over his body without touching the one spot
that ached the most.

"I'm taking my time," she whispered, her mouth against
the flesh of his shoulder. "I want you so bad, baby. But I
don't want this to end too fast." Shani made the act of
wearing the condom an act of erotic play.

She pushed him down on the bed. Eric moaned deep
in his throat as she lowered herself onto him. The gentle
rocking motion propelled them both to cries of pleasure.
The lingering motion went on for a long, luscious time
until Eric began to buck beneath her. With one elbow
braced on the bed, he lifted his pelvis while clutching her
waist. His thrusts sent shudders through her. Shani dug
her fingernails into his shoulders.

"Now, baby," Eric said through clenched teeth. "Now."

Shani let control of her passion slip just enough. Ecstasy
raked her body like thousands of needles. Tiny needles of
both pleasure and pain.

"Please, please. Oh, Eric!"

His cries were a mixture of grunts and groans incompre-
hensible except for her name repeated with each bone
shaking stroke as he climaxed. Shani crumpled in a heap
on his chest. Eric eased her down to stretch beside him
on the sheets. Minutes stretched into an hour before either
spoke.

"Now that you've seduced me and made me into an
obsessed man . . ." Eric began.

"Say what?" Shani poked him in the ribs.

"That's right, young lady. You have to take responsibility

for your actions and do right by me. I'll need treatment."
Eric combed his fingers through the tangle of her thick
hair.

"What kind of treatment?" Shani snuggled into the
crook of his arm.

"Regular doses of your voice, your face, and . . ." He
squeezed her thigh beneath the sheet. "Everything else
your hot little imagination can cook up."

"Well under the circumstances it's the least I can do."
She giggled.

"Good. And about our politics," he said lifting her face
to his, "Don't ever suppose what I believe could lead me
to intentionally hurt you. Promise you'll trust me, Shani,"
he whispered.

"I promise, baby. I promise." Shani gave him an ardent
kiss that rekindled smoldering embers.

Chapter Four

"Hey good-lookin'." Eric planted a solid kiss on his mother's cheek.

"Hello, dear," Adeline Aucoin said. She gave him a maternal pinch of his cheek in return. "Well, you look okay I guess. Getting plenty of rest?"

Eric shrugged. "Enough. I try not to work late too many nights in a row. Yum-yum, you've been baking again." He reached for a plate of brownies under a round glass cover on the kitchen counter.

"Your favorite." Adeline beamed at his sighs of satisfaction.

"You must be feeling pretty good then."

Eric gazed at his mother, searching for signs that she was in pain. Adeline suffered from rheumatoid arthritis, high blood pressure, and asthma. Though she had never been strong, her health had grown worse in the last four years. There were days she could not get out of bed without assistance. Dalton Aucoin treated his wife with a tender concern in stark contrast to the brusque manner he usually displayed.

"Tip top." Adeline smiled at him. "Really dear, you shouldn't worry about me," she replied seeing the small crease remain in his forehead. She patted his arm to reassure him.

"What did the doctor say?" Eric knew from his father that she'd had her checkup the previous day.

"I'm doing well all things considered, baby." To prove her point, she walked over to the refrigerator. "You need something to wash that down."

She poured him a glass of milk much as she'd done when he came home from school as a boy. Adeline sat next to him at on a stool. With long fingers showing slight swelling from arthritis, she arranged the ankle-length green silk lounge dress. Her hair was a lustrous silver gray perfectly styled. Adeline was meticulous with her hair, makeup, and dress. And despite her illnesses, she was still a handsome woman at fifty-three.

"Now I want to catch up on you. How is work coming along? I hear a real fight over the budget is shaping up."

"Yes, a lot of sacred cows are on the carving board. It's not going to be pretty or polite this session," he said referring to the upcoming legislative term. "There are some pretty determined folks on both sides."

"Indeed. One in particular seems to have made quite an impression. On the media, I mean." Adeline pretended not to notice his darting glance.

Eric cleared his throat. "Oh? Think I'll have some more milk." He went to the refrigerator.

"There to your right on the top shelf," she pointed to the red and white carton. "An attractive, articulate young woman was shown tearing into you at one of your committee meetings. Now what is her name? Morton, Morrison . . ."

Eric came back and gave her an admonishing look. "Mama, let's cut the cat and mouse game. You've got a better pipeline of information than the FBI."

Adeline looked innocent. "Why I don't know what you mean."

"Mama." Eric stared at her hard.

"Well it just so happens my friend Imogene Hampton's son is a member of the Mid-City Board of Directors. She says . . ." Her voice trailed off at his frown. "I wasn't being nosy. Immy and I got to talking one day over coffee after garden club meeting."

"Sure." Eric looked skeptical. "And it just happened to come up."

"Immy might have said she saw you two having lunch." Adeline fussed with her hair. "Of course I told her she must have been mistaken. Eric would most certainly have introduced me to her, I said."

"Mama, we only started seeing each other a few weeks ago. And you haven't met every woman I've dated in the last seven years."

Adeline's finely shaped eyebrows went up. "Only the two you were serious about. Or thought you were serious about. Thankfully you came to your senses both times."

"Mama—"

"I know you too well, Eric Paul Aucoin. If it meant nothing, you would have mentioned having met her over lunch when I first brought it up." She waved a finger in front of his nose. "She seems a . . . nice young woman from all I hear." The word "nice" was said in an disparaging tone meant to provoke him into talking. It worked.

"Shani is a caring committed professional and yes, Mama, she is a very *nice* person. Someone who cares about other people. Unlike most of the silly women you've shoved at me." Eric wore a sour expression.

"I don't shove women at you, Eric," Adeline said in an injured voice. "I've merely introduced you to some of most beautiful young ladies from the finest families in Baton Rouge."

"With nothing heavier on their minds than the next shopping trip in New Orleans or Houston."

"Don't be ridiculous. Jalisia Minor is a top marketing consultant. Why you don't see her anymore is a mystery to me. The poor girl adores you."

"Jalisia works, if you can call it that, for her uncle. She's looking for a husband so she can explore new frontiers of credit," Eric retorted.

"Nonsense. And what about Helene Cavalier? She's top assistant to the secretary of the Department of Health and Hospitals."

Eric laughed. "Who made it clear when we first met that she had an income requirement for any man she'd let in her life. Don't get me started, Mama. I could tell you things about those lovely ladies that would curl your hair."

"Don't be crude, Eric." Adeline looked away in an attempt to hide the spark of interest his spicy tidbit caused.

But Eric was not deceived. "You'd love to hear it. And no doubt you'll get the full details by sundown tomorrow." He grinned at her.

"Don't try to change the subject. Shani Moore doesn't seem to have much in common with you." Adeline walked with some effort to the den beckoning him to follow. She sat on a large sofa with huge stuffed pillows. A fire burned brightly in the brick fireplace.

"You mean her family background." Eric poured his mother a glass wine.

"I meant what I said. Thank you." She took a delicate sip of her one drink for the day. "Relationships are hard enough these days. It helps when you share the same views."

"We don't differ that much," Eric stared into the fireplace.

The yellow flames brought back the searing heat that had flashed through his body when he made love to Shani. She worked a kind of sorcery on his senses. Memories of her smile, the sound of her voice in his ear set his heart thumping and his mind reeling.

"My goodness. Things have gone that far then." Adeline clucked her tongue.

"What?" Eric started. He wiped perspiration from his upper lip with a handkerchief.

She gave him a wise smile. "It doesn't take a mind reader to know this Shani Moore has a special place in your heart. Just be careful. Opposites attract, but fights that electrify and stir passion early in a relationship can become bitter later on."

"That won't happen to us, Mama." Eric took her hand.

"Hello, hello. What this? Are you all right, darlin'?" Dalton sat next to his wife to peer at in with an anxious frown. "What's wrong, son?"

Adeline kissed her husband's cheek then wiped away her lipstick from it. "Nothing is wrong, Dalton. My what a pair of worriers you are."

Dalton's shoulders relaxed. He grinned at his wife with affection. "Not me woman, I just want to know what you two are cooking up. What about a drink, son? Your mother won't object," he teased.

"No thanks, Dad. I've got to keep a clear head these days."

Adeline stood up. "That's my boy. Now y'all have to excuse me. I'm going to bed and watch a little television."

"I'll try not to disturb you when I finally turn in." Dalton said. He watched her walked away with a stiff gait. Seams of worry were etched into his face. "Your mother tries to hide just how bad she feels most of the time, Eric. I know it."

Eric pushed away his own fears. His voice had a forced heartiness even to his own ears. "Mama is doing much better. It's been over a year since she was in the hospital. Look how she's gotten back into the swing of her social life."

"Maybe you're right. Still, I'm going to get her to slow down some." Dalton turned an appraising eye on Eric. "Now, what about you? Are you keeping a clear head?"

Eric lounged against the chair back. "Yep. I've been spending my days working on building coalitions and nights pouring over budget figures for three of the largest state departments. I don't intend to be caught off guard when the session begins."

"Good, do your home work. Don't let distractions trip you up, son. Or hormones rule your head." Dalton got up and went to the bar. He poured himself a glass of Chivas Regal.

Eric sat up straight. "What have my hormones got to do with anything?" A sinking feeling began in the pit of his stomach.

"Women are a gift, Eric. I'm the first to say so. But the wrong woman can be curse." Dalton waved his glass to punctuate his words.

"Dad, you're talking in riddles."

"I'm talking about that social worker you've been seen with lately. The one that's over . . . what's it called? Oh yeah, Mid-City Center. A lot of misguided social engineering that only helps people stay dependent." Dalton gave a grunt of disapproval.

"Dad, Mid-City has some very fine initiatives. And so what if I'm seeing Shani?"

Eric's jaw jutted out in a defensive expression that bordered on sullen. His father was making him feel like he was ten years old and had just broken a neighbor's window with his softball. Still, these were some of the same thoughts he'd had trying to convince himself not to get any closer to Shani. Now here he was defending the social programs his own party held in such low esteem. His conservative colleagues, Senator Raymond in particular, would not be pleased to say the least. It was obvious his father was thinking along the same lines.

"Son, you need to look to the future. I mean your future in politics, in the party. We need to establish credibility with men like Raymond." Dalton took a swig of his drink.

Eric spoke in a tight voice. "My record should more

than speak for itself. The party doesn't rule my personal life."

"Listen, Eric, I understand." Dalton winked at him. "I was young and single once. Have your fun, boy. But don't advertise it."

Eric had a hard time checking his anger. He and his father had discussed his romantic escapades many times before. Yet this was very different. What he felt was different.

"Shani means a lot to me, Dad," he said speaking with measured deliberation.

Dalton eyed him steadily for several minutes. "I see. Then you need to rethink that, boy." He rose and put his now empty glass on the bar. "We've worked too hard to see it all unravel because you're infatuated."

Eric gripped the arm of the chair. "You mean you've worked too hard."

Dalton whirled to face him. "Damn right. For years being a conservative has gotten me scorn from the liberal black leaders; so-called leaders living off our community like parasites. And the white conservatives treated me like dirt, hell worse than dirt sometimes. But I held on to my principles and worked to build something for you. Don't throw it away for a little—"

Eric shot from his chair. "Don't say it, Dad." He turned his back to Dalton.

Dalton looked taken aback then contrite. "I'm sorry, son. I didn't mean to disrespect the young lady. But think of the consequences."

"My objectives haven't changed. Raymond knows that. I don't think anyone can question my commitment to the party platform." Eric took a deep breath and faced him. "My private life has nothing to do with it."

"Don't be naive, Eric. They're watching you like a hawk."

"Then I'll tell them exactly what I've just told you. Dad,

Shani is a beautiful person. I want you to get to know her as a person, not a political label."

"Son, I'm sure she's a nice person . . ."

"I've invited her to our Christmas party at the club." Eric went to his father and put a hand on his arm. "Please, don't make this hard for us. Shani would really like to meet you and Mama. And it's important to me that you give her a chance."

After a long moment, Dalton covered Eric's hand with his own large one. "All right, son. I'll give it a try," was all he would venture. "But maybe an intimate dinner here just the four of us would be a more personal way to get acquainted first."

Eric brightened. "Hey, that's a great idea. Shani will be thrilled when I tell her. Thanks, Dad." He gave his father a rough embrace. "Well, I better get going. Lots of work to do."

"No problem, son. I'll see you later." Dalton smiled at him, but the smile faded when Eric turned away. His face became a rigid mask.

"And this is my office," Eric said sweeping a hand around. He wore a nervous smile. "The scene of the crime. What do you think?"

Shani stood between the door and his desk twisting the strap of her leather purse. She was not at ease either. Eric's last comment echoed her thought, making her wonder if it was written on her face. This is where plans were hatched to change the face of social service funding.

"Very nice," she replied with a smile. "Is your father here?" Shani resisted the urge to glance over her shoulder. Meeting Dalton Aucoin was the second cause of her discomfort.

"Oh, he's on a conference call with couple of our satellite offices. He'll be here in a minute. Come on, honey, sit down. You look tired." Eric closed the door and fixed her a cup of coffee from the pot in his office.

Shani sat down. "You know how it is when you supervise a bunch of people. Why folks won't do right is a mystery to me." She shook her head then tasted the coffee. "Hey, your secretary makes great coffee."

"That is a sexist remark. Nedra didn't make it." Eric grinned at her expression of surprise.

"You mean . . .?"

"Yep, Trumaine," Eric said with a laugh.

Shani gave his knee a playful swat. "Very funny."

"It's good to see you smile. You seemed really down all through lunch."

"Trying to rescue people from drugs seems like a losing battle some days. We can't seem to counter the call of street life." Shani closed her eyes and rubbed her temples.

"Baby, I'm sure you've gone to the limit trying to help them. So if you're beating yourself up thinking you could have done more, don't." Eric kissed her hand. "Mid-City is a lifeboat in a sea of troubles because of you."

"That's what worries me about the cuts, Eric. It's all about having the resources to give these kids choices. Jobs, help with tutoring, a mentor, or sometimes just a hand to hold can be lifesavers," Shani said.

"Eric, I have that report— Oh hello, Ms. Moore. Sorry, the door wasn't completely closed so I thought it was okay to come in." Despite his words, Trumaine entered the room with confidence.

Shani smothered the dislike that rose in her chest at the sight of him for fear he would see it in her eyes. "Hello, Trumaine. How are you?"

"Fine. I won't take long, Eric. Nedra printed out this report and I've proofed it. Give me a call if you have any changes." Trumaine handed Eric a bound stack of papers.

"Great, Trumaine. Efficient as ever." Eric flipped through it before putting it on his desk.

Trumaine turned to Shani. "So how are things at Mid-City? Still running smoothly I hope."

"Routine. The same as with any organization. There are good days and bad." She felt foolish for being so paranoid.

"I heard that. Well, I'm on my way. Nice seeing you again. Senator, I'll meet with you at four, right?" Trumaine headed for the door.

"We're still on, Tru." Eric sat next to Shani again. "He's been a rock for me. A good assistant you can trust is worth his, or her, weight in gold."

"Amen. Elaine keeps me from losing my mind some days. Eric, about this dinner—"

"Sorry it took so long to get here." Dalton strode in and gave Shani a quick kiss on the check. "So this is Ms. Shani Moore. Welcome to our little corner of the business world." He stepped back and studied her with an open, benevolent smile on his face.

Shani was caught off guard. "Pleased to meet you, Mr. Aucoin," she stammered.

"Call me Dalton, sugar."

He settled his large frame in a chair around a coffee table in a corner of Eric's office. Eric and Shani sat on the small sofa.

"I'm so glad to finally meet you. Eric has been singing your praises to his mother and me. Thank you, son." Dalton accepted a large mug of coffee from him.

Shani flushed with pleasure. "It's a nice to meet you, too."

"Shani, Dad and Mom are both great cooks." Eric patted his father's knee with affection.

"And Adeline and I are looking forward to seeing you tomorrow night at dinner. You'll love Eric's mother. She's the sweetest woman in the world."

Shani shifted in her seat. "I'm looking forward to meeting her, too." But not being under a magnifying glass with *two* sets of critical eyes scouring out every little blemish.

"So Eric tells me you're a social worker." Dalton fixed his imposing gaze on her.

"Yes," Shani said. She shifted in her seat. "I'm at Mid-City Community Development, Inc."

"Doing some good things there I hear. Of course, some programs should put more responsibility on folks to pull themselves up out of poverty. The trouble with most of these social workers, no offense, honey, is they think money is the answer to everything. It's obvious all the liberal ways of tackling these problems haven't worked. I know you agree with me on that." Dalton gave a curt nod.

"Yes, well certainly mistakes have been made. We—" Shani began.

"Big mistakes, Shani." Dalton went on before she could finish. "The answer isn't to increased the money flow to what isn't working. We need a return to family values in the black community."

"Dad, Shani has some programs that stress just those values. Tell him about the Teens Lending a Hand program, honey." Eric spoke up with animation.

"Well, yes. As a matter of fact—" Shani began.

Dalton's wrist watch alarm trilled a series of beeps. "Time for my next meeting. This time I'll be talking to Shreveport. What headaches I get just thinking about Louis and that crew. Goodbye, my dear. See you tomorrow night, kids." He bustled out after giving Shani a firm squeeze on the upper arm and Eric a clap on the back.

Shani inhaled and exhaled. "My goodness."

Eric chuckled. "Dad can be overwhelming at times."

"My head is spinning. He's a powerhouse." Shani gazed after the tall man.

"But he can be a real softie, too. Really." Eric laughed at the incredulous look she gave him.

"I hear he's faced down some of the toughest opponents, white and black, in this state to become successful in business. And he's not reluctant to tell some black leaders when he thinks they're wrong, which is often."

"But he will fight just as hard to right injustice or help someone in need. I can't wait for you two to get to know each other. And my mother, too. This is going to be the best holiday ever. My older sister, LeeAnne, is flying in a couple of days before Christmas." Eric put an arm around her.

Shani felt butterflies fluttering in the her chest at the thought of being judged by yet another formidable member of the Aucoin clan. LeeAnne was senior vice president of retail sales for a large corporation. She lived in Atlanta with her husband and two children. One more appraising set of eyes to contend with in a few days.

"Yes, wonderful." Shani's voice was thin with anxiety.

Eric pulled back to scan her face. "What's wrong? You sound less than enthusiastic. My family isn't that bad." He gave her chin a gentle pinch.

Shani bit her lip. She formed her words with care. "Eric, my family isn't like yours. Mama and Daddy worked hard to give us what we needed, but we very were poor. Brendon and I worked our way through college. And then there's J.J."

"Shani, I—"

"No, let me finish. My baby brother is in prison, Eric. He's serving a sentence on a drug charge." Shani let out a long breath.

"I know. Brendon is a computer analyst. His wife's name is Janine, they have two kids. J.J. has been in trouble since he was fourteen. I've known for a while now. And it's okay."

Shani went rigid. "Have you been investigating me or something? I'm not asking for your approval or begging you to excuse my family tree."

"That's not what I meant, Shani," Eric put in with a worried look.

"Well, it sure sounded like it. Furthermore, I don't like having a background check run on me by my dates." Shani pushed him away and stood up.

"Shani, wait a minute. You gave an interview to a newspaper reporter the day of the committee hearing. The reporter did a story on you and mentioned those things." Eric held out his hands in a gesture of conciliation. "Remember?"

Shani did remember the story. The story was supposed to be on the center but the reporter included information on her family as well. She felt a twinge of guilt for her fit of temper.

"I said a few things and the reporter did research. But I'm not ashamed of my family," she added in a defensive voice. "J.J. is going to turn his life around."

Eric took her in his arms again. "I'm sure he will. With you for a sister he's got a lot to be thankful for all ready. Did you really think so little of me? That I'd look down on J.J. and your parents?"

Shani was grateful to feel the hard arms around her. She rested against his chest. "I'm sorry, Eric. It's just that we've had to face a lot of folks passing judgment on us. Forgive me?" she murmured.

The scent cologne on his neck was glorious. Shani put her arms under his suit jacket around his body. Passion, warm and sweet, flowed from his hard body into hers.

"Baby, there's nothing to forgive. Now I better let you go before we set off the sprinkler system in here." Eric touched the tip of his tongue to the soft inside of her mouth for a second before letting her go. "Oh, man. How many hours until we meet tonight?"

Shani's legs were unsteady. "Too many. Now I'm going to have one heck of a time concentrating for the rest of the day. And this meeting with the city parish Human Services staff promises to be too dull for words."

"You can steel yourself for the ordeal while you drive the six blocks over there," Eric chuckled. "And I'll make it up to you tonight." He winked at her.

"I'm holding you to that." At least she could daydream about his embrace to get through what promised to be a drab afternoon of tedium.

*   *   *

"So what have you got, Trumaine?"

Dalton rocked back in the deep red leather captain's chair behind the massive, highly polished oak desk in his office. The picture window at his back over looked the street below and a small park. Dalton was proud of his office. For him it represented his triumph over all those who said he could not make it.

"Some very interesting information, sir. An ex-employee has given me evidence that could be quite helpful." Trumaine placed brown folder in front of Dalton. He leaned down to point at a paragraph. "Look at that."

"Interesting is right." Dalton balanced his bifocals on the end of his nose to read. "How widespread is this theft of goods from Mid-City."

"My source, frankly she's had her fingers stuck to property not hers, says it's the rule not the exception. And Ms. Moore has been ineffective in controlling it." Trumaine pressed his lips together.

"Ex-employee. Fired?"

Trumaine nodded. "Yes."

"Then she isn't credible. Happens all the time, they'll say. She's out for revenge because she got caught stealing." Dalton drummed his fingers on the blotter.

"There are indications that this has happened before, sir. And there's something else." Trumaine lifted the top page to show him the next one. "Involving Ms. Moore allowing a drug addict to remain on a payroll even though this addict has dropped out of the job training program."

"You mean Shani Moore is collecting the paycheck?" Dalton's head came up with a snap.

Trumaine gave a small sigh of disappointment. "Well not really, sir. The paycheck has been stopped, but under the guidelines, this M. Campbell should have been dropped from the list weeks ago. Bad management, pure and simple."

"It's not much, Trumaine. I'd hoped for more."

"I did the best I could with such a short time frame, sir. Besides, with the proper handling a little can go a long way." Trumaine's lips twitched with the trace of a cunning grin.

Dalton looked at him with interest. "How's that?"

"We don't have to prove anything. Just show inept management and questionable results for the money being spent." Trumaine lifted a shoulder. "The appearance of impropriety can be just as damaging. And the new conservative majority legislature won't need much convincing."

"You're right. With the rosy filter taken off his eyes, Eric should come back to his senses." Dalton swiveled his chair around to gaze out of the window. "He won't give up his career to support her when this comes out."

"Novelty, sir. I've been there myself a time or two." Trumaine let out a gruff laugh.

Dalton glanced at him sideways. "Yes I know." He suppressed a smile of satisfaction at the flash of worry that flittered across Trumaine's thin face for an instant. "But how do we know the reporter will use it?"

"He was already doing a series on scandals involving funds mishandled by the Department of Health and Hospitals. I know the guy, he'll grab it like a dog goes after a juicy soup bone." Trumaine wore a smug look.

"Very good." Dalton let his gaze wandered around for a few seconds. The downtown buildings were decorated with garlands and red bows. "We need to get my son back on track. Humm, it will come out when Eric wanted to introduce her to our social circle," he murmured to himself as though Trumaine was no longer in the room.

Trumaine wrinkled his long nose at the prospect. "There would certainly be talk about *that*. Not to mention how fast it would get back to Senator Raymond."

Dalton did not answer or seem to notice Trumaine was still present. "Yes, the timing is just right."

Chapter Five

"Come in, My'iesha." Shani held open the front door to the center.

Several other girls from the neighborhood had told her that My'iesha was pacing back and forth outside. Shani did not waste a minute. She did not want to miss an opportunity to connect with the skittish young woman again. My'iesha presented a tough exterior, gained from being bounced around ten foster homes by the time she was sixteen. She ran away at seventeen and was forced to do whatever she could to live. Though quick to insist she needed no one, her presence meant she was crying out for help. But she looked as though she might take flight.

"Please," Shani said.

My'iesha stood still, looking down the street instead of at Shani. "I can't stay long."

"Sure. Just a quick cup of coffee."

"All right I guess." My'iesha responded with a toss of her head. She sauntered past Shani. A childlike sketch of a Christmas tree topped with a gold star caught her eye.

"Kids decorated. Hey, look at little Yusef's drawing. Pretty good for a seven-year-old," she said examining it.

"Yes, the children worked real hard on our decorations." Shani swept a hand around her. Not only were there drawings, but the children had hung garlands and made a two large wreaths for the double doors leading into the center. "They started right after Thanksgiving."

"Not bad." My'iesha did not move from the drawing. She stared at the signature.

"Yusef has asked about you several times," Shani said.

My'iesha's shoulders went rigid. "Yeah, well workin' in some after-school daycare is a pain."

"You volunteered to help out a couple of days a week after your part-time job. The kids loved your puppet shows."

"I ain't got time for none of that." My'iesha retorted in a tough girl voice.

Shani said nothing until they got to her office. When the door was closed, she poured hot water for the coffee. "This will take the chill off."

"Thanks." My'iesha took the mug and slumped into one of the chairs facing Shani's desk.

"So how've you been?"

"'Kay." My'iesha mumbled with her head down.

"Yusef isn't the only one who misses you. Maybe you could drop by sometime when Mrs. Martin is here. All the ladies in the senior citizens crafts class said to tell you hi."

My'iesha shifted in her seat. "What did you tell them? About me not being around anymore?"

"Just that you had a lot going on."

"Yeah, that's no lie," My'iesha said with a grunt. Silence stretched between them. "I guess you disgusted with me."

"I'm worried about you. Life is rough without friends." Shani sat next to her.

"You want me to come back?" My'iesha said in a little girl voice.

"Very much," Shani replied. She held her breath waiting.

"But how I'm gonna get my job back? You must have given it to somebody else by now." She relaxed a little.

"No, I kept it open for you."

My'iesha looked up at her with liquid eyes. "How did you know I'd come back?"

"Because I know how much pride you took in doing a good job and how much it meant to you," Shani said with feeling.

"Well, maybe I can go by there next Tuesday." My'iesha plucked at a loose thread on the tight skirt she wore.

"Fantastic. I'll call them today. I'm glad you're back. My'iesha." Shani put her hand on My'iesha's shoulder. "We're going to be okay."

My'iesha could no longer stop the tears. She put down the cup and lay her head on Shani's shoulder.

"That was a wonderful meal, Mrs. Aucoin." Shani sat next to Eric in the large den.

She could not help but be impressed with her surroundings. The foyer of the spacious house was made festive with white lights strung around two tall potted trees. Fresh garlands draped over the windows of the formal living room and dining room, both decorated by professionals in ivory, green, and gold. The house smelled of a refreshing combination of pine and cinnamon. After dinner, Mrs. Aucoin had insisted they be informal and relax in the den.

"Now let's have Dalton fix us a drink. He just loves playing bartender," Adeline winked at her.

"And I'm good if I do say so myself." Dalton called out from behind the bar. "Here we go. Chardonnay for you, sweetheart. Ginger ale for my son whose driving, and brandy for his lady." He sat on the wide arm of the chair Adeline occupied with a glass of bourbon for himself. "So Shani, you're from Baton Rouge?"

"Actually I was born in Evangeline Parish, but my parents moved to Baton Rouge when I was a baby." Shani took a sip of the brandy.

"And you have a master's degree. What school?" Dalton kept his tone casual.

"Undergraduate at Southern, master's at LSU." Shani cleared her throat. This was the part of the evening she'd dreaded. Soon Mrs. Aucoin would jump in with questions of her own.

"I understand you have two brothers. What do they do?"

"Dad—" Eric cut in before Shani could speak. He frowned at Dalton.

"No, Eric. It's okay. My older brother, Brendon, is a computer analyst. My youngest brother, J.J., is in prison."

Dalton's expression showed no surprise. "I see." He glanced at Eric then Adeline. "How unfortunate."

"Both my parents are dead. They were poor, working people. My mother finished high school. My father never did. I don't have any educated, well-to-do relatives or a fancy family history." Shani spoke in an even tone without hostility, a tone that said "take it or leave it."

Adeline's handsome features clouded over. "Dalton, you should be ashamed. You sound like a police officer questioning a suspect." She faced Shani. "Excuse my husband, Shani. He can be hard to take sometimes."

Dalton waved away his wife's admonishment. "What's everybody getting so upset about? I was just making conversation. Getting acquainted."

Shani scanned his face. "Is there something else you want to know, Mr. Aucoin? A lot of people are curious about my younger brother. It's natural."

She was used to the questions and shocked whispers behind her back. It was obvious Mr. Aucoin wanted to see if she would mention J.J. being in prison. And he wanted Eric and his wife to hear it.

"That's quite enough, Dalton," Adeline said in a sharp voice. "Shani, this is our first meeting and we know quite enough for now. I don't believe in spilling family secrets to those you barely know." She smiled at Shani with genuine fondness. "But I do hope we will become closer."

"Thank you, Mrs. Aucoin. I'd like that."

Shani was so touched, tears came to her eyes. She took a deep breath and blinked them back. Adeline's warm, maternal personality reminded her of how much she missed her mother.

"My son looks at you the way I've never seen him look at another young woman. I have a feeling we'll be seeing more of each other." The twinkle in Adeline's eyes returned.

"Mama, please," Eric said with an embarrassed expression.

Dalton glanced at his wife and son. His stern expression relaxed. "Sure, there will be plenty of time for spilling family secrets. Hell, we've got more than a few Aucoins who've been in jail at one time or another. My wife's family couldn't keep their hands off other folks livestock." He guffawed.

"Dad! That was almost eighty years ago." Eric's troubled look shifted to one of relief. He gripped Shani's hand to reassure her.

Adeline laughed. "More recent than that, sweetie. Now, what about Christmas? Shani, you must join us."

For the next few hours the conversation moved from making plans for the holidays to sports. To Shani's surprise, she did not feel as though the talk was forced or superficial. Could she fit into Eric's life? Of course, J.J.'s crime was more serious than cattle theft. Would Adeline still be so understanding when she learned he had been a drug dealer? She felt a growing affection for the kind, gentle woman who seemed so different from her husband. Dalton Aucoin. Shani doubted there was little he did not know about her all ready. Yet he had never treated her with anything but a courtly kind of old fashion courtesy. Maybe her fears were unfounded.

Back at her apartment, Shani poured them each a cup of hot herbal tea. "This will help us sleep."

Eric frowned at the steaming brew. "Not what I had in mind." He ducked her playful swat with a chuckle. "Just joking. I've got an early day tomorrow. I'd better drink this and go. It's eleven all ready."

"Yeah, I need to get a fresh start myself. I've got back-to-back meetings all day." Shani settled onto the sofa near him. "So do you think tonight went okay?"

Eric put down his cup. "Honey, it went really well. Dad's opinionated, pushy sometimes, and a bit of a snob, but he's a good person at heart. Honestly, I thought he'd be worse." He grinned.

"Hey, it's normal that your father would want to know. He cares about you and your career. Who you associate with can ruin your career as a politician." Shani bit her lower lip. She had been a fool not to have realized it before now. Dalton's questions hit home with the force of dynamite. Those same questions would be asked by others. The answers could be weapons used against Eric.

"My constituents are not that narrow-minded." Eric moved close to her. "So don't worry about my career."

"But you might have lots of problems because of me." Shani let out a sigh of dismay.

"And we'll handle them. Together," he said in a soft voice.

"But—"

Eric silenced her with a kiss. Shani melded her body to his, anxiety dissolved at the touch of his tongue to hers. "Eric, this is serious," she mumbled. Her breath quickened with each brush of lips brushed against her neck. His hands moved up her thighs to her breasts.

"Baby, you can't tell how serious I am?" he whispered. "I want you, Shani. And nothing will come between us. Nothing."

In a soft haze of desire, they found their way to her bed. They lay together naked within minutes of frantic undressing. Once again his strong body moved with hers in a rhythmic dance of passion. He moved with enough speed to lift her close to the edge of ecstasy, then slowed leaving her crying for more. And more he gave. Shani trembled at the delicious torture of delay.

"Eric," Shani moaned.

Over and over she said his name, her voice rising with the strength of each thrust. His cries told her he would delay no longer. First Shani came, a shower of bright colors exploding in her head. Eric groaned holding her tight as he shuddered inside her. They went limp in each other's arms, gasping for breath. For a long time neither spoke. They enjoyed holding each other. Eric combed his fingers through Shani's thick hair while she pressed her cheek to his broad chest.

"Now isn't this better than any old herbal tea?" Eric's chest rumbled with mirth.

Shani giggled. "You got that right."

"And I don't want you worrying about my career. Even if it did make a difference, which it won't, I couldn't give you up now. I love you too much." Eric lifted her chin to gaze into Shani's eyes.

"I love you, too. I love you like crazy." Shani kissed him long and hard.

Terrilyn came into the living room of her spacious townhouse carrying a huge bowl of popcorn. "I saw Robert the other day. Claudia dumped him."

"Ah, too bad," Shani said in a voice heavy with sarcasm.

"He asked about you. Honey, he wants you back bad. It was written all over his pitiful face. Go girl. Two fine men after you is good for the ego."

"You called Robert a low down, no good mongrel. Now you sound like he's the catch of the day." Shani stared at her friend in mock outrage.

"He's a dog to his heart, girl. No question. But he's a

fine dog with money." Terrilyn popped a kernel into her mouth.

The two women were dateless, Eric was working late and Terrilyn's latest flame was working a night shift. So they decided to spend Friday night watching movies and eating snacks to console themselves. They sat on Terrilyn's sofa bed that she bought for when her mother or one of her sisters came from Shreveport to visit. Propped against oversized pillows, they were snug and ready to cry over their favorite movie, *Black Orpheus*.

"Having Robert slither back does nothing for my ego, Terrilyn. He doesn't care about me." Shani arranged the heavy cotton throw over her legs.

"Even better. Honey, rub that wound raw. Let the little mangy puppy do a slow burn thinking about some other man giving you good love."

The corners of Shani's mouth turned up with the trace of a grin. "You're wicked. Darn, this video tape is acting strange."

"Surprise, surprise. We've played the thing a zillion times. Maybe it's worn out." Terrilyn tried to help clear the picture by pressing buttons on the remote.

"Or maybe you should invest in a new VCR. They delivered this one in a horse and buggy." Shani dodged a pillow.

"Look. I give up. But have no doubt I'm going to buy a new copy of this classic. Let's see what's on the movie channel." Terrilyn turned to a local station and was about to switch when Shani stopped her.

"Wait, it's the ten o'clock news."

"Who cares? Look, the television guide says *The Color Purple* is on Channel thirty-two starting . . . now. I could watch that movie another dozen times at least, girl."

Shani grabbed the remote from her. "No you don't. There's Eric." She pointed to the screen.

"Who is that cutie next to him? Oh, I love those soulful eyes." Terrilyn leered.

"Trumaine Delacrosse, Eric's aide. Now will you hush?"

"Senator Raymond and a group of freshman legislators have mapped out a plan to address the serious fiscal problems of this state." A black female reporter spoke into the camera before the picture switched back to the group of about fifteen men who stood in the lobby of the state capitol building in downtown Baton Rouge.

Senator Raymond, with thick gray hair and a puffy face, stood at a podium with microphones positioned in front of him. "We believe that a drastic change in the way we do business in state government is necessary. No longer can will we allow those who will not work to live off the sweat of hard-working, decent men and women. Our message to them is simple, the party's over."

All fifteen of the men, including Eric, applauded his words.

The female reporter came back on camera. "Among the areas targeted for reduction are block grants to several community centers where there has been evidence of poor administration or misapplication of funds. According to Senator Raymond, details will soon follow. This is Cynthia Bienville for Channel two."

Shani and Terrilyn sat silently for several seconds.

Terrilyn finally broke the tense quiet. "I can see those wheels of suspicion turning. Don't jump to conclusions."

"But did you see him cheerleading that old bag of wind? What am I supposed to think?" Shani wanted to cry. "Maybe Eric is a liar and just using me."

Terrilyn turned down the sound of the television. "You told me that Eric never claimed to be a converted liberal after you two got together. But he did promise to consider input from you and other social workers."

Shani chewed a finger and stared at the picture of a weather map. "How can I be sure he'll stick by that when he's faced with all his party members?"

"He's only one man, Shani. He can't change everyone or do it alone. He can only try." Terrilyn shrugged.

Shani felt better as she digested her words. "As usual you're brilliant."

"You just figured that out?" Terrilyn quipped. "Lets get another round of drinks before we get into Whoopi's premier performance." She padded into the kitchen in her bunny slippers.

"You're absolutely right. I'm being so childish. Of course, Eric will be outnumbered when it comes to defending agencies like Mid-City. But he can make a difference." Shani smiled at the strawberry flavored soft drink Terrilyn handed her. "My favorite."

"Hey, nothing but the best for our slumber party. And for me, old fashioned Barq's root beer. Now, here's to Senator Aucoin. A man for all seasons." Terrilyn raised a clear mug filled to the top.

"To Senator Aucoin. A man after my own heart." Shani clinked her glass against the mug.

"He's after more than that, honey. And count your lucky stars for it." Terrilyn winked at her.

"Every day, sugar. Every fun-filled day." Shani snickered with her. They spent the rest of the night watching movies and talking about everything under the sun.

Chapter Six

Only six days until Christmas. What a difference a few weeks made. Shani sang along with the carolers grouped in front of a huge, elaborately decorated tree in the middle of the mall. Unlike her previous shopping trips, the festive mood made the task easy. Enjoyable even. She glanced at her watch and hurried to the next store. The smell of leather drew her toward a row of briefcases and portfolios. There it was. A leather covered calendar and weekly planner. Perfect for a busy senator, Shani mused feeling a flush of happiness at the thought of giving it to Eric.

She whizzed through the rest of mall picking up items for everyone on her list. The only time her mood darkened was when she picked out a Sony Walkman for J.J. Another Christmas separated from him. And this year would be even worse when she went to visit him Sunday without Brendon. Yet she could not stay sad for long. A glance at the bright green holiday shopping bag, Eric's wrapped gift nestled in among the rest of her treasures, lifted her up again. Somehow she would make things right between her brothers. This Christmas was filled with hope and a kind of newness.

Back at the office, Shani dove into the pile of messages on her desk with gusto. Elaine chattered away through the open door as she worked about her plans for the holidays.

"Yeah, honey. I can't wait. I've been saving up all year for my new sound system. Me and Wayne gonna celebrate pushing the last of our kids out of the nest by throwing the best darn New Year's Eve groove fest in this old town." Elaine snapped her fingers to the beat of Otis Redding singing "Merry Christmas, Baby" coming from the radio on her desk.

"Sounds good to me." Shani laughed.

"Yep. You and Senator Aucoin are coming, right?"

"Yes indeed. When I told Eric, he grinned from ear to ear. We'll hit your place first then go to the big ball down at the Raddisson. It's going to be one stupendous beginning to 1997," Shani murmured.

"I heard that."

Elaine gave a low chuckle. Shani's eyes widened in embarrassment. Shani hadn't realized she'd spoken aloud.

"I mean . . .," she stammered to find the right words.

Elaine glanced up at her when she came out carrying signed memos and letters. "You mean great parties are always nice." She wore a knowing grin.

"Yes, they are." Shani went back into her office smiling. She tapped out a beat on her desk. "Bringin' all them good ole presents for my baby an' me, ha-ha-ha," she sang along with the gravel voiced soul music legend.

"Merry Christmas, baby." Elaine took up the song. "You sho did treat me nice."

They both dissolved into giggles. Suddenly Elaine's voice was cut off by the ring of the telephone.

"Merry Christmas, Mid-City Center. How may I help you? Yes she's in." Elaine put the call through. "Senator main squeeze on line two."

Shani was still laughing when she pushed the button. "Hello, Eric. Yes I know you're working late tonight."

"Now don't be that way. You know how it is." Eric's voice was soft and placating.

"But it's almost Christmas. I'll bet none of those other lawmakers are putting in overtime like this. Typical Type A behavior."

"We've made a lot of headway with our proposals. And I'm wrapping up the last of a few loose ends now. We're ready to bring this state back to fiscal responsibility." Eric switched back to his businesslike tone.

Shani cradled the phone and shuffled a stack of papers. "Save it for the news conference, mister," she teased. "What about tonight? Or must I languish in loneliness once more?"

"Take heart, lovely one. I'll be all yours in a few short hours."

"Can't wait."

"Bye, love." Eric's voice went low and sensuous.

"Bye, honey." Shani sighed and sank back against the back of her chair. She stared up at the ceiling.

"Can I come in?" Paulette stood in the door.

"Sure. Get some coffee."

"In a minute. Have you read today's paper?"

"No. Yesterday's either. Honey, I've been wrapping gifts and trying to get the last of these presents. Cortana Mall opened at seven this morning with a lot of stores having a special pre-Christmas sale and it was wild." Shani's bright mood faded when she noticed Paulette's expression. "What's wrong?"

Paulette's face was taut with anger. She slapped a newspaper down on Shani's desk. "Look at that."

Shani read aloud. "Theft Widespread at Local Help Centers." The headline was bad enough but it got worse. "Conservative senate investigation spearheaded out of—" Shani broke off for several seconds as a sick feeling began through her midsection. "Out of freshman Senator

Aucoin's office supports the need for changes in the way some social programs are administered."

"It seems Senator Aucoin used his visits to build a case against us." Paulette pressed her lips together. She moved with short jerky motions filling a mug with black coffee. She thumped down the container of creamer. "Of all people, he takes the word of a woman who is a known liar."

Shani's heart pounded as she read the article silently. The thin sheets slipped from her fingers when she was done. "There must be a reason for this."

"Hell yes there's a reason!" Paulette blurted. "Senator Raymond and his minions want to shut us down."

"No, Paulette. Eric told me he wouldn't . . ."

Her voice trailed off because she remembered his words. Eric had never promised he would protect the programs if there was evidence of poor management. But he must see that this so-called evidence did not come from a credible source. Shani stared out the window at the weathered, wood frame homes just across the street. A child no more than two years old played in the dirt with two older children. All three wore ragged, thin sweaters. Had she been so blinded by emotion that she'd given Eric the ammunition needed by his conservative party leaders? Shani closed her eyes to stop the tears pushing to form.

"Shani, these guys have all the conviction of religious zealots when it comes to social programs. Or social engineering as they call it." Paulette glanced at Shani. When she spoke her tone was sympathetic. "Maybe Eric didn't know the information he had about Mid-City would be twisted to show us in the worse possible light."

Shani turned from the window to look her in the eyes. "You don't believe that and neither do I. Eric is very practical and no dummy."

"Eric isn't quoted in this article." Paulette picked up the newspaper and scanned the article again. She had the posture of someone grasping at straws. "His aide Trumaine

Delacrosse gave a statement that the inquiry is continuing."

"Eric knows everything that goes on in his office, Paulette." Shani's anguish hardened into to fury.

"I've worked for other people and run my own private practice. It's very possible not to know everything your employees are doing. It was months later that I found letters one of my former secretaries was supposed to have sent out. I wanted to call her up and fire her again." Paulette leaned forward in her chair. "All I'm saying is, give him a chance to explain."

Shani squinted at her. "Why are you defending him? I know how you feel about black conservatives."

Paulette sank back against the chair. "And I know finding that special person doesn't happen very often. Two years ago, I broke it off with Reginald. I thought he was too rigid and conservative. You know what? He's married to a woman who makes me look like a right-wing reactionary. They have a beautiful baby girl."

"This is more than a difference in political views now. Eric may have used me, lied to me, to further his political career and impress Senator Raymond." Shani could not keep her voice from wavering.

Paulette stood up. "I won't try and dress it up, sugar. This looks pretty bad," she said pointing to the newspaper. "Make him explain. Bring him to his knees to beg forgiveness and swear to make it right. But don't be too quick to write him off."

Shani tried to call Eric but his secretary told her he was gone to some afternoon meeting. She closed up in her office after Paulette left. Fruitless hours of trying to concentrate on the new five-year plan, memos to staff, and the quarterly budget report left her spent. A tap on the door made her glance up from the rows of figures on a spreadsheet.

"Yes? Oh, Elaine." Shani rubbed her tired eyes.

"Have a good evening. I'm going home now."

"It's five already?" Shani glanced at the clock on her credenza. She was shocked at how time had passed. In one hour, Eric would be at her apartment.

"Yeah, and my husband is probably burning up chicken even as we speak. His night to cook," Elaine said with a laugh. Her laughter died when she saw the gloom on Shani's face. "Listen, I know it's none of my business but . . . Give Senator Aucoin a chance to explain."

"Oh, you can bet I want him to tell me all about this one," Shani shot back.

Elaine came into the room and sat opposite her. "I mean, take time to hear what he's saying. You still may not agree, but listen without judgment. My mama taught me that not long after I got married. Her and Daddy were together forty-two years."

"Thanks, Elaine. I'll try to remember that." Shani tried to lift the corners of her mouth into a smile and only half succeeded.

"Good night." Elaine hesitated at the door. "And take care."

"Bye."

Shani was touched by Elaine's concern. She was both anxious and reluctant to see Eric. Part of her was poised to demand answers, another part wanted to avoid what promised to be a painful confrontation. As she changed clothes, she tried to follow Elaine and Paulette's advice.

"I'll keep calm and ask him about the article. Let him talk without interrupting," she said the words trying to make her outrage subside. She glanced at herself in the full length mirror on the bedroom closet door. "After all, there could be a reasonable explanation." The woman staring back at her looked far from convinced. At that moment, the double chimes of her doorbell sounded.

Shani took a deep breath and opened the door. "Hi.

How've you been?'' She resisted the urge to avoid the kiss on her forehead.

"Whew! What a grueling day. But knowing I'd end it with you made it bearable. Sorry I'm late. But the meeting went on way past the time it should have. Then I ran by the house to change.'' He took off his leather jacket to reveal a forest green sweater, striped cotton shirt underneath, and dark brown pants. "I was tired of wearing that suit and tie.''

"Oh, I see." Shani sat next to him, her back straight.

Eric crossed an ankle over one knee. "So how's my sweetie doing? Your day was better than mine I hope." He dropped a muscular arm behind her on the sofa's back.

"It started out okay. Then it went downhill real fast. But of course you know about it.'' She shot him an accusing glance. His casual behavior was infuriating. Did he think his charms were so over powering she would forgive anything?

"I do?"

"Yes, since you saw fit to trash my reputation in the *Advocate.*" Shani picked up the newspaper from her coffee table and waved it.

"What? Oh, the article about problems at help centers. Baby, I told you we would be looking into them. And—''

"But did you ask for reactions from us?'' Shani's ire sprang forward like a hot spark. "You planned this all along. I should have seen it coming.''

"Now hold on, I didn't trash your reputation.'' Eric spoke in an unruffled tone. "Trumaine described problems in his report identified long ago. Some of them you and other directors pointed out.''

"Widespread theft common at the agencies? I don't recall ever saying that. How could you listen to the allegations of one disgruntled ex-employee and splash it all over the wire service?'' Shani glared at him.

"What?'' Eric took the paper from her hand. A frown creased his face as he saw the headline. "I didn't see this edition. I've been swamped and Trumaine only gave me a summary of major stories, including this one. This isn't the way it was supposed to be done."

"What do you take me for? You want to destroy our credibility so we won't have any chance to get funding." Shani turned her face from him. "You're good, I have to give you credit."

"What does that mean?" Eric's jaw clenched.

"It means you used your oily charm to dazzle me. You knew all the right words to lull me into trusting you. How you cared about the poor but wanted the money to be used wisely. Self-determination is what our community needs. But that's not the best part. No, your most impressive performances were when you said how special I was to you," Shani said in a hoarse voice. "And now you think I'm so in love I'll accept any thin lie you offer me?"

"Honey, that's not true at all! Shani, you have to believe me." Eric clutched her arm. "I didn't know the reports of theft would be made the focus by this reporter. Even more important, I never lied about my feelings for you."

Shani twisted from his grasp. "I tried to convince myself all afternoon you couldn't have known about it. But this sentence kept ringing in my head." She jabbed a finger at the last paragraph. "According to Senator Aucoin, these programs are aimed at keeping the poor dependent and provide jobs for social workers. I've heard you say that at least a half dozen times."

"And it's what I believe." Eric drew himself up to his full height. "Look, if these programs can stand up to scrutiny then you've got nothing to worry about. But I resent being accused like this. You always knew my views."

"So you admit being behind this?" Shani was flabbergasted despite her early suspicions. What brass to show such arrogance. How could she have misjudged him so much?

"Shani, you knew all along all of the budget items were under a microscope." Eric's face was like a gathering storm of thunder and lightening. "I think we'd better both stop before we say things that can't be taken back."

Shani stared at him coldly. "I wonder just how far you'd go to get ahead politically. What with Congressman Johnson announcing he won't run for the House of Representatives next election. Your name has been mentioned more than once." She remembered a speech in which Eric talked about his ambition to run for Congress one day.

Eric looked at her through narrowed eyes that glinted with indignation. "And you're willing to defend programs that waste the taxpayers money even when it's obvious every dollar must count in the black community. Save the status quo no matter what. Is that it?"

"So you don't bother to deny your agreement with this hatchet job of an article," Shani spat at him. "I should have known."

Eric picked up his jacket. "Maybe we haven't known each other long in terms of time, but I thought you knew what kind of person I am." He walked to the door. "Obviously I was wrong."

Shani felt a warm flow down her cheek and tasted salt. She turned from him. "You counted on using the famous Eric Aucoin charisma. Didn't work this time, pal. That's what you were wrong about." She made her voice hard as steel.

"If that's the way you see it fine. It's best I found out early in the game. Who needs this?"

When the door slammed behind him, Shani felt the jolt more than on a physical level. She collapsed onto the sofa and gave in to the urge to weep. A tidal wave of loss washed over her that left her feeling weak and more lonely than she had since losing her mother.

Brendon's fine black brows drew together over chocolate brown eyes. "You sick? Looks like you haven't slept in weeks." He paused in wrapping gifts for Colin and Kara.

He and Janine used Shani's apartment as a hiding place for their Christmas toys. With Christmas only two days away, they did the usual. Ate dinner out then came over to get everything that needed assembling put together.

Janine slapped his arm. "Nice going, Brendon. Make her feel even better by telling her she looks awful," she muttered.

Shani came back into the living room with three cups of hot cocoa. "It's okay, Janine. He's never been one for diplomacy." She managed a feeble smile.

Brendon ignored his wife's reproof. "Shani, what's wrong? You know better than to try and hide anything from me. I can look at you in two seconds and see something bad has happened."

"It's just . . ." Shani bit her bottom lip unable to go on.

His eyes went wide with fear. "Is it J.J.? Did he get hurt in prison? You don't want to tell me because of the way I've been acting, is that it?"

"No, no," Shani said in a rush to calm the his rising panic. "J.J. is doing fine. This has nothing to do with him."

Brendon let out a long, slow breath. His relief was visible as he clasped Janine's hand on his arm. "Then what? Work got you down? I've told you about running yourself ragged at that center. Why you don't go into private practice with this psychiatrist friend of mine is beyond me."

Janine shook her head at him. "Brendon, you sure can miss the boat sometimes."

"I don't know what you mean. If it's one thing I understand, it's my little sister. She's got herself all worked up about a misguided kid or poor welfare mother with no more foodstamps." Brendon went back to wrapping a doll for Kara. "You've got to learn some day not to take all the world's problems on your shoulders. You'll wind up with an ulcer."

"Wrong again, Mr. Perceptive. Shani, I read that article." Janine wore a sympathetic expression.

"What article?" Shani busied herself tying a ribbon.

"The one that has probably caused big trouble between you and Eric Aucoin," Janine said.

"Shani and Senator Aucoin?" Brendon blinked as though waking up from a nap.

"Brendon, I mentioned it to you several times. You said, 'That's nice, baby.'" Janine turned to Shani. "He's been up to his neck in work for weeks."

"Yeah, I remember something about Shani having a date. But with Senator Aucoin? He's a staunch conservative." Brendon gazed at his sister in amazement.

Janine gave a short laugh and pointed him to the extra bedroom Shani used as an office where other toys still waited to prepared. "Here, sweetie. Put this pin ball machine together. I'll catch you up later."

Brendon took the large game from her. "Don't be such a smart aleck. And I'm not going anywhere. Besides, I saw the article you're talking about, and now I do remember about Shani and Senator Aucoin." He seemed close to sticking his tongue out at her.

"Lord, I'm so humiliated. Why don't we just rent a billboard that says 'Shani Moore, proof that you can be the same kind of fool twice.'" Shani spoke in an acrid voice.

"Oh, come on. You knew the guy's politics when you met him. At least he was always honest. Something you can't say about a lot of public officials. In fact, I have to agree with some of what he says—" Brendon held up a finger in preparation of launching a discourse.

"Honey, please," Janine cut in. "Shani, from the look on your face, I'd say you had one mean argument with him. Right?"

"It was awful. I got angry, one word led to another, and well you know." Shani pushed aside the green shiny paper in her lap.

"Too awful for a reconciliation?" Janine put an arm around her shoulders.

"It's not just an argument. He used our relationship to

get information against Mid-City. And not only could we be hurt. Every center in this state might suffer."

"Are you sure his party or maybe another legislator didn't use his name to avoid being called racists? They do stuff like that you know. Don't be too quick to think he's a bum." Brendon wore a self-satisfied expression at the surprise his comment brought. "Pretty perceptive of me, huh? I haven't been that immersed in work."

"Amazingly, he could be right." Janine rubbed her chin in thought. "What did Eric say about the article?"

"He claimed not to have known they would go the sensational route and use that theft allegation." Shani kicked a wad of paper across the carpet. "Either way, he's being used. And had the nerve to get an attitude with me."

"I guess so if you jumped the brother," Brendon snorted. "I'd catch a 'tude myself if you called me a liar to my face."

Janine sent him a scathing glance. "What my husband must mean is harsh words lead to hard feelings. But if he wasn't guilty, he should have just answered the questions."

"Excuse me, I know what I meant. Look, Shani, I know how strongly you feel about those programs. Maybe you didn't give the guy much of a chance to tell his side. Maybe the man just made a mistake."

"Eric Aucoin didn't make a mistake. I'm sure of it. Now the subject is closed," Shani said in a firm voice.

"Okay. If you say so." Brendon cocked an eyebrow at his wife.

"And don't give any eye signals behind my back either." Her foot bumped against a gift bag under her small Christmas tree. One of J.J.'s gifts, homemade tea cakes from her grandmother's recipe. "Besides, you don't practice what you preach." Shani pointed a finger at his nose.

"Meaning?"

"Meaning J.J. has very little to look forward to during Christmas except visits from us. Why can't you forgive him?" Shani shoved thoughts of Eric away to focus on a different source of pain.

"It's not the same. J.J. hurt Mama with his wild behavior. And his being in prison is a disrespect to her and Daddy's memory." Brendon had a stubborn set to his square jaw.

"He's ashamed of himself, Brendon. He needs us to stand by him." Shani wanted to shake reason into him.

Janine looped her arm through his. "Sweetheart, we both know how torn up you're going to be if you don't see him. You're miserable," she said to him in a soft voice.

"J.J. is not going to put my entire family in prison with him. He made his choices. Now let him deal with the consequences. Let's drop it." Brendon stormed out of the room.

Janine nodded to Shani. "Talk to him alone. This is something only you can help him work through."

Shani followed him into her office. She pushed aside empty boxes that only recently held toys and other gifts now wrapped. "Brendon, I know you feel partly responsible for J.J., but it's not your fault. He did make certain choices."

Brendon stood with his back to her staring out the window into the night. "I was so into high school, the band, and Charlene. Or was Darlene?" He gave an grunt of self-disgust. "I can't even remember her name. J.J. was drifting from mischief into crime while I went to parties and hung out with my buddies. Oh, I remembered my promise to Daddy. I lied to myself that a few lectures and taking him to the movies once in a while was the best I could do."

Shani stepped closer to him. "You were only a teenager yourself. I counsel parents much older than you were at the time who can't figure out how to save their kids from the streets. It really isn't your fault, Brendon."

He turned to her, his face drawn with torment. "You don't think I failed you both?"

Shani hugged him to her. "No, no. J.J. and I looked up to you. We always thought we'd never be able to be half the person you are today. J.J. understands your anger. He doesn't think he's worthy of you."

"Mama used to clap her hands and laugh with joy seeing us running to get our presents Christmas mornings. She would say . . ." Brendon could not go on.

"She'd say, 'Ain't nothin' like bein' with family on Christmas. Thank you, Jesus. I can feel your daddy smilin' down on us, too,'" Shani finished for him. "Please, come with me Sunday."

Brendon wiped his eyes. "Here are his presents." He pointed to a large bag. He wore a sheepish expression, "We went overboard and spoiled him as usual."

"Now you can give them to him yourself. By the way, he agrees you shouldn't bring the children." Shani squeezed his hand.

"Thanks little sister." Brendon shook off his somber mood. "Now quit stalling. You suggested I buy this contraption, and you're going to help me put it together." He held up a wide sheet of instructions with tiny print.

"My goodness! We're going to be here all night."

For the next hour, the three of them wrestled to finish. Shani was relieved to the see tension melt from her older brother. He laughed with ease as though a weight was lifted from his shoulders. The holiday would not be so bad after all. Then she thought of Eric. The bright lights and shiny wrapping seemed to go dim. She continued to chatter with them, but her heart was not in it.

"Bye, sis. See you Sunday," Brendon said. He kissed her forehead.

"Take all this stuff and put it in the trunk, babe. I'm coming." Janine loaded his arms with tools and bags. "Thanks for everything, sugar."

"Hey, you don't have to thank me. I love wrapping presents for our beautiful babies."

"I'm not talking about that. Thanks for helping Brendon unload that heartache he's been lugging around for

months." Janine hugged and kissed her. "About Eric
Aucoin, from what I hear he's a good person."

"Janine, I just don't know what to think."

"Try to work it out once more. No accusations, just
openly share the hurt you feel. Talk to him."

"It's not so simple." Shani hugged herself against the
cold that came from inside, not the chill night air.

Janine sighed. "Honey, it never is. But from the light
in your eyes when you talked about him, I'd say don't give
up without a fight. Promise you'll consider what I've said?"

Shani said nothing but nodded in response. Alone, she
faced the bleak truth. There was no way to bridge the gulf
between her and Eric. He had taken advantage of her.
Maybe planned it from the beginning. No, it was over. A'
least this time she hadn't spent years being deceived. And
she had survived last New Year's Eve without someone
special to hold at midnight. She would make it through
to the dawning of 1997 as well.

"Come in, Trumaine," Eric said in a clipped tone. He
drummed his fingers on his desk. For the last twenty-four
hours he'd simmered, unable to confront him. Trumaine
had taken the previous day off. "I left messages on your
answering machine."

"I spent the night in New Orleans with a friend after
we finished shopping at the River Walk. You ready for
Christmas?" Trumaine strolled in and poured himself a
cup of coffee.

Eric ignored his question. "Tell me about this article."
He held up the newspaper.

"Which article is that?" Trumaine took a sip from the
cup. He squinted at the fine print.

"The one 'spearheaded out of my office,'" Eric
snapped. "The one that implies Shani Moore and several
community center directors are incompetent at best and

thieves at worst. The article you summarized for me but left out a few rather important details.''

"You and I discussed gathering information for our reports to Senator Raymond. But I told you there were problems at those agencies. I provided that information to Senator Raymond's office as we agreed.''

"But you decided what information to send. An allegation made by an angry woman fired from her job is not the basis to make judgments about an entire organization,'' Eric said, his voice rising.

"Senator Raymond specifically asked for a complete report and I gave it to him. It was their decision to use the reports of pilfering.''

"I see,'' Eric said.

"In more than one instance, programs were being mismanaged,'' Trumaine defended his actions. "I thought the purpose of our investigation was to expose these abuses.''

"But based on credible evidence. Not hearsay and unconfirmed rumors. And definitely not from such a suspect source as some woman fired when she was caught stealing,'' Eric said.

"Senator Raymond—''

"Senator Raymond doesn't run my office,'' Eric cut him off. He stood up and planted both fists on the desk top. "You listen to me, and listen to me good. I decide what goes out of this office to Senator Raymond or any of the party leaders. Frankly, I think you knew damn well how that information would be put to use.''

Trumaine faced him with a cool expression. "He expected to get very specific information to use. Of course, I understand your relationship with Ms. Moore is at a delicate stage. But so is your political career. It's in your best interest to . . . work closely with Senator Raymond.''

"My relationship with Ms. Moore isn't any of your business.'' Eric spoke with such heat that Trumaine's cool exterior faltered for a split second. "And as for 'working with Senator Raymond,' I won't jump when he speaks just to advance my political career. Apparently you have your own career ambitions in mind."

Trumaine paused before he spoke. "Senator Raymond is a powerful man in this state."

"And known for rewarding loyalty." Eric had a sour taste in his mouth.

"Bucking men like Raymond is political suicide. And I plan a steady rise. I thought you had the same plans. Until now." Trumaine's lips curled with a hint of derision.

Eric crossed his arms. "Oh I'll be moving up. But not with my lips planted firmly on anyone's rear end. And if Senator Raymond expects that, then he can go jump."

Trumaine raised both eyebrows. "You want to be careful with that kind of talk or you could find yourself neutralized."

"I will not be an errand boy for him or anybody!" Eric shouted.

Dalton strode into the office and shut the door with a bang. "Lower your voice, son. Some influential businessmen who meet with Raymond regularly are in this building and roam these halls all the time. Now what is going on?"

Trumaine faced Dalton. "A small disagreement about strategy."

"Hardly," Eric retorted. "Acting without my approval and deciding to misrepresent my position makes this disagreement anything but small. Did you see this article, Dad?" He handed Dalton a copy of the newspaper.

Dalton didn't take it. "I'm sure Trumaine did what he felt was best for you and the party. Don't be so hot-headed, son. After all, you don't win a war without firing shots. If we're going to get anywhere with the party, we have to be bold."

Eric became still as a statue. "You knew about this," he said in a quiet voice. It was not a question.

"Trumaine," Dalton said with a nod toward the door. He waited until the door closed behind him. "Now look,

Eric, Raymond wants results. He isn't going to settle for some soft-peddled kind of approach."

"This is too much." Eric turned his back on Dalton.

Dalton went on. "And I agree with him. All those social agencies have accomplished is to give folks an excuse to do nothing, be nothing."

"You, Trumaine, and Senator Raymond, huh? Everybody is in agreement on what I should do. How about asking me?" Eric threw the paper down on his desk.

"The story was all ready in the works. You knew that. We added what we thought was pertinent information gathered in the last few weeks. Listen, if you're worried about that social worker—"

Eric's eyes flared with indignation. "Shani is angry and justifiably so. It's obvious you didn't care about getting facts, only smearing the community centers."

"Nothing in that paper is a lie, young man. Look at it again," Dalton said, his voice sharp and defensive. "You've said as much about these social programs time and again."

Eric hung his head. "Why did you do this, Dad? To go behind my back and attack the woman I love . . ." He sank down into his chair.

Dalton gave a grunt of cynicism. "The woman you love. How many women have you been through since college? You averaged about one each year."

"Dad—"

"Tell me their names," Dalton pointed an index finger at him.

"Dad, you don't understand—"

"That's what I thought. Listen, here, boy. I worked long and hard to give my children what I never had. I won't see you throw away your career. Now if you take time to consider, you'll see I'm right." Dalton sat back in his chair. He wore a look of stern paternalism, the look of a father who was used to being obeyed and did not doubt he would be.

Eric sat up straight. He stared hard at his father for

several seconds. "Don't ever talk down to me like that again. I'm way past being ten years old. No one, including you, will dictate to me how I conduct my career. Or my private life."

"You watch your mouth, son. And as for Ms. Moore, she's hardly more than a passing fancy." Dalton sat forward, his knuckles taut from gripping the arms of the chair. "She's not for you."

"Shani Moore is one of the finest women in the world. Don't ever disrespect her again," Eric continued ignoring his father's wrathful scowl. His voice was harsh. "I'm going to fire Trumaine and issue a statement denouncing this article."

"Now wait a minute young man!" Dalton jumped up. "I won't stand for any such thing!"

"You don't have a choice, Dad. I make my own decisions. You taught me that." Eric return his father's look of fury with a steady gaze.

"But, your political career will be over in this state. You won't be able to get any legislation through. Don't be a fool, boy!" Dalton rubbed a large hand over his eyes. "This woman has got you behaving irrationally."

"That's enough!" Eric shouted causing his father's head to jerk up with shock. "My feelings for Shani have nothing to do with it. That article was underhanded. I want no part of such tactics. We have nothing else to talk about."

Dalton stood with his hands at his side balled into fists. He was the picture of impotent fury. "I thought you had more sense. Don't come crawling to me when you realize how stupid you've been." He stormed from the office.

Eric slumped back into his chair feeling exhausted. How could his father know so little about him? How could he not see how much Shani meant to him? Eric went over in his mind the talks he'd had with Dalton about her. All the time his father was pretending to understand. And now because of Dalton, he may have lost Shani. He pounded the desk top with his fist.

"You all right, Senator Aucoin?" Nedra, his secretary, peered around the door frame. She appeared ready to take flight if need be.

Eric wiped a palm over his face and sighed. "Yeah sure, Nedra. Hold all my calls." He turned on the computer on his desk. "I've got a lot of work to do."

For the rest of the day, he lost himself in work. At least he could take control of one part of his life that had gone awry. Eric was determined to make a positive difference in the upcoming legislation, and do it the right way. Programs that were not helping the people they were designed for must be changed or eliminated so the money could reach the community. With shrinking resources and a backlash against from the middle-class, excesses and abuses would have to end.

But Shani was never far from his mind no matter how hard he tried to banish her. He could smell the sweet scent of her skin or hear her laugh it seemed. More than once he stared at the monitor for long periods without seeing it. A cold empty feeling settled inside his chest. One he feared would be there for a long time. What a sorry end to the old year and a grim beginning to the new one. What would he have to celebrate December thirty-first at midnight?

Chapter Seven

Outside the wind blew making the already forty-degree temperature feel more like below freezing. Shani and Terrilyn agreed they were tired of turkey and dressing. They sat in China Gardens waiting on their lunch orders.

"Brendon came with me to Angola. He and J.J. talked the whole time." Shani stirred the hot tea in her cup.

"That's great." Terrilyn stared at her.

"Yeah. Even with J.J. still behind bars, feels like those wounds in my family are really healing now. Brendon is genuinely proud of how J.J. has taken college courses."

"When will J.J. get out?" Terrilyn said.

"Hopefully before March. It looks good for him. At last he's got some reason for hope." Shani smiled for a moment before her lips sagged down again.

"He's a smart guy. Sounds like he got a made up mind to move in a better direction. I'm happy for him, Brendon, and for you."

Shani nodded. "At least Christmas was good for them this year. I mean for us." She avoided returning Terrilyn's gaze. "Don't start."

"What did I say?" Terrilyn held out both hands.

"It's what you're about to say. Don't go there, Terrilyn." Shani shot her a warning glance before staring back into her tea again.

"I just think you're being too hasty."

"Terrilyn, it's no use." Shani's eyes mirrored the hurt she felt. "Eric and I just can't make it. I was kidding myself that he really cared about me. You'd think Robert would have taught me a lesson."

"Hey, now. Don't be so down on yourself."

"Another New Year's Eve sitting at home eating popcorn and drinking sparkling fruit juice. Oh, well. At least I won't feel all tired out from partying and drinking all night," Shani said with a laugh devoid of humor.

"I'm putting my foot down this year, girlfriend. You are coming to the Circle of Friends Social Club's New Year's Eve party at the Hilton. I'm sure Jamal can hook you up with one of his buddies." Terrilyn's boyfriend of the moment was a funloving high school coach.

Shani's head whipped back and forth. "Forget it. I'm not interested in a blind date."

"Just one night of dancing and having a good time. That's all the commitment either of you need to make. What do say?"

"Well . . ." Shani mentally ran through a list of ways to be diplomatic yet firm. She did not want to hurt Terrilyn's feelings. After all, she was only trying to help. No one else knew just how miserable New Year's Eve had been for her last year. But go on a date? No, she could not do it.

"Have mercy, look who just walked in and he's headed this way," Terrilyn said in a hurried whisper.

"Two lovely ladies. How are you, Shani?" Robert leaned down and kissed her forehead. "Hello, Terrilyn." He spoke with practiced charm.

Terrilyn stared at him with an impassive expression to show she was not moved. "Hi."

"Hello, Robert." Shani wished he would leave soon. "How are you?"

"Can't complain. This is still your favorite place to eat I see. I don't get over this way much since I moved to my new condo." Robert smiled at them. His manner suggested he was in a talkative mood.

"Really? Where?" Terrilyn said. She jumped when Shani's foot kicked her ankle beneath the table.

Robert sat down next to Shani in the booth and got comfortable. "Those new luxury units on Concord Avenue. Three bedrooms, two and a half baths, and covered parking. You should see it." He stared at Shani for several seconds.

"So how is Claudia?" Shani shot back. "With her talents, she must have helped you decorate."

"I haven't seen Claudia in a while. Terrilyn, could you give us a minute?" Robert spoke with a delicate tone that implied she was a woman of understanding who would not refuse.

"I've got to visit the ladies' room anyway." Terrilyn screwed up her face when she turned away from him.

"What was that all about, Robert? We don't have a thing to talk about." Shani did not bother to look at him.

"Let's at least be on good terms if not friends. I'll settle for that if I have to, though . . ." Robert put an arm around the back of the seat. "Not a day goes by that I don't regret behaving like such a fool. Let me make it up to you, baby."

Shani rubbed her temples. How easy it would be to give in. She was so tired of being angry. And he had helped her get through some rough days after the death of her mother. "Friends is all we can be now, Robert."

"I just don't want you to hate me. Let's call a truce, deal?" Robert leaned close to her.

Shani gazed at him for several seconds. "Deal." She blinked when he pressed his lips to hers.

"Still sweet," Robert grinned at her.

Shani pushed him away in time to see Eric standing at

the cash register with a bag of take out food. He was frozen in the act of handing money to the cashier. To her horror, he headed straight for them.

"Hello, Shani. Guess I don't have to ask how you're doing," Eric said. His brown eyes sparkled with resentment. His gaze flickered to Robert. "Pretty well, I see."

Shani swallowed hard. "Hi." Then she got angry. Why should she feel guilty? Eric Aucoin did not own her. He could take his attitude and stuff it. "I'm doing quite well as a matter of fact." She lifted her chin in defiance.

"Robert Saucier, Senator. Nice to meet you." Robert was the picture of a smug, triumphant suitor as he stuck out his hand.

Eric stared at his hand for a second then glanced past Robert to Shani. "Right."

Robert dropped his hand. Still smiling, he broke the long moment of silence that stretched between them. "I've been following you're career with a lot of interest."

Eric shifted his focus back on Robert. He looked at him with open dislike. "Have you really?"

"Oh yes. It takes a lot of guts to be a black conservative, especially in this state. I mean, helping dismantle all those programs black leaders fought for long and hard, some even died. Yes, sir. Lots of nerve." Robert wore the ghost of a smile.

"Apparently Senator Aucoin thinks all those people were wrong and he's right. Everyone should pull themselves up by their bootstraps. The problem is, most poor people don't even have boots," Shani said.

"I think sometimes we don't give our people enough credit for being able to achieve before we jump in to help them. But I don't want to debate this here. Shani, I'll call you later. We need to talk," Eric said in a strained voice.

"Baby, don't forget we're going over to my place later for coffee and brandy," Robert put in before she could answer. He sat down, put a possessive arm around Shani and looked up at Eric. "I've just got a new condo and a new sound system. Shani is crazy about my collection of rhythm and blues classics."

Shani's anger at Eric won out over her urge to put Robert in his place. "Goodbye, Eric. I'm sure you have to rush off to continue the conservative revolution." Her voice was pure venom.

Eric stood clutching the bag of food so tight, his hands shook. He whirled around and walked away with long strides. Terrilyn, who had watched the scene from a distance, came back to the table.

"Whew! I thought we were going to have a big problem there for a while," Terrilyn mumbled. She watched Eric push the door so hard as he left it banged against the wall. "Mercy!"

"Well, ladies. Shall we order?" Robert was in high spirits. He rubbed his hands together.

Shani gave him a cutting look. "I've lost my appetite. Come on, Terrilyn." She tried to get past him.

"Hey, but I . . ." Terrilyn pointed to the hovering waitress ready to take their order. She stopped when Shani's eyes flashed her a warning. "Yeah, I'm not so hungry."

"Wait a minute, babe. Come on over to my place." Robert put his arm around Shani's waist and put his lips close to her ear. "You know it's true. You used to love sipping brandy and listening to Luther Vandross on my CD player."

Shani lifted her face to his. Her lips curved into an inviting smile. "Robert, there's only one thing wrong with that scene. You." She shoved him aside and headed out of the restaurant with Terrilyn right behind her.

"Oowee, girl," Terrilyn said in a voice breathless from giggling. "You're on a roll today."

"Yeah, and it's all down hill." Shani got in the passenger seat of Terrilyn's Honda Accord. "As if I wasn't feeling bad enough. Both of the men who've used me show up at once. A nice reminder of what an idiot I've been." Her bottom lip trembled.

"Stop that. They're the idiots, not you. Eric for letting his stupid politics get in the way of holding onto a fantastic woman, and Robert . . . Honey, we don't have time to list all the things wrong with that sorry excuse for a man." Terrilyn gave Shani a pat on the shoulder and started the car.

"But I chose them both, Terrilyn. What does that say about me?" Shani turned to her desperate for an answer.

Terrilyn turned to her. "It means you can make a mistake like anybody else. I've been there."

"But in this case, my heart was stomped on. Twice." Shani wiped her eyes with tissues from a dispenser in Terrilyn's car. "But I'm not going to walk around feeling sorry for myself. They can both get stuffed."

"Good for you, girl. And to start the new year right, have a blast at one of the finest parties in town. What about it?" Terrilyn winked at her.

Shani sniffed a couple of times. "Why not? Sure. Count me in."

"Fantastic! We're going bring 1997 in right, girlfriend."

Shani smiled at her. Terrilyn chattered about the parties being given and how they could attend more than one. Shani nodded in all the right places, but her mind was far away. The way Eric's eyes had clouded with contempt when he looked at her cut like a knife. Any deep secret hopes that she and Eric could be together were now dashed. But she would go on without him. She had no choice.

"We've got a serious problem." Paulette closed the door to Shani's office. "My'iesha."

Shani felt a stab of fear. She knew what Paulette was going to say, but she asked anyway. "She saw the article?"

Paulette nodded yes. "She's convinced you know."

"I don't understand." Shani frowned at her.

"That she was in on the stealing around here. She was giving the merchandise to her old man for a while. And he would fence it. She's ranting and raving that you stabbed her in the back.''

Shani's eyes were wide with shock. "My'iesha is stealing from the center?"

"Not now, no. But in the first two months after she started the program. Then she left that low life and started to straighten out her life."

"Just when you think things can't get worse, they do." Shani closed her eyes and massaged her temples.

"Now she's all paranoid. She's still using, I'm afraid. I hope we can work through this—" Paulette spread her hands. She was cut short by My'iesha's entrance.

"You paid me back, huh? Told that damn reporter all that stuff." My'iesha stood with feet apart in an aggressive stance just inside the door.

"The article said nothing about you for one thing." Shani spoke in a calm voice. "And the information came from those conservative legislators. It said so in the article. Let's talk about this without shouting or accusations."

My'iesha strode farther into the room. "You been runnin' around with one of them legislators, too. Didn't think I knew that. Yeah, I know that and a lot more. You been feedin' him all that crap."

"Why would I do something to hurt the center? You know how hard we've worked together for everything we have here. It doesn't make any sense." Shani could see by the wild look in her eyes that logic would not pierce the fog of suspicion.

"My'iesha, please. You need to go into detox like we talked about. There's a bed available." Paulette moved between them.

My'iesha grabbed Paulette by the arm and yanked her out of the way. She jabbed a finger at Shani. "LeVar been right about you all the time. Now he's gonna be after me thinkin' I ratted him out to the cops. I gotta find him so he'll know the truth."

Shani did not go closer. My'iesha would feel cornered

and might lash out with violence. "If LeVar does think that, then you should try to stay far away from him. He won't believe you, My'iesha. When the police don't come after him, maybe he'll know you didn't inform on him."

"I'm through listenin' to you. LeVar been the only one I could count on. He's gonna take good care of me." My'iesha walked backward looking from Shani to Paulette. "You two are always plottin' somethin'. Well, it won't work. You hear me? I'm not gonna be your chump no more!"

Shani took one cautious step toward her. "My'iesha, let us help you."

My'iesha spun around and stomped out. The sound of her pounding footsteps echoed down the hall. Paulette and Shani stood still for a full minute before they both slumped down into chairs with despondent sighs.

Paulette looked at Shani. "You think he'll hurt her?"

"You kidding? He's beaten her up for less than this."

"I knew the answer. Guess I was hoping you'd say something different."

"And I don't think she'll have to go looking for him. LeVar will find *her*. We've got to do something. But I don't know what." Shani raked fingers through her hair.

"Let's get some of the other staff in here. They've hit bottom before." Paulette referred to several counselors who were recovered addicts. "They might have some ideas." Paulette dialed the phone.

"Okay," Shani said. She stared down at the newspaper article. "Eric Aucoin should know just how dangerous playing politics at the expense of these people can be. He and his kind are despicable. If something happens to that young woman . . .".

Shani could only think of how self-involved she had been. Thinking only of herself and how much she missed him. The real consequences of his actions hit home now. She must see Eric as another foe. Paulette's voice, low and urgent, brought her back from her somber thoughts.

"They'll be down in about ten minutes," Paulette hung up the phone.

"Okay. But I intend for Senator Aucoin to take responsibility for his part in all this." Shani punched the buttons on the phone. "Yes, may I speak to Senator Aucoin. This is Shani Moore. Hello, Eric. I'm ready to talk."

Eric sat across from Detective McElroy Landry in the most popular coffee house in town. The Coffee Cafe was buzzing with activity as early morning customers came in for café au lait or strong dark roast south Louisiana coffee. Mac and he had been good friends since they played college football together. Now Mac was a respected narcotics cop.

"How's it going, Mac," Eric said.

"Doing what I can against the forces of evil. I haven't seen you since the last time you were on duty doing your reserved police officer thing. How's it going?" Mac straddled a chair making it look child-sized under his tall frame.

Eric grinned. "Pretty good. I managed a few rounds over the past months. But I'm going to have to give it up though. Too busy."

"The hazards of being an emerging statesman I guess," Mac teased.

When they both got coffee orders, Eric got down to business. "What do you know about a LeVar Stewart, Mac?" he said in a low voice leaning both elbows on the table.

Mac's thick black eyebrows went up a notch. His pleasant ebony face was transformed in an instant to a solemn mask.

"He went from a nobody to drug king pin just a few years short of his twentieth birthday. He did it by taking out anybody who stood in his way." Mac shrugged. "The man is a one-man crime wave."

"Damn," Eric said.

"You planning to make him and his kind a political issue?"

"It's personal." Eric shook his head when he saw Mac's eyes go opaque with worry. "Not me. Someone close to me is afraid he's going to hurt a young woman."

"You got a name?"

"Yeah, My'iesha Campbell. She was in a drug treatment program until recently. You saw an article in the paper about the community centers?" Eric stared down into the creamy liquid in his mug.

"Uh-huh. You did some kinda investigation about theft and bad management. I skimmed over it before going to the sports section as usual." Mac grinned.

"Well, my former assistant gave a lot of the information for that article without my approval. He even went so far as to name this young woman," Eric said.

"Not good."

"It gets worse. This Stewart guy now thinks she informed on him."

Mac let out a low whistle. "That is very bad news, my brother. LeVar is vicious when he even *thinks* someone's done him wrong."

"Look, Mac, I feel responsible for her being in danger. I should have kept Trumaine on a short leash," Eric said tapping the table top with a large fist. "But now that the damage is done, I've just got to do something about it. Can you help?"

Mac rubbed his chin. "Give me a minute." He got up and went outside to his car. Once inside, he started talking into his cellular phone.

Eric glanced around the bright dining room. Early morning sunshine splashed through the wide windows giving everything and everyone a golden, happy glow. He thought of Shani's smile, a smile he had not seen for some time now. At least not for him. How his spirits had risen when she called only to plunge at her words of condemnation. Eric still felt the sting of hearing her controlled voice stabbing through the phone. In that moment, all his explanations about the report and his party actions shriveled up into nothingness. A young woman's life was in jeopardy because he had been careless. Staring out to the parking lot, he prayed Mac would find a way to save My'iesha. The tall man turned a few female heads when he came back into the restaurant.

Mac placed the cellular phone next to his now cold mug of coffee. "I've got good news and bad news. The good news is LeVar is wanted on a warrant and we're all ready looking to take him down. This time he could get a hefty sentence if he's convicted. That's a big if, but better than nothing."

Eric checked his rising hope. "What's the bad news?"

"There was a drive-by shooting. Three guys shot, two dead and the third is in critical condition. Word is, LeVar and his gang are responsible. He's on a revenge rampage."

Eric hung his head. Like Shani, he wanted a way to stop the killing. Somehow leaders along the political spectrum must agree to approaches they could all support.

"And one of his former girls is supposed to be a target."

"My'iesha?" Eric's head jerked up. He felt anxiety tighten in his chest at Mac's sober nod. "What can we do? There's got to be a way to help her."

"Maybe she ought to leave town for a while. That way we won't have to worry about her getting killed before he's caught."

"Shani doesn't know where she is. In fact, My'iesha is looking for LeVar. She thinks she can explain herself to him," Eric said.

"Definitely a bad idea. That's like helping a rattlesnake sink his fangs into a major artery." Mac sat in thought for several minutes. "I've got an idea, but it involves your friend. Does she have any clue where My'iesha could be?"

"Maybe. But I don't want Shani put in any danger, Mac." Eric felt even greater fear at the possibility that she could be hurt as well.

"What's your idea, Detective? Hello, I'm Shani Moore.

Sorry I'm late." Shani ignored the stunned look on Eric's face.

"What are you doing here?" Eric pulled out a chair for her next to him. A faint whiff of her fragrance stirred sweet memories.

"You told me about meeting here with Detective Landry, remember?" Shani turned to Mac. "Now, about that idea?"

Eric's beeper went off. "It's my office."

"Here. Use my phone." Mac handed him the cellular phone.

While Eric walked off to call in, Mac explained his plan to Shani. She listened and interrupted only to ask a couple of questions. Mac paused mid-sentence to stare at Eric with a frown.

"Something is very wrong. Eric looks like he just got hit by a truck," Mac said.

Eric came back, his face stiff with grief. "My mother has been taken very ill. Dad's at the emergency room with her. I've got to go."

Shani put a hand on his arm. "I'm so sorry, Eric. Can I do anything?"

Eric's hand closed on hers. "I'll call you later?" His eyes searched hers for comfort.

"Of course," Shani replied.

"Let me know how your mama is doing, man. You know how I feel about that special lady." Mac put a hand on Eric's shoulder.

Eric could only nod in gratitude before hurrying off. Shani and Mac watched him leave. Both wore frowns of concern for him and his parents.

"Like my grandma says, if it ain't one thing, it's two," Mac said.

Shani sighed. "And that's the truth."

* * *

"She's going to be all right, son." Dalton gripped Eric's arms tight. "It was a very mild stroke." His face showed the strain of fear at losing the woman he loved.

"But she couldn't talk or move her right arm," Eric said. His insides churned at the thought of his mother suffering.

"Her speech came back though it's still a little slurred. And she can move her arm just not too much." Dalton let go of Eric and twisted his hands together as he talked. "She's going to bounce back. Of course she going to need physical and speech therapy. She'll be back to her old self in no time."

Eric could see that his father was trying to reassure himself. Dalton's hand shook as he wiped his brow with a monogrammed linen handkerchief. For the first time, Eric realized how much his parents were a part of each other. All day, Eric had waited with his father for the test results. Now in the twilight of early evening, the white lights of the small waiting seemed eerie and forbidding. He put his hand on Dalton's back to console him.

"Of course she will. Mama is a fighter." Eric hoped his face did not show the uncertainty he felt. "Let's go in."

The hospital room door swished open and Dalton went inside ahead of Eric. At first it seemed Adeline was asleep in the darkened room. The only light came from the television.

Dalton scowled. "Now who left that on," he said in a harsh whisper. He reached for the remote that hung over the bed rail.

"Me. Don't to-ouch it," Adeline said. "It's Wednesday and I never miss m-my favorite shows." Her lips curved into a mischievous smile. There was a slight droop to one side of her mouth. "Come on in here you two and give me some sugar."

Dalton leaned down brushing a tendril of hair from her face as he did so. He pressed his lips to hers for a long moment, his eyes closed. Eric almost felt a need to leave them alone. The tenderness and love between them was a palpable thing filling the air, making the antiseptic hospital atmosphere seem less impersonal. Seeing the bond between his parents, Eric felt a pang deep inside. How he needed to make things right with Shani. There was no doubt in his mind that she was the one he wanted, needed, to share his life and his heart.

"How's my sweet thing feeling?" Dalton continued brush her hair with his fingers.

"Like a weak kitten. I hope you didn't forget to bring my blue nightgown. Soon as they take out this IV, I'm going to wear my own things. There's my baby." Adeline held up her left arm to welcome Eric.

"Hey, darlin'. You look marvelous." Eric smiled and kissed her cheek.

"Don't lie to me, Eric Paul Aucoin. I look like hell." Adeline shook a finger at his nose. She gazed at him, then Dalton. "But so do you. Both of you got those smiles plastered in place trying not to look scared."

"We were, but now we've gotten the good news that—"

"That I ha-ad a str-roke? What do you call good news?" Adeline said with a grunt.

Eric cleared his throat and forced cheer into his voice. "Well, not that of course. But it wasn't as serious as it could have been. The doctor says—"

"That they can remove the blockage and reduce the chance of another one. I know. They've been poking and pulling on me since I got here. They took so much blood, I was beginning to wonder if Dracula wasn't on staff here." Adeline shifted on the raised bed.

Eric gave a low laugh. He was encouraged to hear his mother joking. "Those lab techs do only seem to come at night or early in the morning before the sun comes up. Seriously, Mama, Doctor Mills is very optimistic you can make a full recovery."

"Yeah, sweetie. We'll be doing the swing out at the spring

fraternity dance. You wait and see." Dalton held his wife's hand.

"Now there's a reason to have some therapist ordering me around. Going to that dance so I can watch Odessa Trahan paw you at every opportunity." Adeline pursed her lips. "She's tried to get her hands on him since we were in college. But I snapped him up."

Dalton gave a groan. "You gonna start on that. It's been over thirty years, Adeline." His eyes were alight with amusement to share this old argument they'd had for years, never in anger but to tease each other.

"Well, she can just retract those claws because I'm not going anywhere for a long time." She caressed her husband's jaw. "So get that worried look off your face." Her voice was soft.

Dalton held her hand to his cheek. His eyes filled with unshed tears. "We'll be fine, you and me."

"Yes, dear. Just fine." Adeline's eyebrows came together, giving her a severe look. "Now there is some unfinished business between you two."

"Adeline, don't you let that weigh on your mind. You've got to concentrate on getting well." Dalton blinked. A look of guilt crossed his rugged features.

Eric took his father's cue. "Yeah, Mama. The most important thing is—your health."

"Hu-ush up. Dalton," she said, fixing him with a look of censure. "You owe your son an apology."

"Now, Adeline, don't get worked up." Dalton patted her hand.

"Dalton Augustin Aucoin, tell him," Adeline said in a voice of quiet strength.

Dalton took a deep breath. "Forgive me, son. I had no right to interfere the way I did." He stared down at the floor.

"And?" Adeline urged him on with a sharp nod.

"And . . . I was wrong to go behind your back and help

Trumaine feed all that stuff to the news reporter." Dalton scratched his head with a nervous movement of his hand.

Adeline sighed and settled back with a pleased expression. "That's a start. Eric, tell your father he's forgiven. Go on."

"Mama, we—"

Adeline made an attempt to sit up by holding on to rail. "Don't ma-ake me-e get up out of this bed, boy."

Eric's eyes widened with alarm. He stepped forward and placed his hands on both her shoulders. Dalton gave her a gentle but firm push back against the pillows.

"Adeline, you are the most willful little woman." Dalton gazed up at Eric. His eyes were full of emotion. "Best do as you're told, son. Am I forgiven?"

"Sure," Eric said in a voice strangled with unspoken feelings for the man he admired more than anyone else. "Sure you are, Dad." He hugged Dalton's neck.

Adeline nodded at them. "Now talk to each other." Her eyes were already half-closed. "I'm going to take a little nap. I can rest easier now."

Eric and Dalton left only after her low, regular breathing assured them she was asleep. They returned to the small waiting room down the hall.

"My apology wasn't just to keep your mama from getting upset. I had no right to come between you and Shani. It was wrong." Dalton looked away. "Adeline means the world to me. When you find the woman who makes you feel like a king even when the whole world is beating you down, well there's just no way to replace that."

"I believe you, Dad." Eric was moved.

"Is there anything I can do to make things right between you two?"

"Thanks, but no. Something was bound to test our relationship." Eric lifted his shoulders. "Maybe it's just as well we broke up. Could be our differences are just too big."

"You think so?" Dalton rubbed his chin and gazed off into the distance. "Maybe, maybe not."

Eric's head lowered, his chin touching the top of his open collar. "I'm afraid it's not, Dad. Anyway," he said looking up again, "at least there's good news about Mama. Listen, why don't you go home and rest. I'll stay here tonight."

"Humm? Oh no, I don't . . . Well okay. I'll go take a shower and change. But I'll be back in a few hours." Dalton slapped Eric's back. "You take the early shift. I'll be back by ten or ten-thirty."

"But you've been up since four this morning," Eric protested. "The last thing I need is for both of you to be sick."

"Trust me, son. My place is with Adeline. Now go on in there. That lounge chair is surprisingly comfortable. My thoughtful secretary is on her way with some food for me. You eat it. I'll get something on the way home." Dalton pulled him along.

"I'm not all that hungry."

"You will be. Now quit arguing with me. When I'm through, things are going to work out right." Dalton gave a cheerful wave goodbye before stepping through the open doors of the elevator. "You'll see."

"What?" Eric blinked in puzzlement at his words. "Dad, wait a minute."

The doors clicked shut leaving him to wonder about the mysterious grin his father wore.

Chapter Eight

"Sure you want to go through with this?" Mac said to Shani. He glanced around with an uneasy grimace on his dark features. "This isn't the safest place to be in the daytime, much less after dark."

They sat in his unmarked car outside a rundown boarding house on East Boulevard. Several blocks down the street a group of young men stood on a corner laughing and shoving each other. Cars drove up to them then sped off after a hasty transaction. Rap music blared from a ramshackle house about a block down East Boulevard behind them. Mac took his eyes off the boarding house only to check their surroundings through the rearview mirrors.

"We both know that My'iesha could disappear fast. If she's here, I want to be with you to talk to her." Shani was so intent on what she would say to My'iesha, she did not feel afraid for herself. Her fear was for the young woman who teetered on the edge of being another murder statistic.

"Let's just hope LeVar isn't up there with her. Things could get ugly real quick." Mac slipped a hand inside the wool blazer to pat his shoulder holster. He shot a look of fury at the group of young men. The fifth car to stop in the last fifteen minutes pulled away. "Wish I could bust those little punks."

"When I see guys like that, it makes me wish I knew the answer to harness all that potential. All going to waste on a street corner or in a prison cell." Shani felt a pall settle over her. The dreary houses with litter strewn in the front yards and in the gutters made for a dark scene. She did not wonder children growing up here would do desperate, dangerous things to escape.

Mac grunted. "More often these days, they end up in a body bag." He pointed to a window. "Look, a light just went on. Somebody's home. You ready?"

Shani's heart thumped, but she put her hand on the door handle. "Yes." She unwrapped the woolen scarf around her neck and let it slide down to the seat.

Mac put his arm out. "Eric is going to kill me when he finds out about this. Maybe we should put this off."

"We've been over that, Mac. He's got enough on his mind with Mrs. Aucoin being ill."

Mac sucked air into his lungs. "Yeah, he's been at the hospital with only a couple of breaks for the last twenty-four hours. Thankfully Ms. Adeline is doing so good."

Shani thought of the anguish in Eric's hazel eyes after hearing the news that his mother was hospitalized. His pain had been her pain. And she shared his joy and relief when he called to tell her Mrs. Aucoin's condition was improving. But the joy was tempered by the knowledge that they would not, could not be together. The newspaper story and the effects of it stood between them like a stone wall. Shani again thought of how foolish she'd been to think their differences could be overcome. Maybe love was not enough. Once they left the sweet haze of their romantic cocoon, the real world slammed them back into being on opposing sides with a vengeance. And they had to live in the real world. The real world of Shani's commitment to programs Eric wanted to destroy. She felt the familiar sadness settle into her heart at the thought. Now she must move ahead and stop feeling sorry for herself.

Shani stared at the weathered wooden porch that sagged on one side. "So we agreed not to call Eric. Besides, we're just going in to talk My'iesha out of this mess."

"It's up to you." Mac continued to watch the window.

"I just hope I can. LeVar knows how to sweet talk needy young women starved for affection. If he's gotten to her . . ."

"From all you've said, he got to her a while ago. Now the question is, can she break free?" Mac followed her gaze. "And will she listen to you?"

Shani opened the car door. "We're about to find out."

At that moment, a shout went up from the group of young men.

"Who done stole my money!" a loud voice boomed.

Curses rang out. Mac muttered a few choice words and kicked open the driver's side door of the sedan. Shani craned her neck around to see two men pounding each other and two others jump into the fray. Mac barked the location of the disturbance into his police radio unit.

"Looks like crowd control is going to be needed for this. Better get over there before some fool starts shooting. Stay here. I'll let the uniforms take over and be back."

More people had gravitated to the scene. He covered the three blocks with long strides. A marked police car came from the opposite direction lights flashing.

Shani sat for fifteen minutes before she began to worry that My'iesha would run if she noticed all the activity. Especially if she saw the police car. After several more minutes of silent debate and courage gathering, Shani decided to enter the boarding house.

"After all, how bad can it be? There's a light in the entrance," she murmured.

Her footsteps across the porch sounded too loud. She pushed open the door and entered a hallway lit with a naked bulb set in the ceiling. The worn stairway railing wobbled as she climbed the steps.

Eric sat next to the hospital bed. He stared into the darkness outside, his mood matched the grim looking shadows thrown by the building onto the ground below. The happiness he felt was not complete. With a glance at his sleeping mother, he felt a jab of guilt to be thinking of himself at such a time. Yet he could not help it. Shani had been glad to hear from him, of that he was certain. But the reserve in her voice over the telephone hurt more than a little. For a brief moment, he wanted to believe they could find a way back to each other. When she looked at him that day he got the call about his mother, her eyes were filled with emotion. He felt the familiar pull between them. Now he realized the loss of something precious. And it seemed Shani would not be able to forgive him.

"Well hello there. Don't tell me you haven't been home or gotten something to eat." Adeline's voice was alert though she'd been sleeping on and off for most of the time since being admitted to the hospital.

"Hello, beautiful." Eric got up and kissed her forehead. "How're you feeling? Can I get you anything?"

"Some water, please." Adeline sipped through the straw. "Umm, that's better. Other than feeling a little weak, I'm just fine." She put the plastic cup aside and stared at her son. "Goodness, you look beat."

Eric straightened his shirt collar and sweater. "I'm okay."

"Where's Dalton?"

"He's down the hall on the phone. Business calls. He didn't want to disturb you."

"I see. I look a sight." Adeline began to brush her hair while looking into a small mirror set in the combination table and vanity positioned next to the bed. "What's your excuse?"

"I don't understand." Eric sat back down.

"Eric, you can't deceive me. For the first time, I saw your eyes gleam in a very special way just at the mention of a woman's name. Now that gleam is gone."

"Mama, don't trouble yourself about my problems. You've got to think of getting better. I'll survive."

"Humph, I wonder."

Eric tried to make his voice sound light, but knew he'd failed. "You've got therapy sessions and a new diet to follow. And I expect you to obey the doctor's orders."

"Don't lecture me, young man. I know exactly what I have to do, thank you very much. And don't try to change the subject." Adeline shook a finger at him. "Have you spoken to Shani?"

"Yes, she sends best wishes and told me to tell you she's glad to hear you're doing so well." Eric turned his face away.

"How sweet. But that's not what I'm talking about and you know it. What about you two? Have you made up?"

"Mama . . ." Eric drew in a sharp breath. "We're not going to make up. It's over. The most we can be are cordial acquaintances."

"Nonsense."

"Mama, you don't understand."

Adeline put the hair brush down. "Ha! I was learning about love before you were even thought of, sugar. And don't tell me you can't make it because she's a liberal social worker and you're a conservative. All silliness."

"It's not so simple as labels. It's how we act on our convictions."

"Eric Paul Aucoin, you must be trying real hard to be stupid because there are no dumb people in our family. You sure didn't inherit it." Adeline squinted at him.

"Mama!—"

"I don't want to hear it," she broke in. "Sitting around here with that 'poor pitiful me' look on your face. Both of you share a drive to do the best thing for people, that's why she's a social worker and you went into politics. Maybe you disagree on the methods, but so what? You share the same values and have some of the same ideas."

"Hey, babe. What's up?" Dalton strolled in wearing a big smile when he saw Adeline awake and looking refreshed. He brushed his lips across hers.

Adeline's eyes twinkled at the sight of her husband. "Sit down. Maybe you can help talk sense to this child."

"Mama, Shani and I have some very real problems we can't overcome. I wish . . . we could but, that's just the way it is." Eric felt an ache at his words. What he wanted to believe and reality were two different things. There was no denying that Shani could never feel the same for him.

"I don't think it has to be that way, son. She misses you just as much." Dalton spoke up.

"No, she doesn't." Eric shook his head. He was still turned away from them.

"Oh yes she does," Dalton said with a certain ring to his voice.

Eric faced him. "Why do you say that? Dad, you haven't been talking to her have you?" He wore a tense expression that threatened to turn into anger.

Dalton blinked. "Uh, I'm just saying . . . I bet she's missing you real bad. From the way you two were all lovey-dovey, I could tell she's as crazy about you as you are about her." He cleared his throat. "That's all I meant."

"Why don't we call her right now? I'd love to say hello." Adeline gestured toward the phone at her nightstand. She yawned. "These darn pills keep me sleepy. Hurry up before I doze off again."

Eric swallowed hard. He stood with his hand on the receiver for several seconds before picking it up. After the tenth ring, he hung up. "She's not there." A picture on the television caught his eye. "Turn up the sound, Dad."

A mug shot appeared on the screen as a reporter spoke. "Police believe this man, LeVar Stewart is responsible for the last drive by shooting in Easy Town. Crime Stoppers is offering a cash reward for information that leads to his arrest and conviction.''

Eric remembered what Mac had said right before he got the call at the restaurant about his mother. Shani had not been home twice before when he'd tried to call. He punched in the number to Mac's desk phone at the station.

"Hey, Eric." His partner, Bill, answered. "No, he went out after some woman tied up with this Stewart scum ball. Some ratty place on East Boulevard. How's Mrs. A?"

Eric answered him in a mechanical fashion before hanging up. His mind raced with terrible possibilities. He knew how much Shani wanted to save My'iesha. Could she be in danger now? And was she with Mac? East Boulevard was a high crime area well known to him. He had visited an angry group of people who lived there about efforts to clean it up.

"Eric, is anything wrong?" Adeline frowned up at him.

"No, Mama. Look, I'm going to find Shani." Eric gave her hand a quick squeeze.

"Oh, that's wonderful, dear. Don't let a good thing get away." Adeline waved at him, all ready she was struggling to keep her eyes open.

Dalton followed him to the door. "Something's wrong," he whispered. "Tell me what's going on."

Eric smiled. "Nothing, Dad. Really. Now take it easy. I'll be back in the morning, okay?" He patted his father's back and walked off before Dalton could say more.

"Honey, open the door please," Shani said in a low, urgent voice. "I know you're in there. My'iesha?"

"What you doin' here? Go way," My'iesha called back. She sounded tense.

Shani heard a thump and a furtive rustling sound. "Let's talk. Just let me in for ten minutes."

"I'll see you at the center. Tomorrow maybe. Now go away." My'iesha seemed closer to the door.

"It's got to be now. I promise not to lecture you or stay for longer than ten minutes."

After a few seconds, there was the rattle of locks being opened. Slowly the door swung back into the room. My'iesha, looking drawn with dark circles under her eyes, peered out at her. Shani smiled and stepped inside. The door shut with a bang.

"What you want? Got no right harassing me like this," My'iesha rasped. Her whole body shook.

Shani approached but stopped short when My'iesha backed up against the wall. "I'm worried about you. LeVar is on a rampage. Word is out he intends to hurt you bad."

"He gonna listen to me," My'iesha said. "I'm gonna explain to him. I didn't tell the police nothin'. I swear." She rubbed her nose and sniffed hard several times.

"How many times have you used in the last day or so?" Shani moved closer, more concerned about getting her some help than being attacked. Still, she kept her arms by her sides in case My'iesha lashed out in a drug-induced rage.

"Get offa me," My'iesha warned as she inched away. "I mean it."

"Honey, let me help you. LeVar has shot two people that I know of in the last few days. Instead of trying to find him, you should be hauling butt hoping he doesn't find you." Shani planted her feet apart.

"I ain't listenin' to that crap. It's a bunch of lies just like in the newspaper. You and Senator Aucoin set me up!"

Shani shook her head. "You should know me better than that."

My'iesha's mouth turned down in a little girl expression of misery. Large tears rolled down her cheeks. "I thought you was my friend. Different from all them other social workers, psychologists, and stuff."

"I do want to help you. Just come with me." . . . Shani

stepped ever closer. She reached out her across the few inches between them.

My'iesha stared down at Shani's hand. In an instant, her face twisted with rage. "No! You ain't turnin' me in to go to jail. I ain't goin'."

She swung wild. The flat of her hand slapped Shani's shoulder with enough force to make her rock back. Shani shuffled back to regain her footing but My'iesha lunged at her again.

"Stop it! My'iesha, stop!" Shani wrapped her arms around the thin frame. My'iesha tried to break loose from the tight lock, but Shani held her fast.

"Let go of me. Take your filthy, no-good hands off me," My'iesha sobbed. She struggled for a few minutes, but fatigue and emotion left her physically drained. "No, no, no," she cried in a sad sing song voice as Shani cradled her.

Shani eased them both down onto the sagging bed. "It's going to be all right, sweetie. Shh, now."

Eric parked on the opposite side of the street behind a dark green sedan. Everything looked quiet, too quiet. He glanced around looking for a sign of his friend or Shani then walked to Mac's car. His heart gave a lurch when he recognized Shani's woolen scarf on the floor in front of the passenger seat. With care, he climbed the steps to the boarding house. Stale cooking smells hit him when he opened the door leading to a dank hallway. Music and shouting came from behind several of the battered doors. Someone sang a popular rap song in a drunken fashion. One dim yellow bulb hung from a long wire to light it. A stairway of dark, scarred wood led up and to the right.

I hope Mac is up here with her. Eric climbed the steps wincing at the creaks that sounded loud enough to be heard miles away.

A door cracked open to reveal the head of a middle-aged man. The man blinked at Eric with bloodshot eyes then shut the door real quick. Eric tried not to think about how many ways he could be ambushed as he continued up to the third floor. Mac's partner, distracted by another case, had told him where they expected to find My'iesha. When he got to the third-floor landing, he squinted in the darkness. He went to the fourth door with a rusty "3D" hanging at a lopsided angle. Muffled sobbing sent a chill through him.

"Shani?" He knocked hard. "Shani, are you there?" A bump and unrecognizable sounds from within pushed him into to panic. "Open up!" He slammed his shoulder against the peeling painted wood panel.

Shani jerked the door open. "Bring out every gangster within a five-mile radius, why don't you."

Eric stumbled into the room from the momentum of another attempt to batter his way in. "You all right? I heard crying like someone was hurt." He steadied himself and whirled around in a circle looking for danger.

"I'm fine," Shani said. She felt a rush of warmth at the sight of him on guard. Ready to defend her. "It's just My'iesha and me."

"Oh." Eric looked a little embarrassed. But soon his eyes blazed with annoyance. "You shouldn't have come in here without Mac. LeVar could have been in here wired up and packing a gun. He wouldn't hesitate to shoot."

"You're right," Shani murmured.

"Taking crazy chances with you life like this is . . ." Eric huffed in growing anger.

"Stupid, I know." Shani shut the door behind him. "I didn't stop to think. I was just so afraid that My'iesha would slip away from us. I didn't want to lose a chance to keep her from LeVar."

"Well, uh, yeah. No harm done since you're both safe." Eric lost steam, thrown off balance by her ready agreement with him. He gazed at My'iesha who sat staring at him with big dark eyes.

"Right," Shani said. She was amused by the confusion her meek response caused. "My'iesha, this is Senator Aucoin."

"Hi," My'iesha said in a soft whisper. She hugged herself and rocked.

Shani sat next to her again. She put her arm around My'iesha's thin shoulders. "He wants to help you, too."

"Then why did he tell lies to that reporter? He tryin' to get rid of the work program. And he got LeVar thinkin' I ratted him out to the cops." My'iesha shot an accusatory glance at Eric.

Eric sat down in one of two chairs part of an old dinette set. "My'iesha, I'm sorry for the way that newspaper article was written. I didn't know about it, believe me." His jaw tightened at the reference to Trumaine.

"But you tryin' to close Mid-City down. I heard you say so on television." My'iesha's expression of distrust remained.

"No, not really. I just want to make sure the money gets to those it's intended to help." Eric gazed at Shani. "Mid-City is doing a fantastic job in Easy Town. The records confirm that."

"Then they won't close down the jobs program or the drug counseling?" My'iesha leaned forward, wanting to believe but still wary. Her face showed the ravages of a lifetime of hopes dashed. She twisted a pulled thread of the oversized sweater that hung on her slight frame. "When I worked in that office, it was the first time I really started to think I could be somebody."

"No money has been cut off. And even though some may try to, I'll work damn hard to save it. It's one of the programs that's effective and saves money. Every person who makes it, pays taxes. That's what I'm going to say to the legislators." Eric looked at her. His strong jaw set with determination and genuine concern shown in his eyes. "We're all going to work hard to make it all right. Okay?"

My'iesha looked to Shani for confirmation. At her nod,

she turned back to Eric. "Okay," My'iesha said in a more confident voice.

"Good, now let's get out of this place." Eric stood up.

Shani rose with her arm still around My'iesha. "I second that motion."

A knock shook the old door on it's hinges. "Hey, girl. Open up. It's me, LeVar."

All three froze for several seconds. My'iesha gasped and shrunk back away from the door. Eric put a forefinger to his lips.

"I sent word by one of his boys for him to come here," My'iesha whispered low. Still, her voice seemed ring out in the stillness.

"You in there, Leo told me." LeVar pulled at the door knob. "One way or the other, I'm comin' in," he barked. After several seconds, he changed his tone. "Come on, baby. I got somethin' special just for my special lady. Don't I always treat you good? LeVar gives good love, don't he, baby?"

Eric walked to the window on tip toes. There was no escape that way. Maybe LeVar would be convinced the room was empty and leave. Eric glanced at Shani.

"Now what?" she lip synched to him.

Eric started toward them to respond when the door bounced inward with a boom. My'iesha shrieked and went limp with fright.

"I'm tired of messin' 'round. You hear me? Ain't nobody gonna screw up my business." LeVar kicked the door to punctuate each sentence.

Eric pushed the two women into a far corner. He crouched to the right of the door, fists raised. The flimsy lock popped loose as wood splintered around it. LeVar rushed into the room with one arm extended. Eric punched the side of his head causing it to snap back. LeVar staggered forward. Before he could recover, Eric swung both fist down on the back of his neck. The gun in LeVar's hand fell and slid across the floor. Shani crawled toward it. LeVar let out a groan of rage. He shook Eric from his back and started for her. Eric delivered a series of rapid punches that made LeVar's head bounce as though on springs. Eric rammed him into a wall with such force that the window panes rattled. LeVar slumped to the floor with a moan, his hand flailing the air in a vain attempt at defense.

Suddenly Mac's tall frame was a silhouette in the doorway. He took in the scene with a quick professional gaze before his stance relaxed. He crossed to Eric.

"I'll take over from here, brother," Mac said.

Eric stepped back. "He's all yours," he said in a breathless voice.

Mac stood over LeVar, his gun still in hand. "I got more bad news for you, man. You're under arrest."

He motioned two uniformed police officers into the room. They handcuffed LeVar and rattled off his Miranda rights in a practiced monotone.

Eric went to Shani and My'iesha. "You both okay?" He scanned them both for evidence of injury.

"We're not hurt." Shani could feel My'iesha trembling. "I think we better get her to a hospital. She might be going into shock."

Mac led a paramedic inside the already crowded little room. "Here we go, ma'am. Let's get you checked out." He spoke in a soothing tone, very unlike the hard as steel cop he'd been only a few minutes earlier.

"You comin'?" My'iesha did not let go of Shani's arm.

"Sure, honey. You go on. I'll be there in a minute." Shani brushed back her hair. She turned to Eric and Mac. "Well, thank goodness for Buffalo Soldiers to the rescue."

"Aw, shucks ma'am," Mac said in an exaggerated Texas drawl. He grinned at her. "Don't mention it. Are you two okay? Wanna see the paramedics?"

"No," they said in unison.

"Well then, both of you get some rest. See you later."

He slapped Eric on the back before going off to confer with his lieutenant.

She hesitated before joining My'iesha in the Emergency Medical Services van. Shani gazed up at Eric.

"I'm going with her. She's scared—."

"Of course. I'll follow." Eric nodded. He did not reach with his hands, but looked at her with tenderness, reaching out with his heart.

"Will you?" Shani wanted to take a step toward him but the memory of angry words, her angry words, held her in place. Had she any right to believe what she saw in his eyes?

"Anywhere, anytime." Eric wrapped her in his arms. "Just try and stop me," he murmured in her ear.

Attached to every chair placed around the tables scattered in the huge ballroom, colorful helium filled balloons danced and bounced as people passed. Elegantly dressed couples dipped and swayed to the soulful rhythm of a popular local band. Shani laughed out loud, less at the antics of a nearby couple who shimmied down to the floor in imitation of a long ago dance from their youth, than with the sheer joy of being happier than she could ever remember in her life. Feeling Eric's arms cradling her, she thought of how different this holiday was from a year ago. New Year's Eve 1996 was as sparkling as any champagne. And 1997 would burst forth bright with the promise of a new beginning. Looking up into his eyes, Shani felt lighter than the balloons.

"Having a good time?" Eric spoke close to her ear.

"I'm having a marvelous time, the time of my life." She pressed closer to him.

"Did I mention how beautiful you look in this sexy number?" Eric held her at arm's length. His gaze lingered on the low neckline of her emerald green satin bodice. The full black velvet skirt swished around her ankles.

"You're not half bad yourself." She gave him a wink. His broad shoulders and chest wore the tuxedo jacket with as much ease as any causal shirt.

"Thanks, my lady." He pulled her back close to him. "It's almost midnight. The new year is going to be wonderful."

"To think, only a few weeks ago things looked very bleak. But My'iesha is back on the right track and in treatment."

"That's great, babe. Having LeVar in jail and probably going to prison doesn't hurt," Eric said.

"Amen. Things are looking up for my family, too. My brothers are closer than ever. J.J. has a job waiting for him thanks to Brendon."

"And to think, my father actually tracked you down to say he was responsible for that article. So I have him to thank for this night. Yeah, family matters are looking good," Eric said, his voice filled with contentment.

"The new year can't come fast enough for me." Shani snuggled closer to him.

"Me too," he murmured. "Yes, it looks like 1997 is going to be full of action for both of us."

"Yes, with the session coming up for you and me working on new programs with a scaled down budget."

"Oh, yeah. I guess that too," Eric said with a shrug.

Shani look up at him. "We're not talking about the same thing. What's up?"

"You'll find out," he said with the impish grin of a man with a secret.

"Hey, everybody. Here's the count down." One of the party hosts called to the crowd from the microphone on the bandstand. A big screen television mounted high over their heads came on as the lights were dimmed. The ball, lit with red lights to look like a gigantic apple, in New York's Time Square started it's descent.

"Seven, six, five," Shani and Eric yelled with the others. She molded her back to his chest feeling his rising excitement. His hands crossed at her waist.

"One. Happy New Year!" Hundreds of voices blended with the sound of corks being popped and horns blowing.

"Happy New Year, baby," Eric whispered. His kiss was long and deep. "Will you marry me?"

Shani, all ready left breathless with the heat of desire, uttered a tiny cry. "Yes, yes." She placed both hands on his face and kissed him hard. "Yes!"

"Now, you're going to be very busy picking out your engagement ring and planning our wedding." He chuckled.

"That's the way to start a New Year." She laughed with him.

The band started another tune, and they swung in a circle. The sultry contralto of a female singer came through the speakers. As she sang, Shani felt as though the singer had chosen her song just for them. Shani, her cheek resting against Eric's solid shoulder, hummed along with the words "Caught Up in the Rapture (of Love)."

ABOUT THE AUTHOR

Lynn Emery is the pseudonym for Margaret E. Hubbard who lives with her family in Baton Rouge, Louisiana. She has written two novels for Arabesque.

Gwynne Forster lives in New York City, New York. She is a demographer for the United Nations and has traveled the world. She has written two books for Arabesque.

Carmen Green, a native of Buffalo, New York, now lives in Lawrenceville, Georgia, with her husband and three children.

DANGEROUS GAMES   (0-7860-0270-0, $4.99)
by Amanda Scott

When Nicholas Barrington, eldest son of the Earl of Ulcombe, first met Melissa Seacort, the desperation he sensed beneath her well-bred beauty haunted him. He didn't realize how desperate Melissa really was . . . until he found her again at a Newmarket gambling club—being auctioned off by her father to the highest bidder. So, Nick bought himself a wife. With a villain hot on their heels, and a fortune and their lives at stake, they would gamble everything on the most dangerous game of all: love.

A TOUCH OF PARADISE   (0-7860-0271-9, $4.99)
by Alexa Smart

As a confidence man and scam runner in 1880s America, Malcolm Northrup has amassed a fortune. Now, posing as the eminent Sir John Abbot— scholar, and possible discoverer of the lost continent of Atlantis—he's taking his act on the road with a lecture tour, seeking funds for a scientific experiment he has no intention of making. But scholar Halia Davenport is determined to accompany Malcolm on his "expedition" . . . even if she must kidnap him!

Available wherever paperbacks are sold, or order direct from the Publisher. Send cover price plus 50¢ per copy for mailing and handling to Penguin USA, P.O. Box 999, c/o Dept. 17109, Bergenfield, NJ 07621. Residents of New York and Tennessee must include sales tax. DO NOT SEND CASH.

ROMANCES ABOUT AFRICAN-AMERICANS!
YOU'LL FALL IN LOVE
WITH ARABESQUE BOOKS FROM PINNACLE

SERENADE   (0024, $4.99)
by Sandra Kitt

Alexandra Morrow was too young and naive when she first fell in love with musician, Parker Harrison and vowed never to be so vulnerable again. Now Parker is back and although she tries to resist him, he strolls back into her life as smoothly as the jazz rhapsodies for which he is known. Though not the dreamy innocent she was before, Alexandra finds her defenses quickly crumbling and her mind, body and soul slowly opening up to her one and only love, who shows her that dreams do come true.

FOREVER YOURS   (0025, $4.50)
by Francis Ray

Victoria Chandler must find a husband quickly or her grandparents will call in the loans that support her chain of lingerie boutiques. She arranges a mock marriage to tall, dark and handsome ranch owner Kane Taggart. The marriage will only last one year, and her business will be secure, and Kane will be able to walk away with no strings attached. The only problem is that Kane has other plans for Victoria. He'll cast a spell that will make her his forever after.

A SWEET REFRAIN   (0041, $4.99)
by Margie Walker

Fifteen years before, jazz musician Nathaniel Padell walked out on Jenine to seek fame and fortune in New York City. But now the handsome widower is back with a baby girl in tow. Jenine is still irresistibly attracted to Nat and enchanted by his daughter. Yet even as love is rekindled, an unexpected danger threatens Nat's child. Now, Jenine must fight for Nat before someone stops the music forever!

Available wherever paperbacks are sold, or order direct from the Publisher. Send cover price plus 50¢ per copy for mailing and handling to Penguin USA, P.O. Box 999, c/o Dept. 17109, Bergenfield, NJ 07621. Residents of New York and Tennessee must include sales tax. DO NOT SEND CASH.